Karl Elze

Notes on Elizabethn Dramatists

Karl Elze

Notes on Elizabethn Dramatists

ISBN/EAN: 9783337412487

Printed in Europe, USA, Canada, Australia, Japan

Cover: Foto ©Andreas Hilbeck / pixelio.de

More available books at **www.hansebooks.com**

NOTES ON ELIZABETHAN DRAMATISTS

BY

KARL ELZE, PH. D., LL. D.

A NEW EDITION IN ONE VOLUME.

HALLE:
MAX NIEMEYER.
1889.

TO THE MEMORY OF GOTTFRIED HERMANN.

PREFACE.

Twenty years have elapsed since I first ventured on publishing conjectural emendations on the text of Shakespeare and other Elizabethan dramatists. It was but natural that at the outset they should have come as 'single spies' and that they should have gradually increased in number on being combined with metrical comments and going hand in hand with my lectures. The result of these studies was laid before the public in my Notes on Elizabethan Dramatists the first series of which was published in 1880; a second Series followed in 1884, and a third in 1886. Having thus grown upon me I might almost say unawares, these critical and metrical observations wanted suitable arrangement and unity, a want which must have been keenly felt by every reader and may even have stood in the way of the circulation of the three volumes. Under these circumstances I have felt it incumbent on me to remedy this defect and have now re-arranged, revised, and corrected the whole and brought it to the compass of a handy single volume.

The fond hope to which I gave expression in the preface to the first Series that I should not be obliged, at some future day, again to withdraw (as I had done before) part of the conjectural emendations contained in that volume, has like many other hopes sadly deceived me and I now concur in the persuasion of Gottfried Hermann, my great teacher in textual criticism, that a true verbal critic must be no less ready to withdraw his conjectures than to make them. I now firmly believe, that this is a drawback incident on all verbal criticism. The loss thus caused to the bulk of my book has been more than compensated by the addition of fresh matter, especially the notes on K. Richard II. and Othello.

I must not fail to inform the reader that the designation of 'triple ending' has been substituted for 'trisyllabic feminine ending' which latter term I had borrowed from Mr. Fleay. 'Triple ending' is indeed a far simpler and more convenient name and moreover perfectly corresponds with 'triple rhyme'; a regular progression is thus obtained of single, double, and triple rhymes and endings. Should some one or other of my German readers require an English authority for these terms, he may be referred to Dr. Guest's History of English Rhythms (2d Ed., by W. W. Skeat), p. 115 and to Dr. Furnivall's paper on Fletcher's and Shakespeare's Triple Endings in The Academy, July 10, 1880, p. 27 — 28. I need hardly add that the change I have made is exclusively in the name. Most willingly I should also have altered the designation 'syllable pause line', if my endeavours to find out a more suitable name for this kind of verse had been crowned with success.

The addition to the main title 'with Conjectural Emendations of the Text' which appears on the title-pages of the original three volumes has been omitted in the present edition merely in order to give the title greater conciseness.

Halle, January 1889.

K. E.

CONTENTS.

ANONYMOUS PLAYS.

       Note

Appius and Virginia .   394

Arden of Feversham .   . 1. 4. 81. 394

The Birth of Merlin   2—7. 103. 258

A Comedy of King Cambises .   . 394

Damon and Pithias .   . . 19

Edward III.   . .   . .   8—12. 336. 392. 394. 402

Fair Em   4. 13—89. 107. 114. 176. 177. 210. 255. 268. 274. 305. 335. 382. 392

Histrio - Mastix .   . . 90. 125. 394

Locrine   . .   4. 91. 114. 183. 402

The London Prodigal   92—95

A Lover's Complaint   .   263

The Merry Devil of Edmonton   . 96. 274

The Miseries of Enforced Marriage 95

Mucedorus   .   2. 4. 97—183. 263. 274. 305. 335. 452

Nobody and Somebody   184. 392

The Play of Stucley   99. 103

Ram - Alley .   .   4. 9. 81. 95. 301

The Second Maiden's Tragedy   4

The Seven Deadly Sins   290

The Shoemakers' Holiday 11

Soliman and Perseda 4. 185. 255. 282

The Three Lords and the Three Ladies of London   .   125. 183

A Warning for Fair Women .   99. 262. 391. 392

The Wife Lapped in Morel's Skin   . . . , . 394

A Yorkshire Tragedy   . . 177

VIII

ASCHAM.

Note

The Scholemaster .   . 125

BEAUMONT AND FLETCHER.

The Honest Man's Fortune   4
The Humorous Lieutenant .   394
A King and No King   . . .   343
The Knight of the Burning Pestlo   391
The Knight of Malta   392. 394
The Queen of Corinth   4

CHAPMAN.

Alphonsus   186. 250. 392
The Ball 288
Eastward Ho! . .   394
Revenge for Honour 402
The Widow's Tears . ,   566

CHESTER.

Love's Martyr   215

COOKE.

Greene's Tu Quoque   187. 293. 392

DAVENPORT.

The City Nightcap   95

DEKKER.

Old Fortunatus   394

DEKKER AND MIDDLETON.

Honest Whore   95. 136. 254. 301. 302. 402. 452
The Roaring Girl 301. 311

DEKKER AND WEBSTER.

Westward Ho!   125. 188—192. 301. 320. 389. 395. 402. 474

FIELD.

A Woman is a Weathercock .   . 193—196. 335

FORD.

The Lover's Melancholy   437
'Tis Pity She's a Whore   301. 437

GLAPTHORNE.   Note

The Hollander . .   . 197
The Lady's Privilege   .   4
Albertus Wallenstein   . 4. 394

GREENE.

Dorastus and Fawnia 4. 81. 336
Friar Bacon and Friar Bungay .   19. 198—204
Dramatic Works 402

HARRINGTON.

The Anatomie of the Metamorphosis of Ajax   19

HAUGHTON.

Englishmen for my Money   105. 205. 268

HEYWOOD.

The English Traveller   523
The Four Ps.   . 392
If you know not me, you know nobody .   384. 392
Love's Mistress   394

JONSON.

Every Man in His Humour   28. 287. 343. 389
Every Man out of His Humour   . 391
Cynthia's Revels   . 394
Volpone .   34. 281. 394
Alchemist   . . .   4
Catiline   .   15. 34. 335
The Devil is an Ass   . . . 392
The Tale of a Tub   28
The Sad Shepherd   430
Epicoene   . . . 392
Bartholomew Fair   392. 394
Epigrams   . . . 288

KYD.

Cornelia   . 29. 193. 209—211. 343
Jeronimo   4
The Spanish Tragedy   . 81. 206—208. 394

MARLOWE.

Note

Tamburlaine . 212—215. 239. 259. 392. 394. 402

Doctor Faustus . . 215—219. 394

The Jew of Malta 2. 4. 220. 221. 283. 392

Edward II. 4. 15. 57. 81. 106. 206. 222—239. 255. 259. 274. 277. 305. 335. 391. 396

Dido, Queen of Carthage 120. 240. 254. 263. 394

Hero and Leander . . 394

MARSTON.

The Insatiate Countesse 2. 81. 231. 241—247. 263. 286

Antonio and Mellida . . . 394

The Fawn . . . 19

The Malcontent . 19. 254. 290

What You Will 380

Works 268. 277. 651

MASSINGER.

The City Madam . 268

MIDDLETON.

A Chaste Maid in Cheapside . 136

The Mayor of Queenborough . 95. 394

Old Law . 81

NASH.

Summer's Last Will and Testament . 240. 250. 384. 394

Pierce Pennilesse . 7. 391. 394

PEELE.

The Old Wives' Tale 4

SAM. ROWLEY.

When you see me, you know me . . 248. 249. 301. 392. 394

WILL. ROWLEY.

A Match at Midnight 301. 392

SHAKESPEARE AND FLETCHER.

The Two Noble Kinsmen . . . 250. 288

SHAKESPEARE.   Note

The Tempest   2. 4. 29. 193. 210. 251 — 266. 274. 287. 305. 359. 392. 394.
437. 452
The Two Gentlemen of Verona   255. 263. 267 — 269. 392. 499
The Merry Wives of Windsor   66. 81. 268. 270 — 276. 392
Measure for Measure .   2. 4. 95. 110. 136. 277
The Comedy of Errors .   2. 4. 19. 101. 103. 392
Much Ado about Nothing   . . 2. 359. 391. 394
Love's Labour's Lost 391. 392. 517
A Midsummer - Night's Dream . . . . . 4. 66. 263. 278 — 280. 392. 402
The Merchant of Venice   4. 66. 281 — 287. 343. 364. 391. 392. 394. 559
As You Like It 4. 254. 288. 335. 452
The Taming of the Shrew   2. 4. 255. 289 — 302. 392. 452
All's Well that Ends Well   . . . 2. 4. 7. 239. 303 — 306. 556
Twelfth Night   2. 4. 81. 136. 156. 282. 303. 307 — 334. 392. 452. 479
The Winter's Tale   2. 4. 82. 145. 268. 335. 343. 389. 392. 403. 436. 458
King John . . .   . 4. 274. 281. 336 — 340. 391. 394. 410
Richard II.   4. 107. 233. 255. 323. 336. 341 — 377. 392. 394. 402. 415. 420.
437. 442. 499
1 Henry IV.   . 2. 4. 238. 298. 344. 378 — 380. 391. 392
2 Henry IV.   . 290. 344. 394. 402
Henry V.   4. 255. 381. 392. 525
1 Henry VI.   . . 2. 232. 391. 392
2 Henry VI.   . 4. 274. 385. 392. 442. 499
3 Henry VI. 2. 290. 392. 433. 505
Richard III.   2. 4. 107. 255. 259. 263. 274. 277. 364. 458. 505
Henry VIII. 381. 391. 392. 410. 442. 517
Troilus and Cressida 66. 305. 392. 458
Coriolanus   2. 4. 11. 277. 338. 384. 387. 392. 436. 440. 458
Titus Andronicus   4. 53. 268. 386. 389. 402
Romeo and Juliet .   . 15. 101. 291. 382. 391. 442
Timon of Athens   2. 4. 98. 255. 383. 384. 391. 544
Julius Caesar   2. 4. 274. 385 — 388. 394. 458
Macbeth 2. 4. 244. 301. 452. 537
Hamlet   4. 81. 193. 205. 263. 279. 303. 335. 336. 389 — 402. 410. 452. 566. 573
King Lear .   2. 4. 23. 392. 403. 516. 542
Othello . ‘. .   . . . 4. 274. 389. 404 — 449. 452
Antony and Cleopatra . .   . . 4. 263. 269. 305. 343. 437. 450 — 496
Cymbeline . . .   2. 4. 239. 259. 384. 387. 410. 419. 437. 489. 497 — 604

XII

Note

Pericles .	4. 274. 398. 452. 455. 479. 605—669
Venus and Adonis	156. 254
Lucrece .	391. 523
Sonnets	394

SPENSER.

Faeric Queene	7. 19. 254. 336. 384. 386. 503

WEBSTER.

The Duchess of Malfi	254. 324. 392
The White Devil	. 392

I.

Then is there Michael, and the painter too,
Chief actors to Arden's overthrow.

*Arden of Feversham, III, 5 (ed. Delius, 45. — Ed. Warnke
and Præscholdt, 41).*

Is *Chief* to be taken as a so-called monosyllabic foot — followed by
a trochee! — or are we to read: —

Chief actors *both* to Arden's overthrow?

II.

Toclio. Me, Madam! 's foot! I'd be loath that any man
should make a holy-day for me yet:

In brief, 'tis thus: There's here arriv'd at court,
Sent by the Earl of Chester to the king,
A man of rare esteem for holiness,
A reverend hermit, that by miracle
Not onely sav'd our army,
But without aid of man o'erthrew
The pagan host, and with such wonder, sir,
As might confirm a kingdom to his faith.

*The Birth of Merlin, I, 1 (ed. Delius, 5. — Ed. Warnke
and Præscholdt, 5).*

These lines should thus be regulated: —

Toclio. Me, ma'am! 'S foot! I'd be loth that any man
Should make a holiday for me yet.
In brief, 'tis thus: there's here arriv'd at court,
Sent by the Earl of Chester to the king,
A man of rare esteem for holiness,
A reverend hermit, that by miracle
Not only sav'd our army, but without
The aid of man o'erthrew the pagan host,
And with such wonder, sir, as might confirm
A kingdom to his faith.

The monosyllabic pronunciation of *madam* (in the first line) is too frequent to call for any further remark; scan: —

Me, ma'am! | 'S foot! I'd | be loth | that an|y man.

The second line wants the tenth syllable; it is what may be termed a catalectic blank verse. Such catalectic verses have been pointed out by Dr. Wilke in his 'Metrische Untersuchungen zu Ben Jonson' (Halle, 1884), p. 14, 15 and 52, and after him by Schipper (Englische Metrik, II^, 38), whereas S. Walker (Versification, p. 289) assured his readers that 'lines wanting the tenth or final syllable, are unknown to Shakespeare, as they are certainly at variance with his rhythm.' Dr. Abbott, Shakespearian Grammar, s. 505 seqq., makes no difference between catalectic lines in our sense and those that want the last foot. According to Schipper the omission of the last syllable is restricted to those cases where there is a break in the sentence; the instances, however, which I am able to add to the quotations made by Dr. Wilke and Prof. Schipper will sufficiently show that such a restriction is not born out by the facts. Before turning to Shakespeare I shall introduce a few cases in point from his predecessor Marlowe. In 'The Jew of Malta' I find the following: —

1. What right had Cæsar to the Empire?

Marlowe, (Works, ed. Dyce, in 1 Vol., 1870, p. 145 b.)

Dyce *empery* which hitherto has been considered an almost indispensable correction.

2. To read a lecture here in Britain.   *(Ib., l. c.)*

Dyce proposes to insert *to you* between *lecture* and *here.*

3. And all his life-time hath been tirèd.   *(Ib., 146 a.)*

4. And bring with them their bills of entry.   *(Ib., 146 b.)*

5. I have no charge, nor many children.   *(Ib., 147 b.)*

6. Earth's barrenness, and all men's hatred.   *(Ib., 150 a.)*

7. Of labouring oxen, and five hundred.   *(Ib., 150 b.)*

I have little doubt that Dr. Abbott and his adherents will prefer to draw out these last four lines to their proper length by pronouncing *ent-e-ry, child-e-ren, hat-e-red,* and *hund-e-red.*

8. Seducèd daughter? Go, forget not.'   *(Ib., 152 b.)*

Dyce proposes to read: 'forget *it* not.'

9. Farewell; remember to-morrow morning.   *(Ib., l. c.)*

10. I would you were his father too, sir.   *(Ib., 155 b.)*

Printed as prose by Dyce and others.

11. Yes, madam, and my talk with him was.   *(Ib., 157 a.)*

Dyce proposes to add *but* at the end of the line.

12. What, is he gone unto my mother?   *(Ib., 160 a.)*

13. Are there not Jews enow in Malta?   *(Ib., l. c.)*

In both old and modern editions this passage is differently arranged.

cf. A. W. p. 145–6 on these passages. Wagner rejects (no doubt strongly) Elze's position).

14. And common channels of the city. *(Ib., 174b.)*
15. We rent in sunder at our entry. *(Ib., 176b.)*
    According to Dr. Abbott's theory we must pronounce *ent-e-ry*.

As to Shakespeare, I feel almost certain that his plays abound with catalectic blank verse, but am content with quoting some few that have been collected with a view of comparing at the same time the different scansions given by Dr. Abbott.

16. Who hadst | deserv'd | more than | a pris|on.
                                        The Tempest, I, 2, 362.
    Abbott, p. 372, scans: —
    Who hádst | desérv|ed mó|re thán | a príson.

17. Say again, where didst thou leave these varlets. *Ib., IV, 1, 170.*
    Abbott, p. 378, takes *Say* to be a monosyllabic foot.

18. And pún|ish them | t' your height | of pleas|ure.
                                 Measure for Measure, V, 1, 240.
    This line may also be scanned: —
    And pun'sh | them to | your height | of pleas|ure.
    Abbott, p. 373, dissyllabizes *your*, 'unless', he adds, '"pleasure" is a trisyllable.'

19. But moo|dy and | dull mel|ancho|ly.
                              Comedy of Errors, V, 1, 79.
    Abbott, p. 381, prolongs both *moody* (so as to make it a trisyllable) and *dull*. 'Some may prefer', he continues, 'to read "dull" as a monosyllable, but I can find no instance of "meláncholý" to justify such a scansion.' Had this scansion *(mó-ody* and *dú-ll)* been proposed by a German scholar, it would have been condemned unmercifully by all English critics.

20. Good Mar|g'ret. Run | thee to | the par|lour.
                                 Much Ado, III, 1, 1.
    Abbott, p. 416, scans this line: —
    Good Már|garét. | Rún | thee tó | the pár|lour.
    The line may indeed be considered as a syllable pause line (see note IV) just as well as a catalectic verse.

21. Vincentio's son brought up in Florence.
                          The Taming of the Shrew, I, 1, 14.
22. Gentlemen, importune me no further. *Ib., I, 1, 48.*
23. No worse than I, upon some agreement
    Me shall you find ready and willing. *Ib., IV, 4, 33—4.*
24. If you will tarry, holy pilgrim. *All's Well, III, 5, 43.*
25. And lasting in her sad remembrance. *Twelfth Night, I, 1, 32.*
26. The like of him. Know'st thou this country. *Ib., I, 2, 21.*
    Need I advert to the well-known remedy (formerly adopted by myself) of lengthening the words *pilgrim, remembrance,* and *country?*

27. He straight declined, droop'd, took it deeply.
>> *The Winter's Tale, II, 3, 14.*

Abbott, p. 381, pronounces *declinèd* and dissyllabizes *droop'd.*

28. What wheels, racks, fires? What flaying, boiling.
>> *Ib., III, 2, 177.*

Abbott, p. 380, prolongs *boiling,* so as to make it a trisyllable.

29. Did ever so long live. No sorrow.   *Ib., V, 3, 52.*
Abbott, p. 416, thinks a foot omitted after *live.*

30. But tell | me, is young | George Stan|ley liv|ing?
>> *Richard III., V, 5, 9.*

Abbott, p. 383 and 416, offers no fewer than three different scansions of this line. The verse, he says, may either be explained by a pause: —

But téll | me, ' | is yóung | Géorge [*sic*] Stán|ley lív|ing?,

'or "George" may be a quasi-dissyllable, or, possibly,

But téll me, |
Is yóung | George Stán|ley líving?'

In my conviction, the second and third scansions are positively wrong, whereas the first scansion would make the verse a syllable pause line (see note IV) which after all may be just as right as declaring it a catalectic verse.

31. With winged haste to the lord marshal.   *1 Henry IV., IV, 4, 2.*
Abbott, p. 387, *már|(e)shál.*

32. Or horse or oxen, from the leopard.   *1 Henry VI., I, 5, 31.*
Abbott, p. 379, *lé|opárd,* which, he says, occurs often in Elizabethan authors; in Shakespeare, however, the word is nowhere else used as a trisyllable.

33. Men for their wives; wives for their husbands.
>> *3 Henry VI., V, 6, 41.*
Abbott, p. 379, dissyllabizes *wives.*

34. Well, let them rest: come hither, Catesby.
>> *Richard III., III, 1, 157.*

35. Here comes his servant. How now, Catesby.   *Ib., III, 7, 58.*
Abbott, p. 385, pronounces *Catesby* as a trisyllable.

36. They thus directed, we will follow.   *Ib., V, 3, 297.*
I cannot agree with Dr. Abbott (p. 412), who thinks that perhaps part of the following line should be combined with this.

37. This found I on my tent this morning.   *Ib., V, 3, 303.*

38. At a poor man's house: he us'd me kindly.
>> *Coriolanus, I, 9, 83.*
Abbott, p. 380, draws out *kindly* into a trisyllable.

39. In our first way. I'll bring him to you. *Ib., III, 1, 334.*
Abbott, p. 373, dissyllabizes *our.*

40. How, traitor! Nay, temperately; your promise. *Ib., III, 3, 67.*

> Abbott, p. 374, dissyllabizes *Nay*. Here the same dilemma presents itself as in Nos. 20 and 30, viz. whether we are to consider this line as a catalectic blank verse with an extra syllable before the pause, or as a syllable pause line (see note IV): —
>
> How, trai|tor! ⏌ | Nay, tem|perately; | your prom|ise.
> Similar lines are numerous.

41. You've added worth unto it and lustre.
> *Timon of Athens, I, 2, 154.*

42. He humbly prays your speedy payment. *Ib., II, 2, 28.*
> Compare Abbott, p. 378.

43. The heart of woman is. O, Brutus. *Julius Cæsar, II, 4, 40.*
> Compare Abbott, p. 375.

44. And betimes I will to the weird sisters. *Macbeth, III, 4, 133.*
> Abbott, p. 382, dissyllabizes *weird*.

45. They've travelled all the night. More fetches. *Lear, II, 4, 90.*

46. And leave eighteen. Alas, poor princess. *Cymbeline, II, 1, 61.*

Two more instances may be added from Mucedorus (ed. Warnke and Prœscholdt, p. 38 — 9) and from The Insatiate Countess, A. III, *ad fin.* (The Works of John Marston, ed. J. O. Halliwell, III, 160). In Mucedorus we read: —

47. Segasto cease, these threats are needless,
> and in The Insatiate Countess; —

48. And their lusts [qy. lust's?] past, avarice or bawdry.

> The adherents of Dr. Abbott will probably prefer to pronounce *bawdry* as a trisyllable. Another means of extending the line to the customary five feet might be found in the transposition *bawdry or avarice.*

The result may be summed up in the following three conclusions: 1. There are undoubtedly lines which cannot possibly be explained otherwise than on the principle of the omission of the fifth arsis; such lines are, e. g., Nos. 1, 2, 8, 10, 11, 12, 13, 14, 19, 21, 23, 28, 29, 33, 36, 42, 43, 47. — 2. Other lines, though in all likelihood catalectic verses just as well as the former, yet admit at the same time of a different scansion, viz. by the lengthening of vowels or by the insertion of an *e* between a mute and a liquid, or a liquid and a sibilant; such are Nos. 5, 6, 7, 15, 18, 24, 25, 26, 31, 38, 40. — 3. A third class is formed by those lines which may be scanned either as catalectic blank verse with an extra syllable before the pause, or as syllable pause lines, especially such in which the arsis is wanting at the end of the first hemistich; see Nos. 20, 30, 40, and compare note IV. As a rule I prefer scanning verses of the second category as catalectic, and verses of the third class as syllablc pause lines.

I revert once more to the passage at the head of this note in order to add a remark on the eighth line where the addition of the article before *aid* has been objected to by Messrs. Warnke and Prœscholdt *ad loc.* on the ground that, 'as Shakespeare says *with aid of s. b.* we seem not to be permitted to add *the* in the phrase *without aid of s. b.*' The learned editors have overlooked Macbeth, I, 3, 146: But with the aid of use.

III.

> Dispatch it quickly, there's not a minute's time
> 'Twixt thee and thy death.
>> *Proxi*[*mus*]. Ha, ha, ha! [*A stone falls and kills Proximus.*
>> *Merl*[*in*]. Ay, so thou may'st die laughing.
>>> *Ib., (Del., 68. — W. and Pr., 60.)*

The second line is evidently to be joined with Merlin's speech, the verse being continued spite of the interruption caused by the laughter of Proximus; see Abbott, s. 514. We must either run the two words *thee and* into one another and scan: —

> 'Twixt thee and | thy death. | Ay, so | thou may'st | die laugh ¦ ing,

or *thy* must be expunged.

At the next page (Del., 69. -- W. and Pr., 60) the following passage 'gives us pause': —

> '*MERLIN strikes his wand. Thunder and lightning. Two dragons appear, a white and a red; they fight awhile and pause.*
> *Vort.* What means this stay?
> *Merl.* Be not amaz'd, my lord, for on the victory
> Of loss or gain, as these two champions' ends,
> Your fate, your life, and kingdom all depends;
> Therefore observe it well.
> *Vort.* I shall; heaven be auspicious to us.'

Instead of *stay* qy. read *play*? Apart from the fact that the Ed. pr. (1662) reads *Champions,* not *champions',* there is no doubt some corruption also in the third line, but it baffles my endeavours to detect and amend it. In the last line we must, of course, pronounce *au-spi-ci-ous,* if we do not prefer to make the line a catalectic one, i. e. a blank verse without the last arsis: —

> I shall; | heaven be | auspi | cious to | us.

Some pages further on (Del., 76. — W. and Pr., 67) we read: —

> This brought the fiery fall of Vortiger,
> And yet not him alone: &c.

(Qy. read: *his alone?* By the way it may be remarked that in the old edition (1662) this speech of Merlin, like numerous others that are evidently meant to be metrical, is printed as prose.

IV.

Prince. Nay, noble Edol, let us here take counsel,
It cannot hurt,
It is the surest garrison to safety.

Ib., (Del., 71. — IV. and Pr., 62).

Arrange and write: —

Prince. Nay, noble Edol,
Let's here take counsel, it cannot hurt,
It is the surest garrison to safety.

Some twenty lines lower down we meet with a striking parallel, as far as the division of the lines is concerned: —

Prince. Hold, noble Edol,
Let's hear what articles he can enforce.

As to the second line, Messrs. Warnke and Prœscholdt have rightly guessed that it belongs to a class of verses which for want of a more appropriate name, may be called syllable pause lines, i. e. lines in which the pause, to use the words of the Clarendon Edition of Hamlet (p. 124, note on I, 1, 95), 'takes the time of a defective syllable', be it either unaccented or accented. In the latter case the first hemistich corresponds exactly with what I have designated as catalectic lines; it is in this respect as in many others the image of the verse, and the one serves to confirm the other. The majority of these syllable pause lines are reduced to regular metre by Dr. Abbott (s. 484) by the prolongation, or, so to say, dissyllabification of some monosyllable contained in them. In my second edition of Hamlet (p. 126), I have instanced some such lines and I now beg leave to offer another instalment collected at random which, however trifling in number compared to the infinite multitude of these verses, yet will go far not only to establish the fact of their existence, but to throw a flood of light upon them. I shall first give a list where the pause serves as substitute for an unaccented syllable, or, to look at it from a different point of view, where the second hemistich begins with a monosyllabic foot. German readers will no doubt be conversant with Prof. Schipper's most ingenious and learned exposition not only of this metrical peculiarity, but of blank verse in general (Englische Metrik, Vol. I, Bonn, 1881, p. 439 seqq.), and will be aware that those lines in which the pause stands for an unaccented syllable, correspond to Nos. 9 and 11, and when beginning with a monosyllabic foot, to Nos. 13 and 15 of his table (p. 440). My

second list will comprise lines in which the pause does duty for an
accented syllable, lines, for which there is no room in Schipper's
table of the various licenses of blank verse, but which have been
treated by Dr. Abbott in s. 507 seq., though not in a very satisfactory
manner. It will hardly be necessary to advert to the circumstance,
that, while even a very slight pause may sometimes be deemed sufficient to stand for an unaccented syllable, none but a strongly marked
one, or, still better, a break in the line, will serve as substitute for
an accented syllable. Thus, for instance, the verse in Fair Em (ed.
Delius, p. 46; ed. Warnke and Prœscholdt, p. 53): —

> Here is the Lady you sent me for,

has so slight a pause that it would be unsafe to take it for a syllable pause line; indeed no other means of reducing this line to
regular metre seems to be left than the insertion of *whom* after *Lady*.
Our investigation promises to be so much the more attractive, as
most of these lines, in both classes, have been differently scanned
not only by Dr. Abbott, but also by other critics, and the reader will,
therefore, find himself called upon to decide in favour of one or the
other theory. At the same time he will be surprised to see how
large a number of conjectural emendations, both old and new, will
become needless and may be dismissed from doing service any longer
in the critical revision of the text. To prevent misunderstandings,
it may be as well to premise the remark that I shall denote the
unaccented syllable *(thesis)* by ◡ and the accented *(arsis)* by ⊥.

A. LINES IN WHICH THE PAUSE STANDS FOR AN UNACCENTED SYLLABLE.

1. Yea, his | dread tri|dent shake. | ◡ My | brave spir|it.

> *The Tempest, I, 2, 206.*

Theobald duplicates *brave*; Hanmer, *That's my brave*. Abbott,
p. 377, scans: —

> Yea, his | dread tri|dent shake. | My bra|ve spir|it.

Instead of *brave* the word *shake* might just as well have been
dissyllabized.

2. Make the | prize light. | ◡ One | word more; | I charge | thee.

> *Ib., I, 2, 452.*

Pope added *Sir* before *One*.

3. Letters | should not | be known; | ◡ rich|es, pov|erty.

> *Ib., II, 1, 150.*

Pope, *wealth, poverty*; Capell, *poverty, riches*; Prof. W. Wagner,
no riches. Pope and Capell read *poverty* as a trisyllable, as
they had no knowledge yet of triple endings.

4. No sov'|reignty. | ◡ Yet | he would | be king | on't.
Ib., II, 1, 156.

The insertion of *And* before *Yet* in Prof. W. Wagner's edition of Shakespeare is needless.

5. Or night | kept chain'd | below. | ◡ Fair|ly spoke.
Ib., IV, 1, 31.

'Fairly', says Steevens *ad loc.*, 'is here used as a trisyllable.'

6. Makes this | place par|adise. | ◡ Sweet, |.now si|lence.
Ib., IV, 1, 124.

Hanmer, *Now, silence, sweet.*

7. Which is | most faint; | ◡ now, | 'tis true.   *Ib., Epilogue, 3.*

Pope, *and now.* Abbott, p. 377, dissyllabizes *faint.* Of course it makes no difference that this is a line of four feet only.

8. Which was | to please. | ◡ Now | I want.   *Ib., Epilogue, 13.*

Pope, *For now*; Abbott, p. 378, *plé-ase.*

9. Gaoler, | ◡ take | him to | thy cus|tody.
The Comedy of Errors, I, 1, 156.

Hanmer, *Jailor, now*; Capell, *So, jailer*; S. Walker, Versification, p. 153 seq., *Go, gaoler.*

10. But room, | ◡ fai|ry, here | comes Ob|eron.
A Midsummer-Night's Dream, II, 1, 58.

Pope, *But, make room*; Johnson, *faëry*; Seymour, *But, fairy, room, for here*; Abbott, p. 381, *ro-om.*

11. And so | all yours. | ◡ O, | these naugh|ty times!
The Merchant of Venice, III, 2, 18.

Pope, *Alas these*; S. Walker, Versification, p. 137, dissyllabizes *yours.*

12. Villain, | I say, | ◡ knock | me at | this gate.
The Taming of the Shrew, I, 2, 11.

13. Like the | old age. | ◡ Are | you read|y, sir?
Twelfth Night, II, 4, 49 seq.

Abbott, p. 377, dissyllabizes *age.*

14. Poison'd, | ill fare, | ◡ dead, | forsook, | cast off.
K. John, V, 7, 35.

Hanmer, *oh! dead.* S. Walker, Versification, p. 139, and Abbott, p. 370, dissyllabize *fare.*

15. Your grace | mistakes; | ◡ on|ly to,| be brief.
K. Richard II., III, 3, 9.

Rowe, *mistakes me*; Delius, *mistaketh.* According to Abbott, p. 385, the *e* mute in *mistakes* is to be sounded.

16. Yea, look'st | thou pale? | ◡ Let | me see | this wri|ting.
Ib., V, 2, 57.

Hanmer, *come, let*; Malone, *pale, boy?* Abbott, p. 377, dissyllabizes *pale.*

17. Farewell, | kinsman! | ◡ I | will talk | to you.

1 K. Henry IV., I, 3, 234.

FA, *Ile talk*; Pope, *my kinsman*; Capell, *Fare you well*. S. Walker, Versification, p. 140. Abbott, p. 370, scans: —

Fáre|well, kins|man! I | will talk | with [*sic*] you.

18. Touch her | soft mouth | and march. | ◡ Fare|well, host|ess.

K. Henry V., II, 3, 61 seq.

S. Walker, Versification, p. 140. — Printed as two incomplete lines in the Globe Edition.

19. She's tick|led now; | ◡ her | fume needs | no spurs.

2 K. Henry VI., I, 3, 153.

FBCD, *can need*; Dyce and S. Walker (Crit. Exam. III, 156)' *fury*. — Abbott, p. 382, says: 'It may be that "fume" is emphasized in:

She's tick|led now. | Her fu|me needs | no spurs.

(Unless "needs" is prolonged either by reason of the double vowel or because "needs" is to be pronounced "needeth").' — In my opinion the context sufficiently shows that *her* is to be emphasized.

20. My lord, | ◡ will | it please | you pass | along?

K. Richard III., III, 1, 136.

FA, *wilt* (which may be right, although it reduces the line to four feet); modern Edd., *will't*. Compare Cambr. Ed. and Dyce *ad loc.*

21. Doth com|fort thee in | thy sleep; | ◡ live, | and flou|rish.

Ib., V, 3, 130.

Thy omitted in Ff. *Thou* added after *live* by Rowe and Collier's Ms. Corrector.

22. When steel | grows soft, | ◡ as | the para|site's silk.

Coriolanus, I, 9, 45.

Abbott, p. 379, dissyllabizes *steel* and adds: '"Soft" is emphasized as an exclamation (see 481), but perhaps on the whole it is better to emphasize "steel" here.' — I think, neither the one, nor the other.

23. We'll sure|ty him. | ◡ A|ged sir, | hands off. *Ib., III, 1, 178.*

See Dyce *ad loc.* Abbott, p. 378, dissyllabizes *We'll*.

24. Why dost | not speak? | ◡ What, | deaf: not | a word?

Titus Andronicus, V, 1, 46.

FB, *no, not a word*; Dyce conjectures: *what, not a word*; Abbott, p. 378, *dé-af.* Or should we scan: —

Why dost | not speak? | What, deaf? | ◡ Not | a word?

25. Titus, | ◡ I | am come | to talk | with thee.   *Ib., V, 2, 16.*

Dyce, *I now am come.* Abbott, p. 415, classes this verse with the 'Lines with four accents where there is a change of thought.' His scansion is this: —

Títus, | ´ | I (am)'m cóme | to tálk | with thée.

26. Long live | so and | so die. | ◡ I | am quit.
Timon of Athens, IV, 3, 398.

The insertion of *So* before *I,* proposed by Hanmer and adopted by modern editors, is needless.

27. Cæsar | has had | great wrong. | ◡ Has | he, mas|ters?
Julius Cæsar, III, 2, 115.

Craik and Dyce: *Has he not*; S. Walker, Crit. Exam., II, 259, *my masters.* Abbott, p. 330, takes the last two feet to be trochees, 'unless "my" has dropped out', and then adds: 'Even here, however, "wrong" may be a quasi-dissyllable (480).' Thus Abbott is at a loss how to decide between three different scansions to which I have now added a fourth.

28. Lucius, my gown. | ◡ Fare|well, good | Messa|la.
Ib., IV, 3, 231.

Hanmer, *Now farewell*; S. Walker, Versification, p. 141, *Fare you well* (compare *infra* No. 54); Abbott, p. 370, *Fa-re.*

29. 'Gainst my | captiv|ity. | ◡ Hail, | brave friend.
Macbeth, I, 2, 5.

Abbott, p. 377, *more suo* dissyllabizes *Hail.*

30. Horri|ble sight! | ◡ Now | I see, | 'tis true.   *Ib., IV, 1, 122.*
Pope, *Nay now*; Steevens, *Ay, now.* See Dyce *ad loc.* Abbott, p. 379, dissyllabizes *sight.*

31. Died ev|'ry day | she liv'd. | ◡ Fare | thee well.
Ib., IV, 3, 111.

Pope, *Oh fare*; Dyce, *livèd*; S. Walker, Versification, p. 139 seq., dissyllabizes *Fare.*

32. Thence to | a watch, | ◡ thence | into | a weakness.
Hamlet, II, 1, 148.

Compare Abbott, p. 377.

33. Pull off | my boots: | ◡ hard|er, so.   *K. Lear, IV, 6, 177.*
Abbott, p. 381, *bó|ot [sic].*

34. Anto|nius dead! | ◡ If | thou say | so, vil|lain.
Antony and Cleopatra, II, 5, 26.

Whether we read *Antonius* with Delius, or *Anthony's* with FBCD is quite immaterial as far as the scansion is concerned. S. Walker, Versification, p. 48, *do say*; Anonymous in Cambr. Ed., *thou villain*; Abbott, p. 378, *dé-ad.*

35. Obey | it on | all cause. | ⌣ Par|don, par|don.   *Ib., III, 11, 68.*

Capell, *causes*; Theobald, *O, pardon.* Abbott, p. 329 seq., thinks this to be perhaps an instance of two consecutive trochees (compare No. 27) and sees ˙ no ground for supposing that 'pardon' is to be pronounced as in French. In his opinion the difficulty will be avoided, if the diphthong in 'cause' be pronounced as a dissyllable.

36. Enough | to fetch | him in. | ⌣ See | it done.   *Ib., IV, 1, 14.*

'In all probability', says Dyce *ad loc., 'See it be done'* [proposed by Pope]. Abbott, p. 379, lengthens *See.*

37. What, all | alone? | ⌣ well | fare, sleep|y drink.

Marlowe, The Jew of Malta, A. V (Works, 174 b).

S. Walker, Versification, p. 139, dissyllabizes *fare.*

38. *Tanti,* | ⌣ I | will fawn | first on | the wind.

Marlowe, Edward II. (ed. Tancock), I, 1, 22.

Qq: *I'll.* 'Something has dropt out from this line', remarks Dyce *ad loc.,* and Mr. Fleay (Marlow's Tragedy of Edward II., Lon., 1877), after extolling Dyce's emendation *fawn* instead of *fanne,* adds: 'The line still wants a foot.' W. Wagner, in his edition of Edward II. (Hamburg, 1871) p. 6, thinks he 'might easily get the legitimate number of feet by reading: —

Tanti: I will first fawn *upon* the wind.'

All these criticisms and suggestions simply fall to the ground, as it cannot be doubted that the pause after *Tanti* replaces a defective syllable.

39. His head | shall off: | ⌣ Gav|eston, | short warn|ing.

Ib., II, 5, 21.

Mr. Fleay, p. 123, writes *Gauston* and pronounces *war'ning* as a trisyllable.

40. My lord! | ⌣ Sol|diers, | have him | away.   *Ib., II, 5, 25.*

Mr. Fleay, p. 123, pronounces *lor'ds* [*sic*].

41. My lord, | ⌣ we.| shall quick|ly be | at Cob|ham.

Ib., II, 5, 107.

Dyce, W. Wagner, Mr. Keltie (The British Dramatists, Edin., 1875) and Mr. Tancock *we'll,* thus introducing a catalectic verse. Or is this the reading of the Qq?

42. Is 't you, | my lord? | ⌣ Mor|timer, | 'tis I.   *Ib., IV, 1, 12.*

Mr. Fleay, p. 124, *lor'd,* as a dissyllable.

43. Come, come, | ⌣ keep | these preach|ments till | you come.

Ib., IV, 6, 112.

Dyce, W. Wagner, Mr. Keltie, and Mr. Tancock print this passage as prose. Mr. Fleay, p. 127, *p'reachments,* as a trisyllable.

44. Help, un|cle Kent! | ◡ Mor|timer | will wrong | me.

Ib., V, 2, 109.

Mr. Fleay, p. 128, *Mor'timer,* as a word of four syllables.

45. To mur|der you, | ◡ my | most gra|cious lord.   *Ib., V, 5, 43.*

Mr. Fleay, p. 128, *g'racious.*

46. Tell me, | ◡ sirs, | was it | not brave|ly done?

Ib., V, 5, 113.

Mr. Fleay, p. 129, *B'ravely,* as a trisyllable.

47. Betray | us both; | ◡ there|fore let | me fly.   *Ib., V, 6, 8.*

Whilst Dyce, W. Wagner, and Mr. Tancock are silent about this line, Mr. Fleay, p. 114, gives the following scansion of which the less is said, the better it will be: —

    Betray us both, therefóre let mé fly.
        Y. Mor.   Fly
    To th' savages.

48. That same | is Blanch, | ◡ daugh|ter to | the king.

Fair Em, (Del., 8. — W. and Pr., 10. — Sim., II, 416.)*

Simpson's (or Chetwood's?) conjecture *(the daughter)* as well as my own *(sole daughter)* I now consider as needless. See note *ad loc.*

49. Ah, Em, | ◡ faith|ful love | is full | of jeal|ousy.

Ib., (Del., 16. — W. and Pr., 19. — Sim., II, 425.)

Both Simpson's and my own conjectures may be dismissed as needless. *Jealousy* is, of course, to be pronounced as a triple ending.

50. My lord, | ◡ watch|ing this | night in | the camp.

Ib., (Del., 36. — W. and Pr., 42. -- Sim., II, 447.)

My conjecture *(in watching)* seems needless. See note *ad loc.*

51. Comedy, | ◡ play | thy part | and please.

Mucedorus, (Del., 3. — W. and Pr., 21. — Hazlitt's Dodsley, VII, 203.)

No addition seems to be wanted.

52. To match | with you. | ◡ Her|mit, this | is true.

Ib., (Del., 44. — W. and Pr., 66. — H's D., VII, 247.)

Messrs. Warnke and Prœscholdt read, on their own responsibility, *Ay, hermit,* &c.

53. That man|ners stood | ◡ un|acknowl|edgèd.

Ib., (Del., 53. — W. and Pr., 75. — H's D., VII, 256.)

Mr. Hazlitt's Dodsley, without a remark: —

    That manner stood unknowledged.

---

* The explanation of these abbreviations will be given in the first note on Fair Em.

54. Ready | to pay | with joy. | ⌣ Fare|well both.

Beaumont and Fletcher, Queen of Corinth, IV, 2.

S. Walker, Versification, p. 143, needlessly conjectures *Fare you well both.* Compare No. 28.

55. Since you've | so litt|le wit. | ⌣ Fare | you well, | sir.

The Second Maiden's Tragedy, I, 1 (The Old English Drama, Lon., 1825, I, 4).

The verse preceding this may likewise be considered as a syllable pause line, however slight its pause may be: —

'Tis hap|py you | have learnt | ⌣ so | much man|ners.

S. Walker, Versification, p. 143, knows no better means of scanning this line than by dissyllabizing *learnt,* although he feels by no means sure.

56. Would pierce | like light|(e)ning. } ⌣ I | believe. [?]

Glapthorne, The Lady's Privilege.

Compare S. Walker, Versification, p. 18 seq.

57. For with | my sword, | ⌣ this | sharp cur|tle axe.

Locrine (Malone's Suppl., II, 257).

The critics of the last century might have repeated *my*: —

For with | my sword, | this *my* | sharp cur|tle axe.

B. Lines in which the pause stands for an accented syllable.

58. This king | of Na|ples, ⌣́ | béing | an en|emy.

The Tempest, I, 2, 121.

Enemy is to be read as a triple ending. Or should we pronounce *being* as a monosyllable (according to Abbott, s. 470) and scan: —

This king | of. Na|ples, being | an en|emy?

59. A treach|erous ar|my lev|ied, ⌣́ | one mid|night. *Ib., I, 2, 128.*

Not: lév|ied, óne | midníght!

60. And were | the king | on't, ⌣́ | what would | I do?

Ib., II, 1, 145.

Abbott, p. 418, regulates this line by giving the full pronunciation to the contraction *on't,* whereas the late Prof. W. Wagner in his edition of Shakespeare suggested *what would I not do?*, although the following line clearly shows this conjecture to be inconsistent with the sense of the passage.

61. Ay, sir; | where lies | that? ⌣́ | If't were | a kibe.

Ib., II, 1, 269.

Dyce, *and where,* &c. Perhaps it might be as well to scan: —

Ay, sir; | ⌣ where | lies that? | If't were | a kibe.

62. Just as | you left | them; ⏌ | all pris|oners, sir.   *Ib., V, 1, 9.*

Pope, *all your prisoners*; Dyce, following Collier's so-called Ms. Corrector, *all are prisoners*. The one is as good, or as bad, as the other.

63. Their clear|er reas|on. ⏌ | O good | Gonza|lo.   *Ib., V, 1, 68.*

Pope, *O my good*; S. Walker (Crit. Exam. III, 7), *O thou good*. This latter conjecture has been installed in the text by Dyce. Abbott, p. 3.75, gives the following scansion of the line, which I do not quite understand: —

Their cléa|rer réa|son.   O˝, | ˋ góod | Gonzálo.

He adds that he has not found *reason* a trisyllable in Shakespeare.   See *infra* No. 84.

64. Till death | unloads | thee. ⏌ | Friend hast | thou none.
Measure for Measure, III, 1, 28.

Pope, *unloadeth*. Abbott, p. 380, is of opinion, that 'possibly "friends" [*sic*] may require to be emphasized, as its position is certainly emphatic.' I am surprised that he has not thought of making *unloads* a word of three syllables.

65. O me! | you jugg|ler! ⏌ | You can|ker blos|som.
A Midsummer-Night's Dream, III, 2, 282.

Capell, *You jugler, you!* Abbott, p. 364, pronounces *jugg(e)ler*.

66. Like a | ripe sis|ter: ⏌ | the wom|an low.
As You Like It, IV, 3, 88.

FBCD: *but the woman*. Abbott, p. 365, classes this line with those cases where '*er* final seems to have been sometimes pronounced with a kind of "burr", which produced the effect of an additional syllable', the second syllable of sister thus taking the place of two syllables. See *infra* Nos. 75 and 78. After all, *ripe sister* may be a corruption.

67. Of great|est just|ice. ⏌ | Write, write, | Rinal|do.
All's Well that Ends Well, III, 4, 29.

FB: *Write and write*; Hanmer, *Write, oh, write*. Abbott, p. 379, dissyllabizes the first *Write*. To me it seems highly improbable, that the same word should first be pronounced as a dissyllable and immediately after as a monosyllable. It should be observed, however, that the line might just as well be classed with those catalectic blank verse (with an extra syllable before the pause) of which I have treated in note II.

68. The doct|rine of | ill-do|ing, ⏌ | nor dream'd.
The Winter's Tale, I, 2, 70.

FB inserts *no* after *ill-doing*; see S. Walker, Crit. Exam., II, 256 and Dyce *ad loc*. According to Abbott, p. 411, it is a line with four accents, without a pause in the middle of the line; he declares such lines to be *very* rare, except in The Taming of the Shrew.

69. And no|ble Dau|phin, ⹋ | albeit | we swear. *K. John, V, 2, 9.*

'Albeit', says Al. Schmidt s. v., 'in John V, 2, 9 of three, everywhere else of two syllables.' Such an anomaly might have roused a suspicion in the learned lexicographer.

70. Never | believe | me. ⹋ | Both are | my kins|men.
Richard II., II, 2, 111.

Pope, *They are both.* Abbott, p. 415.

71. Bring him | our pur|pose. ⹋ | And so | farewell.
1 K. Henry IV., IV, 3, 111.

S. Walker, Versification, p. 141, note: 'The three first quartos read *purposes* [which is no doubt the better reading], the others and the folios *purpose.'*

72. You have | not sought | it. ⹋ | How comes | it then?
Ib., V, 1, 27.

Pope, *sought it, sir?* Dyce adds *Well* before *How.* Abbott, p. 415, declares this line to be one of four accents, 'unless *comes* is *cometh.'*

73. Lord Doug|las, ⹋ | go you | and tell | him so. *Ib., V, 2, 33.*
Theobald, *go you then*; Abbott, p. 365, pronounces *Doug[e]las.*

74. For worms, | brave Per|cy. ⹋ | Farewell, | great heart.
Ib., V, 4, 87.

S. Walker, Versification, p. 140. — Abbott, p. 370, pronounces *Farewell* as a trisyllable. — The reading of the Qq, *Fare thee well,* has certainly the better claim to genuineness.

75. I pray | you, un|cle, ⹋ | give me | this dag|ger.
Richard III., III, 1, 110.

Hanmer, *uncle then*; Keightley, *gentle uncle.* Dyce, *ad loc.* Abbott, p. 365, says that by a kind of burr the *er* final in *dagger* 'produces the effect of an additional syllable;' compare *supra* No. 66.

76. Were you | in my | stead, ⹋ | would you | have heard?
Coriolanus, V, 3, 192.

Abbott, p. 376, dissyllabizes *you* in the first foot: —
Were yó|u ín | my stéad, | would yóu | have héard?

77. A broth|er's mur|der. ⹋ | Pray can | I not.
Hamlet, III, 3, 38.

78. We'll teach | you. ⹋ | Sir, I'm | too old | to learn.
K. Lear, II, 2, 135.

Abbott, p. 365, dissyllabizes *Sir* by 'a kind of burr' again. Ff *I am,* which may, or may not be a correction.

79. Of quick, | cross light|ning? ͝ | To watch, | poor per|du.

Ib., IV, 7, 35.

S. Walker, Versification, p. 17, and Abbott, p. 365; Abbott pronounces *light[e]ning*.

80. 'Tis mon|strous. ͝ | Ia|go, who | began't? *Othello, II, 3, 217.* Abbott, p. 364, pronounces *monst(e)rous*.

81. Thou kill'st | thy mis|tress: ͝ | but well | and free.

Antony and Cleopatra, II, 5, 27.

Abbott, p. 365, *mist(e)ress*.

82. Be free | and health|ful. ͝ | So tart | a fa|vour. *Ib., II, 5, 38.* Abbott, p. 378, pronounces *healthful* as a word of three syllables. Dyce, on the other hand, assures his readers, that *why*, added by Rowe, is 'absolutely necessary for the sense of this passage.'

83. To taunt | at slack|ness. ͝ | Canid|ius, we. *Ib., III, 7, 28.* Abbott, p. 365, *slack(e)ness*.

84. Lord of | his rea|son. ͝ | What though | you fled?

Ib., III, 13, 4.

S. Walker, Crit. Exam., II, 156 seq., proposes *What an though*, 'unless *What although* be allowable.' Cf. Dyce, *ad loc.* Abbott, p. 415, seems inclined to pronounce *re-a-son*, but does not remember an instance. See *supra* No. 63.

85. A mang|led shad|ow. ͝ | Perchance | to-morrow.

Ib., IV, 2, 28.

Pope, *It may chance* for *Perchance*; Steevens, *Nay, perchance.* Abbott, p. 414.

86. Being | so frus|trate. ͝ | Tell him, | he mocks. *Ib., V, 1, 2.* Capell, *frustrated*; Hanmer, *he but mocks*; Steevens, *that he mocks*; Malone, *he mocks us by*; Abbott, p. 365, *frust(e)rate.*

87. Try man|y, ͝ | all good, | serve tru|ly, nev|er.

Cymbeline, IV, 2, 373.

Johnson (or Capell?), *many, and all.* This conjecture has been adopted by Dyce, 'the line, as he says, halting intolerably from omission.' Abbott, p. 377, dissyllabizes *all.*

88. Go search | like no|bles, ͝ | like no|ble sub|jects.

Pericles, II, 4, 50.

Steevens, *noblemen* instead of *nobles*; Abbott, p. 364, *nob(e)les*, with a mark of interrogation.

89. Farewell, | Zaa|reth; ͝ | farewell, | Temainte.

Marlowe, The Jew of Malta (Works, ed. Dyce, in 1 Vol., p. 148 a).

90. My lord, | be go|ing: ⏑ | care not | for these.
> Marlowe, Edward II. (ed. Tancock), IV, 6, 92.

Mr. Fleay and Prof. W. Wagner, as usual, resort to the re-solution of *care*.

91. Keep them | asun|der: ⏑ | thrust in | the king. *Ib.*, V, 3, 53.

Mr. Fleay, p. 128, says: '*Thr'ust*, or rather *thur'sl* with the *r* transposed, as in *burn* for *bren*.' — The line cannot be taken for a verse of four feet with an extra syllable before the pause, but must be declared to be a blank verse, as from l. 51 to l. 60 we have a regular στιχομυϑία.

92. Cannot | transmute | me. ⏑ | Perti|nax, Sur|ly.
> B. Jonson, The Alchemist, II, 1, 79.

Modern edd., *my Surly*.

93. More an|tichrist|ian ⏑ | than your | bell-found|ers.
> *Ib.*, III, 1, 23.

Or should we scan: —

More an|tichrist|i-an | than your | bell-found|ers?

94. Call out | Caly|pha, ⏑ | that she | may hear.
> Geo. Peele, The Old Wives' Tale (Greene and Peele,
> ed. Dyce, in 1 Vol., 1861, 450b).

Dyce *ad loc.* needlessly conjectures, *call that she* &c.

95. For all | thy for|mer kind|ness, ⏑ | forget.
> Beaumont and Fletcher, The Honest Man's Fortune, I, 1.

S. Walker, Versification, p. 22, proposes to read *kindnesses*.

96. That's all | thou art | right lord | of; ⏑ | the king|dom.
> The Birth of Merlin, (ed. Delius, 73. — Ed. Warnke
> and Præscholdt, 64.)

97. And so | I leave | thee. ⏑ | Farewell, | my lord.
> Jeronimo (Hazlitt's Dodsley, IV, 356).

S. Walker, Versification, p. 141, dissyllabizes *Fare*.

98. The time | that does | succeed | it. ⏑ | Farewéll.
> Glapthorne, Alb. Wallenstein, II, 2 ad fin.

S. Walker, Versification, p. 143, reads *Farewell* as a trisyllable.

99. And sweet | Perse|da, ⏑ | accept | this ring.
> Soliman and Perseda (H's D., V, 260).

100. Grac'd by | thy coun|try, ⏑ | but ten | times more.
> *Ib.*, V, 264.

101. Erast|us, ⏑ | to make | thee well | assur'd. *Ib.*, V, 320.

102. Perse|da, ⏑ | for my | sake wear | this crown. *Ib.*, V, 339.

103. And seeing | her mis|tress ⏑ | thrown on | the ground.
> Ram-Alley (H's D., X, 280).

This line, like so many others, seems to admit of different scansions; *mistress* may be pronounced as a trisyllable, and *upon* may be substituted for *on*, if so much liberty be conceded to the critic.

104. Her life | and be|ing, ⊥ | and with|out which. *Ib., X, 288.*

For the accentuation *without*, about which S. Walker, Abbott, Al. Schmidt (Shakespeare-Lexicon) and others are silent, compare, e. g., Coriolanus III, 3, 133: —

That won you without blows! Despising,

and Mucedorus (ed. W. and Pr.) II, 2, 78: —

Vile coward, so without cause to strike a man.

Cf. W. Wilke, Metrische Untersuchungen zu B. Jonson, 43.

105. I know't, | sweet Al|ice; ⊥ | cease to | complain.
Arden of Feversham, (ed. Del., 16. — W. and Pr., 14.)

106. Some see | it ⊥ | without | mistrust | of ill.
Fair Em, (Del., 16. — W. and Pr., 18. — Sim., II, 425.)
The conjectural emendations of Chetwood (*see it plain*, adopted by Delius) as well as of Messrs. Warnke and Prœscholdt *(see't)* seem to be uncalled for.

107. Now, Mar|ques, ⊥ | your vil|lainy | breaks forth.
Ib., (Del., 34. — W. and Pr., 41. — Sim., II, 446.)
Simpson repeats *now* after *Marques*; Messrs. Warnke and Prœscholdt think that *your* may 'be pronounced as a dissyllable.'

108. I tell | thee, Man|vile, ⊥ | hadst thou | been blind.
Ib., (Del., 50. — W. and Pr., 57. — Sim., II, 463.)
I formerly suggested to read *haddest*, which form occurs in Chaucer (Works, ed. Morris, IV, p. 311, l. 248); in The Faerie Queene, I, 2, 18; in Greene's Dorastus and Fawnia (Shakespeare's Library, ed. Hazlitt, I, IV, 77, *bis*), and elsewhere, but am now satisfied that we have to deal with a syllable pause line. (Jahrbuch der Deutschen Shakespeare-Gesellschaft, XV, 350).

109. Now, El|ner, ⊥ | I am | thine own, | my girl.
Ib., (Del., 50. — W. and Pr., 57. — Sim., II, 463.)
Messrs. Warnke and Prœscholdt say: 'We must either pronounce *Elner* as a trisyllable (*Eliner* [properly *Elinor* and *Elnor*]), or consider the line with Simpson as a verse of four accents, and read *I'm.*'

110. Mine, Man|vile? ⊥ | Thou nev|er shalt | be mine.
Ib., (Del., 50. — W. and Pr., 57. — Sim., II, 463.)
In the Jahrb. d. D. Sh.-G., XV, 350, I proposed to insert *No* before *thou*, but now withdraw that conjecture.

2*

111. Segas|to, ⊥ | cease to | accuse | the shep|herd.
> *Mucedorus, (Del., 23. — W. and Pr., 43. — H's D., VII, 224.)*

The transposition *(the shepherd to accuse)* proposed by the late Prof. W. Wagner (Jahrb. d. D. Sh.-G., XI, 67) and adopted by Messrs. Warnke and Prœscholdt, is needless.

112. To 't, Bre|mo, to | it; ⊥ | essay | again.
> *Ib., (Del., 31. — W. and Pr., 52. — H's D., VII, 233.)*

Qq: *To it, Bremo, to it; say again.* The correction *essay* is due to Mr. Hazlitt.

113. Now, Bre|mo, ⊥ | for .so | I heard | thee call'd.
> *Ib., (Del., 41. — W. and Pr., 63. — H's D., VII, 244.)*

My conjecture *(for so do I hear)*, although received into the text by Messrs. Warnke and Prœscholdt, yet appears to be needless.   (Jahrb. d. D. Sh.-G., XIII, 71.)

V.

> *Prince.* Look, Edol: Still this fiery exhalation shoots
> His frightful horrors on th' amazed world.
> > *Ib., (Del., 74. — W. and Pr., 65.)*

Arrange: —
> *Prince.* Look, Edol:
> Still this fiery exhalation shoots &c.

Still is to be considered as a so-called monosyllabic foot (cf. Abbott, 482).

VI.

> Nor shall his conquering foot be forc'd to stand,
> Till Rome's imperial wreath hath crown'd his fame
> With monarch of the west, from whose seven hills
> With conquest, and contributary kings,
> He back returns —
> > *Ib., (Del., 78. — W. and Pr., 68.)*

Qy. read: —
> *With'* [i. e. *With the] monarchy of th' west, &c.?*

VII.

> Tenebrarum precis, divitiarum et inferorum deus, hunc Incubum
> in ignis æterni abyssum accipite —
> > *Ib., (Del., 82. — W. and Pr., 72.)*

Qy. read, — Tenebrarum *princeps,* divitiarum et inferorum deus, &c.? Nash's Pierce Pennilesse is inscribed 'To the High and Mightie Prince

of Darknesse', &c. Compare All's Well that Ends Well, IV, 5, 44 — 5:
The black prince, sir; alias, the prince of darkness; alias, the devil.
— Spenser, The Faerie Queene, I, 1, 37: —

    Great Gorgon, Prince of darknesse and dead night.

To the objection raised by Messrs. Warnke and Prœscholdt (p. 85)
I cannot attach any weight.

VIII.

> The sin is more, to hack and hew poor men,
> Than to embrace, in an unlawful bed,
> The register of all rarieties
> Since leathern Adam 'till this youngest hour.

Edward III., II, 2 (ed. Del., 33. — W. and Pr., 32).

Instead of *rarieties* Delius reads *varieties*, Moltke (Doubtful Plays of
Wm. Shakespeare) *fair rarities*. Ever since I proposed, in the Jahrb.
d. D. Sh.-G., XIII, 78, to read *heathen Adam*, Dr. F. J. Furnivall has
lost no opportunity of falling foul of this conjecture and holding it
up, with manifest zest, to ridicule and contempt, although he might
have known that it has been withdrawn at p. 327 of the very same
volume in which it was published. He not only upholds the original
text, but in the Transactions of the New Shakspere Society, Dec. 9,
1881, p. 10*, even praises as 'admirable' the expression *leathern
Adam,* which he takes to mean 'Adam clad in skins, or his own
skin, or leather.' This interpretation has partly been repeated in
The Academy for July 22, 1882, p. 60, where Dr. Furnivall maintains
the expression to be equivalent to 'Adam clad in skins.' He seems
to have given up the grotesque notion that the adjective *leathern*
might refer to Adam's own skin and might mean 'Adam clad in his
own skin, or leather!' The skin of a man may certainly be designated as leather, either by way of joke, or in good earnest; see
Halliwell, Dictionary, s. *Lether* (3). But this is vastly different from
calling a naked man a leathern man. The explanation 'clad in skins'
might indeed be supported by a reference to Genesis, III, 21: 'Unto
Adam also and to his wife did the Lord God make coats of skins
and clothed them.' But who ever heard of people clad in skins,
such as the ancient Britons or Germans, being called leathern? The
true meaning of the word lies in a very different direction and has
been pointed out to me by my late lamented friend Ed. Müller, the
learned author of the 'Etymologisches Wörterbuch der englischen
Sprache.' To all appearance *leathern*, in the passage under discussion, is a corrupted form of O. E. *leþer, liþer, leþerand* = 'nequam,
malus', 'vile, hateful.' See Stratmann, Dictionary, s. *Luđer,* and
Halliwell, Dictionary, s. *Lether* (2). Adam is called *leathern,* i. e.
leþer, nequam or hateful, because through his fall paradise was lost

to mankind. If this be the correct explanation, as I have little doubt
it is, it would seem preferable to deviate as little as possible from
the spelling of the old editions (1596 and 1599), both of which read
Letherne Adam, and to print *lethern.* I am indeed ignorant by whom
the misleading spelling *leathern* was introduced into the text.

IX.

Next, — insomuch thou hast infring'd thy faith,
Broke league and solemn covenant made with me, —
I hold thee for a false pernitious wretch.

Ib., (Del., 48. — W. and Pr., 46).

This is the uniform reading of the quartos, with the exception of
most pernitious in the second quarto (1599) which in this particular
has been followed by various modern editors, amongst others by
Capell (compare his Prolusions; or, Select Pieces of Antient Poetry,
Lon., 1760). It seems, in fact, that the two adjectives *false* and
pernitious do not well agree with one another, although they give an
unexceptionable sense. Qy.: a false *perfidious* wretch? Compare Ram-
Alley (Dodsley, ed. Hazlitt, X, 371): —

Shame to thy sex,
Perfidious perjur'd woman, where's thy shame?

(Jahrb. d. D. Sh.-G., XIII, 80.)

X.

And with a strumpet's artificial line
To paint thy vitious and deformed cause.

Ib., (Del., 49. — W. and Pr., 46).

Read: artificial *lime.* (Jahrb. d. D. Sh.-G., XIII, 81.)

XI.

Upon my soul, had Edward prince of Wales,
Engag'd his word, writ down his noble hand,
For all your knights to pass his father's land,
The royal king, to grace his warlike son,
Would not alone safe-conduct give to them,
But with all bounty feasted them and theirs.

Ib., (Del., 75. — W. and Pr., 71).

Grammar, I think, requires either: —

Had not alone safe-conduct *given* to them,

or: —

But with all bounty *feast both* them and theirs.

As, however, these alterations might be thought too bold, a contraction may be suggested: —

But with all *bounty'd* feasted them and theirs,

i. e., of course, *bounty had.* — Messrs. Warnke and Prœscholdt *ad loc.* refer their readers to Coriolanus, IV, 6, 35 and to The Shoemakers' Holiday, III, 3, 61 (according to their own numbering).

XII.

> *Sec. Cit.*   The sun, dread lord, that in the western fall
> Beholds us now low brought through misery,
> Did in the orient purple of the morn
> Salute our coming forth, when we were known;
> Or may our portion be with damned fiends.

Ib., (Del., 82. — W. and Pr., 78).

One or two verses seem to be wanting between the fourth and fifth line. The king thinks himself cheated, as he has required the foremost citizens of the town to be delivered to him, whereas, he says, only *servile grooms* or *felonious robbers of the sea* are forthcoming; consequently he declares his promise null and void. The second citizen, however, denies this charge and solemnly assures the king that up to that very morning he and his fellow hostages had been indeed the chiefest citizens of their town. The missing verses, therefore, may have been to the following effect: —

> when we were known
> *To be the chiefest men of all our town;*
> *Of this, my sovereign lord, be well assur'd,*
> Or may our portion be with damnèd fiends.

(Jahrb. d. D. Sh.-G., XIII, 83.)

XIII.

> Nor bear I this an argument of love.

Fair Em, (ed. Delius, 3. — Ed. Warnke and Prœscholdt, 5.
Simpson, The School of Shakspere, II, 409.)

Qy.: *in* argument? i. e. in token. Compare 1 K. Henry IV., II, 5, 45: —

> This day, in argument upon a case.

Ib., V, 1, 46: —

> In argument and proof of which contract.

XIV.

Why should not I content me with this state,
As good Sir Edmund Trofferd did the flaile?

Ib., (Del., 4. — W. and Pr., 6. — Sim., II, 411.)

Read either: *Trofferd did with' (wi'th')* flail or *Trofferd with the flail.*
Instead of *Trofferd,* exhibited by both quartos, Delius reads *Trostard;*
perhaps, however, neither the one, nor the other is what the author
wrote. The knight alluded to is no doubt meant to be the same
personage as Sir Thomas Treford who occurs in A. V, sc. 1, l. 263,
although Sir Thomas Treford is there designated as a shepherd.
Delius, in this latter passage, reads *Sir Edmund Treford,* Simpson,
Sir Edmond Treford.

XV.

And thou, sweet Em, must stoop to high estate
To join with mine, &c.

Ib., (Del., 4. — W. and Pr., 6. — Sim., II, 411.)

This is the reading of the old copies. Delius reads: *stoop thy high
estate,* whereas Simpson suggests that *to high* may be a misprint for
to like; this, however, as Messrs. Warnke and Prœscholdt justly
remark, 'would little agree with the following *to ioyne with mine.*'
The author most probably wrote or meant to write *stoop too high
estate,* the spelling *to* instead of *too* being of great frequency in the
old copies; compare, e. g., A. I, sc. 4, l. 40: —

What! comes he to, to intercept my loue?

The sense is: Sweet Em, thou must stoop (thy) high estate likewise,
in order that thy estate may join or agree with mine. It might be
objected, that, if this was the author's meaning, he would have placed
too in the accented part of the foot; however we frequently find that
a word which bears the emphasis, i. e. 'the stress laid upon a word
in pronouncing a sentence', does not always bear the rhythmical
accent (the ictus) or stand in the arsis. See, e. g., lower down
(I, 3, 50): —

A sweet | *face,* an | exceed|ing dain|tie hand;

Marlowe, Edward II., I, 4, 128: —

O might | I keep | *thee* here | as I | do this.

The antithesis between *face* and *hand* in the former and between *thee*
and *this* in the latter line, seems to require that *face* and *thee* should
have been placed in the arsis. Compare also Marlowe, Edward II.,
II, 1, 34: —

A vel|vet cap'd | *cloak,* fac'd | before | with serge;

Romeo and Juliet, I, 1, 234 seq.: —

> Examine other beauties. ·
> *Rom.*   'Tis the way
> To call | *hers* ex|quisite, | in quest|ion more.

Ib., I, 2, 31: —

> And like | *her* most | whose mer|it most | shall be.

Ib., III, 1, 185: —

> I beg | for just|ice which | *thou,* prince, | must give.

We should have expected the words *cloak, hers, her* and *thou* to stand in the accented part of the rhythm. Still more to the point is the position of *too* in the following lines taken from B. Jonson's Catiline (I quote from Moxon's edition of The Works of B. Jonson, in 1 Vol., London, 1853): —

> And they | *too* no | mean aids. | Made from | their hope *(287b).*
> Shun they | to treat | with me | *too?* No, | good la|dy *(297a).*
> In being | secure: | I have | of late | *too* plied | him *(299a).*
> A trick | on me | *too!* It | is some | men's mal|ice *(302a).*
> Hath sent | *too* to | his ser|vants, who | are man|ly *(302b).*
> And send | them hence | with arms | *too,* that | your mer|cy *(303b).*

On the transitive use of the verb *to stoop* see Al. Schmidt, Shakespeare - Lexicon, s. *Stoop.*

XVI.

You will have the cramp in your finger at least ten weeks after.
Ib., (Del., 7. — W. and Pr., 9. — Sim., II, 414.)

Chetwood: *fingers.* This is one of those few of Chetwood's alterations that deserve the notice of the critics.

XVII.

That graceth him with name of Conqueror.
Ib., (Del., 7. — W. and Pr., 9. — Sim., II, 415.)

I take this to be a case of absorption and feel sure that we should write *with'* or *wi'th'.*

XVIII.

> *Marq.* That same is Blanch, daughter to the king,
> The substance of the shadow that you saw.
Ib., (Del., 8. — W. and Pr., 10. — Sim., II, 416.)

S. Walker, Versification, p. 206 seqq., has endeavoured to show that *daughter* is sometimes used as a trisyllable, although in some cases

he is doubtful, whether the passage ought not rather to be amended.
Simpson has added the article *the* before *daughter*. I should prefer
sole daughter; *sole daughter, sole son, sole child,* and *sole heir* being,
as it were, proverbial phrases of almost daily occurrence. Lower
down (Del., 39. — W. and Pr., 46. — Sim., II, 451) we are, in fact,
told that Blanch is the king's 'only daughter',

> 'The only stay and comfort of his life.'

There is, however, no need of conjecturing at all, the verse being
evidently a syllable pause line; scan: —

> That same | is Blanch, | ◡ daugh|ter to | the king.

XIX.

> Ill head, worse-featur'd, uncomely, nothing courtly,
> Swart and ill-favour'd, a collier's sanguine skin.

> *Ib., (Del., 8. — W. and Pr., 10. — Sim., II, 416.)*

What does *Ill head* mean? We do not want a substantive here, but
an adjective that will serve, as it were, as a positive to the comparative *worse-featured*. In a word, I think we ought to read *Ill-
shaped*. That the shape of the lady cannot be passed over with
silence becomes evident from William the Conqueror's eulogy on the
beauty of Mariana twenty lines below. There he says: —

> A modest countenance; no heavy sullen look;
> Not very fair, but richly deck'd with favour;
> A sweet face; an exceeding dainty hand;
> A body, were it framèd all of wax
> By all the cunning artists of the world,
> It could not better be proportionèd.

By the way, it may be remarked that instead of *framed all of wax*
Delius erroneously reads *formed &c.*. The passage aptly quoted by
Simpson from The Comedy of Errors, IV, 2, 19 seqq. speaks strongly
in favour of my suggestion. It is to the following effect: —

> He is deformèd, crookèd, old and sere,
> Ill-faced, worse-bodied, shapeless everywhere;
> Vicious, ungentle, foolish, blunt, unkind,
> Stigmaticall in making, worse in mind.

Compare also Greene, Friar Bacon and Friar Bungay (The Works of
Rob. Greene and Geo. Peele, ed. Dyce, in 1 vol., London, 1861,
p. 163b): —

> *Miles. Salve,* Doctor Burden!
> This lubberly lurden,
> Ill-shap'd and ill-fac'd,
> Disdain'd and disgrac'd,
> What he tells unto *vobis*
> *Mentitur de nobis.*

Marston, The Malcontent, I, 7 (Works, ed. Halliwell, II, 222): *faire-shapt*; ib., III, 2 (Works, ed. Halliwell, II, 247): *well shapt*; ib., III, 150 (Works, ed. Halliwell, III, 150): *well-shap'd*.

As to the '*collier's sanguine skin*' the following lines from Damon and Pithias (Dodsley, ed. Hazlitt, IV, 80) may be compared: —

> By'r Lady, you are of good complexion,
> A right Croyden sanguine, beshrew me.

On these lines Dodsley has the following foot-note (by Reed): 'From the manner in which this expression [viz. *sanguine*] is used by Sir John Harington, in "The Anatomie of the Metamorphosis of Ajax", 1596, sig. L, 7, it seems as though it was intended for a sallow hue. "Both of a complexion inclining to the oriental colour of a *Croyden sanguine*."' — Croydon, it will be remembered, was famous for its colliers, and as a sanguine skin or complexion is particularly ascribed to the men of Croydon it may probably mean rather a swarthy than a sallow hue which seems to be corroborated by the passage under discussion. Spenser, Faerie Queene, III, 8, 6, however, speaks of 'a lively sanguine' as almost identical with 'perfect vermily': —

> The same she tempred with fine Mercury
> And virgin wex that never yet was seald,
> And mingled them with perfect vermily;
> That like a lively sanguine it seemd to the eye.

Compare Marston, The Fawn (The Works of John Marston, ed. J. O. Halliwell, II, 28): '*Her*[*cules*]. Fore Heaven! you are blest with three rare graces — fine linnen, cleane linings, a sanguine complexion, and I am sure, an excellent wit, for you are a gentleman borne.' Mr. Halliwell (p. 296) takes the opportunity of quoting the following passage from the Book of Knowledge, ed. 1049, p. 35: 'A sanguine man is large, loving, glad of cheer, laughing, and ruddy of colour, stedfast, fleshly, right hardy, mannerly, gentle, and well nourished.'

XX.

> *King Den.* Mariana, I have this day receivèd letters
> From Swethia, that lets me understand
> Your ransom is collecting there with speed,
> And shortly hither shall be sent to us.
> *Mar.* Not that I find occasion to mislike
> My entertainment in your Grace's court,
> But that I long to see my native home.
>   *Ib., (Del., 8. — W. and Pr., 10. — Sim., II, 416.)*

Evidently there is something wanting here; Mariana's speech should begin with a line somewhat to the following effect: —

> *It glads my heart to hear these joyful tidings;*
> Not that I find occasion to mislike, &c.

Instead of 'to mislike', which is an emendation by Simpson, the
quarto of 1631 reads 'of mislike'; Delius, 'of misliking'.

XXI.

I'll gage my gauntlet gainst the envious man
That dares avow there liveth her compare.
> *Ib., (Del., 9. — W. and Pr., 11. — Sim., II, 417.)*

So far as I know *compare* is used without exception as an abstract
noun and is equivalent to *comparison,* in which sense it occurs in
our very play, II, 1, 154.

XXII.

Wm. Conq. Yea, my Lord; she is counterfait in deed,
For there is the substance that best contents me.
> *Ib., (Del., 9. — W. and Pr., 12. — Sim., II, 417.)*

This is the reading of the quartos. Simpson proposes to read, either: —
For there's the substance that doth best content me,
or: —
For there's the substance best contenteth me.
I should prefer: —
For *there's* | the sub|stance ι | that best | contents | me,
or (what would 'best content me'): —
For *there's* the substance that *contents me best.*

XXIII.

These jars becomes not our familiarity.
> *Ib., (Del., 10. — W. and Pr., 12. — Sim., II, 418.)*

Not an Alexandrine, but a regular blank verse; pronounce *familiar'ty*
as a word of four syllables. Compare K. Lear, I, 2, 4: —
The curiosity of nations to deprive me,
where, according to S. Walker, Versification, p. 201, Shakespeare no
doubt pronounced *cúrious'ly.*

XXIV.

Full ill this life becomes thy heavenly look,
Wherein sweet love and virtue sits enthroned.
Bad world, where riches is esteem'd above them both,
In whose base eyes nought else is bountiful!
> *Ib., (Del., 10. — W. and Pr., 13. — Sim., II, 418 seq.)*

Is the third line perhaps to be classed with those Alexandrines of which Abbott in his Shakespearian Grammar, s. 499, gives such curious instances? Or are we to admit an emendation and read: —

> Bad world, where riches is esteem'd *'bove both?*

Chetwood, according to Simpson, reads: —

> Bad world! where riches 'bove both are esteemed most.

This would be getting out of the frying-pan into the fire. According to Messrs. Warnke and Prœscholdt, however, the line, as altered by Chetwood, runs thus: —

> Bad world! where riches are esteemed most,

'and not *is* esteemed most, as Del., p. XI, erroneously states.' The best means to dispose of the excrescence of this perplexing line seems to be to place *Bad world!* *extra versum* as an interjectional line. In the fourth line the adjective *beautiful* would seem to be imperatively demanded by the context instead of *bountiful* which is out of place here.

XXV.

> *Mount.* Nature unjust, in utterance of thy art,
> To grace a peasant with a princess' fame!
>> *Ib., (Det., 11. — W. and Pr., 13. — Sim., II, 419 seq.)*

For *fame* Chetwood writes *frame*; neither can be right. Perhaps we should read *face* which would agree much better both with Mountney's subsequent praise of 'her beauty's worthiness' and Manvile's eloquent lines (I, 4, 4—5): —

> Full ill this life becomes thy heavenly look,
> Wherein sweet love and virtue sits enthroned.

Twelve lines below Simpson needlessly adds *out* —

> And she thou seekest [out] in foreign regions.

Read *seek'st* (with Delius) and pronounce *re-gi-ons.*

XXVI.

> *Val.* Love, my Lord? of whom?
> *Mount.* Em, the miller's daughter of Manchester.
>> *Ib., (Det., 12. — W. and Pr., 14. — Sim., II, 421.)*

Em may be considered as a monosyllabic foot; by the repetition of *of,* however, a regular ten syllable line might be obtained: —

> *Of* Em, the miller's daughter of Manchester.

XXVII.

I' faith, I aim at the fairest; &c.

Ib., (Del., 14. — W. and Pr., 16. — Sim., II, 422 seq.)

The arrangement of these capping verses in Messrs. Warnke and Prœscholdt's edition was proposed by me in the Jahrb. d. D. Sh.-G., XV, 345.

XXVIII.

Trot[*ter*]. Yes, woos, but you did.

Ib., (Del., 14. — W. and Pr., 17. — Sim., II, 423.)

Woos which has been omitted by Delius without a remark, is a corruption (by 'ablaut') of *wis (iwis, ywis)* = certain, sure. B. Jonson, Every Man in his Humour, I, 1: *Step*[*hen*]: No, wusse; but I'll practise against next year, uncle. Ib., IV, 2: *Down*[*-right*]: Come, you might practise your ruffian tricks somewhere else, and not here, I wuss. Id., A Tale of a Tub, I, 2: —

Clay. No, wusse. Che lighted I but now in the yard,
Puppy has scarce unswaddled my legs yet.

See also Mr. Henry B. Wheatley's notes on the two passages in Every Man in his Humour (B. Jonson's Every Man in his Humour, ed. H. B. Wheatley, 1877) p. 126 and p. 186.

XXIX.

But time and fortune hath bereaved 'me of that.

Ib., (Del., 15. — W. and Pr., 17. — Sim., II, 424.)

A pseudo-Alexandrine. Read and scan either: —

But time | and for|tune's b'rea|vèd me | of that,

or: —

But time | and for|tune hath b'rea|vèd me | of that.

Compare notes on Kyd's Cornelia (H's D., V, 213) and on The Tempest, I, 2, 296 seq.

XXX.

Man. Ah, Em! were he the man that causeth this mistrust,
I should esteem of thee as at the first.

Ib.; (Del., 15. — W. and Pr., 17. — Sim., II, 424.)

A verse of six feet; the words *Ah, Em!* are to be placed in an interjectional line.

XXXI.

Two gentlemen attending on Duke William,
Mountney and Valingford, as I heard them named,
Ofttimes resort to see and to be seen.

Ib., (Del., 15. — W. and Pr., 18. — Sim., II, 424.)

The second line might easily be regulated by being enclosed in parentheses and by the expunction of *as*: —

(Mountney and Valingford I heard them named).

The name of *Valingford,* however, here and elsewhere seems to have been used as a dissyllable by the poet; thus, e. g., on p. 23 (W. and Pr., p. 27; Sim., II, 433) and p. 28 (W. and Pr., p. 33 seq.; Sim., II, 439), if I am not mistaken in the conviction that these passages, now printed as prose, were originally written in verse. The former passage, printed as verse, would run thus: —

'Zounds! what a cross is this to my conceit!
But Valingford, search the depth of this device.
Why may not this be some feign'd subtlety
By Mounteney's invention, to th' intent
That I, seeing such occasion, should leave off
My suit, and not persist to solicit her
Of love? I'll try th' event. If I perceive
By any means th' effect of this deceit
Procurèd by thy means, friend Mounteney,
The one of us is like to repent our bargain.

On p. 28 (W. and P., 33 seq.) the following verses may be restored: —

Mount. Valingford, so hardly I digest an injury,
Thou'st proffer'd me, as, were 't not I detest
To do what stands not with the honour of my name,
Thy death should pay the ransom of thy fault.

Injury, in the first line, is. to be pronounced as a dissyllable. The third line is not an Alexandrine, but a blank verse with an extra syllable before the pause, however slight that pause may be: —

To do | what stands | not with th' hon|our of | my name.

Similar lines with extra syllables before slight pauses are A. II, sc. 1, l. 121; A. II, sc. 3, l. 2; A. III, sc. 1, l. 72; A. III, sc. 1, l. 107. It cannot be denied, however, that another, and perhaps a safer, arrangement of the passage may be devised, viz.: —

Mount. Valingford,
So hardly I digest an injury,
Thou'st proffer'd me, as, were 't not I detest
To do what stands not with the honour of my name,
Thy death should pay the ransom of thy fault.

XXXII.

Ah me, whom chiefly and most of all it doth concern,
To spend my time in grief, and vex my soul, &c.

Ib., (Del., 16. — W. and Pr., 18. — Sim., II, 425.)

Dele, *chiefly and*; or place *Ah me* extra versum.

XXXIII.

For which I am rewarded most unthankfully.

Ib., (Del., 16. — W. and Pr., 19. — Sim., II, 425.)

I am now persuaded that the scansion of this line proposed by me
in the Jahrb. d. D. Sh.-G., XV, 345, and adopted by Messrs. Warnke
and Prœscholdt, is hardly right. It seems much more natural to
take *unthankfully* for a triple ending and to scan the verse thus: —

For which | I am | reward|ed most | unthank|fully.

XXXIV.

And so away? What, in displeasure gone,
And left me such a bitter sweet to gnaw upon?
Ah, Manvile, little wottest thou
How near this parting goeth to my heart.

Ib., (Del., 16. — W. and Pr., 19. — Sim., II, 425.)

Chetwood duplicates *Manvile* (in l. 113) in order 'to restore the
legitimate number of feet', and Simpson proposes to read *to gnaw on*
(in l. 112). Both are manifestly wrong. Arrange, of course: —

And left me such a bitter sweet to gnaw

Upon? Ah, Manvile, little wottest thou, &c.

Compare for similar *enjambements* Guest, History of English Rhythms
(2d Ed.), 154 seq. W. Wilke, Metrische Untersuchungen zu B. Jonson, 66. B. Jonson, Catiline, III, 8 (Folio; Works, Lon., 1838, in
1 Vol., III, 3, p. 288a): —

The flax and sulphur are already laid

In, at Cethegus' house; so are the weapons.

Volpone, V, 2 (Folio; Works, &c., V, 1, p. 199b): —

Shew them a will: open that chest, and reach

Forth one of those that has the blanks.

To think that ll. 111 and 112 are meant for a couplet, would be a
mistake. It is true that the following verses (114—115, 116—117,
120—121) are rhymed, but they read rather as casual rhymes than
as couplets written on purpose; moreover these casual couplets are
interrupted by the unrhymed lines 118—119, which contain no sign of
corruption and offer no handle for the correcting activity of the critic.

XXXV.

Nor shall unkinduess cause me from him to start.

Ib., (Del., 17. — W. and Pr., 19. — Sim., II, 426.)

To need not be expunged as has been done by Messrs. Warnke and Prœscholdt in accordance with a suggestion made by Simpson *ad loc.* The line has an extra syllable before the pause, however slight the latter may be: —

Nor shall | unkind|ness cause me | from him | to start.

Compare A. II, sc. 3, l. 5 (see note XL): —

And makes | him conceive | and con|ster his | intent,

and A. III, sc. 1, l. 107 (see note XLVII): —

Or court | my mis|tress with fab|ulous | discour|ses.

XXXVI.

I speak not, sweet, in person of my friend,
But for myself, whom, if that love deserve
To have regard, being honourable love;
Not base affects of loose lascivious love,
Whom youthful wantons play and dally with,
But that unites in honourable bands of holy rites,
And knits the sacred knot that God's —

Ib., (Del., 17. — W. and Pr., 20. — Sim., II, 426 seq.)

Instead of *loose lascivious love* read *loose lascivious lust.* Compare *ante* (Delius, 6. — W. and Pr., 7. — Sim., II, 413): —

Let not vehement sighs,
Nor earnest vows importing fervent love,
Render thee subject to the wrath of lust —

which Chetwood has wrongly altered to *the wrath of love.* — For the faulty repetition of *love* cf. *infra* note LXI. In the last line but one omit *honourable* before *bands*; it is likewise owing to faulty repetition.

XXXVII.

You keep a prattling with your lips,
But never a word you speak that I can hear.

Ib., (Del., 17. — W. and Pr., 20. — Sim., II, 427.)

The first verse may easily be completed by the addition of *I see* at the end of the line: —

You keep a prattling with your lips, *I see,*
But never a word you speak that I can hear.

XXXVIII.

Em. Speak you to me, sir?
Mount. To thee, my only joy.
Em. I cannot hear you.
Mount. O plague of fortune! O hell without compare!
What boots it us, to gaze and not enjoy!

Ib., (Del., 18. — W. and Pr., 20 seq. — Sim., II, 427.)

I cannot agree with Simpson, who remarks on the fourth line —
'Dele *oh*' [before *hell*]. — Instead of *enjoy* in the fifth line Simpson
suggests *hear*, which, he adds, would rhyme with *compare*. Apart
from this somewhat questionable rhyme, *hear* cannot be right, since
it is applicable only to Em. According to my conviction a verb
or phrase is wanted which applies to both Em and Mountney, for
Mountney asks, *What boots it us?* Qy. *and not converse?* Or a line
to the following effect may have dropped out: —

and not enjoy
The sweet converse of mutual love between us.

XXXIX.

This may be but deceit,
A matter feignèd only to delude thee,
And, not unlike, perhaps by Valingford.
He loves fair Em as well as I —

Ib., (Del., 18. — W. and Pr., 21. — Sim., II, 428.)

I strongly suspect that a line has dropped out after *Valingford*, which
may have been to the following effect: —

Is she incited to this artful fraud.

XL.

Em. Jealousy, that sharps the lover's sight,
And makes him conceive and conster his intent.

Ib., (Del., 21. — W. and Pr., 25. — Sim., II, 431.)

Simpson proposes to read: *Ah, Jealousy,* but I have little doubt that
Jealousy should be pronounced as a word of four syllables: *Je-a-lous-y.*
The same dissolution occurs in *creature, treasure* and similar words;
see note XLIII. S. Walker, Versification, 136 seqq. Crit. Exam., II,
19 seqq. Abbott, s. 484; and Hazlitt's Dodsley, V, 22, where *treasure*
is twice to be pronounced as a trisyllable (Those bloody wars have
spent my tre-a-sure; And with my tre-a-sure my people's blood).
In the second line *him* is to be elided and read as an enclitic:
makes'm, if it should not be thought preferable to consider it as an
extra syllable before the pause and to scan the line: —

And makes | him conceive | and con|ster his | intent.

See *ante,* note XXXV, and compare Lord Byron, Sardanapalus, II, 1
(Poetical Works, in 1 vol., Lon. 1864, p. 254 b): —

May I | retire? | _ Say. _ Hush! | let him go | his way.

Mark Antony Lower, The Song of Solomon [in] the Dialect of Sus-
sex, &c. Lon., 1860, p. IV: —

Set'n down, and let'n stan;
Come agin, and fet'n anon.

XLI.

Here cometh Valingford;
Shift him off now, as thou hast done the other.

Ib., (Del., 22. — W. and Pr., 25. — Sim., II, 431.)

Qy.: *Now shift him off, &c.?* I do not think, that the author meant
to point out metrically an antithesis between *him*, i. e. Valingford,
and *the other,* i. e. Mountney. Such an antithesis, in the mouth of
Fair Em, would be too formal.

XLII.

Infortunate Valingford, to be thus cross'd in thy love! — Fair Em,
I am not a little sorry to see this thy hard hap. Yet nevertheless,
I am acquainted with a learned physician that will do anything for
thee at my request. To him will I resort and inquire his judgment,
as concerning the recovery of so excellent a sense.

Ib., (Del., 22. — W. and Pr., 25. — Sim., II, 432.)

This passage is an instance of metrical composition that has degen-
erated into prose by the negligence or ignorance of transcribers and
compositors. With the aid of a few slight alterations it may thus
be restored: —

Infortunate Valingford, to be thus cross'd
In love! — Fair Em, I'm not a little sorry
To see this thy hard hap, yet ne'ertheless
I am acquainted with a learned physician
That will do any thing for thee
At my request; to him will I resort
And will inquire his judgment as concerning
Th' recovery of so excellent a sense.

After the third line there is no doubt a gap that should be filled up
by some such line as the following: —

yet ne'ertheless
I fairly hope, all will be well again;
I am acquainted &c.

The fifth line may easily be extended to a regular blank verse by
the addition of *he can* after *any thing.*

3*

XLIII.

Val. Yet, sweet Em, accept this jewel at my hand,
Which I bestow on thee in token of my love.

Ib., (Del., 23. — W. and Pr., 27. — Sim., II, 432.)

The words of address should form an interjectional line and the
verses thus be regulated: —

Val. Yet, sweet Em,
Accept this jewel at my hand, which I
Bestow on thee in token of my love.

Chetwood, who wants the words *Em* and *on thee* to be expunged,
is evidently wrong.

A similar instance occurs a few pages farther on (Del., 32. —
W. and Pr., 38. — Sim., II, 443): —

Em. Trotter, lend me thy hand; and as thou lovest me, keep
my counsel, and justify whatsoever I say, and I'll largely requite thee.

The following verses may easily be restored: —

Em. Trotter,
Lend me thy hand, and as thou lov'st me, keep
My counsel, and justify *whate'er* I say,
And *largely I'll* requite thee.

Let me add a third passage (Del., 33. — W. and Pr., 39. — Sim.,
II, 444): —

Em. Good father, let me not stand as an open gazing-stock
to every one, but in a place alone, as fits a creature so miserable.

Omit *as* after *stand* and arrange: —

Em. Good father,
Let me not stand an open gazing-stock
To every one, but in a place alone
As fits a creature so miserable.

It is a well-known fact, that *creature* is frequently pronounced as a
trisyllable; see S. Walker, Versification, p. 136 seqq. Crit. Exam.,
II, 19 seqq. Abbott, s. 484 (p. 378). Compare note XL.

XLIV.

Mar. My lord, you know you need not to entreat,
But may command Mariana to her power,
Be't no impeachment to my honest fame.
Lub. Free are my thoughts from such base villainy
As may in question, Lady, call your name.

Ib., (Del., 24. — W. and Pr., 28. — Sim., II, 433 seq.)

Qy. either: *honest name,* or: *call your fame?* The same word should
surely be repeated.   Compare A. III, sc. 2, l. 141 seq.: —

I hold that man most shameless in his sin
That seeks to wrong an honest lady's name.

XLV.

It would redound greatly to my prejudice.

Ib., (Del., 24. — W. and Pr., 28. — Sim., II, 434.)

The emendation *'T would,* proposed by Simpson, is not sufficient to
restore the metre of this line. Nor can I agree with Messrs. Warnke
and Prœscholdt who are of opinion that we should pronounce
redound as a monosyllable, if we do not choose to follow Simpson;
the position of this monosyllabic *r'dound* in the unaccented part of
the foot can hardly be imputed even to so loose a versifier as the
author of Fair Em. Most probably we have to deal with a syllable
pause line, although the pause be ever so slight: —

It would | redound | ⌣ great|ly to | my pre|judice.

Prejudice in this case to be pronounced as a triple ending. Should
this scansion find no acceptance, we seem to be driven to the remedy
of transposing the words: —

'T would greatly to my prejudice redound.

XLVI.

For princely William, by whom thou shalt possess.

Ib., (Del., 25. — W. and Pr., 29. — Sim., II, 435.)

Simpson proposes to print *b'whom* and Messrs. Warnke and Prœscholdt
say that *by* is to be slurred. In my opinion the line has an extra-
syllable before the pause and should be scanned: —

For prin|cely Will|iam, by whom | thou shalt | possess.

XLVII.

Or court my mistress with fabulous discourses.

Ib., (Del., 27. — W. and Pr., 32. — Sim., II, 437.)

Simpson *ad loc.* proposes to read: —

Or with discourses fabulous court my mistress,

which would be too artificial and select a construction for the homely
language of our play. I myself suggested: —

Or court with fabulous discourse my mistress.

Both these corrections are needless, as the text is quite correct, the line having an extra syllable before the pause although this pause be one of the slightest. Scan: —

> Or court | my mis|tress with fab|ulous | discour|ses.

See *ante* note XXXV. (Jahrb. d. D. Sh.-G., XV, 346.)

XLVIII.

> *Mar.* My lord, I am a prisoner, and hard it were
> To get me from the court.
>> *Ib., (Del., 27. — W. and Pr., 32. — Sim., II, 438.)*

My suggestion in the Jahrb. d. D. Sh.-G., XV, 346, although it has met with the approval of Messrs. Warnke and Prœscholdt, yet seems needless, since *prisoner* may be pronounced as a triple ending before the pause.

XLIX.

> *Mount.* Thou know'st too well she hath:
> Wherein thou couldst not do me greater injury.
>> *Ib., (Del., 29. — W. and Pr., 34. — Sim., II, 440.)*

This is the division of the lines in the Qq, whereas the three modern editions have added *Wherein* to the first line, clearly with a view to cut down the second line to the compass of a blank verse. But even according to the arrangement of the Qq the second line is by no means a verse of six feet, as *injury* is evidently to be pronounced as a triple ending, so that there is no occasion whatever for an alteration.

L.

> For when I offered many gifts of gold,
> And jewels to entreat for love,
> She hath refused them with a coy disdain,
> Alleging that she could not see the sun.
>> *Ib., (Del., 29. — W. and Pr., 34 seq. — Sim., II, 440.)*

In A. II, sc. 3, l. 41 seqq. Em does not allude to the sun, but says: —

> What pleasure can I have
> In jewels, treasure, or any worldly thing
> That want my sight that should discern thereof?

It may, therefore, be suspected that the poet instead of *the sun* wrote *the same* which in the *ductus literarum* would come very near the spelling of the old copies *(sunne).* The only objection to which

this conjecture seems to be open, is that the next line begins with
the very same words: —

The same conjectured I to be thy drift,

although it seems difficult to say whether this circumstance does not
speak rather in favour of my suggestion than otherwise.

LI.

Val. In my conjecture merely counterfeit:
Therefore let us join hands in friendship once again,
Since that the jar grew only by conjecture.
    Moun. With all my heart: yet let us try the truth thereof.
    Val. With right good will. We will straight unto her father,
And there to learn whether it be so or no.
Ib., (Del., 30. — W. and Pr., 35. — Sim., II, 441.)

In the second line Messrs. Hazlitt and Simpson read *let's join*. There
is little difficulty in reducing this line to a blank verse; read,
either: —

Therefore in friendship let's join hands again;

or: —

Therefore join hands in friendship once again;

or, as proposed by Messrs. Warnke and Prœscholdt *ad loc.*: —

Therefore let's once again join hands in friendship.

Nevertheless the reading of the Qq may indeed have proceeded from
the author's pen who would seem to have admitted a few regular
Alexandrines; compare I, 4, 63 (where, however, *My lord* might easily
be expunged); II, 1, 70 (*Ah, Em,* might be printed as an interjectional line); II, 1, 102; II, 1, 165; V, 1, 86 (compare, however,
my note *ad loc.*); V, 1, 143; V, 1, 215 (although *utterly* had better
be taken for a triple ending before the pause). Perhaps also Mountney's reply to Valingford's proposal should be added to the number
of these Alexandrines: —

With all my heart: yet let us try the truth thereof.

Instead of *We will* in the fifth line, which is the uniform reading
of the old copies, Delius and Messrs. Warnke and Prœscholdt justly
write *We'll.* In the last line there is certainly some corruption as
it violates all grammar. Perhaps we should write either: —

To learn there whether it be so or no,

or: —

And there we'll learn whether it be so or no.

(Jahrb. d. D. Sh.-G., XV, 346 seq.)

LII.

And get we once to seas, I force not then
We quickly shall attain the English shore.
            Ib., (Del., 30. — W. and Pr., 35. — Sim., II, 441.)
Qy. read, *sea* for *seas?*

LIII.

Since first he came with thee into the court.
            Ib., (Del., 33. — W. and Pr., 40. — Sim., II, 445.)
Simpson: *in to the court*; compare, however, V, 1, 104: —
    When first I came into your highness' court.
The use of the preposition *into* is generally restricted to those cases
in which *court* stands for a court of justice, whereas *court* in the
sense of the residence and surroundings of a prince is generally
preceded by *to* or *unto*; see, e. g., I, 1, 78: —
    Will go with thee unto the Danish Court.
In the line in Titus Andronicus, IV, 3, 61: —
    Kinsmen, shoot all your shafts into the court,
the word *court* has a different meaning and the construction does
not therefore contradict the rule.. (Jahrb. d. D. Sh.-G., XV, 349.)

LIV.

To steal away fair Mariana, my prisoner.
            Ib., (Del., 34. — W. and Pr., 40. — Sim., II, 445.)
Chetwood's alteration: *fair Marian, my captive,* shows him to have
been ignorant of the peculiar characteristics of the Elizabethan blank
verse. The line is quite right as it stands, *Mariana* having an extra
syllable before the pause and *prisoner* being a triple ending: —
    To steal | away | fair Ma|ria|na, my pris|oner.

LV.

Or I shall fetch her unto Windsor's cost,
Yea, and William's too, if he deny her me.
                        [*Exit Sweno.*
            Ib., (Del., 35. — W. and Pr., 41. — Sim., II, 447.)
The last line may either be taken for an Alexandrine, or for a blank
verse; in the former case *Yea* is to be read as a monosyllabic foot,
in the latter *Yea, and* must be joined so as to form one syllable,
which, on account of the pause, seems unusual and harsh. The
stage-direction has been altered by Delius to *Exeunt all,* and this

alteration has been adopted by Messrs. Warnke and Prœscholdt. An attentive perusal of the scene, however, will convince the reader that Sweno, after employing his attendants to take both Lubeck and Mariana to prison, has remained alone on the stage and that consequently the stage-direction of the Qq is quite correct and requires no alteration whatever.

LVI.

> *Wm.* Hence, villains, hence! Dare you lay your hands
> Upon your sovereign!
> *Sol.* Well, sir; will deal for that.
> But here comes one will remedy all this.
>
> > *Ib.*, *(Del., 35 seq. — W. and Pr., 42. — Sim., II, 447.)*

Arrange: —

> *Wm.* Hence, villains, hence!
> Dare you lay your hands upon your sovereign!
> *Sol.* Well, sir, we'll deal for that!
> But here comes one will remedy all this.

How, added by Del., and *to*, added by Sim., are needless. *Dare* is a monosyllabic foot and *sovereign* a triple ending.

LVII.

> *Soldier.* My lord, watching this night in the camp
> We took this man, and know not what he is.
>
> > *Ib.*, *(Del., 36. — W. and Pr., 42. — Sim., II, 447.)*

Is the first line to be scanned as a verse of four feet: —

> My lord, | watching | this night | in th' camp?

Or is *lord* to be pronounced as a dissyllable? Cf. Marlow's Tragedy of Edward II., ed. by the Rev. F. G. Fleay, London, 1877, p. 117. Or are we to call in the aid of an emendation and read: —

> My lord, *in* watching this night in the camp?

Compare sixteen lines lower down: —

> In knowing this, I know thou art a traitor.

Or have we to deal with a syllable pause line: —

> My lord, | ◡ watch|ing this | night in | the camp?

Compare note IV.

LVIII.

> *Wm. Conq.* In knowing this, I know thou art a traitor;
> A rebel and mutinous conspirator.
> Why, Demarch; knowst thou who I am?
>
> > *Ib.*, *(Del., 36. — W. and Pr., 42. — Sim., II, 448.)*

Simpson adds the indefinite article before *mutinous* and thus produces a verse of six feet. The line is quite right as it stands, since *rebel* is to be pronounced as a monosyllable. *Why* is, of course, to be considered as a so-called monosyllabic foot.

LIX.

Dem. Pardon, my dread lord, the error of my sense,
And misdemeanour to your princely excellency.
Wm. Conq. Why, Demarch, what is the cause my subjects
are in arms?
Dem. Free are my thoughts, my dread and gracious lord,
From treason to your state and common weal.
Ib., (Del., 36. — W. and Pr., 43. — Sim., II, 448.)

There are no differences in the readings, except that Delius puts a semicolon after 'Demarch' and a comma after 'cause'. The substitution of 'excellence' (pronounced as a dissyllable) for 'excellency' in the second line seems to be indispensable to the restoration of the metre. The words 'Why, Demarch' form an interjectional line; and in the last line we should insert the definite article before 'common weal'. The whole passage, therefore, ought to be printed: —

Dem. Pardon, my dread lord, the error of my sense,
And misdemeanour to your princely *excellence.*
Wm. Conq. Why, Demarch,
What is the cause my subjects are in arms?
Dem. Free are my thoughts, my dread and gracious lord,
From treason to your state and *th'* common weal.

LX.

Only revengement of a private grudge,
By Lord Dirot lately proffered me.
Ib., (Del., 36. — W. and Pr., 43. — Sim., II, 448.)

Which is the right scansion of the second line? Are we to pronounce *lately* as a trisyllable (Abbott, s. 477): —

By Lord | Dirot | láte|ly prof|fer'd me?

Or have we to deal with a syllable pause line: —

By Lord | Dirot | ◡ late|ly prof|fer'd me?

Or has the original position of the words been perverted and did the poet write: —

Proffer'd | me late|ly by | *the* Lord | Dirot?

Thus a dilemma not only with two, but with three horns, if I may say so, presents itself to the reader, to whose judgment the decision must be left.

LXI.

> *Amb.* Marry thus: the king of Denmark and my Sov'reign
> Doth send to know of thee, what is the cause,
> That, injuriously, against the law of arms
> Thou hast stol'n away his only daughter Blanch,
> The only stay and comfort of his life?
> Therefore, by me
> He willeth thee to send his daughter Blanch,
> Or else forthwith he will levy such an host,
> As soon shall fetch her in despite of thee.
> > *Ib., (Del., 39. — W. and Pr., 45 seq. — Sim., II, 451.)*

Arrange and read: —

> *Amb.* Marry thus:
> The king of Denmark and my sovereign
> Doth send to know of thee, what is the cause,
> That thou hast stol'n, against the law of arms,
> Injuriously away his daughter Blanch,
> The only stay and comfort of his life?
> Therefore by me he willeth thee to send her,
> Or else forthwith he'll levy such an host,
> As soon shall fetch her in despite of thee.

The reiterations of *only* in the fourth and fifth, and of *his daughter Blanch* in the fourth and seventh lines are evident 'dittographies', if this technical term of German critics may be introduced into English; it might, I think, conveniently supersede the somewhat heavy and vague circumlocution of S. Walker, Crit. Exam., I, 276. A similar dittography has occurred already in note XXXVI. Critics of such thorough-going conservatism as to shield even glaring dittographies, may perhaps prefer to read the third and fourth lines thus: —

> That, 'gainst the law of arms, injuriously
> Thou'st stol'n away his only daughter Blanch.

The sixth and seventh lines have been contracted by Chetwood into the following: —

> Therefore by me he wills thee send her back.

Needlessly bold and needlessly harsh.

LXII.

> Our subjects, erst levied in civil broils,
> Muster forthwith, for to defend the realm.
> > *Ib., (Del., 40. — W. and Pr., 46. — Sim., II, 452.)*

The trochee *levied,* in the first line, not being preceded by a pause, seems hardly admissible, and it may, therefore, be surmised that the poet wrote: —

> Our subjects, *levied erst* in civil broils, &c.

LXIII.

Mil[*ler*]. Alas, sir, blame her not; you see she hath good cause,
being so handled by this gentleman: &c.

Ib., (Del., 43. — W. and Pr., 49. — Sim., II, 455.)

These words produce the impression on the reader's mind that an
adverb is wanted before *handled*; say, for instance, 'so *cruelly* handled.'

LXIV.

Sweno. Rosilio, is this the place whereas the Duke William
Should meet me?
Ros. It is, and like your grace.

Ib., (Del., 43. — W. and Pr., 50. — Sim., II, 455.)

This is the reading of the Quartos, whereas Delius, Simpson and
Messrs. Warnke and Prœscholdt have adopted the following arrangement: —

Sweno. Rosilio, is this the place whereas
The Duke William should meet me?
Ros. It is, and [an't, *Del.*] like your grace.

This, I apprehend, is even farther from the mark than the old text,
corrupted though it be. In my opinion the author wrote: —

Sweno. Rosilio,
Is this the place whereas Duke William
Should meet me?
Ros. It is, an't like your grace.

This arrangement agrees with the old copies in so far as it divides
the lines after *William,* which word, occurring as it does at the end
of the line, is plainly to be pronounced as a trisyllable. In the
same way *Grumio* in The Taming of the Shrew is generally used
as a trisyllable at the end of the line, but only exceptionally occurs
as such in its body. — Need it be added that in the last line the
pause 'takes the time of a defective syllable'? Compare note IV.

LXV.

Sweno. Rosilio, stay with me; the rest be gone. [*Exeunt.*

Ib., (Del., 43. — W. and Pr., 50. — Sim., II, 456.)

Both here and nine lines *infra* the Qq have the insufficient and misleading stage-direction *Exeunt* which has been retained by Messrs.
Warnke and Prœscholdt as well as by Simpson. Delius has added
Attendants in the second passage, whereas in the first passage he has
omitted the stage-direction altogether. It admits of no doubt that in
both places the stage-direction *Exeunt* can have no other meaning
than *Exeunt Attendants* and that consequently in both places the
latter word should be received into the text.

LXVI.

Sweno. William,
For other name and title give I none
To him, who, were he worthy of those honours
That fortune and his predecessors left,
I ought by right and human courtesy
To grace his style the Duke of Saxony.

Ib., (Del., 44. — W. and Pr., 51. — Sim., II, 457.)

William, which both in the Qq and in Delius's and Simpson's editions is joined to the following line, has justly been placed *extra versum* by Messrs. Warnke and Prœscholdt. The same correction has been made with respect to *Sweno* in A. V, sc. 1, 1. 97. — The last line was altered by Simpson to: —

To style his grace the duke of Saxony,

and I formerly concurred in this apparently ingenious alteration. A passage in The Merry Wives of Windsor (II, 2, 297), however, speaks greatly in favour of the reading of the Quartos as given above; it runs thus: 'Ford's a knave, and I will aggravate his style; thou, Master Brook, shalt know him for knave and cuckold.' *Style* means *title, official designation, mode of address.* But even this explanation does not clear away all difficulty and I am still afraid that there is some corruption lurking at the bottom of the passage. Chetwood reads: To grace his style with [!] King of England; Delius: To grace his style with Duke of Saxony. For *human courtesy* I formerly felt tempted to substitute *common courtesy.* Compare W. Irving's Tales of the Alhambra (London, 1878), p. 182: I could not do less in common hospitality. Cotter Morison, Macaulay (London, 1882), p. 23: We are bound in common equity to remember this fact. C. M. Ingleby, A Complete View of the Shakspere Controversy &c. (London, 1861), p. 41: No man of honourable feeling, or indeed of common humanity, &c. However, the old text is right; compare A Midsummer-Night's Dream, II, 2, 57 (in human modesty); The Merchant of Venice, IV, 1, 25, and Troilus and Cressida, IV, 1, 20 (human gentleness). (Jahrb. d. D. Sh.-G., XV, 348.)

LXVII.

Wm. Herein, Sweno, dost thou abase thy state,
To break the peace which by our ancestors
Hath heretofore been honourably kept.

Sweno. And should that peace for ever have been kept,
Had not thyself been author of the breach.

Ib., (Del., 45. — W. and Pr., 51. — Sim., II, 457).

Instead of *abase thy state* Delius reads *abuse thy state*. — There can
be little doubt that the first line of the King of Denmark's speech
wants correction; read: —

And that peace should for ever have been kept.
(Jahrb. d. D. Sh.-G., XV, 348.)

LXVIII.

And think you I conveyed away your daughter Blanch?
> *Ib., (Del., 45. — W. and Pr., 51. — Sim., II, 457.)*

Dele either *away* or *Blanch*.   *Away* may have lingered in the transcriber's recollection since he wrote in A. IV, sc. 2, l. 6 (according
to W. and Pr.): —

Thou'st stolen away his onely daughter Blanch.

To convey, without *away,* is used by the author of our play in A. IV,
sc. 2, l. 14: —

Saying, I conveyed her from the Danish court. .

Your daughter Blanch occurs five lines lower down (Del., 45; &c.),
likewise at the end of a verse; it seems, therefore, not unlikely that
Blanch was added to the line under discussion through faulty anticipation.

LXIX.

Sweno. Thou didst confess thou hadst a Lady hence.
> *Ib., (Del., 45. — W. and Pr., 52. — Sim., II, 457.)*

Sweno speaks as if he was still in Denmark, although the scene has
been shifted to England where he has landed with his troops. Is
this an oversight of the author, or has the word *hence* crept in by
way of corruption, or how is it to be explained? Should we read,
perhaps, *thence* instead of *hence*?

LXX.

Yet, Demarch, go and fetch her straight.
> *Ib., (Del., 46. — W. and Pr., 52. — Sim., II, 458.)*

The only means of scanning this perplexing line is to take *Yet* for
a monosyllabic foot and to suppose a pause which takes 'the time
of a defective syllable' to fall either after *Demarch* or after *go*: —

Yet, | Demarch, | ⌣ go | and fetch | her straight,

or: —

Yet, | Demarch, | go ⊥ | and fetch | her straight.

It seems, however, far more natural and easy to reduce, by a slight transposition, the verse to a regular line of four feet: —

Yet go, | Demarch, | and fetch | her straight.

(Jahrb. d. D. Sh.-G., XV, 348.)

LXXI.

Enter Rosilio with the Marques.

Ros. Pleaseth your highness, here is the Marques and
Mariana.

Ib., (Del., 46. — W. and Pr., 52. — Sim., II, 458.)

The words *and Mariana* have justly been added to the stage-direction by Delius. — Rosilio's speech which in both old and modern Editions forms a line of six feet with a double ending, should be arranged thus: —

Ros. Pleaseth your Highness,
Here is the Marques and Mariana.

The second line is a catalectic blank verse; see note II. — Compare ll. 88 and 89 of the same scene: —

Dem. May it please your Highness,
Here is the Lady [*whom*] you sent me for.

LXXII.

Lub. Duke William, you know it's for your cause
It pleaseth thus the king to misconceive of me,
And for his pleasure doth me injury.

Ib., (Del., 46. — W. and Pr., 53. — Sim., II, 459.)

The true arrangement of these lines I now think to be: —

Lub. Duke William,
You know it's for your cause it pleaseth thus
The king to misconceive of me,
And for his pleasure doth me injury.

As to the fourth line it may be questioned whether we should not write *do* for *doth*.

LXXIII.

Wm. Sweno,
I was deceiv'd, yea, utterly deceiv'd,
Yet, this is she, the same is Lady Blanch,

And, for mine error, here I am content
To do whatsoever Sweno shall set down.
                Ib., (Del., 47. — W. and Pr., 53. — Sim., II, 459.)
Qy.: *Yes,* this is she, &c.?   (Jahrb. d. D. Sh.-G., XV, 349.)

LXXIV.

Mar. When first I came into your highness' court,
And William often importing me of love,
I did devise, to ease the grief your daughter did sustain,
She'ld meet Sir William masked, as I it were.
                Ib., (Del., 47. — W. and Pr., 54. — Sim., II, 459.)
For the first line see *supra* note LIII. — *Often importing* is the
reading of the Qq and of Delius; Simpson: *oft' importing*; Messrs.
Warnke and Prœscholdt: *oft importuning,* as proposed by me in the
Jahrb. d. D. Sh.-G., XV, 349.   Compare A. III, sc. 1, l. 79 seqq.: 'Sir
Robert of Windsor, a man that you do not little esteem, hath long
importuned me of love.' The words *I did devise* clearly form an
interjectional line, which is perfectly in keeping with similar passages
of our play, e. g. III, 1, 23 (Thus stands the case); III, 2, 11 (Wretch
as thou art); IV, 2, 8 (Therefore by me); V, 1, 200 (Or deaf, or
dumb).   The passage should therefore be written and arranged: —

Mar. When first I came into your highness' court,
And William oft *importuning* me of love,
I did devise,
To ease the grief your daughter did sustain,
She'ld meet Sir William mask'd, as I it were.

LXXV.

Unconstant Mariana, thus to deal
With him which meant to thee nought but faith.
                Ib., (Del., 47. — W. and Pr., 54. — Sim., II, 460.)
As it would seem, three different ways of scanning the second line
offer themselves, among which the reader may choose that which in
his judgment is the least doubtful. Firstly: *nought,* like *wrought*
and similar words, may be read as a dissyllable; see Abbott, s. 484
(p. 381).   This scansion, suggested by me in the Jahrb. d. D. Sh.-G.,
XV, 349, has been adopted by Messrs. Warnke and Prœscholdt; it
would, however, produce a trochee, and a trochee in the fourth foot
after a very slight pause seems questionable. The second way of
dealing with the verse would be to class it among the syllable pause
lines and scan it thus: —

With him | which meant | to thee | ⌣ nought | but faith.

To this scansion it may be objected that the pause after *thee* is too
slight to serve as substitute for a defective syllable. Thirdly and
fourthly: the change of *to* into *unto,* or the insertion of *else* after
nought would certainly remove all difficulty, if the latter be not considered too bold an expedient. Nothing, therefore, remains but to
request the reader, in the hackneyed Horatian words: —

Si quid novisti rectius istis,

Candidus imperti.

LXXVI.

Wm. Conceit hath wrought such general dislike,
Through the false dealing of Mariana,
That utterly I do abhor their sex.

Ib., (Del., 48. — W. and Pr., 55. — Sim., II, 461.)

The second line is clearly a catalectic blank verse (see note II).
Diffident critics that are afraid of subscribing to my theory of catalectic verses may perhaps prefer to fill up the line by the addition
of *In me:* —

In me through the false dealing of Mariana.

The pronoun *their,* in the third line, does not only refer to Mariana,
but at the same time to Blanch who is standing beside her.

LXXVII.

Blanch. Unconstant knight, though some deserve no trust,
There's others faithful, loving, loyal, and just.

Ib., (Del., 48. — W. and Pr., 55. — Sim., II, 461.)

I am unable to see why William should be called unconstant, as he
has done nothing to deserve this reproach. Blanch should much
rather upbraid him for his injustice, for William rejects the whole
female sex without exception as being 'disloyal, unconstant, all un-
just', to which sweeping condemnation Blanch justly replies that
some, indeed, deserve no trust, but that there are others faithful,
loving, loyal, and just. May not the reading *Unconstant* be owing to
a faulty repetition from line 142? But what is to take its place?
Ungenerous? Unsparing? Uncourteous?

LXXVIII.

El[ner]. She has stolen a conscience to serve her own turn.
But you are deceived, i'faith, he will none of you.

Ib., (Det., 49. — W. and Pr., 56. — Sim., II, 462.)

These lines, divided at *turn* in the Qq as well as in the editions of
Delius and Simpson, have been printed as prose by Messrs. Warnke

and Prœscholdt; as, however, the scene is entirely written in verse, it seems highly improbable that a speech in prose should have been interposed by the author, especially as no reason whatever is apparent, why it should be in prose instead of verse. On the other hand the lines as printed in the Quartos, in Professor Delius' edition, and in Simpson's School of Shakspere show no regular metre, and are certainly corrupt. I do not see, how a meaning can be extorted from the words *She has stolen a conscience &c.* Let us look at the context. Elner says, that there was no witness by, when Manvile plighted his troth to Em and that, therefore, her claim to his hand is not valid. Em's reply is, that Manvile's conscience is a hundred witnesses, to which assertion Elner would seem bound by the laws of logic to rejoin, that it was not Manvile's own conscience, but a conscience stolen to serve Em's turn, and that Em may rest assured that he will none of her. Thus it appears that for *She hath* we ought to write *He hath*, an alteration which at the same time induces us to expunge *own* before *turn*. Moreover it seems evident that these words, at least the first line, must be spoken aside. In short, the lines, in my humble opinion, would seem to have come from the author's pen in the following shape: —

> *El.* [*Aside*]. He's stolen a conscience to serve her turn;
> But you're deceived, i'faith, he'll none of you.

Conscience is, of course, to be read as a trisyllable; compare l. 184 of our scene: —

> To void the scruple of his conscience.

LXXIX.

> But some impediments, which at that instant happen'd,
> Made me forsake her quite;
> For which I had her father's frank consent.
>
> *Ib., (Del., 49. — W. and Pr., 56. — Sim., II, 462.)*

This is the arrangement of the Qq, altered *in pejus* by the modern editors who have joined *happen'd* to the following line, because they have overlooked the fact that *impediments* is to be read as a trisyllable and that the line has an extra syllable before the pause.

LXXX.

> I loved this Manvile so much, that still my thought, &c.
>
> *Ib., (Del., 49. — W. and Pr., 56. — Sim., II, 462.)*

Much is an extra syllable before the pause; scan: —

> I lov'd | this Man | vile só | much, that still | my thought.

LXXXI.

Of whom my Manvile grew thus jealous.

Ib., (Del., 49. — W. and Pr., 56. — Sim., II, 462.)

This line looks as though it was catalectic, but it is not, since *jealous* is to be pronounced as a trisyllable, *jeal-i-ous*. To the instances of this pronunciation adduced by S. Walker, Versification, p. 154 seq., the following may be added: Arden of Feversham, ed. Delius, 15 (ed. Warnke and Prœscholdt, 14): —

Your louing husband is not Jelious.

Kyd, The Spanish Tragedy (Dodsley, ed. Hazlitt, V, 46): —

Ay, danger mixed with jealous despite.

Ib., (Dodsley, ed. Hazlitt, V, 131): —

To summon me to make appearance (= *appear-i-ance*).

Ram-Alley; or, Merry Tricks (Dodsley, ed. Hazlitt, X, 289): —

But that is nothing for a studient;

Ib., (Dodsley, ed. Hazlitt, X, 347): —

Say then her husband should grow jealous.

Marlowe, Edward II., I, 59: *siluian* (in the old Edd.); Andrew Borde, Introduction of Knowledge (ed. Furnivall for E. E. T. S.), p. 204: *stupendyouse*; Marston, The Insatiate Countesse, A. II (Works, ed. Halliwell, III, 138): *regardiant*; ib., A. V (Works, III, 185): *faviour*; Greene, Dorastus and Fawnia (Shakespeare's Library, ed. Hazlitt, I, IV, 36): *rigorious*. Clement Robinson, A Handful of Pleasant Delights, ed. Arber, p. 9: *studient*; Hamlet, I, 2, 177: *fellowe-studient* (in QB and QC); Merry Wives, III, 1, 38: *studient* (in FA); Twelfth Night, I, 5, 66: *dexteriously*; Milton, Samson Agonistes, l. 1627: *stupendious*. S. Walker's conjectural emendation on Middleton's Old Law, I, 1 (Versification, 156) is thus established beyond a doubt. Compare also Abbott, s. 480 (p. 372) and Storm, Englische Philologie (Heilbronn, 1881), p. 290 seq. (Jahrb. d. D. Sh.-G., XV, 350).

LXXXII.

By counterfeiting that I neither saw nor heard
Any ways to rid my hands of them.

Ib., (Det., 50. — W. and Pr., 57. — Sim., II, 463.)

This division is certainly wrong; the words *nor heard* are to be transferred to the following line (as has been done by Messrs. Warnke and Prœscholdt in accordance with my suggestion) and *any ways* is to be contracted in pronunciation so as to form only two syllables; see note on The Winter's Tale, I, 2, 173. (Jahrb. d. D. Sh.-G., XV, 350).

LXXXIII.

All this I did to keep my Manvile's love,
Which he unkindly seeks for to reward.
Ib., (Del., 50. — W. and Pr., 57. — Sim., II, 463.)

Qy.: *thus* instead of *for*?   (Jahrb. d. D. Sh.-G., XV, 350.)

LXXXIV.

Or else what impediments might befall to man.
Ib., (Del., 50. — W. and Pr., 57. — Sim., II, 463.)

Simpson's correction of this suspicious reading of the Qq: —

Or what impediments else might befall man,

is a modern instance of the truth of the old saying: —

Incidit in Scyllam, qui vult vitare Charybdim.

If an emendation of the line is to be resolved upon, I still adhere
to the alteration proposed by me in the Jahrb. d. D. Sh.-G., XV, 350,
which, I think, is preferable at least in point of rhythm: —

Or what impediments else might man befall.

At the same time, however, I have tried to scan the Quarto-reading
and Messrs. Warnke and Prœscholdt have approved of my scansion: —·

Or else | what 'mped | 'ments might | befall | to man.

Should the reader think this scansion harsh, I shall not contradict
him; let him make his own choice or try to find out something
better.

LXXXV.

Man.   Forgive me! sweet Em!
Ib., (Del., 50. — W. and Pr., 57. — Sim., II, 463.)

Qy.: Forgive me, *my* sweet Em?

LXXXVI.

Val. My Lord, this gentleman, when time was,
Stood something in our light,
And now I think it not amiss
To laugh at him that sometime scorned at us.
Ib., (Del., 51. — W. and Pr., 58. — Sim., II, 464.)

This reading of the Qq, faulty though it manifestly be, has been left
undisturbed by both Delius and Simpson, whereas Messrs. Warnke

and Prœscholdt have adopted the correction proposed by me in the
Jahrb. d. D. Sh.-G., XV, 351: —

> *Val.* My Lord,
> This gentleman stood something in our light,
> When time was; now I think it not amiss
> To laugh at him that sometimes scorn'd at us.

As to the third line, I must now say that *and* need not be omitted;
the line has simply an extra syllable before the pause. — From
these lines forward the concluding part of the play is corrupt, or, at
least, in great disorder. Simpson and his editor Mr. Gibbs, make a
few remarks on this fact, but they are inadequate. Simpson declares
it to be evident that the lines addressed to William the Conqueror
by Manvile: —

> I partly am persuaded as your grace is —
> My Lord, he's best at ease that meddleth least,

must certainly be spoken before William the Conqueror accepts Blanch.
As Mr. Gibbs further remarks, the derision of Manvile by Valingford
and Mountney should begin immediately after Valingford's words:
Then thus (V, 1, 221). Valingford continues: —

> Sir, may a man
> Be so bold as to crave a word with you,

so that the dialogue follows uninterruptedly as far as: —

> *Mount.* I know full well: because they hang too high.

Whilst this dialogue between Valingford, Mountney, Manvile, the King
of Denmark, and the Marquis Lubeck has been going on, William
the Conqueror has evidently been conversing aside with Mariana and
Blanch and has come to an understanding with them. He now
addresses Manvile too, asking him: —

> Now, sir, how stands the case with you?

to which Manvile replies the two lines just quoted: —

> I partly am persuaded as your grace is —
> My Lord, he's best at ease that meddleth least.

I may add, that after this line a verse has evidently been lost which
informs us, with whom we should meddle least in order to be best
at ease, viz. with womankind. William the Conqueror, however, has
meanwhile changed his mind and replies: —

> I see, that women are not general evils

and so on, as far as: —

> And after my decease the Denmark crown.

After this line there is an evident gap; some lines are wanting that
should introduce the question (in l. 255): —

> And may it be a miller's daughter by her birth?

which, by the way, is a rather suspicious line of six feet which
Simpson has tried to regulate (And may't be a Miller's daughter by
her birth). From this line to the end the regular sequence of the
lines seems not to have been disturbed. The original succession of
the lines expressed in numbers according to the numbering of Messrs.
Warnke and Prœscholdt is this: 221 *(Then thus)*, 234—254, 231
—233, 222—230, 255—278. (Jahrb. d. D. Sh.-G., XV, 351 seq.)

LXXXVII.

> *Lub.* In mine eyes this is the properest wench;
> Might I advise thee, take her unto thy wife.
>
> Ib., (Del., 52. — W. and Pr., 59. — Sim., II, 465.)

This is the reading and arrangement of the Qq, whereas the passage
is printed as three lines in Delius' and Simpson's editions. Moreover
Delius reads *my eyes* instead of *mine eyes,* Simpson *to thy wife*
instead of *unto thy wife,* and I myself have suggested *this'* for *this
is,* thus making the line one of four feet only. This suggestion has
been installed in the text by Messrs. Warnke and Prœscholdt. However, I have now come to the conviction that the old text is completely right. Rightly scanned the first verse is no doubt a syllable
pause line: —

In mine | ˈeyes this | ⌣ is | the prop|erest wench.

and the second line has an extra syllable before the pause: —

Might I | advise | thee, take her | unto | thy wife.

Compare V, 1, 218. 248. 264. (Jahrb. d. D. Sh.-G., XV, 352.)

LXXXVIII.

> And, fair Em, frolic with thy good father.
>
> Ib., (Del., 52. — W. and Pr., 59. — Sim., II, 466.)

Simpson, in order to restore the metre, inserted *thou* after *frolic,*
which is contrary to a metrical usage observed throughout our play,
viz. the usage of placing the name of Em (or Blanch) in the accented
part of the rhythm. See A. I, sc. 1, l. 62: —

> But to renown fair Blanch, my sovereign's child

Ib., l. 80: —

> Bright Blanch, I come! sweet fortune, favour me.

A. I, sc. 2, l. 15: —

> And thou, sweet Em, must stoop too high estate

A. II, sc. 1, l. 128: —

> Nay, stay, fair Em. — I'm going homewards, Sir

Ib., l. 149: —

 Sweet Em, it is no little grief to me

Ib., l. 164: —

 Ah, Em, fair Em, if art can make thee whole

Ib., l. 169: —

 He loves fair Em as well as I —

If, therefore, the insertion of *thou* should be deemed necessary, it should take its place not after *frolic,* but after *And*: —

 And thou, fair Em, frolic with thy good father.

However, the line may be both complete and uncorrupted as it has · been handed down to us; if *And* be taken for a monosyllabic foot, the verse may thus be scanned: —

 And, | fair Em, | frólic | with thy | good fa|ther.

This is by no means a smooth and harmonious line, but the versification of our play everywhere shows the author to have been a most negligent versifier and it is not the province of either editor or critic to improve his lines, but merely to restore them where they have been corrupted. (Jahrb. d. D. Sh.-G., XV, 352.)

LXXXIX.

 Em. Em rests at the pleasure of your highness.

  Ib., (Del., 52. — W. and Pr., 60. — Sim., II, 466.)

Em may perhaps be admitted as a monosyllabic foot. The lection *restes* in QA, however, may possibly have been pronounced as a dissyllable. See note on Mucedorus, ed. Del., 49 (his absence *breedes*).

XC.

Are not you Merchants, that from East to West,
From the Antarcticke to the Arctick Poles,
Bringing all treasure that the earth can yeeld?

  Histrio-Mastix, apud Simpson, The School of
   Shakspere, II, 44 seq.

Read: *Bring in* all treasure. — Qy. *Pole*?

XCI.

Come, with your razors rip my bowels up,
With your sharp fire-forks crack my starvèd bones:
Use me as you will, so Humber may not live.

  Locrine in Malone's Suppl. II, 246. — Hazlitt, Suppl.
   Works, 93. — Doubtful Plays (Tauchnitz), 179.

In order to regulate the metre I formerly proposed to read *Use me at will, &c.*, but must now withdraw this suggestion as needless. Scan: —

Use me as | you will, | so Hum|ber may | not live.

Me and *as* are to be run into one another. (Jahrb. d. D. Sh.-G., XIII, 76.)

XCII.

Flow. Sen. I' faith, sir, according to the old proverb:
The child was born, and cried,
Became a man, after fell sick, and died.

*The London Prodigal, I, 1. (Malone, Supplement, II, 455. —
Hazlitt, The Supplementary Works of Wm. Shakspeare, 209.)*

After, in the last line, looks like an interpolation and should be expunged. By the way, it may be remarked that in Mr. Carew Hazlitt's English Proverbs and Proverbial Phrases this 'old proverb' is not to be found.

XCIII.

Sir Lane. Where is this inn? We are past it, Daffodil.
Daf. The good sign is here, sir, but the back gate is before.

Ib., I, 2. (Mal., II, 462. — Haz., 212.)

Qy. read, The *gate* sign instead of The *good* sign? — According to Malone, folios as well as modern editions read *the black gate*; instead of which Malone has restored *the back gate* from the quarto.

XCIV.

Arti. Why, there 'tis now: our year's wages and our vails will scarce pay for broken swords and bucklers that we use in our quarrels. But I'll not fight if Daffodil be o' t' other side, that's flat.

Ib., II, 4. (Mal., II, 480. — Haz., 222.)

Read, in *your* quarrels. The servants do not use their swords and bucklers in their own quarrels, but in those of their masters. 'Sir', says Artichoke to Sir Lancelot, his master, towards the close of the scene, 'we have been scouring of our swords and bucklers for your defence.'

XCV.

M. Flow. Now, God thank you, sweet lady. If you have any friend, or garden-house where you may employ a poor gentleman as your friend, I am yours to command in all secret service.

Ib., V, 1. (Mal., II, 517. — Haz., 241.)

Read: if you have any *field*, or garden-house. *Friend* crept in, by anticipation, from the following line. — Compare Dekker, The Honest Whore, Pt. II, III, 3 (Middleton, ed. Dyce, III, 188): she bids the gentleman name any afternoon and she'll meet him at her garden-house, which I know. — Ram-Alley; or, Merry Tricks, I, 1 (Dodsley, ed. Hazlitt, X, 271): —

> Hither, they say, he usually doth come,
> Whom I so much affect: what makes he here?
> In the skirts of Holborn, so near the field,
> And at a garden-house? he has some punk,
> Upon my life.

Davenport, The City Nightcap (Dodsley, ed. Hazlitt, XIII, 187): Garden-houses are not truer bawds to cuckold-making, than I will be to thee and thy stratagem. — Measure for Measure, V, 1, 212 and 229. — Philip Stubbes's Anatomy of the Abuses in England, ed. Furnivall, Part I, p. 88 seq. and p. 279 seq. — Middleton, The Mayor of Queenborough, III, 1 (Middleton, ed. Dyce, I, 162). — The Miseries of Enforced Marriage (Dodsley, ed. Hazlitt, IX, 538.)

XCVI.

> *Ray[mond].* O, thou base world! how leprous is that soul,
> That is once lim'd in that polluted mud!
> O Sir Arthur! you have startled his free active spirit
> With a too sharp spur for his mind to bear.
>> *The Merry Devil of Edmonton (Dodsley, ed. Hazlitt, X, 230. — Ed. Warnke and Prœscholdt, 22 seq.)*

The old copies (1617, 1626, 1631, and 1655) *that polluted mud*; Dodsley (1744) *thy polluted mud*. — The second *O* spoils the metre and is plainly owing to a dittography; read: —

> Sir Arthur! you've startled his free active spirit.

Several passages in this play are either wrongly printed as prose or wrongly arranged in Hazlitt's Dodsley. Such, e. g., is the following speech by Jerningham at p. 244: 'Blood! if all Hertfordshire were at our heels, we'll carry her away in spite of them', which clearly consists of two regular blank verses, divided after *heels*. By the way it may be remarked that *Blood* is the reading of the later Qq, whereas the copy of 1617 correctly reads *'S blood (Z'blood)*. A wrongly arranged passage occurs at p. 246: —

> *Y. Clare.* We shall anon; nouns! hark!
> What means this noise?
> *Jer.* Stay, I hear horsemen.
> *Y. Clare.* I hear footmen too.

Arrange, of course: —

    Y. Clare. We shall anon; nouns! hark! What means this
                           noise?

    Jer. Stay, I hear horsemen.
    Y. Clare. .   I hear footmen too.

Nouns, by the way, is the reading of the later Qq; Qu. 1617, *zounds.*
Another speech, wrongly printed as prose, is met with at p. 256.
Here Mr. Hazlitt's text is so much the more provoking as in all the
four Qq which I have been able to collate, the passage is divided
quite correctly into two lines: —

    Hil[*dersham*]. Sir Arthur, by my order and my faith,
I know not what you mean.

XCVII.

Most sacred Majesty, whose great deserts
Thy subject England, nay, the world admires.
    *Mucedorus, (ed. Delius, 1. — Ed. Warnke and Præscholdt, 19. —
    Hazlitt's Dodsley, VII, 201.)*

The whole of the Prologue, from l. 3 forward, being in rhyme, I
cannot bring myself to the belief that its very beginning should have
been left rhymeless by the author. Mr. Collier proposes to read
either *desires* in l. 1, or *asserts* in l. 2. I rather think that the original reading in l. 1 was: *aspires.* (Englische Studien, herausgegeben
von Eug. Kölbing, VI, 311.)

XCVIII.

Embrace your council: love with faith them guide,
That both, as one, bench by each other's side.
    Ib., (Del., 1. — W. and Pr., 19. — H's D., VII, 201.)

Qq 1610 and 1615: *Counsell*; later Qq: *Councel* or *Councell*; Mr. Hazlitt: *Council* and *at one.* — The Prologue which first appears in the
edition of 1610, would seem to have been written shortly after the
Gunpowder-Plot to which ll. 9—10 seem to refer: —

Where smiling angels shall your guardians be
From blemish'd traitors, stain'd with perjury.

'Several severe acts', to borrow the words of a writer in the Imperial
Dictionary of Universal Biography (s. James I.), 'were in consequence
[of the Gunpowder-Plot] passed by the Parliament against the Roman
Catholics; but James, partly from timidity, partly from policy, showed
a decided disinclination to carry them into execution.' It would.
seem, as if an allusion to this indecision of the king was to be
traced in ll. 5—6 and as if, accordingly, we should write *counsels*;

especially as this plural seems to be required by the following *them*.
Compare Timon of Athens, III, 1, 27: he would embrace no counsel.
(Kölb., Engl. Stud., VI, 311.)

XCIX.

Why so; thus do I hope to please.

> *Ib., (Del., 3. — W. and Pr., 21. — H's D., VII, 203.)*

I think it highly improbable that the author should have commenced
his play with an incomplete line, however frequently he may have
admitted both shorter and longer lines in its course. I feel convinced that we should add *even: Why, even so; &c.* Compare The
Play of Stucley, l. 348 (Simpson, The School of Shakspere, I, 171):
Master Cross the Mercer, is't even so? A Warning for Fair Women,
A. II, l. 937 (Simpson, The School of Shakspere, II, 305): —

Heaven will have justice showne: it is even so!

(Jahrb. d. D. Sh.-G., XIII, 46 seq.)

C.

Sound forth Bellona's silver-tuned strings.

> *Ib., (Del., 3. — W. and Pr., 21. — H's D., VII, 203.)*

In the Jahrb. d. D. Sh.-G., XI, 63, the late Prof. W. Wagner has
observed that he is unable to attach a meaning to the mention of
Bellona in this passage. Bellona is indeed nowhere represented as
a patroness of music and has nothing to do with either 'silver-tuned
strings' or with wind-instruments which latter seem to be ascribed
to her a few lines below (l. 14 seq.): —

That seem'st to check the blossoms of delight,
And stifle the sound of sweet Bellona's breath.

And what business has Comedy to praise 'sweet Bellona' who is no
comic, but an exclusively tragic character? I cannot help thinking
that there is some corruption lurking at the bottom, but am unable
to offer an explanation how it may have originated, or a cure for
it. By the way it may be remarked that for *stifle* in the Ed. pr.
the later Qq read *still*. (Jahrb. d. D. Sh.-G., XIII, 47.)

CI.

Nay, stay minion, there lies a block.

> *Ib., (Del., 3. — W. and Pr., 21. — H's D., VII, 203.)*

This is the reading of the quartos of 1598 *(staie)*, 1610 and 1615
(Minion); Qq 1619 and 1631: *Nay stay Minion stay, there.* In the
Jahrb. d. D. Sh.-G., XIII, 48, I proposed to read: *Nay, stay, you*

minion, stay, and this conjecture, which no doubt improves the metre, has been installed in the text by Messrs. Warnke and Prœscholdt. *You minion* repeatedly occurs in Shakespeare, e. g., in The Comedy of Errors, III, 1, 54: —

Do you hear, you minion? you'll let us in, I hope?

Ib., IV, 4, 63: —

You minion, you, are these your customers?

Romeo and Juliet, III, 5, 152 seq.: —

And yet 'not proud', mistress minion, you,
Thank me no thankings, nor proud me no prouds.

However, the readings of the earlier as well as the later Qq may be right, if properly scanned. *Nay,* in both cases, is to be considered as a monosyllabic foot and *minion,* in the earliest Quarto, as a trisyllable, although the dissolution of -*ion* usually occurs only at the end and not in the body of the line. If, therefore, this pronunciation should be rejected, the verse, as printed in the first quarto, may perhaps with greater correctness be scanned as a syllable pause line. These, then, are the three scansions: —

Nay, | stay, min|i-on; | there lies | a block
Nay, | stay, min|ion; ⌐ | there lies | a block
Nay, | stay, min|iön, stay | there lies | a block.

The last reading certainly looks like a correction.

CII.

And gain the glory of thy wished port.

Ib., (Del., 3. — W. and Pr., 21. — H's D., VII, 203.)

This is the reading of the earlier Qq; the later Qq: *this wished port.* It seems obvious that instead of *port* we should read *sport,* as suggested by me in the Jahrb. d. D. Sh.-G., XIII, 48. Messrs. Warnke and Prœscholdt have adopted this correction.

CIII.

Flying for succour to their dankish caves.

Ib., (Del., 4. — W. and Pr., 22. — H's D., VII, 204.)

My conjectural emendation *dankish* has been received into the text by Messrs. Warnke and Prœscholdt; the old editions read *Danish,* a reading which cannot lay claim to a gentler appellation than that of nonsense. *Dankish* occurs in the Comedy of Errors, V, 1, 247: —

And in a dark and dankish vault at home.

Another emendation may, however, be offered, viz. *dampish.* Cf. The Birth of Merlin, IV, 1, (ed. Delius, 69): —

Then know, my lord, there is a dampish cave,
The nightly habitation of these dragons,
Vaulted beneath &c.

The Play of Stucley, 668 (Simpson, The School of Shakspere, I, 185): —

When we are lodged within the dampish field.

CIV.

Hearken, thou shalt hear a noise
Shall fill the air with shrilling sound,
And thunder music to the gods above:
Mars shall himself reach down
A peerless crown &c.

Ib., (Del., 4. — W. and Pr., 22. — H's D., VII, 204.)

Qq 1598—1610: *with a shrilling sound. Hark,* before *Hearken,* in Messrs. Warnke and Prœscholdt's edition, is an unnecessary addition of the late Prof. W. Wagner's (see Jahrb. d. D. Sh.-G., XI, 63). The passage, I think, should thus be arranged: —

Hearken! thou'lt hear a noise shall fill the air
With shrilling sound, and thunder music to
The gods above: Mars shall himself reach down
A peerless crown &c.

Exception might be taken to the *enjambement* in the second line, but this drawback is amply compensated by the restoration of three regular lines in lieu of two complete and two incomplete ones. Moreover the versification of our author is, on the whole, so loose and careless that we shall scarcely wrong him by fathering an unstopped line upon him. (Jahrb. d. D. Sh.-G., XV, 340 seq. — Kölb., Engl. Stud., VI, 312.)

CV.

In this brave music Envy takes delight,
Where I may see them wallow in their blood &c.

Ib., (Del., 4. — W. and Pr., 22. — H's D., VII, 204.)

'As there is no antecedent', say Messrs. Warnke and Prœscholdt, 'to which *them* might refer, it would, perhaps, be better to read *men.*' At the same time they refer the reader to l. 64 seq., where the same want of connexion recurs and where no alteration seems suited to remedy it. To me it seems more probable that in both passages something is wanting (after l. 30 and l. 64). Four lines below (l. 34) we have to deal with an Alexandrine which might, however, easily

be reduced to a blank verse by the omission of *my trull.* Compare
Englishmen for my Money (Dodsley, ed. Hazlitt, X, 514): —

Were I as you,
Why, this were sport alone for me to do.

(Jahrb. d. D. Sh.-G., XV, 341.)

CVI.

Thou bloody, envious disdainer of men's joys.

Ib., (Del., 4. — W. and Pr., 22. — H's D., VII, 204.)
Thus Qq (Qu. 1598 *ioye*); Messrs. Warnke and Prœscholdt *'sdainer.*
See Marlowe's Edward the Second, ed. Tancock (Clarendon Press,
1879), p. 160. In my opinion *bloody* has intruded by mistake from
the following line; it is a dittography. Read therefore: —

Thou envious disdainer of men's joys.

(Jahrb. d. D. Sh.-G., XIII, 49.)

CVII.

Whirling thy measures with a peal of death,
And drench thy metres in a sea of blood.

Ib., (Del., 5. — W. and Pr., 23. — H's D., VII, 205.)
Qq: *pleasures* and *methodes.* The conjectural emendations *measures*
and *metres,* introduced into the text by Messrs. Warnke and Prœscholdt,
were proposed by me. *Measure,* in the sense of *dance* is used, e. g.,
in K. Richard II., I, 3, 291; in K. Richard III., I, 1, 8, and in Fair
Em, II, 2, 8; *metre,* in the sense of *verse* or *line,* occurs, e. g., in
K. Richard II., II, 1, 19.   (Jahrb. d. D. Sh.-G., XIII, 50.)

CVIII.

Why then, Comedy, send thy actors forth.

Ib., (Del., 5. — W. and Pr., 23. — H's D., VII, 205.)
In order to improve the metre Messrs. Warnke and Prœscholdt insert
now after *send,* whereas in the Jahrb. d. D. Sh.-G., XV, 341, I contended for the reading of the Qq. If *why* be taken for a monosyllabic foot, the line may thus be scanned: —

Why, | then Come|dy, send | thy act|ors forth.

I have, however, some misgiving whether it may be deemed admissible to disjoin the words *Why then* and to alter the punctuation of
the Qq, especially as two other ways of scanning the line seem to
be open, which involve no change whatever. The first is to pronounce *Comedy* as a trisyllable: —

Why then, | Come|dy, send | thy act|ors forth.

To this scansion it may be objected that, throughout our play, *Comedy* in the body of the line seems always to be used as a dissyllable. This difficulty will be avoided if we class the verse among the syllable pause lines: —

Why then, | Comedy, | ᴗ send | thy act|ors forth.

The reader may make his choice among these different expedients. Thus much is certain, that we shall have to admit a trochee in the second place, if we do not choose to separate *why* from the rest of the line, and that an alteration of the text or the addition of some expletive seems by no means unavoidable.

CIX.

But, my Anselmo, loth I am to say,
I must estrange that friendship.
Ib., (Del., 6. — W. and Pr., 24. — H's D., VII, 206.)

In the Qq these two verses form one line only. Qu. 1668: *enlarge thy friendship.* W. Wagner proposes to read: *my friendship.* The second line may easily be completed by adding *for a while.* On the other hand it may be suggested that the words *loth I am to say,* may possibly be an interpolation by some actor or copyist and that the original line was to the following effect: —

But, my Anselmo, I must estrange that friendship.

(Jahrb. d. D. Sh.-G., XIII, 51.)

CX.

Does mangle verity; boasting of what is not.
Ib., (Del., 6. — W. and Pr., 25. — H's D., VII, 206.)

Verily is a triple ending before the pause, and the second hemistich commences with a trochee *(boasting)*; thus, no alteration whatever is needed. Compare note on Measure for Measure, IV, 3, 131. (Jahrb. d. D. Sh.-G., XIII, 51; XV, 341.)

CXI.

Ansel. Your miss will breed a blemish in the court,
And throw a frosty dew upon that beard,
Whose front Valentia stoops to.
Ib., (Del., 6 seq. — W. and Pr., 25. — H's D., VII, 206.)

However fond of queerness our author may have shown himself in his diction, yet it seems to surpass all bounds to speak of the front of a beard. The late Prof. W. Wagner (Jahrb. d. D. Sh.-G., XIV, 278) suggested *upon his beard,* which I cannot think very plausible. Qy.: *head* instead of *beard?*

CXII.

Though base the weed is, 'twas a shepherd's.

Ib., (Del., 7. — W. and Pr., 25. — H's D., VII, 207.)

This is the reading of the Qq. The late Prof. W. Wagner proposed
to add *once* after *shepherd's,* and Messrs. Warnke and Prœscholdt
have admitted this conjecture into the text. I formerly conjectured
for it was a shepherd's, but am now inclined to consider the line
either as a catalectic verse (see note II) or as a syllable pause line: —

Though base | the weed | is, ⸺ | it was | a shep|herd's.

(Jahrb. d. D. Sh.-G., XIII, 51.)

CXIII.

So, let our respect command thy secrecy,
At once a brief farewell,
Delay to lovers is a second hell.

Ib., (Del., 7. — W. and Pr., 26. — H's D., VII, 207.)

Besides the conjectural emendation of this passage proposed by me
in the Jahrb. d. D. Sh.-G., XIII, 51 seq., and partly adopted by Messrs.
Warnke and Prœscholdt, two others of a more conservative tendency
may be offered. Firstly: the text may be left untouched as printed
in the Qq, provided *So* be taken for a monosyllabic foot, and *secrecy*
for a triple ending. This latter scansion, however, seems somewhat
doubtful, and besides we should have to deal with a couplet of un-
equal lines, which seems doubtful again. These difficulties would be
avoided by the following arrangement of the lines: —

So, let our respect command
Thy secrecy. At once a brief farewell
Delay to lovers is a second hell.

This would involve no alteration whatever, except in the division of
the lines, and it does not matter that the first line is one of four
feet only.

CXIV.

Mouse. O horrible, terrible! Was ever poor gentleman so scared
out of his seven senses?

Ib., (Del., 8. — W. and Pr., 26. — H's D., VII, 208.)

Compare Locrine, IV, 2 (Malone's Supplement, II, 244): O horrible!
terrible! I think I have a quarry of stones in my pocket. — Fair
Em, (ed. W. and Pr.), III, 4, 42 seq.: Ah! that is as much as to say
you would tell a terrible, horrible, outrageous lie, and I shall soothe
it. — Specimens of Cornish Provincial Dialect collected and arranged
by Uncle Jan Trenoodle (London, 1846), p. 14: I do think also

seriously of writing some works of a light and popular sort; or some of what a friend of mine do call, the mysterious, and terrible-horrible school, (books of easy virtue); or some Cornish tales &c. (Jahrb. d. D. Sh.-G., XIII, 52.)

CXV.

Seg. O, fly, madam, fly, or else we are but dead.
Ama. Help, Segasto, help, help, sweet Segasto, or else I die.
Seg. Alas, madam! there is no way but flight.

Ib., (Del., 8. — W. and Pr., 27. — H's D., VII, 208.)

Upon second, I may even say third and fourth, thoughts I have come to the conviction that the alterations of these lines proposed by me in the Jahrb. d. D. Sh.-G., XIII, 52, can as little be upheld as the far bolder reading introduced by Messrs. Warnke and Prœscholdt. *Madam* in the first line is to be pronounced as a monosyllable and in the third as a trochee. The exclamation *Help, Segasto, help* very naturally lends itself to an interjectional line, so that, apart from this alteration in the division of the lines, the old text would remain unaltered: —

Seg. O, fly, madam, fly, or else we are but dead.
Ama. Help, Segasto, help!
Help, sweet Segasto! or else I die.
Seg. Alas, madam! There is no way but flight.

The third line is a syllable pause line; scan: —

Help, sweet | Segas|to! ‿ | or else | I die.

This improvement on the old text would, I think, be complete, if the interjection *O,* which is certainly misplaced, could be transferred to the following line: —

Seg. Fly, madam, fly, or else we are but dead.
Ama. O help, Segasto, help!
Help, sweet Segasto! or else I die.
Seg. Alas, madam! there is no way but flight.

(Jahrb. d. D. Sh.-G., XV, 342.)

CXVI.

Now, whereas it is my father's will.

Ib., (Del., 9. — W. and Pr., 28. — H's D., VII, 209.)

This reading of the Qq requires no alteration whatever, and the conjectures proposed by the late Prof. W. Wagner *(And now)* and myself are needless. *Now* is a monosyllabic foot; scan: —

Now, | whereás | it is | my fa|ther's will.

Compare *infra*, A. II, sc. 1, l. 1: —

    Now, | brave lords, | our wars | are brought | to end.

Two lines below the Qq read *through father's former usury* which, in my humble opinion, cannot be right; I feel convinced that the poet wrote *through's*, and Messrs. Warnke and Prœscholdt have admitted this conjecture into the text. (Jahrb. d. D. Sh.-G., XIII, 53. XV, 342.)

CXVII.

    But tell me, lady, what is become of him, &c.

        Ib., *(Del., 10. — W. and Pr., 29. — H's D., VII, 210.)*

Messrs. Warnke and Prœscholdt read *what's*, but no alteration is required, the line merely containing an extra syllable before the pause: —

    But tell | me, la|dy, what is | become | of him.

Four lines *infra* my conjecture to add *was* after *Yet* has been adopted by Delius as well as Messrs. Warnke and Prœscholdt. Perhaps, however, *Yet* may be taken to be a monosyllabic foot, although it is a short syllable and not followed by a pause. (Jahrb. d. D. Sh.-G., XIII, 53 and XV, 342.)

CXVIII.

    So will the king, my father, thee reward:
    Come, let's away and guard me to the court.

        Ib., *(Del., 11. — W. and Pr., 29. — H's D., VII, 211.)*

It seems not at all unlikely to me that these concluding lines of the scene originally formed a couplet and that accordingly we should read: —

    So will the king, my father, thee reward:
    Come, let's away and to the court me guard.

The same inverted construction occurs in A. II, sc. 1, l. 37: —

    I shall with bounties thee enlarge therefore.

(Kölb., Engl. Stud., VI, 312.)

CXIX.

    When heaps of harms do hover over head,
    'Tis time as then, some say to look about,
    And of ensuing harms to choose the least.

        Ib., *(Del., 11. — W. and Pr., 29. — H's D., VII, 211.)*

The later Qq include the words *some say* in parentheses. Qy. read, *'Tis time then, as some say, &c.?* — (Jahrb. d. D. Sh.-G., XV, 344.)

CXX.

In harmful heart to harbour hatred long.

Ib., (Del., 12. — W. and Pr., 30. — H's D., VII, 212.)

Compare Marlowe, The Tragedy of Dido, Queen of Carthage, A. I, *sub fin.*: —

Forbids all hope to harbour near our hearts.

CXXI.

Seg. [*Aside*]. This seems to be a merry fellow.

Ib., (Del., 13. — W. and Pr., 32. — H's D., VII, 213.)

A regular blank verse would be restored by the insertion of *very* before *merry*. That *very* was frequently interpolated has been shown by S. Walker, Crit. Exam., I, 268 seq. Cf. also *infra* note CLXXXIV. Here we meet with an instance of its omission.

CXXII.

Now, brave lords, our wars are brought to end,
Our foes to foil, and we in safety rest:
It us behoves to use such clemency
In peace, as valour in the wars. It is
As great an honour to be bountiful
At home, as to be conquerors in the field.

Ib., (Del., 14. — W. and Pr., 33. — H's D., VII, 215.)

From Dodsley Messrs. Warnke and Prœscholdt seem to have drawn the conclusion that QD (1610) reads *that our wars* and have printed the line accordingly. This, however, is erroneous; all Qq, which I have been able to collate, QD included, unanimously read *brave lords, our wars,* and the addition of *that* in Dodsley is due to Mr. Hazlitt and as such is enclosed in brackets. As *Now* is to be read as a monosyllabic foot, no correction of the line is required, although the passage would no doubt be improved by the addition of *that* and the transposition suggested by me in Prof. Kölbing's Englische Studien. *To foil* is an emendation of the late Prof. W. Wagner's; Qq: *the foil. It is,* in the fourth line, might, perhaps, be transferred to the following line and *bountiful* be pronounced as a triple ending. In l. 5 *an* has been added by Messrs. Warnke and Prœscholdt in compliance with my conjecture. (Jahrb. d. D. Sh.-G., XIII, 54. — Kölb., Engl. Stud., VI, 312.)

CXXIII.

And reign hereafter, as I tofore have done.

Ib., (Del., 15. — W. and Pr., 34. — H's D., VII, 215.)

No alteration of this reading, uniformly exhibited by all the Qq, is required. The transposition proposed by Prof. W. Wagner in the Jahrb. d. D. Sh.-G., XI, 64 *(as tofore I've)* and adopted by Messrs. Warnke and Prœscholdt, is needless. There is, of course, an extra syllable before the pause.

CXXIV.

> *King.* Then march we on to court, and rest our wearied limbs!
> But Collen, I have a tale in secret kept for thee.
>
> *Ib., (Del., 15. — W. and Pr., 34. — H's D., VII, 216.)*

The second verse may be easily reduced to a blank verse by the introduction of an interjectional line: —

> *King.* Then march we on to court, and rest our wearied limbs!
> But Collen,
> I have a tale in secret kept for thee: &c.

I may add that *kept* is the reading of the earlier Qq, whereas the later copies, from 1619 downwards, read *fil.* (Jahrb. d. D. Sh.-G., XV, 344.)

CXXV.

> *Seg.* Why, Captain Tremelio.
> *Mouse.* O, the meal-man; I know him very well.
>
> *Ib., (Del., 16. — W. and Pr., 36. — H's D., VII, 217.)*

A pun was certainly intended in these lines, but the first half of it has been lost. In order to restore it, we must evidently add *man* after *Tremelio.* The same kind of corruption occurs in l. 44 seq. and in A. III, sc. 3, l. 22. In the former passage the pun is to be completed by the insertion of *knave* after *Tremelio,* and in the latter by the addition of *buzzard* after *shepherd.* *Buzzard* in the sense of a worthless or useless fellow, a blockhead or dunce, occurs pretty frequently; compare, e. g., Piers Ploughman, ed. Thom. Wright, l. 6156 seq.: —

> I rede ech a blynd bosarde
> Do boote to hymselve.

The Three Lords and Three Ladies of London (*apud* Dodsley, ed. Hazlitt, VI, 381): —

> A buzzard? thou buzzard! Wit, hast no more skill,
> Than take a falcon for a buzzard?

Westward Ho!, V, 4 (Webster, ed. Dyce, 1857, in 1 vol., p. 243b): *Ten[terhook]*: Marry, you make bulls [qy. *gulls?*] of your husbands. *Mist. Ten[terhook].* Buzzards, do we not? out, you yellow infirmities! do all flowers show in your eyes like columbines? — The Dramatic

Works of Rich. Brome (Lon., Pearson, 1873) II, 43: The Buzzards are all gentlemen. We came in with the conqueror. Our name (as the French has it) is *Beau-desert*; which signifies — Friends, what does it signifie? — R. Ascham, The Scholemaster, ed. Arber, p. 111: who neuertholesse, are lesse to be blamed, than those blind bussardes, who in late yeares, of wilfull maliciousnes, would neyther learne themselues, nor could teach others, any thing at all. — Milton, Eiconocl., Chap. I: Those who thought no better of the living God, than of a buzzard idol. — The Life and Letters of W. Irving. By his Nephew Pierre E. Irving (Lon., 1877, Bell and Sons, I, 113): Inspired by such thoughts, I open your letters with a kind of triumph; I consider them as testimonies of those brilliant moments which I have rescued from the buzzards that surround you. — Compare Histrio-Mastix, A. II, 1. 289 seq. (*apud* Simpson, The School of Shak-spere, II, 40): —

> Fie! what unworthy foolish foppery
> Presents such buzzardly simplicity.

I have only to add that these three emendations (*man, knave,* and *buzzard*) have been adopted by Messrs. Warnke and Prœscholdt. (Jahrb. d. D. Sh.-G., XIII, 54 and 67.)

CXXVI.

I cannot tell; wherefore doth he keep his chamber else?
>> *Ib., (Del., 17. — W. and Pr., 36. — H's D., VII, 217.)*

I strongly suspect that *him in* should be inserted after *keep*. (Kölb., Engl. Stud., VI, 313.)

CXXVII.

> *Seg.* Well, Sir, away.
> Tremelio, this it is, thou knowest the valour of Segasto,
> Spread through all the kingdom of Aragon,
> And such as have found triumph and favours,
> Never daunted at any time: but now a shepherd,
> Admired in court for worthiness,
> And Segasto's honour laid aside:

My will therefore is this, that thou dost find some means to work the shepherd's death: I know thy strength sufficient to perform my desire, and thy love no otherwise than to revenge my injuries.

> *Tre.* It is not the frowns of a Shepherd that Tremelio fears:
> Therefore account it accomplish'd what I take in hand.
> *Seg.* Thanks, good Tremelio, and assure thyself,
> What I promise, that I will perform.
>> *Ib., (Del., 18. — W. and Pr., 37. — H's D., VII, 218 seq.)*

Apart from differences in the spelling to which no weight can be attached, this is the uniform reading and arrangement of the passage in the Qq, except that Qq 1598 and 1610 read *Admired at in court,* which I feel convinced is a faulty transposition for *Admired is at court.* It need hardly be remarked that, at least as far as the arrangement of the lines is concerned, the passage is a model of corruption. The late Prof. W. Wagner (in the Jahrb. d. D. Sh.-G., XI, 65) has tried to restore the original verses which he thinks to have run thus: —

> Well, Sir, away. Tremelio, this is it:
> Thou know'st the valour of Segasto spread
> Thorough all the kingdom of Aragon;
> And such as have found triumph and favours
> Never daunted me at any time: but now
> A shepherd is admir'd in court for worthiness,
> And all Segasto's honour laid aside.
> My will therefore is this, that thou dost find
> Some means to work the shepherd's death: I know
> Thy strength sufficient to perform — thy love
> No other than to wreak my injuries.

The weak points of this attempt at restoration, some of which have not escaped Prof. W. Wagner himself, have been pointed out and a different arrangement proposed by me in the Jahrb. d. D. Sh.-G., XIII, 56 seq. The latter, adopted with a few slight alterations by Messrs. Warnke and Prœscholdt, seems still capable of improvement and I therefore reproduce it in an amended form, including one or two new readings: —

> *Seg.* Well, Sir, away. Tremelio, this it is.   [*Exit Mouse.*
> Thou know'st the valour of Segasto, spread
> Thorough the kingdom of all Aragon,
> And such as, never daunted at any time,
> Hath triumph found and favours; but now a shepherd
> Admirèd is at court for worthiness,
> And Lord Segasto's honour laid aside;
> My will therefore is this, that thou dost find
> Some means to work the shepherd's death: I know
> Thy strength sufficient to perform my desire,
> Thy love no otherwise than to revenge my injuries.

The fourth line might be improved by a slight transposition: —

> And such as, daunted ne'er at any time.

Desire, in the last line but one is to be pronounced as a monosyllable; compare Induction, l. 39 *(Delighting)*; A. III, sc. 2, l. 52 and A. IV, sc. 1, l. 22 *(departure)*; A. V, sc. 1, l. 55 *(Desiring)*. In the last line *otherwise* is to be pronounced as a dissyllable (see Abbott, s. 466), and *revenge* as a monosyllable, provided it be not thought

preferable to give the line an extra syllable before the pause and
scan it thus: —

Thy love | no oth'r | wise than to | revenge | my in | juries.

Injuries, in either case, is a triple ending. The rest of the passage
seems to defy emendation except by means which, on maturer reflec-
tion, I cannot think justifiable. *What,* in the last line, may be considered as a monosyllabic foot and thus the metre be regulated.

CXXVIII.

Seg. Hold, shepherd, hold, spare him, kill him not:
Accursed villain, tell me what hast thou done?
Ah, Tremelio, trusty Tremelio, I sorrow for thy death,
And since that thou living didst prove faithful to Segasto,
So Segasto now living shall honour the dead
Corpse of Tremelio with revenge.
Blood-thirsty villain, born and bred to merciless murder,
Tell me, how durst thou be so bold,
As once to lay thy hands upon the least of mine?
Assure thyself thou shalt be used according to the law.
Mucc. Segasto cease, these threats are needless,
Accuse not me of murder, that have done nothing,
But in mine own defence.

Ib., (Del., 18 seq. — W. and Pr., 38 seq. — H's D., VII, 219.)

Instead of *shall honour, to merciless murder,* and *Accuse not me* in
the earliest quarto all the other old copies read *will honour, in merciless murder* and *Accuse me not.* Some minor differences may be
left unnoticed. Prof. W. Wagner in the Jahrb. d. D. Sh.-G., XI, 66,
is not far from the mark in declaring the whole passage to be 'hopelessly corrupt', especially as regards its arrangement. Nevertheless
I have made an attempt to restore the original verses to which, with
a few exceptions, I still adhere. The interjection *O* in l. 80, inserted
by me, must certainly be expunged again as the verse belongs to
the well-known class of syllable pause lines. In l. 81 the old text
may likewise be left unaltered; the line is to be scanned: —

Accurs | èd vil | lain, tell me | what hast | thou done.

In l. 84 Prof. W. Wagner's alteration: *didst faithful to Segasto prove*
(Jahrb. d. D. Sh.-G., XIV, 280), seems preferable to my own suggestion:
didst faithful prove unto Segasto. Line 87, though not an Alexandrine,
is yet a verse of six feet and cannot be reduced to a blank verse
without great boldness. The objection raised by Messrs. Warnke and
Proescholdt against my alteration and division of ll. 90 seq. is certainly not unfounded; I doubt, however, whether their own endeavour
to regulate the lines can boast of a better success, and am now able

to offer a different arrangement which implies no alteration of the
old text beside the division of the lines. The climax reached by
the corruption of the passage is shown by ll. 92 seq. which in Hazlitt's Dodsley read as follows: —

> But in mine own defence accuse not me
> Of murther that have done nothing.

The alteration in the division of these two lines proposed by me and
adopted by Messrs. Warnke and Prœscholdt seems needless and had
better be withdrawn. The passage should be arranged and printed
thus: —

> *Seg.* Hold, shepherd, hold! Spare him, kill him not!
> Accursèd villain, tell me, what hast thou done?
> Tremelio, ah, trusty Tremelio:
> I sorrow for thy death and since that thou
> Living didst faithful to Segasto prove,
> So now Segasto living with revenge
> Will honour the dead corpse of Tremelio.
> Blood-thirsty villain: born and bred to merciless murder:
> Tell me, how durst thou be so bold, as once
> To lay thy hands upon the least of mine?
> Assure thyself
> Thou shalt be used according to the law!
>
> *Muce.* Segasto, cease! these threats are needless.
> Accuse not me of murder that have done nothing
> But in mine own defence.

The first line is a syllable pause line, the second and the last but
one have an extra syllable before the pause, and the last but two is
a catalectic blank verse (see note II). (Jahrb. d. D. Sh.-G., XIII,
57 seq. XV, 344. — Kölb., Engl. Stud., VI, 313.)

CXXIX.

> I think his mother sang looby to him, he is so heavy.
> *Ib., (Del., 19. — W. and Pr., 39. — H's D., VII, 220.)*

Looby is the name of a children's dance and its accompanying music.
The words are printed in Halliwell's Nursery Rhymes and Nursery
Tales, p. 75; words and tune in The Baby's Bouquêt. A Fresh
Bunch of Old Rhymes and Tunes. Arranged and Decorated by Walter
Crane (London and New York, George Routledge), p. 54. Compare
Halliwell, Dictionary of Archaic and Provincial Words, s. *Looby*.
Nares, ed. Halliwell and Wright, s. *Looby*. Webster, s. *Looby, Lubber,*
and *Lubberly*.

CXXX.

Now Bremo sith thy leisure so affords,
An endless thing, &c.

> *Ib.*, *(Del.*, *20. — W. and Pr.*, *40. — H's D.*, *VII*, *220.)*

This reading of the Qq, nonsensical though it be, has yet been left untouched by both Delius and Mr. Hazlitt. Prof. W. Wagner proposed *aimless* instead of *endless*. The reading of Messrs. Warnke and Prœscholdt: —

Now, Bremo, sit, thy leisure so affords,
A needless thing. [*Sits down.*]

is due to me; see Jahrb. d. D. Sh.-G., XIII, 58 seq.

CXXXI.

Rend them in pieces, and pluck them from the earth.

> *Ib.*, *(Del.*, *20. — W. and Pr.*, *40. — H's D.*, *VII*, *221.)*

In the Jahrb. d. D. Sh.-G., XIII, 59, I maintained that *and* should be thrown out, but now withdraw this conjectural emendation; the line contains an extra syllable before the pause.

CXXXII.

Who fights with me and doth not die the death? Not one!

> *Ib.*, *(Del.*, *20. — W. and Pr.*, *40. — H's D.*, *VII*, *221.)*

Not one need not be omitted, as proposed by Prof. W. Wagner, but is to be placed *extra versum* as an interjectional line. (Kölb., Engl. Stud., VI, 313.)

CXXXIII.

That here within these woods are combatants with me.

> *Ib.*, *(Del.*, *21. — W. and Pr.*, *41. — H's D.*, *VII*, *221.)*

No Alexandrine, *combatants* being used as a dissyllable; scan: —

That here | within | these woods | are com|b'tants with | me.

Compare Kölb., Engl. Stud., VI, 313 and note on K. Richard II., II, 4, 6.

CXXXIV.

King. Shepherd, thou hast heard thine accusers,
Murther is laid to thy charge:
What canst thou say? thou hast deserved death.

> *Ib.*, *(Del.*, *21. — W. and Pr.*, *41. — H's D.*, *VII*, *221.)*

Arrange and write: —

>   *King.* Shepherd, thou hast heard thine accusers; murder
>   Is laid unto thy charge; what canst thou say?
>   Thou hast deservèd death.

Three lines *infra* I formerly proposed to add *out* and to read: —

>   Not *out* of any malice, but by chance.

However, I now withdraw this conjecture, as I feel pretty sure that *Not* may be read as a monosyllabic foot. The next speech of Segasto: —

>   Words will not here prevail;
>   I seek for justice, and justice craves his death,

may be completely right, although a different division of the lines would seem to possess a still better claim to be considered the author's own, viz.: —

>   Words will not here prevail; I seek for justice,
>   And justice craves his death.

(Jahrb. d. D. Sh.-G., XIII, 60.)

CXXXV.

Come, sirrah, away with him, and hang him 'bout the middle.

Ib., *(Del., 21 seq. — W. and Pr., 42. — H's D., VII, 222.)*

Mr. Hazlitt has omitted *Come,* which is in all the old copies I have been able to collate, and has printed the rest as prose; it is indeed labour thrown away to correct his edition of Dodsley. — *Come, sirrah,* is no doubt to be considered as an interjectional line, while the rest of the line forms a regular blank verse. (Kölb., Engl. Stud., VI, 313.)

CXXXVI.

Come on, sir; ah, so like a sheepbiter a looks.

Ib., *(Del., 22. — W. and Pr., 42. — H's D., VII, 222.)*

Qu. 1598: *Come on sir*; Qq 1610, 1615 and 1619: *Come on sirra*; the later Qq: *Come you, sirrah.* *Sheep-biter* originally meant no doubt a morose or surly cur that bites the sheep in good (or rather sad) earnest; hence a morose or surly fellow. Compare Dekker, The Honest Whore, Part II, II, 1 (The Works of Th. Middleton, ed. Dyce, III, 162): A poor man has but one ewe, and this grandee sheep-biter leaves whole flocks of fat wethers, whom he may knock down, to devour this. — Middleton, A Chaste Maid in Cheapside (Works, ed. Dyce, IV, 33): —

>   Sheep-biting mongrels, hand-basket freebooters.

Twelfth Night, II, 5, 6. Measure for Measure, V, 1, 359 *(sheep-biting face).*

CXXXVII.

Ama. Dread Sovereign, and well beloved Sire,
On bended knee I crave the life of this condemned Shepherd, which
heretofore preserved the life of thy sometime distressed daughter.

 King. Preserv'd the life of my sometime distressed daughter!
 How can that be? I never knew the time
 Wherein thou wast distress'd: I never knew the day
 But that I have maintained thy estate,
 As best beseem'd the daughter of a king.

Ib., (Del., 22. — W. and Pr., 42. — H's D., VII, 222.)

No reader, I think, will deny that this passage bears manifest traces
of corruption. The earliest quarto reads *on bended kees*; instead of
condemned we find *condemn'd* in Dodsley, ed. Hazlitt, VII, 222; and
heretofore has been altered to *tofore* by Messrs. Warnke and Prœscholdt. *Heretofore,* however, is quite correct, as *shepherd* is either
to be pronounced as a monosyllable, or as a dissyllable with an extra
syllable before the pause. In the first line of the king's speech
which is an Alexandrine, the late Prof. W. Wagner wanted *sometime*
to be thrown out (Jahrb. d. D. Sh.-G., XI, 67), whereas in my opinion
Preserv'd should be expunged. I feel convinced that the original
wording and arrangement of the passage was as follows: —

 Ama. Dread sovereign and well belovèd sire,
 On bended knee I crave the life of this
 Condemnèd shepherd, which heretofore preserved
 The life of thy sometime distressèd daughter.
 King. The life of my sometime distressèd daughter?
 How can that be? I never knew the time
 Wherein thou wast distress'd: I never knew
 The day, but that I have maintain'd thy state,
 As best beseem'd the daughter of a king.

As to *state* (for *estate*) the reader may be referred to A. IV, sc. 5,
l. 139: —

 I have no lands for to maintain thy state.
(Jahrb. d. D. Sh.-G., XIII, 60. — Kölb., Engl. Stud., VI, 313 seq.)

CXXXVIII.

 His silence verifies it to be true. What then?

Ib., (Del., 23. — W. and Pr., 43. — H's D., VII, 223.)

A regular blank verse as far as *true. What then?* forms an interjectional line. (Jahrb. d. D. Sh.-G., XIII, 61. — Kölb., Engl. Stud.,
VI, 314.)

CXXXIX.

But all in vain; for why, he reached after me, &c.

Ib., (Del., 23. — W. and Pr., 43. — H's D., VII, 223.)

Omit *for why.*   (Kölb., Engl. Stud., VI, 314.)

CXL.

Indeed, occasion oftentimes so falls out.

Ib., (Del., 23. — W. and Pr., 43. — H's D., VII, 223.)

Qq, Delius, and Mr. Hazlitt: *oftentimes*; W. Wagner conjectured *often.*
The correction *ofttimes* was made by me and has been adopted by
Messrs. Warnke and Prœscholdt; it occurs, e. g., in Cymbeline, I,
6, 62. — From l. 55 to l. 64 we have what, in classical parlance, is
called a στιχομυϑία, i. e. a dialogue where the speeches of the
interlocutors consist of single lines. The present στιχομυϑία is in
rhyme, with the only exception of ll. 57 and 62; the latter being
spoken aside and belonging to the Clown who throughout the play
makes use of prose, cannot be said to form part of the conversation
going on between the king, Segasto, and Amadine and may be left
unnoticed. L. 57, 'therefore, remains the only one without rhyme; it
is, moreover, the only one that is entirely unconnected. Does the
poet mean to say that it ofttimes so falls out that the slaughter of
a man deserves great blame? This would be below the meanest
playwright of the Elizabethan era. In my conviction, there is a gap
between l. 56 and l. 57; a line is wanting in which Amadine takes
the part of Mucedorus against Segasto and points out that no blame
attaches to him for having killed his adversary in fight. This line
which, of course, must have supplied the missing rhyme with l. 57,
may have been to the following effect: —

Ama. *No blame, to kill one's enemy in a rout,*

to which remark the king would then make the appropriate reply: —

Indeed, occasion ofttimes so falls out,

i. e. it occurs, indeed, frequently that a man is killed in a brawl,
and no blame can be laid on the killer. (Jahrb. d. D. Sh.-G., XIII,
61 seq. — Kölb., Engl. Stud., VI, 314 seq.)

CXLI.

King. But soft, Segasto, not for this offence, &c.

Ib., (Del., 23 seq. — W. and Pr., 44. — H's D., VII, 224.)

This seems, indeed, to be a 'hopelessly corrupt' passage and I refrain
from reproducing my explanation given in the Jahrb. d. D. Sh.-G.,
XIII, 62 seq., which I now think unsatisfactory, although it has found
favour with Messrs. Warnke and Prœscholdt.

CXLII.

King. Come, daughter, let us now depart to honour
The worthy valour of the shepherd with rewards.

    Ib., (Del., 24. — W. and Pr., 44. — H's D., VII, 224.)

Printed as prose in Delius's edition, in accordance with all the Qq.
In order to reduce the second line to regular metre Prof. W. Wagner
(Jahrb. d. D. Sh.-G., XIV, 281) proposes to read: —

    The shepherd's worthy valour with rewards,

a conjecture which, in my eyes, is by no means satisfactory. As
three lines *supra* the king says: —

    And for thy valour I will honour thee,

I am led to the belief that in the line under discussion *worthy*
before *valour* has surreptitiously intruded and should be expunged.

CXLIII.

From Amadine, and from her father's court,
With gold and silver, and with rich rewards,
Flowing from the banks of golden treasuries.
More may I boast, and say, but I,
Was never shepherd in such dignity.

    Ib., (Del., 24. — W. and Pr., 44 seq. — H's D., VII, 225.)

Qu. 1598: *tresuries*; Qq 1610 and 1615: *golden treasures*; Qu. 1619:
gold and treasures. — Two lines seem to have been lost in this
mutilated soliloquy of Mucedorus, the one after l. 1, the other after
l. 4. In the former we expect to hear something like the words
I now come laden heavily, while the latter may possibly have run
thus: —

    Am silent and declare but this: as yet, &c.

I am not prepared, however, to affirm that even after the addition
of two such lines the passage will be exempt from all difficulty.
(Kölb., Engl. Stud., VI, 315.)

CXLIV.

The king and Amadine greet thee well,
And after greeting done, bid thee depart the court.
Shepherd, begone!

    Ib., (Det., 24. — W. and Pr., 45. — H's D., VII, 225.)

QA: *greetes, greetings* and *bids.* — I still adhere to the belief that
these lines originally formed a couplet and now think that the couplet
formerly proposed by me, may still be improved by the omission of
well: —

    The king and Amadine greet thee, and greeting done,
    Bid thee depart the court: shepherd, begone!

Amadine is, of course, to be pronounced as a dissyllable. Messrs.
Warnke and Prœscholdt have added *do* before *greet*. (Jahrb. d. D.
Sh.-G., XIII, 63. — Kölb., Engl. Stud., VI, 316.)

CXLV.

> *Ama.* Ariena, if any body ask for me,
> Make some excuse till I return.
> *Ari.* What, an Segasto call?

Ib., (Del., 26. — W. and Pr., 46. — H's D., VII, 227.)

This division of the lines (thus printed in the Qq) can hardly be
right. The arrangement proposed by me in the Jahrb. d. D. Sh.-G.,
XIII, 64, has met with the approval of Messrs. Warnke and Prœscholdt
and seems indeed to be the only one by the help of which we can
hope to overcome the difficulty. It is this: —

> *Ama.* Ariena!
> If any body ask for me, make some excuse,
> Till I return.
> *Ari.*   What, an Segasto call?

The words *any body ask* do not count for more than three syllables;
see note on The Winter's Tale, I, 2, 173.

CXLVI.

> Shepherd, well met, tell me how thou dost?

Ib., (Del., 26. — W. and Pr., 47. — H's D., VII, 227.)

On my conjecture Messrs. Warnke and Prœscholdt have inserted *pray*
before *tell*. This addition, however, I now think needless, as the
verse evidently belongs to the numerous category of syllable pause
lines, and is to be scanned: —

> Shepherd, | well met, | ᴗ tell | me how | thou dost?

The arrangement of the following lines (8—15) as given by Messrs.
Warnke and Prœscholdt was also suggested by me. In l. 13 I formerly
proposed to read: *with all thy heart*, but have now come to the conviction that the true arrangement is either: —

> *Muce.*   Since I must depart
> One thing I crave with all my heart —
> *Ama.*   Say on.
> *Muce.* That in absence, either far or near, &c.

or, which to a conservative critic may seem preferable: —

> *Muce.*   Since I must depart
> One thing I crave —
> *Ama.*   Say on.
> *Muce.*   With all my heart:
> That in absence, either far or near, &c.

That, in the last line, is to be considered as a monosyllabic foot, or, if not, we seem to be compelled to insert *my* before *absence.* (Jahrb. d. D. Sh.-G., XIII, 64 seq. — Notes (privately printed, 1882), p. 16 seq.).

CXLVII.

Muce. Unworthy wights are more in jealousy.
  Ib., (Del., 27. — W. and Pr., 47. — H's D., VII, 228.)
Qu. 1598: *most in ielosie;* all the rest: *more in jealousie.* — Qy.: *worst in jealousy?* which would fall in with our poet's predilection for alliteration. Instances of this alliteration have been given by me in the Jahrb. d. D. Sh.-G., XIII, 65 and by Messrs. Warnke and Prœscholdt in their Introduction, p. 9.

CXLVIII.

Well, shepherd, sith thou sufferest this for my sake.
  Ib., (Del., 27. — W. and Pr., 47. — H's D., VII, 228.)
Apparently a line of six feet: —

Well, shep|herd, sith | thou suf|ferest | this for | my sake.
The right scansion, in my conviction, however, is: —

Well, shep|herd, sith | thou suf|fer'st this | for my | sake,
so that the line proves to be a regular blank verse with a double ending. Compare A. IV, sc. 3, l. 69: —

Ama. Yet give him leave to speak for my sake, [*Bremo*],
where the accent also rests on the pronoun *my.* For *this* in the three earliest copies the later Qq read *thus.* Qu. 1610: *suffrest;* the rest *sufferest.*

CXLIX.

I dare not promise what I may perform.
  Ib., (Del., 27. — W. and Pr., 48. — H's D., VII, 228.)
Mayn't, which Messrs. Warnke and Prœscholdt have received into their text, was suggested by the late Prof. W. Wagner-(Jahrb. d. D. Sh.-G., XI, 67 seq.); the Qq uniformly exhibit *may.* As far as I can see, Professor W. Wagner missed the poet's meaning and even converted it into its contrary. 'I smother up the blast', says Mucedorus, 'because I dare not yet promise what I may (or intend to) perform, when the convenient time is at hand; in other words, I dare not yet hint at my transformation from a shepherd to a prince worthy of becoming the husband of so beautiful a princess.' (Kölb., Engl. Stud., VI, 316.)

CL.

Se. Tis well Segasto that thou hast thy will,
Should such a shhephard, such a simple swaine
As he, eclips thy credite famous through the court.
No ply Segasto ply; let it not in Arragon be saide,
A shepheard hath Segatoes honour wonne.

Ib., (Det., 28. — W. and Pr., 48. — H's D., VII, 229.)

This is the reading of the earliest quarto (1598). Delius, who follows the latest quarto (1668) prints the passage thus: —

Seg. 'Tis well *Segasto,* that thou hast thy will:
Should such a shepherd, such a simple swain as he,
Eclipse thy credit through the court?
No, ply *Segasto,* ply, let it not in Aragon be said,
A shepherd hath *Segasto's* honour won.

The shape in which the lines appear in Dodsley, whether due to some one or other of the quartos, or to Mr. Hazlitt's own correction, cannot possibly have come from the author's pen. It is this: —

Seg. 'Tis well, Segasto, that thou hast thy will,
Should such a shepherd, such a simple swain,
As he eclipse thy credit, famous through
The court? No, ply, Segasto, ply;
Let it not in Arragon be said,
A shepherd hath Segasto's honour won.

This is altogether a wrong arrangement. As to particulars, either the second *such* in the second line, or the lame addition *as he,* must certainly be done away with, if we do not choose to omit *famous,* as it has been done in Qu. 1668 and accordingly by Delius in his edition. The words *No, ply, Segasto, ply* evidently form a line by themselves, whereas the rest was no doubt meant for a couplet. I formerly added *And* before *Let,* but now think that *Let* may well be taken for a monosyllabic foot. Arrange and write therefore: —

Seg. 'Tis well, Segasto, that thou hast thy will:
Should such a shepherd, such a simple swain,
Eclipse thy credit famous through he court?
No, ply, Segasto, ply!
Let it not be said in Aragon:
A shepherd hath Segasto's honour won.

This arrangement has been adopted by Messrs. Warnke and Prœscholdt. (Jahrb. d. D. Sh.-G., XIII, 66. — Kölb., Engl. Stud., VI, 316.)

CLI.

Seg. Why, you whoreson slave, have you forgotten that I sent you and another to drive away the shepherd?

Mouse. What an ass are you; here's a stir indeed, here's message, errand, banishment, and I cannot tell what.

> *Ib.,* (Del., 29. — W. and Pr., 50. — H's D., VII, 230.)

Arrange: —

Seg. Why, you whoreson slave, have you forgotten that I sent you and another to drive away the shepherd? What an ass are you!

Mouse. Here's a stir indeed, &c.   (Notes, privately printed, 1882, p. 17.)

CLII.

Bremo. With this my bat will I beat out thy brains;
Down, down, I say, prostrate thyself upon the ground.

> *Ib.,* (Del., 30. — W. and Pr., 51. — H's D., VII, 232.)

The three earliest copies: *will I beat*; the rest: *I will beat.* Arrange, perhaps: —

Bremo. With this my bat will I beat out thy brains;
Down, down!
I say, prostrate thyself upon the ground.

(Kölb., Engl. Stud., VI, 316 seq.)

CLIII.

Ay, woman, wilt thou live in woods with me?

> *Ib.,* (Del., 31. — W. and Pr., 52. — H's D., VII, 233.)

I strongly suspect: *Say, woman.*   Compare A. IV, sc. 3, l. 61: —

Say, sirrah, wilt thou fight &c.

A. IV, sc. 3, l. 107 seq.: —

Say, hermit, what canst thou do?

Paradise Lost, X, 158: —

Say, woman, what is this which thou hast done?

My conjecture is strengthened by the fact that the Ed. pr. reads, *ay woman, ay* not being spelled with a capital letter; the capital *S* has evidently dropped out.   Qq 1610 and 1615: *Aie woman*; the rest: *Ay woman.*   (Jahrb. d. D. Sh.-G., XVI, 250 seq.)

CLIV.

King. Mirth to a soul disturb'd is embers turn'd
Which sudden gleam with molestation,
But sooner lose their light for it.

> *Ib.,* (Del., 34. — W. and Pr., 56. — H's D., VII, 237.)

The Qq, as far as I have been able to collate them, uniformly read *sight,* which, of course, is a corruption from *light.* The last line might easily be completed: —

But *all the* sooner lose their light for it.

(Jahrb. d. D. Sh.-G., XIII, 69. — Kölb., Engl. Stud., VI, 317.)

CLV.

'Tis gold bestow'd upon a rioter,
Which not relieves, but murders him
'Tis a drug given to the healthful,
Which infects, not cures.
How can a father that hath lost his son,
A prince both wise, vertuous, and valiant,
Take pleasure in the idle acts of Time?
No, no, till Muccdorus I shall see again,
All joy is comfortless, all pleasure pain.

Ib., (Del., 34 seq. — W. and Pr., 56. — H's D., VII, 237.)

This reading of the Qq, though undoubtedly faulty, has not been amended by either Delius or Mr. Hazlitt. Arrange and write: —

'Tis gold bestow'd upon a rioter,
Which not relieves, but murders him; a drug
Given to the healthful, which infects, not cures.
How can a father that hath lost his son,
A prince both wise, virtuous, and valiant,
Take pleasure in the idle acts of *pastime*?
No, no!
Till Mucedorus I shall see again,
All joy is comfortless, all pleasure pain.

Instead of *wise, virtuous* I formerly proposed *virtuous, wise.* This alteration has been adopted by Messrs. Warnke and Prœscholdt and certainly improves the line; nevertheless it may be dispensed with. *Pastime* is positively demanded by the context; it is used by our poet in A. V, sc. 1, l. 72. (Jahrb. d. D. Sh.-G., XIII, 69 seq. — Kölb., Engl. Stud., VI, 317.)

CLVI.

In Aragon, my liege, and at his parture
Bound my secrecy
By his affectious love, not to disclose it.

Ib., (Del., 35. — W. and Pr., 56 seq. — H's D., VII, 237.)

In the earliest quarto this scene is wanting; the two copies of 1610 and 1615: *parture*; the rest: *parting. Affectious loue* is the reading of the earlier quartos; the Qq from 1634 downwards, *affections loue*. The former reading is, to say the least of it, extremely doubtful; the latter is simply absurd. Qy. read, *affection's loss* (loffe-loue) and arrange the lines as follows: —

> In Aragon, my liege,
> And at his 'parture bound my secrecy,
> By his affection's loss, not to disclose it.

Both the emendation *affection's loss* and the alteration in the division of the lines have been adopted by Messrs. Warnke and Prœscholdt. It may be added that S. Walker, Crit. Exam., I, 285, proposes to read *loss* instead of *love* in Venus and Adonis, st. 78, and in Twelfth Night, I, 2, 39. (Jahrb. d. D. Sh.-G., XIII, 72.)

CLVII.

> *K. V.* Thou not deceiv'st me; I ever thought thee
> What I find thee now, an upright loyal man.
> But what desire, or young-fed humour
> Nurs'd within the braine,
> Drew him so privately to Aragon?
> > *Ib., (Del., 35. — W. and Pr., 57. — H's D., VII, 237.)*

Apart from differences in the spelling and punctuation that are hardly worth mentioning, this is the reading and arrangement in Qq 1610 and 1615; in Qu. 1598 the passage is wanting. The later Qq, from 1619 downwards, divide the lines as follows: —

> *King Va.* Thou not deceiv'st me,
> I ever thought thee what I find thee now,
> An upright loyal man.
> But what desire, or young-fed humour
> Nurs'd within his brain,
> Drew him so privately to Aragon?

Arrange: —

> *King.* Thou not deceiv'st me.
> I ever thought thee what I find thee now,
> An upright, loyal man: but what desire,
> Or young-fed humour, nurs'd within the brain,
> Drew him so privately to Aragon?

The various reading *his brain* instead of *the brain* in the two copies of 1610 and 1615, is immaterial. (Jahrb. d. D. Sh.-G., XIII, 72. — Kölb., Engl. Stud., VI, 317 seq.)

CLVIII.

> No doubt, she thinks on thee, ·
> And will one day come pledge thee at this well.

> Come, habit, thou art fit for me. [*He disguiseth himself.*
> No shepherd now, an hermit must I be.
> Methinks this fits me very well. `
>
>   *Ib., (Det., 36. — W. and Pr., 58. — H's D., VII, 238.)*

This is the arrangement of the Qq, but the division of the first two
lines as given in Hazlitt's Dodsley, seems preferable: —

> No doubt, she thinks on thee, and will one day
> Come pledge thee at this well.

Thus the short line takes its proper place at the end of one train
of thought and serves to mark the transit to another, in so far as
Mucedorus now turns his attention to the habit he is donning. *Must
I be* is the reading of Qq 1610, 1615, and 1619. The last line
may easily be completed: —

> Methinks this *habit* fits me very well.

(Kölb., Engl. Stud., VI, 318.)

CLIX.

Muce. Thou dost mistake me; but I pray thee, tell me what
dost thou seek in these woods?
Clown. What do I seek? for a stray king's daughter, run
away with a shepherd.

>   *Ib., (Det., 37. — W. and Pr., 58. — H's D., VII, 239.)*

Although all the Qq which I have collated, place the interrogation
after *seek*, yet I strongly suspect that it ought to take its place after
for, and am confirmed in this conviction by the fact that Messrs.
Warnke and Prœscholdt have approved of the arrangement and reading
of these lines proposed by me in the Jahrb. d. D. Sh.-G., XIII, 91, viz.: —

Muce. Thou dost mistake me: but, I pray thee, tell me
What dost thou seek *for* in these woods?
Clown. What do I seek for? A stray king's-daughter, run
away with a shepherd.

Instead of *what dost thou seek* Delius prints *whom dost thou seek*,
this being the reading of Qu. 1668.

CLX.

Clown. Nay, I say rusher, and I'll prove mine office good:
for look sir, when any comes from under the sea or so, and a dog·
chance to blow his nose backward, then with a whip I give him the
good time of the day and strow rushes presently; therefore I am a
rusher, a high office, I promise ye.

>   *Ib., (Det., 38. — W. and Pr., 59. — H's D., VII, 240.)*

Qq 1598, 1615, and 1619: *I'll prove*; Qu. 1610: *I prove.* The
three earliest copies: *for look sir*, the later quartos: *for look you*

sir. — A badly corrupted passage. It seems evident that the poet did not write *sea*, but *seat.* This correction, however, does not suffice to restore sense and grammar; perhaps we should read: *when a dog comes from under the seat or so, and chance to blow, &c.,* or: *when a cat comes from under the seat, or so, and a dog chance to blow, &c.* For, although the Clown jestingly calls himself a 'rusher of the stable', yet his office of strowing rushes was performed in the hall and rooms of the mansion, where cleanliness was no less a desideratum than in the stable. The rushes to be used there were no doubt under the care of a stable-boy or groom and preserved in a stable or shed, from whence they were taken to the mansion whenever they were required. — See The Babees Book, ed. Furnivall, p. LXVI, and my Abhandlungen zu Shakespeare, S. 405.

CLXI.

> *Bremo.* See how she flies away from me,
> I will follow, and give attent to her.
> Deny my love! Ah, worm of beauty,
> I will chastise thee: come, come,
> Prepare thy head upon the block.
>> *Ib., (Del., 39. — W. and Pr., 60 seq. — H's D., VII, 241.)*

The reading of the three earliest copies in l. 1, *flinges away*, is preferable. Qu. 1598 reads *a rend* and *ah worme*, all the rest *attend* and *a worme*; the same quarto also joins the last two lines into one. As to *ah, worm* see A. IV, sc. 5, l. 8 and A. IV, sc. 5, l. 21, where *Ah* has been wrongly expunged by Mr. Hazlitt. Compare also 2 K. Henry IV, V, 3, 17, where the quarto and the second folio read *A sirrah* instead of *Ah, sirrah*. The division of the lines, although it has been retained by Delius and Mr. Hazlitt, is obviously wrong; arrange: —

> *Bre.* See, how she flings away from me! I'll follow
> And give attent to her. Deny my love!
> Ah, worm of beauty, I will chastise thee!
> Come, come, prepare thy head upon the block!

Messrs. Warnke and Prœscholdt have adopted both my arrangement and my readings as proposed in the Jahrb. d. D. Sh.-G., XIII, 70.

CLXII.

> I will crown thee with a complet made of ivory.
>> *Ib., (Del., 39. — W. and Pr., 61. — H's D., VII, 241.)*

This is the reading of the two earliest copies. In the later Qq *I will* and *complet* have rightly been altered to *I'll* and *Chaplet*, whereas *ivory* has been retained, till Delius substituted *ivy* in its room, which, so far as the sense is concerned, is undoubtedly right and will probably be adopted by most succeeding editors, although, in my opinion, it should not be admitted into the text, since it appears from Evans, Leicestershire Words, Phrases, and Proverbs (English Dialect Society, No. 31, London, 1881), p. 297, that *ivory* is a Rutland provincialism for *ivy*. That it cannot be taken for an erratum seems to be proved by the occurrence of another provincialism in A. II, sc. 4, l. 65, viz. *shipstick*, i. e. *shiptick*, which latter, according to Evans, p. 237, is the Leicestershire pronunciation for *sheeptick*. A third provincialism may possibly lie at the bottom óf the pun on the word *errand* (III, 3, 45), pronounced and spelt *arrand* in Leicestershire (Evans, p. 93), all the Qq which I have collated reading indeed *Arrand* or *arrand*. These curious provincialisms, however few, yet seem sufficient to justify the belief that the author of 'Mucedorus' was a native of either Rutland or the adjoining part of Leicestershire, where *ivory* instead of *ivy* may have been a no less current idiom than in Rutland itself, as the dialects of Rutland and Leicestershire 'seem, indeed, to be substantially identical' (Evans, p. 296). Or are we to attribute these provincialisms to a Leicestershire compositor who thus disfigured his London author's pure English and correct spelling? (Kölb., Engl. Stud., VI, 318 seq.)

CLXIII.

Be merry, wench, we'll have a frolic feast,
Here's flesh enough for to suffice us both,
Say, sirrah, wilt thou fight, or dost thou yield to die?
   Ib., (Del., 40. — W. and Pr., 62. — H's D., VII, 243.)
The last line is an Alexandrine which Prof. W. Wagner in the Jahrb. d. D. Sh.-G., XIV, 282, proposes to reduce to regular metre by the omission of *dost thou*. I formerly thought that we should rather omit *thou* before *fight* (compare Abbott, s. 241), but have now come to the conviction that the true arrangement is: —

  Say, sirrah!
  Wilt thou fight, or dost thou yield to die?

Wilt is no doubt used as a monosyllabic foot by the poet; see notes CL, CLXV, &c. — Compare *supra* note CLIII. (Kölb., Engl. Stud., VI, 319.)

CLXIV.

 Ama. Yet give him leave to speak for my sake.
   Ib., (Del., 41. — W. and Pr., 62. — H's D., VII, 243.)
A catalectic verse (see note II), if we do not prefer to complete it by the addition at the end of the name of the person addressed, viz. *Bremo*. Compare Jahrb. d. D. Sh.-G., XVI, 228 seq. and Shakespeare's Tragedy of Hamlet, ed. Elze (1882), p. 146 seq.

CLXV.

Glad were they, they found such ease,
And in the end they grew to perfect amity.
Weighing their former wickedness,
They term'd the time wherein they lived then
A golden age, a goodly golden age.

Ib., (Del., 41. — W. and Pr., 63. — H's D., VII, 243 seq.)

In the first line *that* has been added by Mr. Hazlitt, and Messrs. Warnke and Prœscholdt have adopted this addition, erroneously ascribing it to Qu. 1610. But the verse is either a syllable pause line, or *Glad* is to be read as a monosyllabic foot. In either case it is to be completed by the addition of *perfect* which, according to an ingenious conjecture of Professor W. Wagner in the Jahrb. d. D. Sh.-G., XIV, 282, has slipped down to the second line. Scan, therefore, either: —

Glad were | they, ⌣ | they found | such per|fect ease,

or: —

Glad | were they, | they found | such per|fect case.

The passage should be written and arranged thus: —

Glad were they, they found such perfect ease,
And in the end they grew to amity.
Weighing their former wickedness, they term'd
The time wherein they liv'd a golden age,
A goodly golden age.

(Kölb., Engl. Stud., VI, 319.)

CLXVI.

If men, which lived tofore, as thou dost now,
Wild in woods, addicted all to spoil, &c.

Ib., (Del., 41. — W. and Pr., 63. — H's D., VII, 244.)

Qq 1610, 1615, 1619, and 1621: *Wilde (Wild) in Wood*; Qq 1631, 1634, 1650 [?], and 1668: *Wilde (Wild) in Woods*. Qu. 1598 reads *Wilie in wood* (not *Wily*, as Mr. Hazlitt says) by which reading Mr. Hazlitt has been induced to conjecture *Wildly* and to introduce this conjecture into the text. In the Jahrb. d. D. Sh.-G., XIII, 71, I suggested to add *the* before *woods*, and this suggestion has been adopted both by Delius and Messrs. Warnke and Prœscholdt. Or should *Wild* be read as a monosyllabic foot?

CLXVII.

No, let's live, and love together faithfully,
I'll fight for thee —

> *Bre.*   Or fight for me, or die: or fight, or else thou diest.
> *Ama.*   Hold, Bremo, hold.
>
> *Ib., (Del., 42. — W. and Pr., 63. — H's D., VII, 244.)*

This is the uniform reading of all the old copies which I have collated; Mr. Hazlitt and Messrs. Warnke and Prœscholdt *let us live.* The old copies, however, are right, *No* being a monosyllabic foot and *faithfully* a triple ending. Those critics that do not approve of this scansion had better place *No extra versum* than alter the reading; the rest of the line will then form a regular blank verse. — With respect to the following line it may be observed that Bremo does not want Mucedorus to fight for him, but to fight with him (just as in A. III, sc. 4, l. 19 he wanted Amadine to fight with him), or he will slay him forthwith; see *supra* l. 61 seqq. He is about to strike the deadly blow, when Amadine interferes and comes to the hermit's rescue. The first hemistich, therefore, of Bremo's speech cannot possibly have come from the author's pen; the second hemistich *(or fight, or else thou diest)* exactly completes the verse, and Amadine's ejaculation *(Hold, Bremo, hold)* forms an interjectional line. (Kölb., Engl. Stud., VI, 319 seq.)

CLXVIII.

> You promised me to make me your queen.
>
> *Ib., (Del., 42. — W. and Pr., 63. — H's D., VII, 244.)*

This is the reading of Qq 1598 and 1610; Qq 1615, 1619, 1621, 1631, 1634, 1650 [?]: *You promised me to make me queen*; Qu. 1668: *You promised to make me queen.* I suspect that all the quarto-readings are corrupt. Perhaps we should write: —

> You pro|mis'd me | *for* to | make me | your queen,

a correction which would agree with the prevalent use of this pleonastic form of the infinitive in our play. Compare, Induction, 37 (for to please); I, 4, 14 (for to resist); II, 1, 9 (for to give); II, 3, 32 (for to work); III, 2, 38 (for to provide); III, 5, 2 (for to make); IV, 3, 60 (for to suffice); IV, 5, 139 (for to maintain); IV, 5, 144 (for to win). — Two lines below *me* should be inserted after *promised*, as has been conjectured by Prof. W. Wagner (Jahrb. d. D. Sh.-G., XIV, 282), so that ll. 101 and 103 are made to correspond with one another. (Kölb., Engl. Stud., VI, 320.)

CLXIX.

> *Mouse.*   I think he was, for he said he did lead a saltseller's life about the woods.
> *Seg.*   Thou wouldst say, a solitary life about the woods.
>
> *Ib., (Del., 42. — W. and Pr., 64. — H's D., VII, 245.)*

Read: a *solitary's* life &c.

CLXX.

Ama. Not my Bremo, nor his Bremo woods.

Ib., (Del., 44. — W. and Pr., 66. — H's D., VII, 246.)

This is the reading of all the Qq I have collated. Mr. Hazlitt has altered and divided the line, I do not know on what authority or for what reason: —

Ama. Not my Bremo,
Nor Bremo's woods.

I feel convinced that the poet wrote: —

Ama. No, not my Bremo, nor *my Bremo's* woods.

This emendation, as first proposed in the Jahrb. d. D. Sh.-G., XIII, 71 *(Oh, not my Bremo, &c.)* has been introduced into the text by Messrs. Warnke and Prœscholdt. Critics, however, who will allow *Not* to take the place of a monosyllabic foot, may dispense with the addition of *Oh* or *No* to the original line. Compare Mucedorus, ed. Delius, p. XIV.

CLXXI.

Bre. Thou holdst it well; look how he doth,
Thou may'st the sooner learn.

Ib., (Del., 45. — W. and Pr., 67. — H's D., VII, 248.)

Before *look* Mr. Hazlitt has added the stage-direction *To Amadine.* The division of the lines, although invariably the same in all the Qq I have collated (with the only exception of Qu. 1598 where the passage is printed as prose), nevertheless seems to be wrong; arrange: —

Bre. Thou holdst it well.
Look how he doth, thou may'st the sooner learn.

[*To Amadine.*

(Jahrb. d. D. Sh.-G., XIII, 71 seq.)

CLXXII.

Then have at thine, so lie there and die,
A death no doubt according to desert;
Or else a worse, as thou deservest a worse.

Ib., (Del., 46. — W. and Pr., 67 seq. — H's D., VII, 248.)

This is the arrangement of Qu. 1598, whereas all the later Qq join the words *So lie there and die* to the following line. Arrange and point, perhaps: —

So! lie there and die a death, no doubt,
According to desert; or else a worse,
As thou deserv'st a worse.

Thou after *lie*, which has been added by Messrs. Warnke and Prœscholdt, seems a needless correction, as *So!* may surely take the place of a monosyllabic foot. (Kölb., Engl. Stud., VI, 320.)

CLXXIII.

And there a while live on his provision.

Ib., (Del., 46. — W. and Pr., 68. -- H's D., VII, 249.)

Thus the Qq, Delius, and Mr. Hazlitt. I first proposed to add *we* before *live*, but afterwards thought it preferable to write: *on's provision*, which emendation I privately communicated to Messrs. Warnke and Prœscholdt who thought it worthy of insertion in the text. Or should we be justified in supposing the verse to be a syllable pause line and accordingly scan it: —

And there | a while | ᴜ live | on his | provis|ion?

(Jahrb. d. D. Sh.-G., XIII, 72.)

CLXXIV.

Muce. Then know that which ne'er tofore was known,
I am no shepherd, no Arragonian I,
But born of royal blood: my father's of Valentia king,
My mother queen: who for thy sacred sake,
Took this hard task in hand.

Ib., (Del., 49. — W. and Pr., 70 seq. — H's D., VII, 252.)

Arrange and read: —

Muce. Then | know that | which ne'er | tofore | was known,
I am no shepherd, no Aragonian I,
Who for thy sacred sake took this hard task
In hand, but born of royal blood: my father
Is of Valentia king, my mother queen.

A similar disturbance in the original sequence of the lines has been pointed out by the late Prof. W. Wagner in A. I, sc. 1, l. 66 seq., where l. 67 must of course precede l. 66. See Jahrb. d. D. Sh.-G., XIV, 283. — *Then,* in the first line, is a monosyllabic foot. The earliest quarto reads not, as Messrs. Warnke and Prœscholdt erroneously say, *never tofore,* but *nere tofore,* like all the rest *(neere tofore, neretofore).* (Kölb., Engl. Stud., VI, 321.)

CLXXV.

As if a kingdom had befallen me this time.

Ib., (Del., 49. — W. and Pr., 71. — H's D., VII, 252.)

The words *this time* are completely meaningless and spoil the metre; I have no doubt that they should be discarded. (Jahrb. d. D. Sh.-G., XIII, 72.)

CLXXVI.

Her absence breedes sorrow to my soul
And with a thunder breaks my heart in twain.

Ib., (Del.. 49 seq. — W. and Pr., 71 seq. -- H's D., VII, 253.)

Qq 1598 and 1610: *breedes sorrow*; Qu. 1615: *breeds sorrow*; Qq
1619, 1631, 1650 [?], and 1668: *breeds great sorrow*; Qu. 1634:
breedes great sorrow. *Breedes*, like *restes* in Fair Em, V, 1, 273 (see
note LXXXIX), seems originally to have been pronounced as a dissyllable. -- Mr. Collier, according to Messrs. Warnke and Prœscholdt
ad loc., proposed to read: —

And *when asunder* breaks my heart in twain.

As I privately suggested to Messrs. Warnke and Prœscholdt, I think
it more likely that the author wrote: —

And *will asunder break* my heart in twain.

CLXXVII.

Ama. My gracious father, pardon thy disloyal daughter.
King. What, do mine eyes behold my daughter Amadine?
Rise up, dear daughter, and let these embracing arms
Show thee some token of thy father's joy,
Which e'er since thy departure, hath languished in sorrow.

Ib., (Del., 51. — W. and Pr., 73. — H's D., VII, 254.)

Amadine's speech is to be scanned: —

My gra|cious fa|ther, pard'n thy | disloy|al daugh|ter.

Pardon, as a monosyllable, occurs also in Fair Em, V, 1, 191; in
A Yorkshire Tragedy, I, 10 *ad fin.* (Malone's Supplement, II, 675:
To plead for pardon for my dear husband's life); and elsewhere.
Compare Paradise Lost, I, 71 *(prison)*; I, 248 *(reason)*, and II, 878
(iron). In the second line *Amadine* is to be pronounced as a triple
ending (see Jahrb. d. D. Sh.-G., XV, 343); in the third *and* before
let is to be expunged and the reading of the later Qq *(these embracing
arms)* to be adopted in preference to that of Qq 1598 and 1610
(these my embracing arms). The last line is manifestly corrupted;
a blank verse might be restored by the omission of *ever* and the
transposition of *languished in sorrow*: —

Which, since thy d'parture, hath in sorrow languish'd.

As to *d'parture* or *parture* compare *ante* note CLVI.

CLXXVIII.

Muce. No cause to fear, I caused no offence,
But this, desiring &c.

Ib., (Del., 51. — W. and Pr., 74. — H's D., VII, 255.)

But this has been transferred by Messrs. Warnke and Prœscholdt to
the first line which has thus been made to consist of six feet, whereas
the second line has become a regular blank verse.　In my opinion
But this is a metrical excrescence and should form an interjectional
line; it is, however, altogether suspicious as it occurs again ten lines
below: *With all my heart, but this,* and in neither passage does it
seem to be wanted.

CLXXIX.

Prepared welcomes; giue him entertainement.
> *Ib., (Del., 53. — W. and Pr., 75. -- H's D., VII, 256.)*

This is the reading of the quarto of 1610.　Qu. 1615: —

Prepared welcomes, giue him entertainment;

Qu. 1619 (and all the rest): —

Prepared welcomes giue him entertainment.

The progress of corruption cannot be shown more clearly.　I strongly
suspect that the poet wrote: —

Prepare a welcome; give him entertainment,

and Messrs. Warnke and Prœscholdt have installed this conjectural
emendation in the text.　It may be as well to add that this line is
not contained in Qu. 1598.　(Jahrb. d. D. Sh.-G., XIII, 73.)

CLXXX.

My power has lost her might, and Envy's date's expired,
Yon splendent majesty has 'felled my sting,
And I amazed am.
> *Ib., (Del., 55. — W. and Pr., 78. -- H's. D., VII, 259.)*

And before *Envy's* has been added by the editors.　The second line
is wanting in the quartos of 1621 and 1668 and consequently in
Delius's edition also.　In my opinion, the three lines should be thus
arranged: —

My power has lost her might, and Envy's date
Expirèd *is*; yon splendent majesty
Has 'fell'd my sting, and I amazèd am.

Or should we alter *Envy's* to *my*?　A text so grossly corrupted as
that of Mucedorus cannot be healed without boldness, although the
less bold an emendation is, the better claim it possesses on our
approval.　Now, if we read *my*, not only the addition of *and* would
be spared, but also the division of the lines would remain untouched: —

My power has lost her might, my date's expir'd,
Yon splendent majesty has 'felled my sting,
And I amazèd am.

CLXXXI.

Who other wishes, let him never speak —
 Envy.   Amen!
   Ib., (Del., 56. — W. and Pr., 79. — H's D., VII, 259.)
No Alexandrine, but a regular blank verse; scan: —

 Who óth|er wísh|es, let hím | ne'er speák — | Amén!
(Kölb., Engl. Stud., VI, 321.)

CLXXXII.

And pray we both together with our hearts,
That she thrice Nestor's years may with us rest.
   Ib., (W. and Pr., 76, n. 2. — H's D., VII, 259.)
Being enclosed within two couplets these lines may likewise have
formed a couplet in the author's manuscript: —

 And both together with our hearts pray we,
 That she thrice Nestor's years may with us be.
(Kölb., Engl. Stud., VI, 321.)

CLXXXIII.

God grant her grace amongest vs long may raigne,
And those that would not haue it soe,
Would that by enuie soone their heartes they might forgoe.
 Com. The Counsell, Noble, and this Realme,
Lord guide it stil with thy most holy hand,
The Commons and the subiectes grant them grace,
Their prince to serue, her to obey, and treason to deface:
Long maie she raine, in ioy and greate felicitie,
Each Christian heart do saie amen with me, [*Exeunt.*
   Ib., (W. and Pr., 77. — H's D., VII, 260.)
These verses, which conclude the play in the quarto of 1598, have
been transmitted to us in a state of such degeneracy as cannot be
laid to the author's door, however poor a versifier he may have been.
The second line consists of four, the third of six feet; the words
Would that, which begin the third line, have simply slipped down
from the second to the third line, or rather they were written in the
margin and inserted in the wrong place by the compositor. For
realm in the fourth line, however unexceptionable it may be *per se,*
land should be substituted, as with this single exception the concluding speech of Comedy is in rhyme. This alteration is, moreover,
supported by the concluding prayer in The Three Lords and Three
Ladies of London (Hazlitt's Dodsley, VI, 501 seq.). There we read: —

 Her council wise and nobles of this land
 Bless and preserve, O Lord! with thy right hand.

Whether or not the line should be filled up, it is difficult to decide, as it involves, at the same time, the question, whether, instead of *guide it* in the following line, we should not read *guide them*. Both may be easily done, if the requisite boldness be conceded to the emendator. May not the author have written, e. g.: —

> The council and the nobles of this land
> Lord, guide them still with thy most holy hand?

Of the two clauses *Their prince to serve* and *her to obey* in the seventh line one — most probably the second — is certainly a gloss and must be expunged; and the last line but one may be easily reduced to five feet either by the omission of *joy and* or of *great* before *felicity,* in which latter case *felicity* is to be pronounced as a trisyllable (f'licity).* The corresponding line in the concluding prayer of The Three Lords and Three Ladies of London runs as follows: —

> Lord! grant her health, heart's-ease, [*and*] joy and mirth.

The whole passage, therefore, would seem to have come originally from the author's pen in about the following shape: —

> God grant her Grace amongst us long may reign,
> And would that those that would not have it so,
> By Envy soon their hearts they might forego.
> *Com.* The council and the nobles of this land,
> Lord, guide them still with thy most holy hand!
> The commons and the subjects, grant them grace,
> Their prince to serve and treason to deface:
> Long may she reign in joy and felicity,
> Each Christian heart do say Amen with me!

Similar prayers for the sovereign are found at the conclusion of The Trial of Treasure; Like will to Like; King Darius; The Longer thou Livest, the more Fool thou art; New Custom; Locrine; &c. In 'Locrine' the prayer is apparently defective, in so far as a line seems to have been lost which, besides the missing rhyme to *felicity,* contained the very words of supplication, without which the prayer would be pointless. It may have been to the following effect: —

> *God grant her grace amongst us long to be.*

The whole of the concluding passage is this: —

> And as a woman was the only cause
> That civil discord was then stirred up,
> So let us pray for that renowned maid
> That eight and thirty years the sceptre sway'd;

---

* Felicity as a trisyllable occurs in Sir Thomas More's Utopia, ed. Arber, p. 167: —

> Wherfore not Utopie, but rather rightely
> My name is Eutopie: A place of felicity.

See Abbott, s. 468.

God grant her grace amongst us long to be
In quiet peace and sweet felicity;
And every wight that seeks her grace's smart,
Would that this sword were pierced in his heart.

CLXXXIV.

I thankt him, and so came to see the Court,
Where I am very much beholding to your kindness.

> *Nobody and Somebody, (Simpson, The School*
> *of Shakspere, I, 322.)*

Dele *very* in the second line. Compare S. Walker, Crit. Exam. I, 268 seqq.
See also notes CXXI and CCXCVI.

CLXXXV.

The desert plains of Afric have I stain'd
With blood of Moors, and there in three set battles fought,
March'd conqueror through Asia,
Along the coasts held by the Portuguese;
Ev'n to the verge of gold, aboarding Spain,
Hath Brusor led a valiant troop of Turks,
And made some Christians kneel to Mahomet.

> *Soliman and Perseda (Hazlitt's Dodsley, V, 265.)*

And there, in the second line, seems to have slipped out of its place
and to have contracted a slight corruption during this transposition.
Qy. read: —

> With blood of Moors, in three set battles fought,
> *And then* march'd conqueror through Asia, &c.?

Or would it be thought preferable to write: —

> With blood of Moors, and there in three set battles
> Fought *and* march'd conqueror through Asia?

But even this alteration, though nearer to the old text, would I think,
hardly be acceptable without the change of *there* to *then.*

CHAPMAN.

CLXXXVI.

Give me the master-key of all the doors.

> *Alphonsus, (ed. Elze, 43 and 133.)*

The old editions read: —

> Boy, give me the master-key of all the doors.

Another instance to the same effect occurs on p. 52 (cf. p. 135) where the old editions read: —

> Madam, that we have suffer'd you to kneel so long.

In both cases I have thought myself justified by the metre in expunging the words of address *Boy* and *Madam,* as no doubt such words were frequently interpolated by inaccurate actors. In the edition of Chapman's Works (Plays) by Richard Herne Shepherd (London, 1874) where my text of Alphonsus has been followed remarkably closely, without the least acknowledgment, *Boy* has been omitted, whilst *Madam* has been restored from the old edition. There are, however, two other ways of satisfying the requirements of the metre; one is, to place the words *Boy* and *Madam* in interjectional lines: —

> Boy,
> Give me the master-key &c..

the other, to restore the metre by contractions: —

> Boy, gíve | me th' má|ster-keý | of áll | the doórs,

and: —

> Ma'am, thát | we've súf|fer'd yoú | to kneél | so lóng.

I now think the first-named scansion to possess the best claim to have been the poet's own. (Anglia, herausgegeben von Wülcker und Trautmann, I, 344 seq.)

COOKE.

CLXXXVII.

Gera. How cheerfully things look in this place.
> *Greene's Tu Quoque (H's D., XI, 203.)*

In order to reduce this line to regular metre the critics of the last century, such as Pope, Warburton, Capell, &c., would most likely have inserted *all*: —

> How cheerfully *all* things look in this place.

S. Walker would have declared in favour of dissyllabification and Dr. Abbott may probably maintain the same opinion: —

> How che-erfully things look in this place.

A third way would be to read *cheerfully* as a dissyllable and make the line one of four feet: —

> How cheer|f'lly things | look in | this place.

Or should the verse, notwithstanding the slightness of its pause, be classed with the syllable pause lines: —

> How cheer|fully | ⌣ things | look in | this place?

Thus the line may serve as an eloquent instance of the different stages in verbal or rather metrical criticism.

DEKKER AND WEBSTER.

CLXXXVIII.

Too often interviews amongst women, as amongst princes, breed envy oft to other's fortune.

Dekker and Webster, Westward Ho!, I, 2 (Webster, ed. Dyce, 1857, in 1 vol., 213b.)

In The Dramatic Works of Thomas Dekker &c. (London, 1873), where Westward Ho! has been printed from the Quarto of 1607, this passage stands thus (II, 291): too often interviewes amongst women, as amongst Princes, breeds enuy oft to others fortune. — *Oft*, after *too often*, can hardly be right; qy. *of one*? The passage would then read: Too often interviews amongst women, as amongst princes, breed envy *of one* to other's fortune.

— — — —

CLXXXIX.

I heard say that he would have had thee nursed thy child thyself too.

Ib., I, 2 (Webster, ed. Dyce, 214a.)

In The Dramatic Works of Thomas Dekker, II, 292, the passage reads: I heard say that he would haue had thee nurst thy Childe thy selfe to. — *Nursed*, or *nurst*, is to all appearance a mere misprint for *nurse*.

— — — —

CXC.

Mist. Honey[*suckle*]. I think, when all's done, I must follow his counsel, and take a patch; I['d] have had one long ere this, but for disfiguring my face: yet I had noted that a mastic patch upon some women's temples hath been the very rheum [rheuwme, Dekker, Dram. Works, II, 298] of beauty.

Ib., II, 1 (Webster, ed. Dyce, 216a.)

Dyce remarks on the word *rheum*: 'A misprint, I believe: but qy. for what?' I think for *prime*. Another corruption seems still to be lurking in the passage; may not the original reading have been: yet I *have* noted?

— — — —

CXCI.

Such a red lip, such a white forehead, such a black eye, such a full cheek, and such a goodly little nose, now she's in that French gown, Scotch falls, Scotch bum, and Italian head-tire you sent her, and is such an enticing she-witch, carrying the charms of your jewels about her. *Ib., II, 2 (Webster, ed. Dyce, 218b.)*

'Scotch falls, Scotch bum' is an evident dittography. Read either
DUTCH *falls, Scotch bum*, or, *Scotch falls,* DUTCH *bum.* It may be
left to the antiquaries to inquire which of these two conjectural
emendations is countenanced by the Dutch and Scotch fashions of the
time. — In Dekker's Dramatic Works, II, 302, the passage is given
without the least variation, except in the spelling.

———

CXCII.

Whirl[*pool*]. We'll take a coach and ride to Ham or so.
Mist. Ten[*terhook*]. O, fie upon 't, a coach! I cannot abide to
be jolted.
Mist. Wafer. Yet most of your citizens' wives love jolting.
Ib., II, 3 (Webster, ed. Dyce, 222b.)

The last speech comes very inappropriately from Mistress Wafer's
lips, she being a citizen's wife herself. In my judgment it should
be assigned to one of the three gentlemen, Linstock, Whirlpool, and
Sir Gosling Glowworm, most probably to Mr. Whirlpool, as it is he
who has made the proposal of taking a coach. — In The Dramatic
Works of Thomas Dekker &c., II, 311, the prefixes to these three
speeches are: *While* (for *Whirle*[*poole*]) *Tent.* [i. e. *Mist. Tenterhook*];
and *Mab*[*ell*].

———

FIELD.

CXCIII.

'Tis your jealousy

That makes you think so; for, by my soul,
You have given me no distaste by keeping from me
All things that might be burthenous, and oppress me.
A Woman is a Weathercock, (H's D., XI, 13.)

To conclude from these and other lines, the text of this play in
Mr. Hazlitt's Dodsley would seem to have been printed from The
Old English Drama (London, Thom. White, 1830), Vol. II, provided
that this collection itself was not printed from one of the older
editions of Dodsley. It would be time and labour thrown away to
sift this matter and it may suffice to say that Mr. Hazlitt has compared the old copies in a very perfunctory manner, and that numerous
blunders have crept into the text. In the quarto of 1612 the above
lines are given quite correctly: —

Tis your jealousie

That makes you thinke *it* so, for by my soule
You haue [pronounce *You've*] giuen me no distast, *in* keeping
from me, &c.

Iu the same play Mr. Hazlitt has spoiled the following lines (XI, 40): —

> *Strange.* Good [people], save your labours, for by heaven,
> I'll do it: if I do't not, I shall be pointed at, &c.

Qu. 1612 correctly reads: —

> *Stra.* Good, saue your labors, for by Heauen Ile doo't:
> If I doo't not, I shall be pointed at, &c.

For the use of *Good* without a noun, the reader may be referred to The Tempest, I, 1, 3 and to Hamlet, J, 1, 70, passages which are so well known that they ought to have been remembered by Mr. Hazlitt.

Farther on (XI, 66) Mr. Hazlitt prints: —

> *Capt. Pouts.* I will kill two men for you; till then, &c.

and thus spoils the metre again. Qu. 1612 correctly reads: —

> *Capt.* *Sir*, I wil kill two men for you, till then, &c.

In the Old English Drama, II, 49, the address *Sir* has likewise been omitted.

Some similar instances of negligence and corruption of the text may be added from Kyd's Cornelia as printed in Mr. Hazlitt's Dodsley (Vol. V). At p. 205 we meet with the following lines: —

> Under this outrage now are all our goods,
> Where scattered they run by land and sea
> (Like exil'd us) from fertile Italy,
> To proudest Spain or poorest Getuly.

In a foot-note on the last line Mr. Hazlitt remarks: '*Getullum*, in Tripoli. See Hazlitt's "Classical Gazetteer", in v.' Is this negligence or ignorance or both combined together? Mr. Hazlitt ought to have looked up *Gætulia,* under which head the correct explanation is given, an explanation, by the way, which is contained in every Latin Dictionary and known to almost all boys of the upper forms. Two glaring misprints occur at the very next page (p. 206, ll. 9 and 17) where instead of the prefix *Cornelius* we must, of course, write *Cornelia,* and where the Chorus should not say: —

> Why suffer *your* vain dreams your head to trouble,

but: —

> Why suffer *you* vain dreams your head to trouble,

The quarto of 1594 correctly reads both *Cornelia* and *you.*

These blunders and corruptions collected at random are sufficient proofs of the carelessness with which this latest edition of so important and almost indispensable a collection of old plays has been prepared. Readers and students should therefore never be off their guard and in all difficult and doubtful cases should not allow themselves to be deluded into the belief that they are using a correct or critically revised text.

CXCIV.

Scud[*more*].   What means my —
  Nev[*ill*].   This day this Bellafront, the rich heir,
Is married unto Count Frederick,
And that's the wedding I was going to.

Ib., (H's D., XI, 16.)

Mr. Hazlitt's Dodsley here completely agrees with Qu. 1612, except
that the latter has the misprint *whar* for *what*. — If the first two
lines admit of a scansion at all, it can be no other than this: —

What means | my — This | day this | Bell'front | the rich | heir,
Is mar | rièd | unto | Count Fred | erick.

But what critic will impute such unreadable harshness even to one
of the lesser lights of the dramatic galaxy of the Elizabethan age?
I think that *Is* slipped out of its place and that the poet wrote: —

Scud.   What means my —
  Nev.   This day *is* this Bellafront,
The rich heir, married *to* Count Frederick, &c.

CXCV.

Cap.   You haue shew'd some kindnes to me, I must loue you *Sir*,
What did you with his bodie?

Ib., (H's D., XI, 66.)

This is the reading and arrangement of the old copy.   Mr. Hazlitt's
Dodsley (in accordance with the respective passage in The Old
English Drama): —

Capt. Pouts.   You have show'd some kindness to me:
I must love you, sir.   What did you with his body?

Arrange and read either: —

Capt. Pouts.   You | have show'd | some kind | ness to | me: I
Must love you, sir.   What did you with his body?

or: —

Capt. Pouts.   You've show'd | some kind | ness. to | me: I, &c.

CXCVI.

Kath.   Life! I am not married, then, in earnest.
Nev.   So, Mistress Kate, I kept you for myself.

Ib., (H's D., XI, 80 seq.)

Thus Mr. Hazlitt in accordance with Qu. 1612.   Read, *No* for *So*.
Compare note on Pericles, IV, 1, 14, where *No* has usurped the place
of *So*.   *Life* is to be read as a monosyllabic foot.

GLAPTHORNE.

CXCVII.

The Panther so
Breaths odors pretious as the Sarmaticke gums
Of Easterne groves, but the delicious sent
Not taken in at distance choakes the sense
With the too muskie savour.

Glapthorne, The Hollander, (Plays and Poems, 1874), I, 127.

Though this passage contains a manifest corruption, yet it has been reproduced without correction in Miss Phipson's 'Animal-Lore of Shakspeare's Time' (Lon., 1883), p. 23. Instead of 'the Sarmaticke gums' read, of course, 'the *aromatic* gums.' In the unamended line either the article *the* before *Sarmaticke* must be elided, or we must allow an extra syllable before the pause (after the fifth syllable), however slight that pause may be. To the amended line both these metrical liberties must be conceded; scan: —

Breathes ó|dours pré|cious as th' ár|omát|ic gums.

(The Athenæum, Sept. 3, 1887, p. 320.)

GREENE.

CXCVIII.

I have struck him dumb, my lord; and, if your honour please.

*Friar Bacon and Friar Bungay, (Rob. Greene and George Peele,
ed. Dyce, 1861, in 1 vol., 162b. — Old English Drama,
ed. A. W. Ward, Oxf., 1878, p. 70.)*

Dyce rather boldly suggests: *if you please* instead of *if your honour please,* whereas the late Professor Wilhelm Wagner in Professor Wül-ker's Anglia, II, 524, declares the line to be an Alexandrine. In my opinion it is a regular blank verse with an extra syllable before the pause; read and scan: —

I 've struck | him dumb, | m' lord; and if | your hon | our please.

CXCIX.

I have given non-plus to the Paduans,
To them of Sien, Florence, and Bologna,
Rheims, Louvain, and fair Rotterdam,
Frankfort, Utrecht, and Orleans.

Ib., (Greene and Peele, ed. Dyce, 168a. — Old E. Dr., 83).

'This [viz. the last] line', says Dyce, 'is certainly mutilated; and so perhaps is the preceding line: from the Emperor's speech, p. 159,

first col., it would seem that "Paris" ought to be one of the places
mentioned here.' — Dyce is quite right, but the mere addition of
'Paris' is no sufficient cure of the two defective lines. I strongly
suspect that Greene wrote: —

> I have given non-plus to the Paduans,
> To them of Sien, Florence, and Bologna,
> *Of* Rheims, *of* Louvain, and fair Rotterdam,
> *Of* Frankfort, Utrecht, *Paris* and Orleans.

The last line has an extra syllable before the pause and a trochee
after it; scan therefore: —

> Of Frank|fort, U|trecht, Páris | and Or|leáns.

CC.

> All hail to this royal company.
>> *Ib., (Greene and Peele, ed. Dyce, 168 a. — Old E. Dr., 83.)*

According to Prof. W. Wagner (l. c.) this is an unmetrical line which
he corrects by the insertion of *right* before *royal.* Prof. Ward (l. c.)
proposes to read *unto* instead of *to.* To me the line seems to be
quite correct, if considered as a syllable pause line; scan: —

> All hail! | ⌣ to | this roy|al com|pany.

CCL.

> Gracious as the morning-star of heaven.
>> *Ib., (Greene and Peele, ed. Dyce, 168 b. — Old E. Dr., 85.)*

In Prof. W. Wagner's eyes (l. c.) this is a remarkable instance of the
conservative tendency of the editors; he does not hesitate to declare
in favour of Prof. Ward's conjectural emendation (Old E. Dr., 249): —

> Gracious as *is* the morning-star of heaven.

But may not the poet have used *Gracious* as a trisyllable: —

> Graci|ous as | the mor|ning-star | of heaven?

Or it may be a syllable pause line, as there is certainly a pause
after *Gracious*: —

> Gracious | ⌣ as | the mor|ning-star | of heaven?

CCII.

> And give us cates fit for country swains.
>> *Ib., (Greene and Peele, ed. Dyce, 169 b. — Old E. Dr., 87.)*

Professor W. Wagner (l. c., 525) needlessly inserts *but* after *fit.* It is
a syllable pause line: —

> And give | us cates | ⌣ fit | for coun|try swains.

CCIII.

Persia, down her Volga by canoes.
> *Ib., (Greene and Peele, ed. Dyce, 170a. — Old E. Dr., 87.)*

In order to restore the metre Professor W. Wagner (l. c., 525) proposes to read *adown*. The metre, however, is quite correct; scan: —

Persia, | ᴗ down | her Vol|ga by | canoes.

CCIV.

Ah, Bungay, my Brazen Head is spoil'd.
> *Ib., (Greene and Peele, ed. Dyce, 174b. — Old E. Dr., 99.)*

'Query', says Dyce *ad loc.*, 'Ah, Bungay, *ah,* my.' I think there is no need of such an addition; scan: —

Ah, Bun|gay, ᴗ́ | my bra|zen head | is spoil'd.

HAUGHTON.

CCV.

To them, friends, to them; they are none but yours:
For you I bred them, for you brought them up,
For you I kept them, and you shall have them:
I hate oll others that resort to them.
> *Englishmen for my Money, (H's D., X, 508.)*

In the quartos of 1626 and 1631 the second line runs thus:

For you I bred them, for you I brought them up.

Mr. Hazlitt has wrongly expunged the second *I,* as being 'redundant both for sense and measure.' The fact is, that the line contains an extra syllable before the pause and that the context requires the second *you* to be emphasized: —

For you | I bred | them, for you | I brought | them up.

The next line seems to be defective and one feels tempted to insert *'t is* before the second *you*; such an addition, however, is unnecessary, as the line clearly belongs to the category of syllable pause lines: —

For you | I kept | them, ᴗ́ | and you | shall have | them.

Compare Shakespeare's Tragedy of Hamlet, ed. Elze, p. 127.

KYD.

CCVI.

Embass. This is an argument for our Viceroy,
That *Spaine* may not insult for her successe,
Since English Warriours likewise conquered *Spaine*,
And made them bow their knees to *Albion*.

The Spanish Tragedy, (H's D., V, 35.)

Thus Qu. 1633. The first line is evidently a catalectic blank verse
(see note II). Scan: —

This is | an ar|g'ment for | our Vice|roy.

Three lines *infra* the lection *the king* may be queried; perhaps:
thy king: —

Pledge me, Hieronimo, if thou love *thy* king.

Compare Marlowe, Edward II., I, 4, 339 (Works, ed. Dyce, in 1 vol.,
p. 192a): —

Courageous Lancaster, embrace thy king.

CCVII.

Bel. As those that when they love, are loath, and feare
to lose.
Bal. Then faire, let *Balthazar* your keeper be.
Bel. *Balthazar* doth feare as well as we.

Ib., (H's D., V, 102.)

This is the reading of Qu. 1633, the only old copy I have been able
to collate. Mr. Hazlitt's Dodsley *what they love* and *No, Balthazar
doth fear.* Qy. omit *and fear* in the first line which words seem to
have crept in from the third line by a kind of prolepsis. Or should
the words *when they* be expunged?

CCVIII.

And, madam, you must attire yourself
Like Phœbe, Flora, or the huntress,
Which to your discretion shall seem best.

Ib., (H's D., V, 151 seq.)

The first line is either a syllable pause line: —

And, mad|am, ∠ | you must | attire | yourself,

or one of four feet only: —

And, ma'am, | you must | attire | yourself.

Huntress, in the second line, is either to be pronounced as a trisyllable (*hunt-e-ress*; see Abbott, s. 477), or the line may be considered

a catalectic blank verse (see note II). It may even be imagined that *Dian* was lost after *huntress,* a conjecture which may possibly have been made before this; compare Milton's Comus, 441. As to the last line, it may be doubted, whether *which* is to be taken for a monosyllabic foot, or *to* altered to *unto.* Or would perhaps a transposition bring the verse still nearer to the poet's own wording: —

> Which shall | seem best | to your | discre | ti-on?

CCIX.

> Fain would I die, but darksome ugly death
> Withholds his dart, and in disdain doth fly me,
> Maliciously knowing, that hell's horror
> Is milder than mine endless discontent.

Cornelia, (H's D., V, 191.)

I do not know whether the above punctuation has been introduced in the text by Mr. Hazlitt, or by some previous editor of Dodsley. The two quartos of 1594 and 1595 have commas at the end of the second and third lines, but not after *knowing.* In my opinion both these commas should be expunged just as well as that after *knowing,* whereas a comma ought to be placed after *Maliciously.* — The third line admits of a twofold scansion; it may be considered as a syllable pause line: —

> Mali | ciously, | ⌣ know | ing that | hell's hor | ror,

or *Maliciously* may be read as a word of five syllables: —

> Mali | cious | ly, know | ing that | hell's hor | ror.

CCX.

> One selfsame ship contain'd us, when I saw
> The murd'ring Egyptians bereave his life; &c.

Ib., (H's D., V, 213.)

A twofold scansion of the second line seems to be admissible: —

> The mur | dering | Egypt | ians b'reave | his life,

or: —

> The mur | d'ring 'Gypt | ians | bereave | his life.

For the pronunciation *b'reave* compare notes on Fair Em (Del., 15, &c.) and on The Tempest, I, 2, 296 seq.

CCXI.

> Then satisfy yourself with this revenge,
> Content to count the ghosts of those great captains,
> Which (conquer'd) perish'd by the Roman swords.

> The Hannos, the Hamilcars, Hasdrubals,
> Especially that proudest Hannibal,
> That made the fair Thrasymene so desert:
> For even those fields that mourn'd to bear their bodies,
> Now (loaden) groan to feel the Roman corses.

Ib., (H's D., V, 250.)

How is the sixth line to be scanned? Can *That* be allowed to take the place of a monosyllabic foot? If not, we seem to have no choice but to dissyllabize either *made* or, which seems more likely, *fair,* although a rhythmical ear will, I think, in most cases demur to this dissolution of long vowels or diphthongs. Or is the verse to be considered as a syllable pause line, although there is hardly a sufficient pause after *fair*: —

> That made | the fair | ⌣ Thra|symene | so des|ert?

Or are we to scan (contrary to the established usage): —

> That made | the fair | Thrasým|ené | so des|ert?

He who will accept none of these scansions, is driven to introduce an emendation of the text, such as *the fairest Thrasymene* or *the fair lake Thrasymene.* This latter, however, would hardly be acceptable as, according to the context, Thrasymene does not seem to denote the lake, but its environs, or the country of which it forms the centre, a meaning which is not sanctioned by classic usage, but seems to have been suggested to Kyd by his French original (Les Tragedies de Robert Garnier, Conseiller du Roy, &c. A Tholose, par Pierre Iagourt. MDLXXXVIII), p. 141: —

> Et contans les espris de ces vieux Capitaines,
> Qui vaincus ont passé par les armes Romaines,
> Les Hannons, Amilcars, Asdrubals, et sur tous
> Hannibal, qui rendit Thrasymene si roux.
> Ores les mesmes champs, qui sous leurs corps gemirent,
> Dessous les corps Romains accrauantez soupirent: &c.

May not the last couplet have misled the translator and made him think that Garnier meant to say that the fields around the lake, and not the lake itself, were reddened by Hannibal? The same meaning has been attributed to the name by Lord Byron in his Childe Harold, IV, 62 and 65, where, moreover, the final -*e* is fully sounded: —

>   and I roam
> By Thrasimene's lake, in the defiles
> Fatal to Roman rashness, more at home;

and: —

> Far other scene is Thrasimene now;
> Her lake a sheet of silver, and her plain
> Rent by no ravage save the gentle plough.

Thrasymene, with a mute -*e* at the end, completely agrees with the rest of those classic names that are derived from substantives in -*us,* such as Euxine, Nile, Polypheme, Rhene (Faeric Queene, IV, 11, 21; Paradise Lost, I, 353), Tyre, and others. May I hint at the possibility that Byron who in his historical note on stanza 63 (No. XXIII) refers to Polybius, writing as he did in Venice, may not have had access to an English translation of the Greek historian and may have been obliged to look up the original either in the Marciana, or in the library of his friends the Armenians? In Bk. III, Chap. 82 (not 83, as he says) of the original he read τὴν Ταρσιμένην καλουμένην λίμνην and by this Greek form of the name may have been misled to make the word one of four syllables, so much the more so as it fell in with the numbers of his verse.

MARLOWE.

CCXII.

Your grace hath taken order by Theridamas.

1 Tamburlaine. I, 1 (Works, ed. Dyce, in 1 col., 1870, 7b. — Ed. A. Wagner, 1885, l. 46.)

Schipper, in his dissertation *De versu Marlovii* (Bonn, 1867), p. 19, ranks this line with those verses of six feet, which, he says, Marlowe did not hesitate to admit. In my opinion, however, most of his so-called *senarii* are regular five feet lines with triple endings and are to be scanned as follows: —

Your grace | hath ta|ken or|der by | Therid|'mas;

To Mem|phis, from | my un|cle's coun|try of Me|dia;

To en|tertain | some care | of our | secu|r'ties;

Besides, | king Sig|ismund | hath brought | from Christ|'ndom;

Now say, | my lords | of Bu|da and | Bohe|mia.

To these lines quoted by Schipper, the following, likewise taken from Tamburlaine, may be added: —

That will | we chief|ly see | unto, | Therid|'mas *(34a)*;

How through | the midst | of Var|na and | Bulga|ria *(49a)*;

Our ar|my and | our bro|thers of | Jeru|s'lem *(51b)*.

Even in the body of the line *Theridamas* is occasionally used as a word of three syllables; see ib., 57a: —

Both we, | Therid|'mas, will | intrench | our men;

Ib., 60b: —

Welcome, | Therid|'mas and | Techel|les, both;

Ib., 68b: —

Take them | away, | Therid|'mas; see them | despatch'd.

It should not be overlooked that the first and second lines exclude every doubt, as they admit of no other scansion and cannot be taken for six feet lines.

CCXIII.

Myc. Well, here I swear by this my royal seat.
Cos. You may do well to kiss it then.

>   *Ib., I, 1 (Works, 8a. — A. Wag., 97 seq.)*

The second line, in my opinion, should be completed by the addition
of *Mycetes*: —

>   You may do well to kiss it then, *Mycetes*.

CCXIV.

Tamb. Stay, Techelles; ask a parle first.

>   *Ib., I, 2 (Works, 11a. — A. Wag., 325.)*

The metre, I think, requires *parley*. The first foot of the line *(Stay)*
is monosyllabic.

CCXV.

And made a voyage into Europe.

>   *2 Tamburlaine, I, 3 (Works, 49a. — A. Wag., 2769.)*

Although this line may well be taken to be a catalectic verse (see
note II), yet I cannot let it pass unchallenged, but strongly suspect
some corruption. 'A word', says Dyce, 'dropt out from this line',
and Mr. Francis Cunningham, *ad loc.*, does not shrink back from the
following correction: —

>   And [thence I] made a voyage into Europe.

I am persuaded, that Marlowe wrote *Europa*. Cf. R. Chester's Loves
Martyr, ed. Grosart (for the New Shakspere Society), 24: —

>   Welcome immortal Bewtie, we will ride
>   Ouer the Semi-circle of Europa,
>   And bend our course where we will see the Tide,
>   That partes the Continent of Affrica,
>   Where the great cham gouernes Tartaria:
>   And when the starry Curtaine vales the night,
>   In Paphos sacred Ile we meane to light.

Chaucer, The Court of Love, 820 seqq. (ed. Morris, IV, 29): —

>   For yf that Jove had*de* but this lady seyn,
>   Tho Calixto ne *yet* Alcmenia,
>   Thay never hadden in his armes leyne;
>   Ne he had*de* loved the faire Europa;
>   Ye, ne yit Dané ne Antiopa!
>   For all *here* bewtie stode in Rosiall,
>   She semed lich a thyng celestiall.

The shortening of the penult in *Européa* will not seem strange when
we compare *Eúphrates* (1 Tamburlaine, V, 2; Works, 36b) and *Sármata*

(Marlowe, First Book of Lucan, Works 377a), beside the wellknown *Hypérion*, *Titus Andrónicus*, and others. False quantity in classical proper names seems to be privileged. Cf. Marlowe's Doctor Faustus &c., ed. A. W. Ward, p. 271 seq. S. Walker, Versification, 172 seq.

CCXVI.

Faust. So Faustus hath
Already done; and holds this principle,
There is no chief but only Belzebub.

Doctor Faustus, (Works, 83b and 120b.)

Qy. arrange: —

Faust. So Faustus hath already done, and holds
This principle:
There is no chief but only Belzebub?

CCXVII.

For that security craves great Lucifer.

Ib., (Works, 86a and 112b.)

This is the reading of the first quarto (1604). In the second quarto (1616) the line is corrected by the omission of *great*; no such correction, however, is needed, as *security* may well be pronounced as a trisyllable *(secur'ty)*.

CCXVIII.

And Faustus hath bequeath'd his soul to Lucifer.

Ib., (Works, 86b and 113a.)

An apparent Alexandrine. *Lucifer* is to be read as a triple ending.

CCXIX.

Faust. How! now in hell.
Nay, an this be hell, I'll willingly be damn'd here:
What! walking, disputing, &c.
But, leaving off this, let me have a wife,
The fairest maid in Germany;
For I am wanton and lascivious,
And cannot live without a wife.
Meph. How! a wife!
I prithee, Faustus, talk not of a wife.

Ib., (Works, 87a seq. and 114a.)

From a comparison of this reading of the first quarto with that of
the second, we may fairly conclude that the passage in the poet's
Ms. stood as follows: —

  Faust. How now! In hell!
An this be hell, I'll willingly be damn'd.
What! Sleeping, eating, walking, and disputing!
But leaving off this, let me have a wife,
The fairest maid *there is* in Germany;
For I am wanton and lascivious,
And cannot live without a wife.
  Meph.   A wife?
I prithee, Faustus, talk not of a wife.

CCXX.

  Abig. Then, father, go with me.
  Bara. No, Abigail, in this
It is not necessary I be seen.
       The Jew of Malta, (Works, 152 a.)

Arrange: —

  Abig. Then, father, go with me.
  Bara.   No, Abigail,
In this it is not necessary I be seen.

CCXXI.

That I may, walking in my gallery,
See 'em go pinion'd along by my door.
       Ib., (Works, 157 b.)

The second line hardly admits of a scansion, if we do not choose
to pronounce *along*. Perhaps the words should be transposed: —

  See 'em go | along | píni|on'd by | my door,
or, which seems preferable: —

  See them | go along | píni|on'd by | my door.

CCXXII.

  Sec. P. Man. A traveller.
  Gav. Let me see — thou wouldst do well
To wait at my trencher, and tell me lies at dinner-time.
     Edward II., (Works, 183 b. — Ed. O. W. Tancock,
      Oxf., 1879, I, 1, 29 seq.)

Lines 29 and 30 should, of course, be joined into one: —

  Sec. P. Man. A traveller.
  Gav.   Let me see — thou wouldst do well.

In the last line Mr. Fleay takes the words 'at my trencher' to be
probably an insertion; they spoil the metre, he says. May not the
line be scanned: —

T'wait at | my tren|cher, and tell | me lies | at din|ner time?

Dinner-time to be read as a triple ending.

CCXXIII.

My lord, here comes the king, and the nobles,
From the parliament. I'll stand aside.

Ib., (Works, 184a. — Tan., I, 1, 72 seq.)

Although this is the reading of all the four quartos (1594, 1598,
1612 and 1622), the text must nevertheless be pronounced corrupt;
the vocative *My lord* has no antecedent to which it might refer, and
the verse, moreover, consists only of four feet. Dyce, therefore,
transposes the words and reads *Here comes my lord the king*, an
emendation which is greatly preferable to Cunningham's suggestion
By'r lord, here comes the king; for Marlowe, as Mr. Fleay justly
remarks, never makes use of similar oaths and protestations, and if
he did, we should be prepared rather for *By'r lady* than for *By'r
lord*. Mr. Fleay himself tries to heal the corruption by a different
arrangement of the lines: —

Here comes my lord
The king and th' nobles from the parliament.
I'll stand aside.

In my opinion this is far from being an improvement. *My lord* is
no doubt a marginal gloss intended to supersede *the king* and has
been joined to the line by the inadvertency of the compositor, the
author of the gloss having neglected to strike out *the king*. Gaveston
likes to call the king his lord not only when addressing him, but
also when speaking of him; compare, e. g., I, 1, 138 and I, 4, 160 seq.
(ed. Tancock). Read and arrange, therefore: —

Here comes my lord and th' nobles from the parliament.
I'll stand aside.

Parliament is a triple ending. (Anglia, herausgegeben von Wülcker
und Trautmann, I, 348.)

CCXXIV.

Edw. What, Gaveston! welcome — kiss not my hand.

Ib., (Works, 185a. — Tan., I, 1, 140.)

Mr. Fleay, in his edition of this play, prints *welcóme* and on p. 119
observes, that this is Marlowe's usual pronunciation of the word.
Even S. Walker, Versification, 142 seq., takes it for granted that

welcome was frequently pronounced with the accent on the last syllable. A more careful examination of the respective lines, however,
will show that Marlowe does not depart from the regular accentuation
of the word. In the above line *welcome* begins the second hemistich
and may therefore without the least difficulty be taken for a trochee.
The same scansion holds good in A. II, sc. 2 l. 51 and ll. 65 — 68,
where Mr. Fleay prints the word both with and without an accent,
a fact that seems to imply that here he admits two different accen-
tuations of the word. The word has the accent on the first syllable
also in A. III, sc. 1 (6), ll. 34, 46, 57, 66; A. IV, sc. 3, ll. 40 and 41;
A. IV, sc. 4, l. 2; &c. It may be added, that very naturally *welcome*
generally takes its place either at the beginning of the line or at the
beginning of the second hemistich, both of them favourite places of
the trochee. — Compare *infra* note CCCLV.

CCXXV.

K. Edw. But in the mean time, Gaveston, away,
And take possession of his house and goods.
Come, follow me, and thou shalt have my guard
To see it done, and bring thee safe again.
    Gav. What should a priest do with so fair a house?
A prison may beseem his holiness.

Ib., (Works, 186a. — Tan., I, 1, 202 — 7.)

In this passage two distinct speeches would appear to have been
welded together and a disturbance in the original sequence of the lines
to have been thus produced. I strongly suspect that Marlowe wrote: —

    K. Edw. But in the mean time, Gaveston, away,
And take possession of his house and goods.
    Gav. What should a priest do with so fair a house?
A prison may beseem his holiness.
    K. Edw. Come, follow me, and thou shalt have my guard
To see it done, and bring thee safe again.

(The Athenæum, Apr. 9, 1887, p. 491. Cf. ib., Apr. 16, 1887, p. 521
and Apr. 23, 1887, p. 554.)

CCXXVI.

Archb. of Cant. But yet lift not your swords against
the king.

Ib., (Works, 187a. — Tan., I, 2, 61.)

This line does not belong to the archbishop, but to the queen, who
has just been addressed by young Mortimer, and must, of course,
reply to him. She repeats her entreaty in almost the selfsame words
in ll. 80 seq. The archbishop only takes part in the dialogue at l. 68,

and shows no desire to ward off the blow from the king. The present line, therefore, would seem to be inconsistent with his character. That there is some confusion in the old editions is shown by the fact that in l. 77 the prefix *(Archb. of Cant.)* has been omitted, and had to be added by Dyce. (The Athenæum, March 12, 1887, p. 362.)

CCXXVII.

> *Gav.* Edmund, the mighty prince of Lancaster,
> That hath more earldoms than an ass can bear,
> And both the Mortimers, two goodly men,
> With Guy of Warwick, that redoubted knight,
> Are gone toward Lambeth: there let them remain.
>
> *Ib., (Works, 187a seq. — Tan., I, 3.)*

What is the meaning of this unconnected scene, which contains nothing but a communication to Kent by Gaveston, the purpose of which is perfectly incomprehensible? As a rule a scene consists of a colloquy between two or more persons; it may also consist of a soliloquy, but it should not consist of a communication made by one of the *Dramatis Personæ* to another, without eliciting a reply from this second person. After Gaveston's shameful attack on the Bishop of Coventry we shall hardly wrong him by supposing that he is incensed at the convention of the lords and eager to seize on them even in the archbishop's residence, the sanctity of which should protect it from all intrusion of worldly power. He is evidently endeavouring to win Kent over to his sacrilegious project, but is stopped short by that circumspect prince, who already has warned his royal brother not to lay violent hands on the Bishop of Coventry. Thus it will become apparent to whom the words 'There let them remain' ought to be assigned; the scene in the poet's manuscript was no doubt to the following effect: —

> *Gav.* Edmund, the mighty prince of Lancaster,
> That hath more earldoms than an ass can bear,
> And both the Mortimers, two goodly men,
> With Guy of Warwick, that redoubted knight,
> Are gone toward Lambeth —
> *Kent.* There let them remain.

Compare A. III, sc. 3, l. 11 seq. (ed. Tancock): —

> *Y. Mor.* Look, Lancaster, yonder is Edward
> Among his flatterers.
> *Lan.* And there let him be
> Till he pay dearly for their company.

(The Athenæum, March 12, 1887, p. 362.)

CCXXVIII.

Gav. The peers will frown.

K. Edw. I pass not for their anger -- Come, let's go;
O that we might as well return as go.

Ib., (Works, 189b. — Tan., I, 4, 141 seqq.)

Arrange: —

Gav. The peers will frown.
K. Edw.   I pass not for their anger.
Come, let's go!
O that we might as well return as go!

CCXXIX.

Lan. For his repeal, madam! he comes not back.

Ib., (Works, 190b. — Tan., I, 4, 204.)

Mr. Fleay prints *madáme* which, he says (at p. 120), is the spelling
of the quartos and shows the pronunciation. Mr. Fleay, I think,
means to say that the Qq read *madame* (or more strictly speaking,
Madame), the accent being an addition of his own. As to the pronunciation I have no doubt that the word here as elsewhere is to
be accented on the first syllable; I know of no reliable instance to
the contrary. The pause falls after *repeal* and the second hemistich
begins with a trochee. The line should therefore be printed: —

For his repeal, — mádam! he comes not back.

CCXXX.

Lan. On that condition, Lancaster will grant.
War. And so will Pembroke and I.
E. Mor.   And I.

Ib., (Works, 191b. — Tan., I, 4, 292 seq.)

What right has Warwick to speak for Pembroke? And why should
not the latter give his assent *in propriâ personâ* just like the rest?
Marlowe wrote, no doubt: —

Lan. On that condition, Lancaster will grant.
Pem. And so will Pembroke.
War.   And I.
E. Mor.   And I.

This arrangement at the same time regulates the metre of the line,
so that there is no need of that awkward lengthening *Pemb(e)roke*
advocated by Mr. Fleay. The pause after 'Pembroke' simply takes
the place of a defective syllable, as we see in numberless lines of
the Elizabethan dramatists; in other words, the verse is a syllable
pause line. (The Athenæum, March 12, 1887, p. 362.)

CCXXXI.

But tell me, Mortimer, what's thy device
Against the stately triumph we decreed? &c.
Ib., (Works, 194b. — Tan., II, 2, 11 seq.)

A very apt illustration of these and the following lines is contained
in the following passage from Neumayr von Ramssla, Johann Ernsten
des Jüngern, Hertzogen zu Sachsen, Reise &c., Leipzig, 1620, S. 179:
'Endlichen zeigete man I[hro] F[ürstlichen] G[naden] eine kleine
Galeria [viz. at Whitehall], etwa 20 Schritt lang, so hinauss auffm
Fluss gebawet, darinn hiengen auff beyden Seiten etliche hundert
Schild von Pappen gemacht, daran waren allerley *emblemata* vnd
Wort gemahlet vnd geschrieben. Wann Frewdenfest seynd, pflegen
die Höffischen solche *inventiones* zu machen, vnd damit auffzuziehen.
Wer nun was sonderlichs vnd denckwürdigs erfunden, dessen Schild
wird zum Gedächtnüs dahin gehengt. Hinden am Ende dieses Gangs,
ist der Gang etwas grösser, in solchem hiengen auch dergleichen
schilde.' — A similar 'Triumph' or rather 'Masque' with devices &c.
is introduced in Marston's Insatiate Countess, A. II (Works, ed. Halliwell, III, 123 seq.), where the gentlemen 'deliver their shields to
their severall mistresses', after that they dance, &c.

CCXXXII.

To gather for him throughout the realm.
Ib., (Works, 196b. — Tan., II, 2, 144.)

All editors as far as they are known to me are agreed in lengthening
throughout so as to make it a trisyllable (thoroughout), and thus produce a line of ten syllables. To me this seems highly improbable.
The verse may be a syllable pause line, although the pause is rather
slight: —

To gath|er for | him ‿ | throughout | the realm.

I feel, however, more inclined to think the line corrupted in so far
as the object (*money, alms, a ransom,* or some such word) has
been lost: —

To gather *money* for him throughout the realm,
To gather *a ransom* for him throughout the realm.

To gather money occurs in 1 Henry VI., III, 2, 5.

CCXXXIII.

K. Edw. I will not trust them. Gaveston, away!
Gav. Farewell, my lord.
K. Edw.   Lady, farewell.

Niece. Farewell, sweet uncle, till we meet again.
K. Edw. Farewell, sweet Gaveston; and farewell, niece.

Ib., (Works, 199a. — Tan., II, 4, 8—11.)

The second line must be pronounced defective, unless we print the
two speeches as two incomplete lines (which they certainly are not),
or resort (with Mr. Fleay) to lengthening *lord* and *farewell*: —

Gav. Farewell, | my lor|'d.
K. Edw.   La|dy, fa|'rewell.

Even if I could bring my ears to acquiesce in this scansion, there
is yet another obstacle which is not to be overcome by a metrical
makeshift. It passes my belief that the poet should have made the
king disregard his favorite's adieu instead of replying to it. I have,
therefore, no doubt that the original wording of the line was this: —

Gav. Farewell, my lord.
K. Edw.   *Farewell.* Lady, farewell.

A strikingly analogous case occurs in K. Richard II., V, 3, 144, where
farewell has also been lost. All the old copies, with the single exception of QE (which is of no critical value whatever), read: —

Uncle farewell: and cousin adieu.

The true reading has been found out by the Cambridge Editors, viz.: —

Uncle farewell; *farewell, aunt*; cousin, adieu.

The conjectural emendations advanced by Collier's so-called corrector
and Dyce are valueless. (The Athenæum, Apr. 9, 1887, p. 491.
Cf. ib., Apr. 16, 1887, p. 521 and Apr. 23, 1887, p. 554.)

CCXXXIV.

His head shall off. — Gaveston, short warning.

Ib., (Works, 200b. — Tan., II, 5, 21.)

A syllable pause line; scan: —

His head | shall off. | ⌣ Gav|eston, | short warn|ing.

CCXXXV.

Arundel, we will gratify the king
In other matters; he must pardon us in this.
Soldiers, away with him.

Ib., (Works, 201a. -- Tan., II, 5, 41 seq.)

Arrange: —

Arundel, we will gratify the king
In other matters; he must pardon us
In this. Soldiers, away with him.

(Kölb., Engl. Stud., XI, 363.)

CCXXXVI.

When, can you tell? Arundel, no; we wot,
He that the care of his realm remits &c.
Ib., (Works, 201a. — Tan., II, 5, 57 seq.)

The first line should, perhaps, be pointed: —

When? Can you tell, Arundel? No; we wot, &c.

With respect to the second line Dyce refers his readers to A. III, sc. 2, l. 56: —

And, Spenser, spare them not, lay it on,

and to A. IV, sc. 6, l. 92: —

My lord, be going; care not for these.　　　•

Care and *spare,* he says, are both to be read as dissyllables. Mr. Cunningham and Prof. W. Wagner, on the other hand, dissyllabize *re-alm,* a pronunciation justly rejected by Mr. Tancock *ad loc.* In my humble opinion all these verses are syllable pause lines and thus to be scanned: —

He that | the care | ⌣ of | his realm | remits

And, Spen|ser, spare | them not, | ⌣ lay | it on

My lord, | be go|ing: ⌣ | care not | for these.

CCXXXVII.

Mortimer hardly; Pembroke and Lancaster.
Ib., (Works, 204a. — Tan., III, 2, 105.)

Dyce, Cunningham, Keltie, Tancock, and W. Wagner make no comment whatever on this line; I wonder how they may have scanned it. Mr. Fleay writes 'Lancáster' and, consequently, must have scanned: —

Mórti|mer hárd|ly; Pém|broke ánd | Lancás|ter,

which I cannot but think wrong as I know of no instance of the name of 'Lancaster' being accented on the penult. The true scansion of the line, in my conviction, is: —

Mórti|mer hárd|ly; Pémbroke | and Lán|castér.

There is an extra syllable before the pause and both hemistichs begin with a trochee. Should a transposition of the names of 'Pembroke' and 'Lancaster' be thought admissible the line might vie with the best in regularity and smoothness: —

Mórti|mer hárd|ly; Lán|castér | and Pém|broke.

The same remarks hold good with respect to A. III, sc. 3, l. 61: —

These lusty leaders, Warwick and Lancaster.

Mr. Fleay again prints 'Lancáster.' The line has an extra syllable before the pause; scan: —

These lús|ty léa|ders, Wárwick | and Lán·castér.

Here too the flow of the rhythm might be made easier by a transposition of the names: —

These lus|ty lea|ders, Lan|caster | and War|wick.

CCXXXVIII.

Q. Isab. Come, son, and go with this gentle lord and me.
Ib., (Works, 216a. — Tan., V, 2, 105.)

An unmetrical line. *And* before *go* evidently crept in from the preceding line (*and* sorrows for it now), and should be struck out. Marlowe wrote, no doubt: —

Q. Isab. Come, son, go with this gentle lord and me.

The connective *and* easily lends itself to interpolation; two more instances will be found in A. V, sc. 1, l. 87 of our play (where some editors have wrongly expunged *you*) and in the note on 1 K. Henry IV., III, 1, 158. (The Athenæum, Sept. 3, 1887, p. 320.)

CCXXXIX.

I feele a hell of greefe, where is my crowne?
Gone, gone, and doe I remaine aliue?
Ib., (Works, 220a. — Tan., V, 5, 87 seq.)

So Qu. 1598. Qu. 1622 and Mr. Francis Cunningham omit *alive.* Dyce adds *still* before *remaine,* in which reading he has been followed by the late Prof. W. Wagner and Mr. Fleay, whereas Mr. Tancock justly rejects this addition. Mr. Tancock takes *Gone, gone* to be 'two solemn monosyllabic feet' and accordingly scans the line: —

Gone, | gone; | and do I | remain | alive?

In my opinion this is evidently wrong. A second way of scanning the line would be: —

Gone! | gone! and | do I | remain | alive?

The most plausible scansion, however, is to consider the verse as a syllable pause line: —

Gone, gone! | ⏑ and | do I | remain | alive?

As far as the first foot is concerned, this scansion is corroborated by another line taken from our play, (A. IV, sc. 6, l. 103, ed. Tancock): —

Gone, gone, | alas, | néver | to make | return!

The following lines may be aptly compared: —
 Stoop, vil|lain! _ | Stoop, stoop! | for so | he bids.
       1 Tamburlaine, IV, 2 (Works, p. 26 b.)
 Of great|est just|ice. _ | Write, write, | Rinal|do.
       All's Well that Ends Well, III, 4, 29.
 When Im|ogen | is dead. | How, how! | anoth|er.
       Cymbeline, I, 1, 114.
 Swift, swift, | you drag|ons of | the night, | that dawn|ing.
       Ib., II, 2, 48.
 Something's | afore't. | Soft, soft! | we'll no | defence.
       Ib., III, 4, 79.
 And find | not her | whom thou | pursuest. | Flow, flow.
       Ib., III, 5, 157.
 O dark, | dark, dark, | amid | the blaze | of noon.
       Samson Agonistes, 80.
 This, this | is he; | softly | awhile.   *Ib., 115.*
 Out, out, | hyæ|na! These are | thy wou|ted arts. *Ib., 748.*
What will now become of Mr. Tancock's 'two solemn monosyllabic
feet'?

CCXL.

 The sun from Egypt shall rich odours bring,
 Wherewith his burning beams (like labouring bees
 That load their thighs with Hybla's honey-spoils)
 Shall here unburden their exhaled sweets,
 And plant our pleasant suburbs with her fumes.
   Dido, Qu. of C., V, 11 seqq. (Works, 270 a.)

Apart from the parentheses this is the reading of the quarto of 1594
and has been implicitly followed by almost all modern editors. Dyce,
in his first edition of Marlowe (London, 1850), II, 426, adds the
following note: '*her*] If right, can only mean — Egypt's: but qy.
"their"?' In his revised and corrected one-volume edition (1858)
he has inserted this conjectural emendation in the text. Mr. Francis
Cunningham, on the other hand, (The Works of Christopher Marlowe,
p. 342), eagerly defends the old text; 'Mr. Dyce', he says, 'most unnecessarily changes *her* into *their*. As if the fumes came from the
bees and not from *Hybla!*' Dyce certainly knew better; his parentheses clearly show that he referred *their* to *beams*, indeed the only
word to which it can be referred. In my conviction, however, the
lection of the old copy is not a corruption of *their fumes*, but of
perfumes, which word comes much nearer to the original *ductus lit-
terarum* and agrees far better with the context than *their fumes*.

The verb *plant*, although it has passed unquestioned till now, is a
corruption too and I do not feel the least doubt that Marlowe
wrote: —

And *scent* our pleasant surburbs with *perfumes*.

At first sight this may, perhaps, seem tautological, but compare Samson Agonistes, 720: —

An amber scent of odorous perfume.

Mr. P. A. Daniel has pointed out to me a curious parallel passage in
Summer's Last Will and Testament (Hazlitt's Dodsley, VIII, 36),
where Sol addresses Summer in the following words: —

The excrements you bred whereon I feed;
To rid the earth of their contagious fumes,
With such gross carriage did I load my beam
I burnt no grass, I dried no springs and lakes;
I suck'd no mines, I withered no green boughs,
But when to ripen harvest I was forc'd
To make my rays more fervent than I wont.

Although this seems to favour the belief that the two passages, in
Summer's Last Will and Testament and in Dido, Queen of Carthage,
came from the same pen, viz. that of Nash, yet I imagine that I can
distinguish the true Marlovian ring in the passage taken from Dido.
(The Athenæum, May 10, 1884, p. 609 seq. Reply by A. H[all], ib.,
May 17, 1884, p. 644.)

MARSTON.

CCXLI.

The feminine deities strowed all their bounties
And beautie on his face; &c.
The Insatiate Countess, (Works, ed. Halliwell, III, 107.)

The Dramatic Works of John Marston, in point of verbal criticism,
are still 'an unweeded garden', as Mr. Halliwell's edition has no
higher claim than to be a reprint of the old editions. 'The dramas
now collected together', says Mr. Halliwell at the end of his preface,
'are reprinted absolutely from the early editions, which were placed
in the hands of our printers, who thus had the advantage of following
them without the intervention of a transcriber. They are given as
nearly as possible in their original state, the only modernizations
attempted consisting in the alternations of the letters *i* and *j*, and
u and *v*, the retention of which would have answered no useful purpose, while it would have unnecessarily perplexed the modern reader.'
So far, so good. Even the most superficial comparison, however, will

satisfy the student, that besides 'the only modernizations' indicated by Mr. Halliwell, his text contains a large number of other deviations from the old editions, especially in the use of capitals and in punctuation, which are not always slight and immaterial. From Mr. Halliwell's statement it would appear that these deviations are due to the printer or, at best, to the proof-reader, although who that proof-reader was and what he did, is nowhere hinted at. One part of the work there is, however, for which Mr. Halliwell himself is certainly to be held responsible, viz. the selection of those quartos, from which the single plays were reprinted, and this selection is not always a happy one. In the case of 'The Insatiate Countess', e. g., Mr. Halliwell says in his preface that there are three quartos in existence, of the years 1613, 1616, and 1631 respectively. Of the quarto of 1616 I cannot judge, as the British Museum cannot boast of a copy, and I have therefore been unable to compare it; of the other two quartos the earlier (1613) is printed very correctly and the later (1631) very carelessly. Nevertheless it is this latter that was chosen by Mr. Halliwell and placed in the hands of his printers, as can be shown by a number of striking instances. Sometimes both these Qq are at fault, but no attempts have been made by the editor to heal their corruption. In the lines at the head of this note, e. g., we should, I think, read *beauties* for *beautie*, although this is the lection of both Qq. Both Qq, moreover, read *Deities,* not *deities.* Two pages further on (III, 109) we meet with the following most perplexing passage: —

'Enter Mizaldus and Mendosa.

Gui[*do*]. Mary, amen! I say, madame, are you that were in for all day, now come to be in for all night? How now, Count Arsena?

Miz[*aldus*]. Faith, signior, not unlike the condemn'd
malefactor,

That heares his judgement openly pronounc'd;
But I ascribe to fate. Joy swell your love;
Cypres and willow grace my drooping crest.

Rob[*erto*]. We doe entend our hymencall rights
With the next rising sunne. Count Cypres,
Next to our bride, the welcomst to our feast.'

This is a perfect muddle. Roberto, Count of Cypres, and Isabella are on the stage; enter to them, according to the stage-direction, Mizaldus and Mendosa. 'This', says Mr. Halliwell, in his note on the passage, 'like many of the other stage-directions, is clearly erroneous. It should be, "reenter Rogero and Guido (Mizaldus)".' Now, this note itself is clearly erroneous, for I do not find that Rogero was on the stage before, nor are Guido and Mizaldus one and the same person. I feel convinced that the stage-direction should be *'Enter Mizaldus*

and Guido, Count of Arsena.' Moreover the prefixes to the first two
speeches should change places, the first speech being evidently spoken
by Mizaldus and addressed to Guido, Count of Arsena.   The second
speech belongs to Guido; the third is by no means addressed to
Count Cypres, Roberto, the speaker, being himself Count of Cypres,
but to Count Arsena, and this name should be substituted for *Count
Cypres*, an emendation which, at the same time, restores the metre
of the line.   The words, *But I ascribe to fate* are also suspicious,
the verb *ascribe* not being used as an intransitive verb; perhaps
Marston wrote *subscribe.* . *Rights,* of course, stands for *rites.*   Lastly
it may be remarked that both Qq (1613 and 1631) read: *Marry
Amen, I say: Madame,* &c., and that there seems to be no sufficient
reason for an alteration of this pointing.   The correct and original
wording of the passage would therefore appear to have been as
follows: —

'Enter Mizaldus and Guido.

Miz.   Marry amen, I say: madame, are you that were in for all
day, now come to be in for all night?   How now, Count Arsena?

    Gui.   Faith, signior, not unlike the condemn'd malefactor,
That heares his judgement openly pronounc'd;
But I *subscribe* to fate.   Joy swell your love;
Cypres and willow grace my drooping crest.
    Rob.   We doe intend our hymeneall *rites*
With the next rising sunne.   Count Arsena,
Next to our bride, the welcomst to our feast.'

In the lines (III, 119): —

            Then read it, faire,
My passion's ample, as our beauties are,

Mr. Halliwell reproduces the corruption of Qu. 1631, although in the
Qu. 1613 he might have found the correct reading *your beauties.*

At p. 137 we read: —

    Isa.   Your love, my lord, I blushing proclaime it.

Mr. Halliwell's edition again follows the Qu. 1631; the Qu. of 1613
correctly reads *blushingly.*

Pag. 142: —

    Sing, boy (thought night yet), like the mornings larke.

Thus Qu. 1631; Qu. 1613: *though night yet.*   The same misprint is
repeated in the very next line both in Qu. 1631 and in Mr. Halliwell's edition: —

    A soule that's cleare is light, thought heaven be darke.
Compare *infra* note CCLXIII.

Pag. 149: —

    Gni[aca].   I crave your hours pardon my ignorance
Of what you were, may gaine a curteous pardon.

Qu. 1631 again; Qu. 1613 rightly *your Honors pardon*. As the printers or proof-readers of Mr. Halliwell's edition have frequently changed the punctuation, they might as well have placed a colon or semicolon after *pardon* in the first line. By the way the reader's attention may be drawn to the repetition of *pardon* which looks very much like a dittography.

At p. 154 the line: —

Let speare-like musicke breathe delicious tones, &c.

is again due to the quarto of 1631; Qu. 1613: *Sphære-like*.

The line (p. 162): —

What can you answere to escape tortures?

though literally agreeing with both Qq, is evidently defective; the article *the* is to be added before *tortures,* as nobody, I think, will be bold enough to plead in favour of the anomalous and unheard-of accentuation *tortúres*. Or should we write *to 'scape* and thus make the line one of four feet only?

One more instance (from p. 181) and I shall have done: —

This is end of lust, where men may see, &c.

This is taken from Qu. 1631 again; Qu. 1613 rightly: *the end of lust.*

After these instances I hope I shall be justified in asking: What was the use of reproducing such an incorrect edition as the quarto of 1631 'with all its imperfections on its head', when a more correctly printed quarto was at hand which might have been reprinted without causing either the editor or his printers a greater amount of trouble and cost? Mr. Halliwell-Phillipps is a scholar of such high standing and has done such excellent service in the field of Shakespearian literature that he may well bear to be told where he has failed; even the best of us have their shortcomings and cannot boast of unmingled success.

CCXLII.

His sight would make me gnash my teeth terribly.

Ib., A. I, (Works, III, 115.)

Terribly was evidently omitted by the transcriber and added in the margin; the compositor was thus deluded into the belief, that it was the last word of the line. Read: —

His sight | would make | me *ter*|*r'bly* gnash | my teeth.

CCXLIII.

How like Adonis in his hunting weedes,
Lookes this same godesse-tempter?
And art thou come? This kisse enters into thy soule:
Gods, I doe not envy you; for know this

> Way's here on earth compleat, excels your blisse:
> Ile not change this nights pleasure with you all.
>
> *Ib., A. III, (Works, III, 155.)*

Read and arrange: —

> How like Adonis in his hunting weeds
> Looks this same goddess-tempter! And art thou come?
> This kiss enters into thy soul.
> Gods, I *don't* envy you; for know *you* this:
> *What's* here on earth complete, excels your bliss;
> I'll not change this night's pleasure with you all.

CCXLIV.

> What Tanais, Nilus, or what Tioris swift,
> What Rhenus ferier then the cataract,
> Although Neptolis cold, the waves of all the Northerne Sea,
> Should flow for ever through these guilty hands,
> Yet the sanguinolent staine would extant be.
>
> *Ib., A. V, (Works, III, 181.)*

Barring some minor differences in spelling and punctuation the text
of this passage in Halliwell's edition, printed from the quarto 1631
of The Insatiate Countess, agrees with the quarto of 1613. Not even
the most conservative critic, however, can doubt that it is corrupt.
Read and arrange: —

> What Tanais, Nilus, or what *Tigris* swift,
> What Rhenus *fiercer* than the cataract,
> *Can quench hell's fire?* Although *Pactolus' gold,*
> *Although* the waves of all the Northern Sea,
> Should flow for ever through these guilty hands,
> Yet the sanguinolent stain would extant be.

The context clearly shows that something like the words inserted
has been lost after *cataract,* a suspicion which is confirmed by the
irregularity of the metre, in so far as the line *Although Neptolis....
Northerne Sea* must necessarily be broken in two. The Tigris could
not be characterized by a more appropriate epithet than *swift,* as
this river is renowned for its rapid flow; its name means *arrow.*
With respect to the correction *Rhenus fiercer* &c., Milton's *fierce
Phlegeton* (Paradise Lost, II, 580) may be compared. — In writing
this passage the poet evidently had before his mind's eye not only
a line from Horace (Epodes, XV, 20), but also the celebrated soliloquy
of Lady Macbeth (V, 1, 39 seqq.): Out, damned spot! out, I say!....
What, will these hands ne'er be clean? &c. Shakespeare's 'Macbeth'
is said to have been first acted in 1610 (which I think too late a
date), whilst 'The Insatiate Countess' was first published in 1613.

CCXLV.

Abi. Husband, I'le naile me to the earth, but I'le
Winne your pardon.
My jewels, jointure, all I have shall flye;
Apparell, bedding, I'le not leave a rugge,
So you may come off fairely.

Ib., A. V, (Works, III, 191.)

Read and arrange: —

Abi. Husband, I'll nail me to the earth, but *I*
Will win your pardon. My jewels, jointure, all
I have, shall fly; apparel, bedding, I'll
Not leave a rug, so you may come off fairly.

CCXLVI.

Tha[is]. Hee's stung already, as if his eyes were turn'd on
Persies shield.

Ib., A. V, (Works, III, 194).

Read, of course, *Perseus' shield.*

CCXLVII.

Rog. Had I knowne this I would have poison'd thee in
the chalice
This morning, when we receaved the sacrament.
Cla. Slave, knowst thou this? tis an appendix to the letter;
But the greater temptation is hidden within.
I will scowre thy gorge like a hawke: thou shalt swallow
thine owne stone in this letter,   [*They bustle.*
Seal'd and delivered in the presence of —

Ib., A. V, (Works, III, 195.)

Read and arrange: —

Rog. Had I known this, I would have poison'd thee
This morning in the chalice, when we received
The sacrament.
Cla.   Slave, know'st thou this? 'Tis an appendix
To the letter; but the *great* temptation's *hid*
Within. *I'll* scour thy gorge like *to* a hawk [*hawk's?*]:
Thou shalt swallow thine own stone in this letter,
Seal'd and deliver'd in the presence of —   [*They wrestle.*
Sacrament is a triple ending before the pause; cf. note CCCLXXIII.

SAM. ROWLEY.

CCXLVIII.

King. Methinks, thou wert better live at court, as I do; King Harry loves a man, I can tell you.

When you see me, you know me. (ed. Elze), 29.

Compare Sir Robert Naunton, Fragmenta Regalia (1630), ed. Arber, p. 28: 'for the people hath it to this day in proverb, King Harry loved a man.'

CCXLIX.

Gardiner, look here, he was deceived, he says,
'When he thought to find John Baptist in the courts of princes, or resident with those, that are clothed in purple.'
Mother o' God, is 't not a dangerous knave.

Ib., (ed. Elze), 60.

In my note on this passage (at p. 105 of my edition) I have remarked that I had not been able to trace this quotation in Dr. Luther's writings. It has since been pointed out to me and occurs in M. Luther's 'Antwort Auf des Königs in England Lästerschrift' (Luther's Werke, Erlanger Ausgabe, Bd. XXX, S. 8). 'Was suche ich russigter Aschenprödel', writes Luther, 'zu Königs und Fürsten Höfe, da ich doch weiss, dass der Teufel obenan sitzt und sein höhester Thron ist? Ich will den Teufel frumm machen ohn seinen Dank und Christum bei ihm finden: so gibt er mir billig solchen Lohn. Komm wieder, lieber Luther, und *suche noch eins Johannem den Täufer in der König Höfen, da man weiche Kleider trägt, ich mein, du wirst ihn finden.'* The *'weichen Kleider'* have been altered to *'purple garments'* by Rowley. By the way it may be observed that, as far as I know, this reply to King Henry VIII. by Luther was not translated into Latin and therefore must have been read in the original German in London.

SHAKESPEARE AND FLETCHER.

CCL.

You most coarse freeze capacities; ye jane judgements.

The Two Noble Kinsmen, III, 5 (ed. Littledale, 52 and 144 seq.)

Mr. Harold Littledale, the latest editor of this play, extends his note on the above line to an explanation of the much discussed phrase *Up-see Freeze*; *Freeze* he thinks to be equivalent with *Friesland Beer* and *up-see* to mean *drunk, halfseas-over.* This explanation, however, has long been superseded. After what has been said by Nares s. v. and myself in my edition of Chapman's Alphonsus, 138 seq., I should not revert to the subject, if I were not able to bring forward some fresh passages that go far to show that *Upsee Freeze* or *Upsee Dutch* means 'in the Frisian or Dutch manner.' The first of these passages occurs in Jack Drum's Entertainment, A. II (Simpson, The School of Shakspere, II, 165): —

> Pour wine, sound music, let our bloods not freeze.
> Drink Dutch, like gallants, let's drink upsey freeze.

That is to say, the English gallants of the time used to drink in the Dutch or Frisian fashion, i. e. with the German drinking ceremonies, for Dutch, here as elsewhere, means German, and it is a wellknown fact that the German drinking ceremonies at that time had spread over Holland and even reached England. John Taylor, the Waterpoet, in his account of his journey to Hamburgh (Three Weeks, Three Daies &c., Works, 1872, 3) says: 'and having upse-freez'd four pots of boon beer as yellow as gold' &c., which words I take to mean, having drunk four pots of beer after the Frisian manner. That *'Upsee Frieze cross'* means to drink with interlaced arms *(Brüder-schaft trinken)*, as I have conjectured, is confirmed by Nash, Summer's Last Will and Testament *(apud* Dodsley, 1825, IX, 49): 'A vous, monsieur Winter, a frolick upsy freese: cross, ho! super nagulum.' That is, let us cross or interlace our arms, as the Germans do when drinking *Brüderschaft,* and let us 'drench' our glasses 'to the bottom', so that what is left may stand on the thumb-nail. This, in German, is called to this day *die Nagelprobe machen,* and still forms part of the ceremony of drinking *Brüderschaft.* — A fourth allusion to 'Upsy Freeze' is contained in a work of a much later date, viz. in Johann Georg Forster's Briefwechsel herausgegeben von Th[erese] H[uber], geb. H[eyne] (Leipzig, 1829), II, 671; it is in an English letter dated Overberg's Contrays, August 27, 1775, and addressed to George Forster by the distinguished Swedish naturalist Andreas Sparrmann. 'Dear Sir', he writes, 'I'll have the pleasure by means of this letter to shake hands with you *"op sein goede Africanse Boers"*; for, as I have now for some time been in quarters by the Owerbergse peasants, you must give me leave to follow the customs of these good folks, who, without any other roundabout compliments, present their sharp hands, as the New Zealanders their carved noses, when a cordial salute is meant.' — There can be no doubt that *op sein goede Afri-canse Boers* means, 'in the true manner of the African Boers.' (Anglia, herausgegeben von Wülcker und Trautmann, I, 347 seq.)

SHAKESPEARE.

CCLI.

This wide-chapp'd rascal — would thou mightst lie drowning
The washing of ten tides!

The Tempest, I, 1, 60 seq.

I do not recollect whether or not any editor has already remarked
that these words contain an allusion to the singular mode of execution
to which pirates were condemned in England. 'Pirats and robbers
by sea', says Harrison (Description of England, ed. Furnivall, London,
1877, 229) 'are condemned in the court of admeraltie, and hanged
on the shore at lowe water marke, where they are left till three
tides haue ouerwashed them.' According to Holinshed, III, 1271,
seven pirates were hanged on the riverside below London, on March 9,
1577—8. (Anglia, herausgegeben von Wülcker und Trautmann,
I, 338.) —

Prof. John W. Hales (in The Academy of Sept. 1, 1877, 220)
has corroborated the above remark by two passages from Greene's
Tu Quoque and from Stow, *apud* Dodsley, ed. Hazlitt, XI, 188. He
also refers to the description of the Execution Dock at Wapping, in
Murray's Handbook for Kent. 'Ten tides', he justly adds, 'are of
course a comic exaggeration, three tides being no sufficiently severe
punishment for "this wide-chapp'd rascal", the boatsman.'

CCLII.

Pros.   Be collected:
No more amazement: tell your piteous heart
There's no harm done.
  Mir.   O, woe the day!
  Pros.   No harm.
I have done nothing but in care of thee, &c.

Ib., I, 2, 13 seq.

It seems absurd that Miranda should reply by a deep-fetched sigh
and an exclamation of pity to her father's consoling statement that
there is no harm done. Dr. Johnson's conjectural emendation: —

  Mir. O, woe the day! no harm?

does not remedy this defect. In my opinion it admits of little doubt
that the original arrangement of these lines was as follows: —

  Pros.   Be collected:
No more amazement: tell your piteous heart —
  Mir. O, woe the day!
  Pros.   There's no harm done!
  Mir.   No harm?
  Pros. I have done nothing but in care of thee, &c.

After what Miranda has seen, she has little faith in the arguments with which she expects to be comforted by her father, least of all is she prepared to hear such good news as he is about to communicate to her. Nothing, therefore, can be more natural than that she should give vent to her grief and compassion in the exclamation by which she interrupts her father's speech, before he has been able to assure her of the perfect safety of the passengers in the vessel which she saw wrecked. Compare S. Walker, Crit. Exam., II, 188. (Notes, privately printed, 1882, p. 1 seq.)

CCLIII.

Now I arise.   [*Resumes his mantle.*

Ib., I, 2, 169.

Blackstone's discovery that these words do not belong to Prospero to whom they are given in the Folio, but to Miranda, has met with little or no acceptance from later editors, as in the opinion of some of them the meaning is metaphorical and equivalent to: 'now I rise in my narration', or, 'now my story heightens in its consequence' (Steevens). Even if this metaphorical meaning were admissible *per se,* which I am convinced it is not, yet it would jar with the words *Sit still* addressed to Miranda immediately after. The explanation given by Dr. Aldis Wright that 'Miranda offers to rise when she sees her father do something which indicates departure', seems partly to have been suggested by the stage-direction; this stage-direction, however, having been added by Dyce, cannot claim any authority whatever. Staunton's notion that the words *Now I arise* are spoken aside to Ariel, is invalidated by the fact that Ariel is not present, but is summoned afterwards in l. 187. And how can this explanation be made to tally with the words *Sit still?* Staunton is silent on this difficulty. Miranda has been labouring all the while under a strange drowsiness that may or may not have been brought on by her father's enchantment. She now thinks her father's tale at an end and gladly seizes the opportunity of rising in order thus to get the better of her sleepiness. That such is the fact seems to be corroborated by Prospero's admonition of her (in l. 186) to give way without restraint to her 'good dulness'. At the same time the words *Now I arise* in Miranda's mouth form a kind of antithesis to her preceding wish *Might I but ever see that man.* Contrary to her intention of rising and walking about, her father desires her to 'sit still and hear the last of their sea-sorrow'. Mr. Collier (in his second edition) thinks it necessary for Prospero to put on his mantle again and thus to be enabled 'to accomplish what he wishes', viz. to send Miranda to sleep. But granting that her sleepiness be really owing to her father's enchantment (the poet does not even hint at such a fact), the magic process must clearly have begun from the very commencement of Prospero's tale, immediately after he has laid down his robe, as is proved by his repeated questions *Dost thou attend me?, Dost thou hear? &c.* Prospero must therefore be thought sufficiently potent to perform such an easy trick of sorcery without the help of his robe. The moment when he resumes it, is clearly indicated in the text by the words addressed to Ariel in l. 187: *I am ready now.* (Notes, privately printed, 1882, p. 2 seq.)

CCLIV.

'   This blue-eyed hag was hither brought with child
      And here was left by sailors.

Ib., I, 2, 270 seq.

Staunton and Mr. P. A. Daniel (Notes and Conjectural Emendations, 9) ingeniously propose *blear-eyed.* In favour of this suggestion it may be added that Reginald Scot, in his Discoverie of Witchcraft, B. I, Chap. 3 (*apud* Drake, Shakspeare and his Times, II, 478), writes indeed that witches 'are women which be commonly old, lame, *bleare-eied,* pale, fowle, and full of wrinkles.' Dr. Aldis Wright, on the other hand, in his annotated edition of this play, sustains the reading of the folio; '*blue-eyed*', he says, 'does not describe the colour of the pupil of the eye, but the livid colour of the eye-lid, and a blue eye in this sense was a sign of pregnancy'; in proof of which Dr. Aldis Wright quotes a passage from Webster's Duchess of Malfi. Nowhere indeed, if not in the passage under discussion, does Shakespeare mean the colour of the pupil, when speaking of blue eyes, but the livid circles round the eyes or the bluish eyelids; thus, e. g., in As You Like It, III, 2, 393: 'a blue eye and sunken'. This, I think, is corroborated by a passage in Spenser's Faerie Queene, I, 2, 45, where the poet ascribes 'blue eyelids' to Duessa, when she has swooned and lies seemingly dead: —

      Her eylids blew
And dimmed sight with pale and deadly hew
At last she gan up lift.

Here too the adjective 'blue' is to be taken in its old sense, viz. 'livid'; see Dr. Skeat's Etymological Dictionary, s. v. Blue. There are besides two passages in Marston and Webster where the blueness is likewise ascribed to the eye-lids; see Marston, The Malcontent, I, 3 (Works, ed. Halliwell, II, 209): 'till the finne of his eyes looke as blew as the welkin'; Webster, The Duchess of Malfi, II, 1 (Works, ed. Dyce, in 1 vol., London, 1857, p. 67a): —

The fins of her eye-lids look most teeming blue.

Compare also Marlowe, Dido, Queen of Carthage (Works, ed. Dyce,
in 1 vol., p. 258a): —

> Then buckled I mine armour, drew my sword,
> And thinking to go down, came Hector's ghost,
> With ashy visage, blueish sulphur eyes, &c.

Nevertheless great doubts remain concerning the 'blue-eyed hag',
as a very different explanation seems to be suggested by some passages in a living American poet, from which it might be inferred
that, in popular belief, blue eyes may possibly have been thought
characteristic of witches. Mr. J. G. Whittier, who is evidently conversant with the particulars of those persecutions for witchcraft that
so darkly fill the pages of early American history, says (The Vision
of Echard and Other Poems, Boston, 1878, 22): —

> A blue-eyed witch sits on the bank
> And weaves her net for thee;

and again on p. 26: —

> Her spectre walks the parsonage,
> And haunts both hall and stair;
> They know her by the great blue eyes
> And floating gold of hair.

Mr. Surtees Phillpotts, in his edition of The Tempest (Rugby Edition,
London, 1876) *ad loc.*, seems to be of a similar opinion; 'probably',
he says, 'this means that her [viz. Sycorax's] eyes had the cold
startling blue which suggests malignity so strongly. It is difficult
to accept Dr. Aldis Wright's suggestion, that the reference is to the
blueness of the eye-lids.' In Dekker's and Middleton's Honest Whore,
Part II, V, 2 (Middleton, ed. Dyce, III, 237), Penelope exclaims: 'Out,
you dog! — a pox on you all! — women are born to curse thee
— but I shall live to see twenty such flat-caps shaking dice for a
penny worth of pippins — out, you blue-eyed rogue.' Entirely
different are the 'two blue windows' ascribed to Venus in Venus
and Adonis, 1. 482, and the 'lovely e'en o' bonnie blue' of Burns's
Blue-eyed Lass that will live for all time in the poet's song. Thus
it appears that the problem of the 'blue-eyed hag' is as far as ever
from final solution.

--- ---------

CCLV.

> *Ari.*   Pardon, master:
> I will be correspondent to command,
> And do my spriting gently.
> *Pros.*   Do so; and after two days
> I will discharge thee.

Ib., I, 2, 296 seq.

9*

According to the Cambridge editors *ad loc.* 'the defect in the metre of l. 298 has not been noticed except by Hanmer, who makes a line thus: —

> Do so, and after two days I'll discharge thee.'

'Possibly', they go on to say, 'it ought to be printed thus: —

> Do so; and
>
> After two days
> I will discharge thee.'

They feel, however, so much the less certain as 'Shakespeare's language passes so rapidly from verse to prose and from prose to verse, ... that all attempts to give regularity to the metre must be made with diffidence and received with doubt.' — This is very true; nevertheless it would seem as if in the present case the metre might be recovered pretty easily. Arrange and read: —

> *Ari.*   Pardon, master:
> I'll be corr'spondent to command, and do
> My spriting gently.
>   *Pros.*   Do so; and after two days
> I will discharge thee.

At first sight the contracted pronunciation of *correspondent* may seem doubtful, since unaccented syllables are often thought to be slurred only when following the accented syllable; at least Dr. Abbott, s. 468, gives no other instances and in s. 460 offers a different explanation of such words where the unaccented syllable precedes the accented one; according to him they merely drop their prefixes. The following passages, however, go far to establish the slurring of unaccented syllables before the accented one and should therefore be examined so much the more carefully.

The Tempest, I, 2, 248: —

> Told thee no lies, made thee no mistakings, served
> Without or grudge or grumblings.

Pope and Mr. Henry N. Hudson (The Complete Works of Shakespeare. Boston, &c.) omit the second *thee,* 'which', Mr. Hudson assures us, 'spoils the verse without helping the sense.' In my opinion, neither the one, nor the other, is true. Pronounce *m'stakings* and both the metre and sense are as regular as can be wished. Dr. Abbott (s. 460, p. 340), however, thinks it more probable that the second *thee* is slurred.

The Tempest, III, 3, 24 (a syllable pause line): —

> At this hour reigning there. I'll b'lieve both.

The Tempest, V, 1, 145: —

> As great to me as late; and supportable.

Abbott, s. 497, explains this apparent Alexandrine by the omission of an unemphatic syllable, viz. *and,* 'unless "supportable" can be accented on the first', in favour of which accentuation Dyce and Mr. William J. Rolfe (Shakespeare's Comedy of the Tempest, New York, 1871, p. 141) openly declare. Dyce, however, is somewhat diffident and would not be loth to adopt Steevens's conjecture *portable.* Mr. Hudson *ad loc.* remarks: 'The original has *supportable,* which makes shocking work with the metre. Steevens printed *portable,* which keeps the sense, saves the verse, and is elsewhere used by the Poet.' This is a rather summary proceeding. Mr. Rolfe compares *détestáble* (K. John, III, 4, 29. Timon of Athens, IV, 1, 33) and *délectáble* (Richard II., II, 3, 7), both of which, in accordance with Dr. Abbott, s. 492, he takes to be accented on the first syllable. This may pass for *detestable* which in both passages occurs in the body of the line, but with respect to *delectable* it may be submitted, that the usual accentuation may be retained, if the first syllable be slurred: —

Making | the hard | way soft | and d'lect|able.

To revert to the line under discussion (The Tempest, V, 1, 145), it should be scanned: —

As great | to me | as late; | and s'pport|able.

The Two Gentlemen of Verona, V, 4, 86 seq. This passage has generally been printed as prose, and Dyce, who has rightly pointed out that 'it undoubtedly was meant to be verse', yet adds that 'here, as elsewhere in this scene, the verse is corrupted.' Now, this pretended corruption fades as fast as Prospero's pageant, if we pronounce *d'liver* as a dissyllable. The passage, according to Dyce, runs thus: —

> *Val.* Why, boy! why, wag! how now! what is the matter?
> Look up; speak.
> *Jul.*　　　O good sir, my master charg'd me
> To deliver a ring to madam Silvia;
> Which, out of my neglect, was never done.

The Taming of the Shrew, IV, 2, 11: —

Quick proceeders, marry! Now, tell me, I pray;

pronounce *pr'ceeders* and scan: —

Quick pr'ceed|ers, mar|ry! Now, | tell me, | I pray.

Ib., IV, 2, 14: —

O despiteful love! unconstant womankind;

pronounce *d'spiteful.* Dr. Abbott, s. 460 (p. 342) says, that the prefix *(de),* 'though written, ought scarcely to be pronounced.' The same proceeding holds good in the lines: Richard II., IV, 1, 148 *(r'sist);* Richard III., III, 5, 109 *(r'course);* ib., V, 3, 186 *(r'venge).*

In the line taken from Richard II., however, the first *it* (after *Prevent*) may be read as an extra syllable before the pause: —

  Prevent | it, resist | it, let | it not | be so.

Henry V., IV, 8, 84: —

  Full fifteen hundred, besides common men.

This may either be taken for a syllable pause line: —

  Full fif|teen hund|red, ⌣ | besides com|mon men,

or *hundred* may be read as a trisyllable (see Abbott, s. 477): —

  Full fif|teen hund|(e)red, | besides com|mon men.

In either case *besides* is to be pronounced as a monosyllable. Dr. Abbott (s. 484, p. 379) scans the line: —

  Full fif|teen hundred, | besi|des com|mon men,

which is no ways acceptable.

Timon of Athens, III, 3, 8. There can be very little doubt that Mr. Lloyd has hit the mark in suggesting that the name of *Lucius* should be added to this line: —

  Lucius, Ventidius, and Lucullus denied him?

If this is, and I am persuaded that it is, what the poet wrote, we shall have to pronounce *d'nied* and the line will be as regular as can be wished: —

  Lucius, | Ventid|ius, and | Lucul|lus d'nied | him?

Marlowe's Edward II. (ed. Tancock), I, 1, 32: —

  And, as | I like | your d'scours|ing, I'll | have you.

Or should we scan: —

  And, as | I like | your d'scours|ing, *I* | *will* have | you?

Mr. Fleay, in his edition of Edward II., accents *discoursing*, without, however, producing an authority for this shifting of the accent.

Edward II., IV, 5, 6: —

  Give me my horse, let us re'nforce our troops.

Re'nforce is the spelling of the Qq, but has been altered to *reinforce* by the editors, even by Dyce, though he cannot help remarking that the old spelling shows how the word 'was intended to be pronounced.' The old copies of this play also print *Lewne* instead of *Levune* which proves that in this name too the unaccented syllable preceding the accented one was slurred.

Soliman and Perseda (Dodsley, ed. Hazlitt, V, 262): —

  Perseda. Here comes a messenger to haste me hence. —
I know your message, hath the princess
Sent for me?
  Messenger. She hath, and
Desires you to consort her to the triumphs.

Arrange either: —

> *Perseda.* Here comes a messenger to haste me hence. —
> I know your message; hath the princess sent
> For me?
> *Messenger.* She hath, and desires you to consort
> Her to the triumphs,

or: —

> *Perseda.* Here comes a messenger to haste me hence. —
> I know your message;
> Hath the princess sent for me?
> *Messenger.* She hath,
> And desires you to consort her to the triumphs.

In either case *desires* is to be pronounced *d'sires*.

Fair Em (ed. Warnke and Prœscholdt), I, 2, 66: —

> Shall in perseverance of a virgin's due;

pronounce *pers'verance*.

Mucedorus (ed. Warnke and Prœscholdt), Induction, 39: —

> Delighting in mirth, mix'd all with lovely tales;

pronounce *D'lighting*. The line begins with a trochee, and W. Wagner's correction *Delights* should not have been admitted into the text.

Ib., II, 2, 68 seq.: —

> Thy strength sufficient to perform my desire,
> Thy love no otherwise than to revenge my injuries.

Pronounce *d'sire* and, perhaps, *r'venge*; see note CXXVII. I take this opportunity of withdrawing formally my former conjecture *wish* for *desire,* although it has met with the approval of Messrs. Warnke and Prœscholdt. *Other* instead of *otherwise* which has been suggested by Prof. W. Wagner and received into the text by Messrs. Warnke and Prœscholdt, ought to be eliminated again.

Ib., II, 4, 35: —

> I refer it to the credit of Segasto;

pronounce *r'fer*.

Ib., III, 2, 52: —

> Your departure, lady, breeds a privy pain;

pronounce *d'parture*.

Ib., V, 1, 55: —

> Desiring thy daughter's virtues for to see;

pronounce *D'siring*; the line begins with a trochee, just like l. 39 of the Induction.

Even beyond the pale of dramatic poetry we meet with the same peculiarity of rapid pronunciation; thus, e. g., in Sir Thomas More's Utopia, ed. Arber, p. 167: —

Wherfore not Utopie, but rather rightely
My name is Eutopie; A place of felicity.

Pronounce *f'licity*. See note CLXXXIV. In the American Dialect Tales by Sherwood Bonner (New York, 1883) we frequently meet with such abbreviations as *b'lieve*, *b'long*, *'bey* (= obey), *'Onymus* (= Hieronymus; p. 68 seqq.), *p'r'aps*, *'salt* (= assault; p. 35), *s'ppose*, &c.

If, after all these instances which might easily be multiplied, there should still remain a doubt in the reader's mind, let him go in a London omnibus from the Bank to *Cha'ng Cróss*, and the conductor's pronunciation of this name will fully satisfy him of the innate tendency of the English language to slur unaccented syllables no less before than after the primary accent.

There still remains another difficulty in l. 298 of our passage which must not pass without a word of comment. Mr. Phillpotts in his edition of this play (Rugby Edition, 1876) gives the following scansion: —

Dó so; | and áf|ter twó | days.

The numeral *two*, however, should not stand in the accented, but in the unaccented part of the foot, just as it is the case in l. 421: *within two dáys*. The same reason holds good against Hanmer's alteration of the line. The fact is, that *after* is to be pronounced as a monosyllable (compare Abbott, s. 465, and Chaucer, ed. Morris, I, 178). The true scansion of the line, therefore, is: —

My sprí|ting gént|ly. Dó so; | and áft'r | two dáys.

(Notes, privately printed, 1882, p. 3 seqq.)

--- ———

CCLVI.

Pro. Goe make thy selfe like a Nymph o' th' Sea,
Be subiect to no sight but thine, and mine: inuisible
To euery eye-ball else: goe take this shape
And hither come in't: goe: hence
With diligence.   *Exit.*
Pro. Awake, deere hart awake, thou hast slept well,
Awake.

Ib., I, 2, 301 seqq.

The above reading of the folio has been handled by the editors in a somewhat strange and violent manner. In the first line, Pope and almost all his followers have added *to* before *a Nymph*; this preposition is indeed taken from the later folios and, as will be shown, cannot be omitted, on account of the metre. Those editors who do not agree to its insertion, transpose the words *Be subject* from the beginning of the second to the end of the first line. In the second line most editors have struck out *thine and,* partly in order to reduce the line to six feet, partly because they thought the word 'an interpolation of ignorance', as Steevens terms it. Dyce goes so far as to stigmatise the poor words, although contained in all the folios, as 'most ridiculous' Such high words, I regret to say, are no arguments; this kind of criticism amounts to correcting the poet himself, if correcting it be, instead of his copyists and printers. In the fourth line Ritson and others have omitted *goe* before *hence,* and, in consequence, have been obliged to write *in it* instead of *in't.* After all these alterations it is no wonder that modern texts read very differently from what has been transmitted in the folio; in Dyce's third edition the passage stands thus: —

> Go make thyself like to a nymph o' th' sea,
> Be subject to no sight but mine; invisible
> To every eyeball else. Go take this shape,
> And hither come in't: hence with diligence.

The last line is not exempt from the faults of weakness and lameness and it speaks greatly in favour of the old text that, the less it is altered, the better verses are obtained; there is indeed no occasion whatever to depart from it, except in the addition of the preposition *to* in the first line and in the arrangement of the lines, which would appear originally to have been this: —

> Go, make thyself like to a nymph o' th' sea:
> Be subject to no sight but thine and mine,
> Invisible to every eyeball else.
> Go, take this shape and hither come in't: go hence
> With diligence.   [*Exit Ariel.*
> Awake, dear heart, awake! thou hast slept well;
> Awake!

I do not know whether or not this arrangement has been given already in some one or other of the innumerable editions of the poet; all I can say is, that I have never met with it. With the words *Go, take this shape* Prospero, of course, gives Ariel the garment which is to render him invisible to everybody's eyes except his (viz. Ariel's) own and those of his master. (Robinson's Epitome of Literature, Philadelphia, March 15, 1879; Vol. III, 48.)

CCLVII.

>   My prime request,
> Which I do last pronounce, is, O you wonder!
> If you be maid or no?
>
>   *Ib., I, 2, 426 seqq.*

Made in the fourth folio is an evident gloss; the sense is, 'If you

be an (unmarried) mortal woman or a goddess?' Compare The Birth
of Merlin, II, 2 (ed. Del., 33. — W. and Pr., II, 3, 147—151): —

> *Aur.* It is Artesia, the royal Saxon princess.
> *Prince.* A woman and no deity? no feign'd shape,
> To mock the reason of admiring sense,
> On whom a hope as low as mine may live,
> Love, and enjoy, dear brother, may it not?

Compare also Virg. Aen. I, 327 seq. and Odyss. VI, 149 where Ulysses
addresses Nausicaa in the following words: —

> γουνοῦμαί σε, ἄνασσα· ϑεός νύ τις ἢ βροτός ἐσσι κ. τ. λ.

CCLVIII.

> Be of comfort;
> My father's of a better nature, sir,
> Than he appears by speech: this is unwonted
> Which now came from him.
>
> *Ib., I, 2, 495 seqq.*

This would imply, that Prospero generally made a less favourable
impression by his speeches than by his actions, which, of course, is
not what Miranda means to say. It is, on the contrary, only this
one speech, just uttered, that shows him to disadvantage, and this
speech, as Miranda assures Ferdinand, is unwonted. Read therefore: —

> Than he appears *by's* speech: &c.

In order to 'make assurance double sure', it may be added that *by's*
occurs in John Taylor the Waterpoet's pamphlet entitled The Water-
Cormorant his Complaint &c. (London, 1622) at the end of the
'Satire on A Figure flinger, or a couzning cunning man': —

> And though the marke of truth he neuer hits,
> Yet still this Cormorant doth liue by's wits &c.

(Jahrb. d. D. Sh.-G., VIII, 376.)

CCLIX.

> *Gon.* I would with such perfection govern, sir,
> To excel the golden age.
> *Seb.*   'Save his majesty.
> *Ant.* Long live Gonzalo.
> *Gon.*   And, — do you mark me, sir?
>
> *Ib., II, 1, 167 seqq.*

This is the reading and arrangement of the Cambridge Edition.
S. Walker, Crit. Exam., I, 215 (misquoted III, 215 by Dyce, *ad loc.*)
would read: *God save his majesty,* the metre in his opinion requiring

the supplement. But *Save* may well be a monosyllabic foot. Antonio's exclamation as transmitted in the Folio is meaningless; it is intended to chaff Gonzalo, but does not. I think it impossible for Shakespeare to have omitted that point or sting which seems to be imperatively demanded by the context; he wrote, no doubt: *Long live* KING *Gonzalo!* Compare 'king Stephano' in A. IV, sc. 2, l. 221 seqq. As to the arrangement of the passage, I feel certain that it is quite correct in FA and should not, therefore, be altered: the two exclamations form one line, as suggested by S. Walker: —

> *Gon.* I would with such perfection govern, sir,
> T' excel the golden age.
> *Seb.* Save his majesty!
> *Ant.*   Long live king Gonzalo.
> *Gon.* And, — do you mark me, sir?

In the scansion of the third line it makes no difference, whether S. Walker's conjecture be adopted or not. In my eyes this addition is by no means called for; on the contrary I think it highly appropriate and expressive for both exclamations to begin with a strongly accented word; scan: —

> Sáve | his maj' | sty. — Lóng | live king | Gonza | lo.

The same rhythmical movement occurs in 1 Tamburlaine, II, 7, *ad fin.*: —

> Lóng | live Tam | burlaine, | and reign | in A | sia;

in Richard III., III, 7, *ad fin.*, according to the Qq: —

> Lóng | live Rich | ard, Eng | land's roy | al king,

(whereas the Ff read: Long líve | king Rich | ard, &c.); in Cymbeline, III, 7, 10: —

> His ab' solute | commis | sion. Lóng | live Cæ | sar;

and in Marlowe's Edward II. (Works, ed. Dyce, 204 b): —

> Lóng live | King Ed | ward, Eng | land's law | ful lord.

In my eyes a strong accent on *Long* is indispensable in this kind of exclamation.

CCLX.

> *Ant.* It is the quality o' th' Clymate.
> *Seb.* Why
> Doth it not then our eye-lids sinke? I finde
> Not my selfe dispos'd to sleep.
> *Ant.* Nor I, my spirits are nimble:
> They fell together all, as by consent; &c.

> *Ib., II, 1, 200 seqq.*

This reading of the Folio has been altered by all subsequent editors in so far as *Not* has been transferred from the beginning of the fourth to the end of the third line. Since, therefore, the *Editio prin-ceps* cannot be followed verbatim, one more remove farther off from it will not greatly tax our conservatism. In order that 1. 201 may be reduced to a regular blank verse, the passage should be printed thus: —

> *Ant.* It is the quality o' th' climate.
> *Seb.* Why doth it
> Not then our eyelids sink? I find not myself
> Disposed to sleep.
> *Ant.* Nor I; my spirits are nimble.
> They fell together all, as by consent; &c.

Line 200 has an extra-syllable before the pause. *Myself* is, of course, to be pronounced as a monosyllabe (compare *Mylord*). (Notes, privately printed, 1882, p. 9.)

CCLXI.

> And would no more endure
> This wooden slavery than to suffer
> The flesh-fly blow my mouth.

> *Ib., III, 1, 61 seqq.*

In order to complete the second line (1. 62) which to all appearance has been mutilated by some copyist or compositor, Pope reads *than I would suffer,* whilst Dyce adds *tamely* after *suffer*. This latter reading has been transferred, without a remark, to Mr. Hudson's edition, although it may be said to have *nomen et omen*: it is tame, very tame. May not the loss have taken place at the beginning of the line as well as at its end? May we not imagine the poet to have written: —

> And would no more endure
> *At home* this wooden slavery than to suffer
> The flesh-fly blow my mouth?

I own that this is a mere guess, but Pope's and Dyce's conjectures are no more. (Notes and Queries, June 2, 1883, p. 424 seq. — Kölb., Engl. Stud., VI, 438.)

CCLXII.

> *Gon.* All three of them are desperate: their great guilt,
> Like poison given to work a great time after,
> Now 'gins to bite the spirits.

> *Ib., III, 3, 104 seqq.*

Mr. P. A. Daniel corrects *their spirits*; compare however A Warning for Fair Women A. II, l. 1381 (Simpson, The School of Shakspere, II, 322): —

> The little babies in the mothers' arms
> Have wept for those poor babies, seeing me,
> That I by my murther have left fatherless.

In my humble opinion, this use of the article instead of the possessive pronoun is no corruption of the text, but a looseness of speech on the part of the author, which it is not the office of the critic to correct; all critics, however, know from their own experience how extremely difficult it is always to keep clear from errors and mistakes in distinguishing between the peculiarities and inaccuracies of a writer and the lapses of his transcribers and printers.

CCLXIII.

> Therefore take heed
> As Hymen's lamps shall light you.

Ib., IV, 1, 22 seq.

Read, *lamp*. Shakespeare is well aware that Hymen has but one lamp or, properly speaking, torch; in l. 97 of this very scene he says: Till Hymen's torch be lighted. Compare Paradise Lost, VIII, 520 (first ed., VII, 1157): —

> On his hill-top to light the bridal lamp.

The *s* in *lamps* has evidently intruded into the text by anticipation of the initial *s* in *shall*; it is the reverse of what is called absorption and what I believe to have taken place in A. 1, sc. 2, l. 497; see note CCLVIII. At the same time the ὁμοιοτέλευτον, i. e. the similar endings of the preceding words (A*s* Hymen'*s*), may likewise have been instrumental in producing the faulty repetition of this final *s*. Similar instances, where a faulty final letter has been introduced either by the influence of the initial of the next word, or by a ὁμοιοτέλευτον, are pretty frequent. Compare, in the first-named category, Hamlet, I, 1, 162 (planet*s* *s*trike; see my note *ad loc.*). Marlowe's Dido, V, 13, where Qu. 1594 reads: —

> That load their thighs with Hybla's honey*s* *s*poyles,

instead of *honey spoyles*. A Midsummer-Night's Dream, II, 2, 121 seq.: —

> where I orelooke
> Loue*s* stories, written in Loue*s* richest booke,

where the poet in all probability wrote *Loue stories*; see S. Walker, Crit. Exam., I, 255. Mucedorus, (ed. W. and Pr.) II, 3, 5: —

> Now Bremo *sith thy* leisure so affords,
> A needless [Qq: An endless] thing,

instead of *sit, thy*; see note CXXX. The Works of Al. Pope, ed. by
the Rev. Whitwell Elwin, I, 352 (Windsor Forest, l. 201 seq.): —

> Let me, O let me, to the shades repair,
> My natives shades — there weep and murmer there.

The line from Dido may at the same time serve as a specimen of
similar endings: —

> That load their thighs with Hybla's honey spoils.

Still more striking is the corruption in the following ὁμοιοτέλευτα.
The first I take from Marston's Insatiate Countess (A. III, sc. 1, l. 13)
where the Qu. of 1631 reads: —

> Sing boy (thought night yet) like the mornings Larke,

whereas Qu. 1613 exhibits the correct reading *though night yet*; see
note CCXLI. A second and third instance occur in The Two Gentlemen of Verona, I, 3, 88, and in Antony and Cleopatra, V, 2, 216
respectively; the former passage stands thus in FA: —

> Sir Protheus, your Fathers call's for you,

the latter thus: —

> sawcie Lictors
> Will catch at vs like Strumpets, and scald Rimers
> Ballads vs out a Tune.

Read, *father* and *Ballad*. Compare Richard III., II, 2, 63, where QA
(1597) reads *kindreds teares* and A Lover's Complaint, 80: —

> Of one by nature's outwards so commended,

where an anonymous critic [the Cambridge Editors?] ingeniously conjectures *outward*. A glaring instance may also be found in: The
Task: Book I. The Sofa. By William Cowper. With Introduction
and Notes (London and Glasgow: William Collins, Sons, and Company. 1878) p. 12, l. 290 seq.: —

> The sheepfold here
> Pours outs its fleecy tenants o'er the glebe.

Compare S. Walker, Crit. Exam., I, 233 — 268 (The final *s* frequently
interpolated and frequently omitted in the first folio). —, Charles and
Mary Cowden Clarke, The Shakespeare Key (London, 1879), p. 676 seqq.
Abbott, p. 240 seq. (Notes and Queries, June 2, 1883, p. 425. —
Kölb., Engl. Stud., VI, 438 seq.)

CCLXIV.

> Go, bring the rabble,
> O'er whom I give thee power, here to this place.

> *Ib., IV, 1, 37 seq.*

I think we should read: I *gave* thee power, for Ariel has exercised
the power given him by Prospero over the meaner spirits already in

the second scene of the first act, where he directs them to dance and to sing: —

Come unto these yellow sands, &c.

· (Notes and Queries, June 2, 1883, p. 425. — Kölb., Engl. Stud., VI, 439.)

CCLXV.

> *Pros.*   Sweet, now silence!
> Juno and Ceres whisper seriously;
> There's something else to do: hush, and be mute,
> Or else our spell is marr'd.

Ib., IV, 1, 124 seqq.

Dr. Aldis Wright ingeniously remarks, that 'it would seem more natural that these words should be addressed to Miranda'. 'If they are properly assigned to Prospero', he continues, 'we should have expected that part of the previous speech would have been spoken by Miranda. They might form a continuation of Ferdinand's speech, which would then be interrupted by Prospero's "Silence!" Otherwise the difficulty might be avoided by giving "Sweet ..... to do" to Miranda and the rest of the speech to Prospero.' — To me a slight alteration of this latter arrangement would seem to meet all exigencies of the case; I feel certain that the original distribution of these lines was as follows: —

> *Mir.* [*To Fer.*]   Sweet, now, silence!
> Juno and Ceres whisper seriously.
>   *Pros.* There's something else to do: hush, and be mute,
> Or else our spell is marr'd.

I think it an admirable touch of the poet that the whispering of the goddesses should produce in Miranda's timid mind some vague fear lest the pageant should be disturbed by Ferdinand's remarks and some harm be done to her lover and herself by the irritated spirits; her speech, however, must end at *seriously,* for how should she have come to the knowledge that there is *something else to do*? Nobody but Prospero knows what is to come or to be done next and the words *There's something else to do* cannot with propriety be assigned to any other interlocutor, whereas the line *Juno and Ceres whisper seriously* seems to fit no lips so well as those of his daughter. (Notes and Queries, June 2, 1883, p. 425. — Kölb., Engl. Stud., VI, 439 seq.)

CCLXVI.

Leave not a rack behind.   *Ib., IV, 1, 156.*

Dyce eagerly contends for the correctness of Malone's interpretation of this passage, *rack* in the opinion of both these critics being equivalent to *wreck,* whereas they think it completely inadmissible to take the word in the sense of *scud* or *floating vapour,* as has been done by Collier and others. In my opinion, *wreck,* in this passage, would be far too gross and not in keeping with the context. Without reviewing the explanations given by Staunton and other editors, I merely wish to point out a coincidence that has not yet been adverted to and which seems to decide in favour of *rack* = *vapour* or *scud.* It is agreed on almost all hands that in these lines Shakespeare has imitated a well-known passage in the Earl of Stirling's tragedy of Darius which its author winds up with the following lines: —

> Those statelie Courts, those sky-encountring walles
> Evanish all like *vapours* in the aire.

Is it not evident that *rack* was intended by Shakespeare as a substitute for the synonymous *vapours*? And why may he not have connected the word with the indefinite article, unusual though this connection may be? At all events this syntactical anomaly seems highly impressive in so far as it reduces, so to say, the mass of floating vapours to a single particle or streak and seems to imply that all the gorgeousness of earth does not leave behind even a single streak of vapour. (Notes and Queries, June 2, 1883, p. 425. — Kölb., Engl. Stud., VI, 440. — Compare Dr. Brinsley Nicholson's reply in Notes and Queries, Sept. 1, 1883, p. 163.)

CCLXVII.

Speed. Sir Proteus, save you! Saw you my master.
> *The Two Gentlemen of Verona, I, 1, 70.*

The late Prof. W. Wagner in his edition of Shakspere's Works (Hamburg, 1880, Vol. I, p. 87) remarks on this line: 'Some word (like *here* or *now*) seems to have dropped out after *saw you.*' I think not. *Proteus* is either to be pronounced as a trisyllable: —

> Sir Pro|te-us, | save you! | Saw you | my mas|ter,

or, which I think more likely, the verse belongs to the wide-spread class of syllable pause lines: —

> Sir Pro|teus, save | you! ⌣ | Saw you | my mas|ter.

The same alternative occurs again A. I, sc. 3, l. 3: —

> 'Twas of your nephew Proteus, your son,

and A. I, sc. 3, l. 88: —

> Sir Proteus, your father calls for you.

These two lines Prof. W. Wagner passes by without comment.

CCLXVIII.

Come, shadow, come, and take this shadow up,
For 'tis thy rival. O thou senseless form,
Thou shalt be worshipp'd, kiss'd, loved and adored!
And were there sense in his idolatry,
My substance should be statue in thy stead.
Ib., IV, 4, 202 seqq.

For *statue* in the last line Hanmer conjectured *sainted*, Warburton
statued. I think we should read *shadow*, on which word Julia is
evidently playing. *Shadow* is usually opposed to *substance,* so that
also in the above line it seems to be almost necessitated by the
preceding *substance*. This conviction is still strengthened when we
recall the verses in A. IV, sc. 2, where Proteus asks for Silvia's
picture and Silvia promises to send it: —

> *Pro.* Madam, if your heart be so obdurate
> Vouchsafe me yet your picture for my love,
> The picture that is hanging in your chamber;
> To that I'll speak, to that I'll sigh and weep:
> For since the substance of your perfect self
> Is else devoted, I am but a shadow;
> And to your shadow will I make true love.
> *Jul.* [*Aside*]. If 'twere a substance, you would, sure,
> deceive it,
> And make it but a shadow, as I am.

> *Sil.* I am very loath to be your idol, sir;
> But since your falsehood shall become you well
> To worship shadows and adore false shapes, ·
> Send to me in the morning and I'll send it:
> And so, good rest.

Compare also: —

> Love like a shadow flies, when substance love pursues.
> *The Merry Wives of Windsor, II, 2, 215.*

> He takes false shadows for true substances.
> *Titus Andronicus, III, 2, 80.*

> That same is Blanch, daughter to the king
> The substance of the shadow that you saw.
> *Fair Em, (Del., 8. — W. and Pr., 10. — Sim., II, 416.)*

> Each one shall change his name:
> Master Vandal, you shall take Heigham, and you
> Young Harvey, and Monsieur Delion, Ned,
> And under shadows be of substance sped.
> *Englishmen for my Money (Hazlitt's Dodsley, X, 514.)*

> *Har*[*vey*]. Hark, Ned, there's thy substance.   [*Aside.*
> *Wal*[*grave*]. Nay, by the mass, the substance is here,
> The shadow's but an ass.   [*Aside.*
>
>   *Ib.*, (*H's D.*, X, 525.)
>
> One shadow for a substance; this is she.
>
>   *Ib.*, (*H's D.*, X, 549.)
>
> Yet love at length forc'd him to know his fate,
> And love the shade whose substance he did hate.
>
>   *Marston, Works, ed. Halliwell, III, 203.*
>
> Religion's name against itself was made;
> The shadow served the substance to invade.
>
>   *Dryden, Astræa Redux, l. 191—2.*

This would seem to be overwhelming evidence in favour of my conjecture; yet, after all, *statue* may possibly be the right word, since it appears to have been used in a passage or two for a picture, or, strictly speaking, a painted life-size figure. The most striking of these passages occurs in Massinger's City Madam, V, 3 (Works, ed. Hartley Coleridge, 1839, p. 338a): --

> *Sir John.* Your nieces, ere they put to sea, crave humbly,
> Though absent in their bodies, they may take leave
> Of their late suitors' statues.
>
>   *Enter Lady Frugal, Anne, and Mary.*
>
> *Luke.* There they hang: &c.

And about thirty lines *infra*: —

> *Sir John.* For your sport,
> You shall see a masterpiece. Here's nothing but
> A superficies; colours, and no substance.

By the way it may be remarked, that the scene forcibly reminds the reader of Hermione 'standing like a statue' in The Winter's Tale, V, 3. —- Next to Massinger Sir Thomas Overbury must be mentioned, from whose Characters the following passage is quoted by Trench, in his Select Glossary (1859), s. Landscape: 'The sins of other women show in landskip, far off and full of shadow; her's [a harlot's] in statue, near hand and bigger in the life.' As according to Blount's Glossary (quoted by Skeat s. Landscape) 'landscape' expresses 'all the part of a picture which is not of the body or argument', thus answering to the modern 'back-ground', it seems highly probable that *statue* is here meant by Sir Thomas Overbury to signify a figure standing in the fore-ground of the picture. Compare The Complete Works of William Shakespeare, ed. the Rev. Henry N. Hudson, I, 235. Collier, Hist. of Engl. Dram. Poetry (1879), III, 125 seq. (Robinson's Epitome of Literature, March 15, 1879; Vol. III, p. 48.)

CCLXIX.

> *Jul.* O, cry you mercy, sir, I have mistook:
> This is the ring you sent to Silvia.
> *Pro.* But how cam'st thou by this ring? At my depart
> I gave this unto Julia.
>
> *Ib., V, 4, 94 seq.*

Steevens proposed an entirely different arrangement of these and the preceding lines with divers alterations of the text which it is needless to repeat. Pope omits *But* in l. 96. Dyce, following Steevens in this particular, transfers the words *at my depart* to the beginning of the following line, without, however, adding a word of explanation or justification. The Cambridge Editors write *camest* and seem to have taken the line to be one of six feet, with a trochee for its second foot. The simplest and easiest way to regulate the metre, in my opinion, is to add *But* to the preceding line; thus: —

> *Jul.* O, cry you mercy, sir, I have mistook:
> This is the ring you sent to Silvia.
> *Pro.*   But,
> How cam'st thou by this ring? At my depart
> I gave this unto Julia.

Compare Antony and Cleopatra, V, 2, 12 seqq.: —

> Antony
> Did tell me of you, bade me trust you; but
> I do not greatly care to be deceived.

(Notes, privately printed, 1882, p. 11 seq.)

CCLXX.

> *Pist.* The horn, I say. Farewell.
> Take heed, have open eye, for thieves do foot by night:
> Take heed, ere summer comes or cuckoo-birds do sing.
>
> *The Merry Wives of Windsor, II, 1, 126 — 7.*

Arrange: —

> *Pist.* The horn, I say. Farewell! Take heed!
> Have open eye; for thieves do foot by night.
> Take heed!
> Ere summer comes, or cuckoo-birds do sing.

Thus the two Alexandrines are reduced to regular metre. To the next line the following stage-direction should be added: 'Nym has all this while been conversing aside with Page.' Compare Steevens and Dyce *ad loc.*

CCLXXI.

Pist. I do relent: what would thou more of man?

Ib., II, 2, 31.

Relent is the reading of QC and the Ff; QAB (the Cambridge Edition erroneously prints Q_3 instead of Q_2): *recant.* Qy.: *repent?*

CCLXXII.

Fal. Good maid, then.
Quick.   I'll be sworn;
As my mother was, the first hour I was born.

Ib., II, 2, 37—9.

The last line is, of course, to be spoken aside. The meaning is: I'll be sworn that I am a maid just as well as my mother was in the first hour after I was born.

CCLXXIII.

Fal. Fare thee well: commend me to them both: there's my purse; I am yet thy debtor. Boy, go along with this woman. [*Exeunt Mistress Quickly and Robin.*] This news distracts me!

Pist. This punk is one of Cupid's carriers:
Clap on more sails; pursue; up with your fights:
Give fire: she is my prize, or ocean whelm them all!

[*Exit.*

Fal. Sayest thou so, old Jack? go thy ways; &c.

Ib., II, 2, 137—44.

This is one of those corrupt passages that have been transmitted from one generation to the other without exciting suspicion. What is the meaning of the words 'Sayest thou so, old Jack?', if the preceding verses are spoken by Pistol instead of Falstaff himself? And who can realize Pistol as the speaker of two verses that in his mouth are entirely meaningless, verses which evidently form part of Falstaff's soliloquy, after Mrs. Quickly, Robin, and Pistol have left the stage. Arrange, therefore: —

Fal. Fare thee well: commend me to them both: there's my purse; I am yet thy debtor. Boy, go along with this woman.

[*Exeunt Mistress Quickly and Robin.*

Pist. This punk is one of Cupid's carriers.   [*Exit.*

Fal. This news distracts me!
Clap on more sails; pursue; up with your fights:
Give fire: she is my prize, or ocean whelm them all.
Sayest thou so, old Jack? go thy ways; &c.

CCLXXIV.

Farewell, gentle mistress, farewell, Nan.

Ib., III, 4, 98.

In accordance with S. Walker, Versification, p. 140, both Dr. Abbott (s. 475) and Dr. Aldis Wright (in his note on The Tempest, I, 2, 53) have advanced the opinion that the first *fare* in the above line is more emphatic than the second; it is a dissyllable, they say, whereas the second is a monosyllable.* It seems natural, however, that Master Fenton should take leave in a more expressive tone from 'sweet Anne Page' than from her mother, the more so as the latter does by no means favour his suit. In my opinion the verse belongs to those syllable pause lines whose name is legion, and should be scanned accordingly: —

Farewell, | ⏑ gen|tle mis|tress; fare|well, Nan.

The pronunciation *fárewell* seems to have been considered more emphatic, not to say pathetic, than *farewéll*, and, in cases of repetition, a kind of climax is sometimes reached by the transition from *farewéll* to *fárewell*. Compare, e. g., 2 Henry VI., III, 2, 356: —

Yet now farewéll; and fárewell life with thee.

Another passage in point occurs in Richard III., III, 7, 247: —

Farewéll, good cousin; fárewell, gentle friends.

In the touching and heart-felt leave-taking of Brutus (Julius Cæsar, V, 1, 116 seq.) the word is accented throughout on the first syllable. Two passages that would seem to contradict my theory occur in Othello (III, 3, 348 seq. and V, 2, 124 seq.) where the word bears the accent on the first syllable. I have, however, little doubt that the arrangement of the second of these passages is corrupted and that Shakespeare did not make Desdemona say: —

Nobody; I myself; farewell.
Commend | me to | my kind | lord. O, | farewell,

but: —

Nobody; I myself; farewéll! Commend me
To my | kind lord. | O, fáre|well!

The following line in Mucedorus (III, 4, 34) has been declared by Messrs. Warnke and Prœscholdt to be a regular Alexandrine: —

Then Mu|cedo|rus, fare|well, my | hop'd joys, | farewell.

---

* According to Dr. Aldis Wright also the first *year* in The Tempest, I, 2, 53, is to be pronounced as a dissyllable, the second as a monosyllable. I think it much more probable, however, that the first *Twelve* is to be considered as a monosyllabic foot and that the true scansion of the line is: —

Twelve | year since, | Miran|da, twelve | year since.

Thus a uniform and more pleasing rhythmical movement is obtained. Compare S. Walker, Versification, p. 138.

If this scansion were right, the more emphatic accentuation of the
word would indeed precede the less emphatic; but the line, far from
being a regular Alexandrine, is a regular blank verse with an extra
syllable before the pause: —

> Then Mu|cedo|rus, farewéll, | my hop'd | joys, fáre|well.

It cannot be denied, however, that in Fair Em there occurs a line
(V, 1, 208) in which the accentuation *fárewell* indeed precedes the
accentuation *farewéll*: —

> Then fárewell, frost! farewéll a wench that will,

whereas in a preceding passage of the same play (II, 1, 157) we
read: —

> Farewéll, my love!   Nay, fárewell, life and all!

The Merry Devil of Edmonton (Dodsley, ed. Hazlitt, X, 239): —

> *Sir Arthur.*   Farewéll, dear son, farewéll.
> *Mounchensey.*   Fáre | you well. | Ay, you | have done?

Marlowe, Edward II., II, 4, 9 seq. (ed. Tancock): —

> *Gav.*   Farewéll, my lord.
> *Edw.*   [Farewéll.]   Lady, farewéll.
> *Niece.*   Farewéll, sweet uncle, till we meet again.
> *Edw.*   Farewéll, sweet Gaveston; and fárewell, niece.
> *Q. Isab.*   No fárewell to poor Isabel thy queen?

Let me add two more lines concerning which I cannot help differing
from Dr. Abbott (s. 475 and s. 480).   They are K. John, III, 3, 17,
scanned thus by Dr. Abbott: —

> Fáre|well, gen|tle cóus|in.   Cóz, | farewéll,

and Pericles, II, 5, 13, scanned thus: —

> Lóath to | bid fá|rewéll, | we táke | our léaves.

The first verse, in which no gradation of accentuation or emphasis
takes place, I take to be a syllable pause line and the second to
begin with a monosyllabic foot: —

> Farewéll, | ◡ gén|tle cóu|sin.   Cóz, | farewéll,

and: —

> Lóath | to bíd | farewéll, | we táke | our léaves.

The conjecture: 'Farewell, *my* gentle cousin', mentioned by S. Walker,
Versification, p. 140, is unnecessary, if not entirely wrong.   (Notes,
privately printed, 1882, p. 13 seqq.)

CCLXXV.

> Than thee with wantonness: now doth thy honour stand.
>
> *Ib., IV, 4, 8.*

Wantonness is a triple ending before the pause.

CCLXXVI.

And marry her at Eton.   Go send to Falstaff straight.

Ib., IV, 4, 75.

Omit *at Eton* which words have intruded here from the last scene, 1. 194.

CCLXXVII.

As if we had them not.   Spirits are finely touch'd.

Measure for Measure, I, 1, 36.

'In *Measure for Measure*', says Mr. Fleay, 1. c., 84, 'the regular instances [viz. of Alexandrines] are numerous and the change to the third period complete.' Mr. Fleay is quite right as to the frequency in 'Measure for Measure' of that peculiar kind of verse which he calls Alexandrines, and I differ from him only in so far as I take the great majority of them to be blank verse, mostly with a triple ending either at the end of the line, or at the end of the first hemistich, i. e. before the pause. I am perfectly aware that Mr. Fleay's opinions on this head are shared more or less by most English Shakespearians and prosodists, amongst others by Mr. Alexander J. Ellis who in his elaborate work 'On Early English Pronunciation' (III, 943 seq.) has proved a staunch defender of Alexandrines in Shakespeare and an eager, though unsuccessful antagonist of Dr. Abbott. It would be labour thrown away to argue with Mr. Ellis and to examine the details of his theory; I merely mention him lest, at some time or other, my silence should be misinterpreted as ignorance. In the following scansions I shall omit some few of the lines designated as Alexandrines by Mr. Fleay and for brevity's sake shall now and then mark the middle syllable of triple endings by an apostrophe. To begin with the line at the head of this note, it has a triple ending before the pause *(had them not),* while *Spirits* is to be pronounced as a monosyllable.

I, 1, 56: Matters of needful value: we shall write to you.

> Hanmer omitted *to you.* Mr. Fleay writes *t' you* and declares the line to be an Alexandrine 'with Spenserian cesura.' In my opinion the verse should be scanned: —
>
> Matters | of need|ful val|ue: we shǎll | write tó | you.

Compare A. IV, sc. 3, 1. 141: —

> And gen|eral hon|our. I'm | direct|ed bý | you.

I, 3, 37: For what I bid them do: for we bid this be done.

> *Be done* omitted by Pope. *Bid them do* is a triple ending before the pause.   Compare K. Richard III., I, 2, 89: —

> Say that | I slew | them not? Why, then | they are |
> not dead,

and Coriolanus, IV, 1, 27: —

> As 'tis | to laugh | at 'em. My moth|er, you | wot well.

Possibly, however, all these lines may just as well be taken for what are termed trimeter couplets by Dr. Abbott, s. 500 seq.

I, 3, 39: And not | the pun | 'shment. Therefore, | indeed, | my fa | ther.

Indeed omitted by Pope. — Compare Marlowe, Edward II., I, 2, 71: —

> Confirm | his ban | 'shment with | our hands | and seals.

I, 4, 5: Upon | the sis | t'rhood, the vo | t'rists of | Saint Clare.

Pope, *sister votaries*; Dyce, *sisterhood, votarists*.

I, 4, 70: To sof | ten An | g'lo; and that's | my pith | of bus | 'ness.

Pith of omitted by Pope; Hanmer and Dyce end the line at *pith* and thus complete the following line, although they differ in their readings.

II, 2, 9: Why dost thou ask again? Lest I might be too rash.

Dost thou omitted by Hanmer. *Ask again* seems to be a triple ending; the line may, however, be taken for a trimeter couplet, just like II, 2, 12; II, 2, 14; II, 2, 41, and numerous others.

II, 2, 70: And what | a pris | 'ner. Ay, touch | him; there's | the vein.

II, 2, 183: To sin in loving virtue: never could the strumpet.

Dyce and Mr. Fleay justly adopt Pope's correction *ne'er* for *never* and thus make the line a regular blank verse with an extra syllable before the pause.

II, 4, 118: T'have what | we would | have, we speak | not what |
we mean.

Steevens (and Dyce), *we'd*.

II, 4, 128 (not 127): In prof | 'ting by | them. Nay, call | us ten |
times frail.

II, 4, 153 seq. Pope, Dyce (and others?) justly end l. 153 at *world*. Dyce thinks the word *aloud* an interpolation and is surprised that none of the former editors has thrown it out. In my opinion such an omission would be quite uncalled for, as the two lines are thus to be scanned: —

> Or with | an out | stretch'd throat | I'll tell | the world
> Aloud | what man | thou 'rt.
> *Ang.*   Who will | believe | thee, Is | 'bel?

Both *man thou art* and *Isabel* are triple endings; as to the latter compare IV, 3, 119; V, 1, 387; V, 1, 392 and V, 1, 435.

III, 1, 32 seq.   Qy. arrange and scan: —

> For end|ing thee | no soon|er. Thou hast | nor youth
> Nor age, | but, as | 'twere, an af|ter-din|ner's sleep?

III, 1, 61: To-mor|row you | set on. | Is there | no rem|'dy?

III, 1, 89: In base | appli|'nces. This out|ward-saint|ed dep|'ty?
Hanmer reads *appliance*.

III, 1, 151 (not 150): 'Tis best | that thou | diest quick|ly. O hear|
> me, Is|'bel.

The old copies as well as the modern editions, as far as they are known to me, wrongly read *Isabella*. The line has an extra syllable before the pause and a triple ending.

IV, 2, 76 seqq.: The best and wholesomest spirits of the night
> Envelop you, good Provost. Who call'd here of late?
> > *Prov.*   None, since the curfew rung.
> > *Duke.*   Not Isabel?
> > *Prov.*   No.
> > *Duke.*   They will, then, ere't be long.

Arrange: —

> The best and wholesomest spirits of the night
> Envelop you, good Provost! Who call'd here
> Of late?
> > *Prov.*   None, since the curfew rung.
> > *Duke.*   Not Isabel?
> > *Prov.*   No.
> > *Duke.*   *She* will, then, ere't be long.

Isabel is a triple ending or a quasi-dissyllable; compare The Works of John Marston, ed. J. O. Halliwell (London, 1856) III, 110: —

> Isabell | advan|ces to | a sec|ond bed.

Of late ..... *Isabel,* therefore, is a regular blank verse and the Alexandrine is discarded. *They,* in the last line, has rightly been altered to *She* by Hawkins. Compare Abbott, s. 501.

IV, 2, 86 seq.: To qualify in others: were he mealed with that
> Which he corrects, then were he tyrannous.

In the one-volume edition of Shakespeare's Plays and Poems published by Ernest Fleischer, Leipsic, 1833, the words *with that* are transferred to the following line and I am surprised that this correction has not been recorded in the Cambridge Edition. Mr. Fleay recommends the same transposition and it only remains to add, that *tyrannous* is a triple ending which makes the line a correct blank verse.

IV, 2, 103: Profess'd | the con|tr'ry. This is | his lord|ship's man.

IV, 3, 131: By every syllable a faithful verity.

Strange to say, this line is not mentioned by Mr. Fleay. *Verity* is a triple ending; compare *supra* note CX.

IV, 3, 137: There to give up their power. If you can, pace your wisdom.

I strongly suspect that the words *If you can* did not come from the poet's pen and should be struck out.

IV, 3, 145: At Mariana's house to-night. Her cause and yours.

To-night omitted by Pope. Mr. Fleay rightly, though diffidently, suggests *Marian's,* and thus restores a regular blank verse. It has not occurred to Mr. Fleay that the same correction is to be applied to A. V, sc. 1, l. 379 and A. V, sc. 1, l. 408: —

Is all | the grace | I beg. | Come hith|er, Ma|rian.
For Ma|rian's sake: | but as | he adjudg'd | your broth|er.

IV, 5, 6: As cause | doth min|'ster. Go, call | at Fla|vius' house.

Go omitted by Hanmer.

V, 1, 32: Or wring redress from you. Hear me, O hear me, here!
Dyce justly queries *here*; it is certainly an interpolation.

V, 1, 42: Is it not strange and strange? Nay, it is ten times strange.
Omit, with Pope, Dyce, &c., *it is.*

V, 1, 51: That I | am touch'd | with mad|ness. Make not | imposs|'ble.

V, 1, 54 (not 56): May seem | as shy, | as grave, | as just, | as ab|s'lute.

V, 1, 65: For in|equal|'ty; but let | your rea|son serve.

Pope needlessly transferred *serve* to the beginning of the next line in which he omitted the article before *truth.*

V, 1, 74: As then | the mess|'nger, — That's I, | an 't like | your grace.
See S. Walker, Versification, 200 seq. and note CDLI.

V, 1, 101: And I | did yield | t' him: but the | next morn | betimes.
But the omitted by Pope. *Yield to him* is a triple ending before the pause.

V, 1, 233: A mar|ble mon|'ment. I did | but smile | till now.

V, 1, 260: Upon | these slan|d'rers: My lord, | we'll do | it through|ly.

CCLXXVIII.

Can you not hate me, as I know you do,
But you must join in souls to mock me too?

A Midsummer-Night's Dream, III, 2, 149 seq.

The second line, although Dyce is silent about it, is certainly corrupt. Hanmer conjectured *in flouts*; Mason, *in soul*; Tyrwhitt, *ill souls*; Warburton, *but must join insolents*. According to my conviction Shakespeare wrote: —

But you must join in *taunts* to mock me too?

The usual abbreviation 'taũts', if the stroke were obliterated, or altogether left out, could easily be misread for 'fouls'. (The Athenæum, Oct. 26, 1867, 537.)

CCLXXIX.

Merry and tragical! tedious and brief!
That is hot ice and wondrous strange snow.

Ib., V, 1, 58 seq.

Hanmer proposed *and wondrous scorching snow*; Warburton, *a wondrous strange shew*; Upton and Capell, *and wondrous strange black snow*; Mason, *and wonderous strong snow*; Collier and R. Grant White (Shakespeare's Scholar, 220), *and wondrous seething snow*; Staunton, *and wondrous swarthy snow*; Nicholson, *and wondrous staining snow*. The Editors of the Globe Edition have prefixed their well-known obelus to the line. There can be no doubt that the epithet must refer to the colour, and not to the temperature, of the snow; for as ice is the symbol and quintessence of coldness, so is snow of whiteness and purity. Compare, e. g., Psalm LI, 7: Purge me with hyssop and I shall be clean, wash me and I shall be whiter than snow. Hamlet, III, 1, 140: be thou as chaste as ice, as pure as snow. Hamlet, III, 3, 46: —

Is there not rain enough in the sweet heavens
To wash it white as snow?

The incongruity, with the ice, therefore, lies in the temperature; with the snow, in the colour. In so far, Staunton's conjecture *swarthy* highly recommends itself; it is, indeed, the only one that is acceptable among those that have been published hitherto. I imagine, however, that Shakespeare wrote: —

That is, hot ice and wondrous *sable* snow.

To a transcriber or compositor of Shakespeare's works, the words *wondrous strange,* from their frequent occurrence, were likely to present themselves even when uncalled for. (The Athenæum, Oct. 26, 1867, 537.)

CCLXXX.

Tongue, lose thy light;
Moon, take thy flight;
Now die, die, die, die, die. [*Exit Moonshine.*

Ib., V, 1, 309 seqq.

This nonsense which is by no means intentional, can never have come from Shakespeare's pen. The word *tongue* is entirely out of place here and has evidently crept in from Thisbe's next speech (the antistrophe): —

Tongue, not a word:
Come, trusty sword;
Come, blade, my breast imbrue.

Mr. Halliwell-Phillipps has conjectured *sun* for *tongue*; but Pyramus has nothing to do with the sun, and such an address to sun and moon would be too truly pathetic in his mouth. Besides, Pyramus does not address the moon, but rather Moonshine and his Dog, and *tongue,* in my opinion, is nothing but a mistake for *dog.* This granted, we have only to transpose the words *Dog* and *Moon,* and the natural flow of thoughts and words seems fully restored: —

Moon, lose thy light,
Dog, take thy flight,   [*Exit Moonshine.*
Now die, die, die, die, die.

(The Athenæum, Oct. 26, 1867, 537.)

CCLXXXI.

My wind cooling my broth
Would blow me to an ague, when I thought
What harm a wind too great at sea might do.

The Merchant of Venice, I, 1, 22 seqq.

Wind is here understood by the commentators and translators to mean 'breath'. The repetition of the word, however, first in this unusual and immediately after in its customary sense, makes me doubt, since no pun is intended; it seems natural, to take the word in both places in the same sense. Besides, nobody is able to blow himself to an ague by his own proper breath; on the contrary, that which produces an ague must come from somewhere else, it must be a wind, in the ordinary sense of the word, and not a breath. The pronoun 'my' does not subvert this explanation; it is used colloquially and redundantly in the same manner as 'me', 'my', or 'your'. Thus, e. g., King John I, 1, 189 seqq.: —

Now your traveller,
He and his toothpick at my worship's mess;
And when my knightly stomach is suffic'd,

> Why then I suck my teeth, and catechize
> My picked man of countries.

Or Ben Jonson, Volpone, IV, 1: —

> Read Contarene, took me a house,
> Dealt with my Jews to furnish it with moveables &c.

Abbott, s. 220 seq., has omitted to mention this redundant use of 'my' (Jahrb. d. D. Sh.-G., XI, 275.)

' CCLXXXII.

Shy. Three thousand ducats; well.

Ib., I, 3, 1.

The same sum of three thousand ducats occurs also in Twelfth Night, I, 3, 22, where we are told by Sir Toby Belch that Sir Andrew Aguecheek 'has three thousand ducats a year.' In 'Soliman and Perseda' (H's D., V, 308) the same amount is again offered as a reward to him who shall discover and capture the murderer of Ferdinando: —

> And let proclamation straight be made,
> That he that can bring forth the murderer,
> Shall have three thousand ducats for his pain.

CCLXXXIII.

How like a fawning publican he looks.

Ib., I, 3, 42.

Messrs. Clark and Wright in their annotated edition of this play take exception to the above line. 'A "fawning publican",' they say, 'seems an odd combination. The Publicani or farmers of taxes under the Roman government were much more likely to treat the Jews with insolence than servility. Shakespeare, perhaps, only remembered that in the Gospels "publicans and sinners" are mentioned together as objects of the hatred and contempt of the Pharisees.' — The learned editors have overlooked that the poet evidently alludes to St. Luke XVIII, 10—14, where the publican fawns — not indeed on men, but — in Shylock's opinion — on God. Such a contrition before God, proceeding from a humility which is a characteristic of Christianity rather than of Judaism, does not enter into Shylock's soul. Shylock lends a deaf ear to Portia's glorious panegyric of mercy; he will neither show, nor accept mercy. He 'stays on his bond' not only in his relations to his fellow-men, but also in his relations to his Creator. 'What judgment shall I dread, doing no wrong?' and 'My deeds upon my head!' he exclaims, in the true spirit of Judaism. Marlowe's Barabas (A. I) speaks in the very same key: —

> The man that dealeth righteously shall live;
> And which of you can charge me otherwise?

But Shylock is not only incapable of sympathizing with the publican that prostrates himself in the dust and cries for mercy, he is even averse to what he deems an abject behaviour; he hates such a man and brands his humility as fawning. Compare Dr. Furness *ad loc.* (Jahrb. d. D. Sh.-G., XI, 276).

CCLXXXIV.

> *Shy.* Signior Antonio, many a time and oft
> In the Rialto you have rated me
> About my moneys and my usances.

Ib., I, 3, 107 seqq.

Roger Wilbraham (An Attempt at à Glossary of Some Words used in Cheshire, London, 1836, under 'Many a time and oft') says: 'A common expression and means, frequently. — — With which colloquial expression, though common through all England, Mr. Kean, the actor in the part of Shylock, being unacquainted, always spoke the passage, by making a pause in the middle of it, thus: "Many a time — and oft on the Rialto", without having any authority from the text of Shakespeare for so doing.' Compare also Forby, Vocabulary of East Anglia, s. v. Many-a-time-and-often: 'a pleonasm or rather tautology, sufficiently ridiculous, but in very familiar use.'

CCLXXXV.

> The young gentleman, — — is indeed deceased, or, as you would say in plain terms, gone to heaven.

Ib., II, 2, 64 seqq.

Launcelot Gobbo delights in saying things by contraries; he advises his father to 'turn down indirectly to the Jew's house' and assures Bassanio that the suit is 'impertinent' to himself. May he not be speaking here in the same style? May not the 'plain term' he has in his mind be 'gone to hell'? He does not, however, pronounce the ominous word, but after some hesitation corrects himself. The actor therefore should make a significant pause before 'heaven', and we should write, *or, as you would say in plain terms, gone to —* *heaven*. A similar humorous innuendo is contained in the well-known poem of Burns 'Duncan Gray', st. 3: —

> Shall I, like a fool, quoth he,
> For a haughty hizzie die?

> She may gae to — France for me!
> Ha, ha, the wooing o't.

I quote from Allan Cunningham's edition (London, 1842, in 1 vol., 450). In the second line, I think, we should write *dee* for *die*. Compare also G. Eliot, Adam Bede (Tauchn. Ed., I, 22): Chad's Bess wore 'a pair of large round earrings with false garnets in them, ornaments contemned not only by the Methodists, but by her own cousin and namesake Timothy's Bess, who, with much cousinly feeling, wished "them earrings" might come to good [i. e. to grief].' (Jahrb. d. D. Sh.-G., XI, 277 seq.)

CCLXXXVI.

How doth that royal merchant, good Antonio?

Ib., III, 2, 242.

The distinguishing title here given to Antonio is repeated in IV, 1, 29: Enow to press a royal merchant down. It is an *epitheton ornans,* by which the poet wishes to define the social position and princely magnanimity of Antonio, but at the same time it hints at the *terminus technicus* for a merchant adventurer, viz. the Merchant Royal. The business of the Merchant Royal is defined in a passage in Thomas Powell's pamphlet Tom of all Trades; or, The plaine Pathway to Preferment (1631), which is reprinted in Dr. Furnivall's edition of Tell-Trothes New-Yeares Gift (Publications of the New Shakspere Society, Ser. VI, No. 2, 164 seq.). 'I admit', says Thomas Powell, 'the Merchant Royall that comes to his Profession by travaile and Factory, full fraught, and free adventure, to be a profession worthy the seeking. But not the hedge-creeper, that goes to seeke custome from shop to shop with a Cryll under his arme, That leapes from his Shop-boord to the Exchange, and after he is fame-falne and credit crackt in two or three other professions, shall wrigle into this and that when he comes upon the Exchange, instead of enquiring after such a good ship, spends the whole houre in disputing, whether is the more profitable house-keeping, either with powder Beefe, and brewes, or with fresh Beefe and Porridge; though (God wot) the blacke Pot at home be guilty of neyther: And so he departs when the Bell rings, and his guts rumble, both to one tune and the same purpose. The Merchant Royall might grow prosperous, were it not for such poore patching interloping Lapwings that have an adventure of two Chaldron of Coles at New-castle; As much oyle in the Greeneland fishing as will serve two Coblers for the whole yeare ensuing. And an other at Rowsio [i. e. Russia], for as many Fox-skins as will furre his Longlane gowne, when he is called to the Livorie.' — Compare also Marston, The Insatiate Countesse, A. II (Works, ed. Halliwell, III, 124): '*Tha*[*is*]: O! this your device smells of the merchant. What's your ships name, I pray? The Forlorne

Hope?   *Abi*[*gail*]: Noe; The Merchant Royall.   *Tha.* And why not Adventurer?' — From these passages it will be seen that Antonio is both a royal merchant and a Merchant Royal. (Anglia, herausgeg. von Wülcker und Trautmann, I, 340.)

CCLXXXVII.

Stephano is my name; and I bring word.

Ib., V, 1, 28.

Dr. Farmer's well-known remark, that the pronunciation of *Stephano* is always right in The Tempest (i. e. with the accent on the first syllable) and always wrong in The Merchant of Venice (i. e. with the accent on the penult) has been repeated and subscribed to by all subsequent commentators, myself among the number (Essays on Shakespeare, p. 293 seq.). Farmer takes it for granted that Shakespeare was taught the right pronunciation of the name by Ben Jonson in the interval between the bringing out of the two respective comedies, as the first version of Every Man in his Humour, in which Shakespeare performed a part in 1598, contained two characters, Prospero and Stephano, both correctly pronounced. However plausible this surmise may appear, I have nevertheless come to the conviction that Shakespeare may noways have stood in need of any such instruction from his friend B. Jonson. Besides the line at the head of this note the name of Stephano occurs again in line 51 of the same scene: —

My friend Stephano, signify, I pray you.

It strikes me, that in both these lines the name may be pronounced as correctly as in The Tempest, the first line opening with a trochee and the second having a trochee in the second place. I need not point out how frequently a trochee occurs at the beginning of the line; that it is also of pretty frequent occurrence in the second foot has been shown in my second edition of Hamlet, s. 118 (That no reuenew hast, &c.). Compare Abbott, s. 453. Nothing prevents us then from scanning: —

Stépha|no ís | my náme; | and Í | bring wórd

and: —

My friénd | Stépha|no, síg|nifý, I práy | you.

(Notes, privately printed, 1882, p. 10 seq.)

CCLXXXVIII.

Bear your body more seeming, Audrey.

As You Like It, V, 4, 72.

In support of Mr. P. A. Daniel's admirable emendation *more swimming,* the following passages may be added to those that have been quoted

by Mr. Daniel himself. The Two Noble Kinsmen (ed. Harold Little-
dale, p. 146): swim with your bodies. Chapman, The Ball, A. II
(The Works of Geo. Chapman: Plays, ed. R. H. Shepherd, 494):
Carry your body in the swimming fashion. B. Jonson, Epigrams,
No. LXXXII (Works, in 1 vol., London, 1853, 671): —

> Surly's old whore in her new silks doth swim:
> He cast, yet keeps her well! No; she keeps him.

From among modern writers the distinguished American poet William
Cullen Bryant may be cited as giving proof of the sense in which
the phrase is understood. In his poem 'Spring in Town' he says: —

> No swimming Juno gait, of languor born,
> Is theirs, but a light step of freest grace,
> Light as Camilla's o'er the unbent corn.

By the way it may be remarked that it was not Juno, but Venus
to whom languor and a swimming gait were appropriated by the
Greeks.

These quotations, I think, are sufficient to remove all doubts
and to clear the way for the admittance of Mr. Daniel's ingenious
correction into the text, so much the more as the phrase 'to bear
one's self or one's body seeming' can hardly be supported by a
single parallel passage. (Jahrb. d. D. Sh.-G., XI, 284.)

CCLXXXIX.

Even as a flattering dream or worthless fancy.
The Taming of the Shrew, Induction, I, 44.

According to the Cambridge Edition an anonymous critic, identified
since by Dyce *ad loc.*, as Mr. W. N. Lettsom, asks whether this
line which is given invariably to the Lord, does not belong to the
Second Hunter. In my opinion it clearly belongs to the First Hunter;
read therefore: —

> *First Hun.* Believe me, lord, I think he cannot choose.
> *Sec. Hun.* It would seem strange unto him when he waked.
> *First Hun.* Even as a 'flattering dream or worthless fancy.
> *Lord.* Then take him up and manage well the jest: &c.

(The Athenæum, Mar. 12, 1881, p. 365.)

CCXC.

Sincklo. I thinke 'twas Soto that your honour meanes.
Ib., Induction, I, 88 (FA).

It is well known that our knowledge of the player Sincklo, Sincklow,
Sinkclow, or Sincler is due to two blunders in FA, where he is
mentioned in the Introduction to the Taming of the Shrew and in

the third Part of Henry VI, III, 1; to a similar blunder in the
Quarto of the second Part of Henry IV. (V, 4); to the Induction to
Marston's Malcontent; and to the Platt of the Seven Deadly Sins in
Malone's Shakspeare (Vol. III).   Collier, in his Memoirs of the
Principal Actors in the Plays of Shakespeare, p. XXVII, further
informs us that Sincklo's 'Christian name appears to have been
William, that he lived in Cripplegate and had children baptized at
St. Giles's Church, in that parish, in 1610 and 1613.'   'He is called
Sincklowe and Sinckley in the registers', Collier continues, 'but
evidently the same man; and we take it that he had been an actor
under Henslowe and Alleyn at the Fortune, (though his name does
not occur in the "Diary" of the former) and on that account resided
near their theatre, where he continued after he had joined the king's
players.'   This information, however, cannot be considered as reliable,
but, especially in its latter part, is an unfounded hypothesis.   Collier,
moreover, makes a mistake with respect to Sincklo's Christian name,
which was not William, but John, as appears from the Platt of the
Seven Deadly Sins.   If, therefore, the Sincklo who is mentioned in
the registers of St. Giles's should there be called William, it is clearly
not the same person; nay, the identity of this inhabitant of Cripplegate with the actor may at all events' be doubted, even if their
Christian names should coincide, provided he be not expressly designated as a player in the registers, which is not likely, as Collier
would have said so, if it was the case.   An addition to these scanty
materials comes to us just now from a very different quarter which,
though partaking of the general uncertainty that envelops the stage-
history of the Elizabethan era, yet must be welcomed as an interesting
fact.   Before, however, entering on an examination of this new
material we shall do well carefully to survey all the particulars,
especially as they have given rise to mistaken inferences.

    I.   In the Induction of the Taming of the Shrew John Sincklo
performed one of the Players, not the First Player, as Delius erroneously says in his note on 2 K. Henry IV., V, 4 (Stage-direction) and
in his Abhandlungen zu Shakspere, p. 300 and 305.   The speeches
of the Players and their prefixes in FA. are as follows: 1) *Players*:
We thanke your Honor; 2) *2 Player*: So please your Lordshippe to
accept our dutie; 3) *Sincklo*: I thinke 't was Soto that your honor
meanes; and 4) *Plai.*: Feare not my Lord, we can contain our selues,
Were he the veriest anticke in the world.   Whether we assume the
first speech to have been spoken by all the Players at once, or by
the First Player in their name, in neither case are we justified in
identifying Sincklo with the First Player.   No weight would attach
to this circumstance, if Delius did not, as a matter of course, attribute the part of Petruchio to Sincklo, because in his opinion this
part was necessarily performed by the First Player.   After all we
know John Sincklo was a subordinate performer and a clown or

humorous man to boot, who could scarcely have been entrusted with so important a part as that of Petruchio.

II. The Quarto of 2 K. Henry IV. (V, 4) contains the following stage-direction: *Enter Sincklo, and three or four officers,* for which the first Folio substitutes: *Enter Beadles, dragging in Hostess Quickly and Doll Tearsheet.* As, moreover, the Quarto has the prefix *Sinck.* for *1 Bead.* in FA, it follows that the First Beadle was acted by Sincklo. Now this First Beadle is chaffed unrelentingly both by the Hostess and Doll Tearsheet on account of his leanness; he is 'a paper-faced villain', a 'thin man in a censer', a 'filthy famished correctioner', a 'starved blood-hound', 'goodman death', 'goodman bones', a 'thin thing', and an 'atomy'. If, then, we see this part expressly assigned to Sincklo, we shall hardly be wrong in concluding that he was the leanest among all the king's players; is it saying too much, if we imagine him to have been perfect in personifying a gaunt, cadaverous-looking fellow? This leanness is another argument, why Sincklo cannot have performed Petruchio in the Taming of the Shrew.

III. According to FA the stage-direction in 3 Henry VI., III, 1 is: *Enter Sinklo and Humfrey,* &c. instead of: *Enter Two Keepers,* &c. in the Qq. From this it follows that Sincklo played the First Keeper.

IV. In the Induction to Marston's Malcontent Sincklo played a foppish young gentleman sitting on the stage, drinking, smoking tobacco, and criticizing the play, the players, and the audience.

V. In the Platt of the Seven Deadlic Sinnes no less than six different parts are assigned to Sincklo, viz. a Keeper, a Soldier, a Captain, a Musician, Julio (?), and a Warder.

VI. I now proceed to the examination of a publication that seems likely to throw an unexpected light on the person and life of Sincklo. Dr. Johannes Meissner, in his recently published book 'Die Englischen Comödianten zur Zeit Shakespeare's in Österreich' (Wien, 1884, p. 19) informs us, that in the household books of the Emperor Maximilian II., who reigned from 1564 to 1576, not only English musicians, but also 'die Narren Anton und Franciscus, ein ungarischer Narr Stefan, ein spanischer Narr, ein Narr Sinclaw, &c.' are mentioned as court-fools. Maximilian II. seems to have been fond of foreign fools or clowns. It has not occurred to Dr. Meissner that this Sinclaw might be identified with the Sincklo of Shakespeare's company; he nowhere alludes to this latter. Nevertheless it seems not at all unlikely that the German Emperor's fool and the performer in The Taming of the Shrew, in 2 Henry IV., in 3 Henry VI., in Marston's Malcontent and in the Platt of the Seven Deadlie Sinnes may have been one and the same person. Like many others of his fellows Sincklo may have gone to Germany when a young man; he may have been about 25 years of age when he stood in the Emperor's service at

Vienna about the year 1570, so that, at the beginning of the seven-
teenth century, when performing in Shakespeare's and Marston's plays,
he was about 55 years old, for there can be little doubt that the
second part of Henry IV., the third part of Henry VI., and probably
also Marston's Malcontent (printed in 1604) were acted before 1600;
the Seven Deadlie Sinnes, according to Malone's showing, must have
been on the stage in or before 1589, that is to say some thirteen
years after the death of Maximilian II. in 1576, at which time
Sincklo had probably returned to his native country. I do not find
it difficult thus to combine the different dates with the only exception
of those that are said to be contained in the registers of St. Giles's
Church; it seems not very credible that a man who was about
55 years old in 1600, should have had children baptized in 1610
and 1613. The name of Sincklo is of rare occurrence and it is not
at all likely that two different players living at the same time should
have borne it, except they were father and son; those critics, therefore, who are unwilling to settle all the different facts upon one and
the same person, may have recourse to this last-named hypothesis.
At all events it would seem that our knowledge of Sincklo and his
doings has been somewhat enlarged since the days of Malone who,
in his Historical Account of the English Stage, has nothing to say
about him except that 'Sinkler or Sinclo, and Humphrey, were likewise players in the same theatre, and of the same class.' See
Malone's Shakspeare by Boswell, III, 221.

<hr>

CCXCI.

As Stephen Sly and old John Naps of Greece.

Ib., Induction, II, 95.

For the private amusement of himself and friends the poet has
introduced in this Induction allusions to some well-known inns and
boon companions of his own county; recollections, no doubt, of the
haunts and acquaintances of his youth. Such, probably, were old
Sly and his son of Burton (or Barton)-on-Heath, if they should not
be meant for Edmund Lambert and his son John (cf. Elze, William
Shakespeare, 64 and 80); such also Marian Hacket, the fat ale-wife
of Wincot, i. e. Wilmecote, which, according to Staunton's note *ad
loc.*, is to this day popularly pronounced Wincot. With these I do
not hesitate to couple *old John Naps of Greece*; Greece being a
palpable corruption, which is neither remedied by Blackstone and
Hanmer's *old John Naps o' th' Green,* nor by Mr. Halliwell-Phillipps's
old John Naps of Greys or *of Greete,* which latter, Mr. Halliwell-
Phillipps says, was a place situated between Stratford and Gloucester.
On the map of Warwickshire I find a place called Cleeve Priory,
on the Avon, a few miles below Stratford. Shakespeareans who are
acquainted from personal knowledge with the topography of Warwick-

shire, which I am sorry to say I am not, can decide whether this
be a place likely to have been the residence of old John Naps; if so,
I should propose to read: —

As Stephen Sly and old John Naps of *Cleeve*.

This conjecture, I think, is strengthened by our poet's allusion in
Romeo and Juliet, II, 4, 83 seq., to 'bitter-sweetings', a kind of
apple which was, and is to this day, 'grown especially at Cleeve
and Littleton' and is still used as a sauce, in complete accordance
with Mercutio's words in the passage cited. See John R. Wise, Shakspere: His Birthplace and its Neighbourhood (London, 1861), 97.
(The Athenæum, Jan. 18, 1868, 95. Reply by Mr. Halliwell-Phillipps, ib.; Jan. 25, 1868, 133. — Shakespeare's dramatische Werke
nach der Uebersetzung von Schlegel und Tieck, herausgegeben von
der Deutschen Shakespeare-Gesellschaft, VII, 120.)

CCXCII.

To suck the sweets of sweet philosophy.

Ib., I, 1, 28.

S. Walker (Crit. Exam. I, 289) has rightly classed this line among
that species of corruption which he calls 'substitution of words',
where a particular word is substituted for another 'which stands near
it in the context, more especially if there happens to be some
resemblance between the two'; in fact, it is what in Germany is
called a dittography, i. e. a faulty repetition of the same or a similar
word (see Nos. XXXVI and LXI). Walker, however, has left the
verse without correction, whilst an anonymous conjecturer, according
to the Cambridge Edition, proposes *fair philosophy*. The context, I
think, clearly shows the true reading to be: —

To suck the sweets of *Greek* philosophy.

Compare note CCXCVII. (The Athenæum, Jan. 18, 1868, p. 95.)

CCXCIII.

Let's be no stoics nor no stocks, I pray.

Ib., I, 1, 31.

I do not recollect to have seen it remarked, that the same pun occurs
in Greene's Tu Quoque (Dodsley, ed. Hazlitt, XI, 258): —

> Why, villain, I shall have the worst, I know it,
> And am prepar'd to suffer like a stoic;
> Or else (to speak more properly) like a stock;
> For I have no sense left.

The question of priority, in this case, does not seem likely ever to
be settled. (Notes, privately printed, 1882, p. 14.)

CCXCIV.

O yes, I saw sweet beauty in her face,
Such as the daughter of Agenor had.   *Ib., 1, 1, 172 seq.*

In order to restore the rhyme Collier's so-called manuscript-corrector
has substituted *of Agenor's race* for *of Agenor had*. Dyce, however,
both in his Strictures on Collier's New Edition of Shakespeare, 72,
and in his second edition of Shakespeare's Works, has shown that by
this alteration the meaning is destroyed and grammar violated. Should
the line have rhymed originally, — and I incline to this belief, —
another, though still bolder, conjecture might serve the purpose: —

O yes, I saw her *in sweet beauty clad,*
Such as the daughter of Agenor had.

CCXCV.

I will some other be, some Florentine,
Some Neapolitan, or meaner man of Pisa.   *Ib., 1, 1, 209.*

The metre of this reading of FA is right enough, provided that
Neapolitan be pronounced as a triple ending before the pause: —

Some Ne|apol|itan, or mean|er man | of Pi|sa.

However, the comparative *meaner* is suspicious and looks very much
like an ill-advised correction of the editors of the old copies. Capell's
emendation *or mean man,* which also makes good metre, has therefore been justly adopted by Dyce and other editors, and Staunton
very appropriately compares the stage-direction in A. II, sc. 1:
'Lucentio in the habit of a mean man.' Nevertheless I have a
misgiving that somehow or other *some* has dropped out before *mean*
and should be repeated: —

Some Ne|apol|itan, or *some* | mean man | of Pi|sa.

But this does not suffice to restore the line, as it contains a still
greater stumbling-block. In order 'to achieve that maid' with whom
he has fallen in love, Lucentio thinks it necessary to be introduced
to her in an assumed character. His scheme is based on the fiction
that he comes from some other place than he really does (from
Florence or Naples), and he would be at variance with himself and
baffle his intent, if he should pass himself off as a mean man from
Pisa which is his native town. In a word, the mention of Pisa by
the side of Florence and Naples is inconsistent and cannot be right.
I strongly suspect, therefore, that instead of *Pisa* we should read
Milan which in the *ductus literarum* comes near enough to it *(Milā-
Pi/a).* Thus, then, the original wording of the two lines would seem
to have been: —

I will some other be, some Florentine,
Some Neapolitan, or some mean man of Milan.

(The Athenæum, June 11, 1881, p. 783; June 25, 1881, p. 848
(reply by Dr. Brinsley Nicholson); July 2, 1881, p. 16; July 9, 1881,
p. 49. — Notes, privately printed, 1882, p. 14 seq.)

CCXCVI.

Hark you, sir; I'll have them very fairly bound.

Ib., I, 2, 146.

This line cannot be right. In order to restore the metre S. Walker
(Crit. Exam. III, 66) proposes to omit *you*. It seems, however,
preferable to expunge *very* which has evidently crept in by faulty
repetition; it occurs in the preceding line (O very well) and again
six lines below (And let me have them very well perfumed). The
verse is no doubt a syllable pause line and should thus be scanned: —

Hark you, | sir; ⌣ | I'll have | them fair|ly bound.

That *very* is pre-eminently subject to interpolation, has been shown
by S. Walker, Crit. Exam., I, 268 seq. It is, however, no less subject
to omission; see notes CXXI and CLXXXIV.

CCXCVII.

And this small packet of Greek and Latin books.

Ib., II, 1, 101.

S. Walker, Crit. Exam., III, 67, conjectured *pack*. There is, however,
no occasion for a correction, as the word *packet* is to be pronounced
as a monosyllable: *pack't*. The Greek and Latin books that are presented to the ladies, serve greatly to corroborate my conjectural emendation on A. I, sc. 1, l. 28 (*Greek* philosophy). See note CCXCII.

CCXCVIII.

Luc. Fiddler, forbear; you grow too forward, sir:
Have you so soon forgot the entertainment
Her sister Katharine welcomed you withal?
Hor. But, wrangling pedant, this is
The patroness of heavenly harmony: &c.

Ib., III, 1, 1 seqq.

To complete. the fourth line is no very difficult task, and it has been
performed by almost all editors; their conjectures, however, are mere
guesses and do not give us the least explanation as to how the
mutilation may have originated. Theobald's and Hanmer's conjectures,
Collier's *I avouch this is,* and W. N. Lettsom's *This is a Cecilia,*
are equally deficient in this respect. The poorest expedient seems
to me S. Walker's arrangement (Versification, 85), which proves that
in criticism, as well as in poetry, even Homer may sometimes take

a nap. Any attempt to fill up this gap which would lay claim to
something better than an 'airy nothing' ought of itself to indicate
the way in which the beginning of the line became lost; for, in my
opinion, the loss took place at the beginning, and not in the body,
or at the end, of the line. I imagine that Shakespeare wrote: —

    Her sister — tut! But, wrangling pedant, this is &c.

The copyist or compositor omitted the first two words because he
had just written them or set them up in the same place in the
preceding line, and the third was overlooked through its similarity
to the following *but.* The copyist or compositor catching this *but,*
fancied that he had already written or set up the three preceding
words. Compare note on 1 K. Henry IV., III, 1, 158. (The Athenæum, Jan. 18, 1868, p. 95.)

CCXCIX.

    Pet. Come, where be these gallants? Who's at home?
    Bap. You 're welcome, sir.
    Pet.   And yet I come not well.
    Bap. And yet you halt not.
    Tra.   Not so well apparell'd
As I wish you were.
    Pet. Were it better, I should rush in thus.
But where is Kate? Where is my lovely bride?
How does my father? — Gentles, methinks you frown.

Ib., III, 2, 89 seqq.

The arrangement and disposition of this passage is, no doubt, corrupt.
It is an unfit remark in Petruchio's own mouth that he does not
come well, nor does it harmonize with his subsequent question: —
'And wherefore gaze this goodly company?' On the contrary he
would have the company believe that he comes quite well as he
comes, and that he gives no occasion for staring at him. This
difficulty is, indeed, removed by the ingenious conjecture of Capell;
there are, however, others still remaining. I do not think it likely
that Tranio should join in the conversation at its very beginning;
moreover, it is not his business to express a wish about Petruchio's
apparel. The words 'Not so well apparell'd As I wish you were'
evidently belong to Baptista; and in the old piece, the corresponding
words ('But say, why art thou thus basely attired?') are in fact
spoken by the father of the bride. In so far I agree with W. N.
Lettsom's arrangement, *apud* Walker, Crit. Exam., III, 68. For the
emendation of the following verse, 'Were it better, I should rush in
thus', a number of conjectures have been offered. Its supposed corruption, however, merely arises from a misunderstanding, or rather
misconstruction. All the editors, whom I have been able to collate,

refer these words to the preceding lines; their meaning, according to Dyce, being, 'Were my apparel better than it is, I should yet rush in thus.' But the pointing of the folio which has a colon after 'thus' shows that the line is to be connected with the following verses; and the position of 'thus' at the end of the line confirms this construction. Petruchio, in answer to Baptista's reproaches, here imitates an amorous coxcomb and asks if it were better to have come in after *this* manner, and with *these* questions. With the words, 'Gentles, methinks you frown', he resumes his own manner and tone. Only on the stage can the truth of this interpretation be made fully apparent. The passage should accordingly be printed: —

> *Pet.* Come, where be these gallants? Who 's at home?
> *Bap.* You 're welcome, sir; and yet you come not well.
> *Pet.* And yet I halt not.
> *Bap.* Not so apparell'd as I wish you were.
> *Pet.* Were it better I should rush in thus? —
> [*Imitating a coxcomb.*
> But where is Kate? Where is my lovely bride?
> How does my father? *(Resuming his own manner again.)*
> Gentles, methinks you frown.

In the first line, S. Walker (Crit. Exam., II, 144) proposes to read *Come, come*; it may, however, as well begin with what is called a monosyllabic foot. In the correction of the fourth line W. N. Lettsom has led the way by expunging *well* before *apparell'd*; he also substitutes *Nor* for *Not,* whereas in my arrangement the original reading is retained. (The Athenæum, Jan. 18, 1868, 95.)

CCC.

> Welcome; one mess is like to be your cheer.
> Come, sir; we will better it in Pisa.
> *Ib., IV, 4, 70 seq.*

Capell's alteration has been conclusively refuted by Dyce. The second line is a syllable pause line; scan: —

> Come, sir; | ⏑ we | will bet|ter it | in Pi|sa.

(The Athenæum, Jan. 18, 1868, 95.)

CCCI.

> Why, then let's home again. Come, sirrah, let's away.
> *Ib., V, 1, 152.*

Here and elsewhere the editors content themselves with the general remark that women just as well as men were frequently addressed *sirrah.* With the exception of Dyce (Webster, Westward Ho!,

A. I, sc. 2, p. 214a) and Dr. Furness (Macbeth, p. 221, n. 30) none of them, as far as I know, ever thought it worth his while to lay before his readers some instances of this curious use of the word; and I, therefore, indulge in the hope that the following batch of parallel passages may prove no unwelcome addition to those quoted by Dyce and Furness. Sam. Rowley, When you see me, you know me, ed. Elze, p. 58: —

King. Go, fetch them, Kate. Ah, sirrah, we have women doctors. William Rowley, A Match at Midnight (Dodsley, ed. Hazlitt, XIII, 29): 'Tis pudding-time, wench, pudding-time; and a dainty time, dinner-time, my nimble-eyed, witty one. Woot be married to-morrow, sirrah? Ib., XIII, 29: Sirrah, woot have the old fellow? — Ford, 'Tis Pity She's a Whore, II, 6 (Works, ed. Hartley Coleridge, p. 34a): Sirrah sweetheart, I'll tell thee a good jest. — The Roaring Girl (The Works of Middleton, ed. Dyce, II, 491): How dost thou, sirrah? (viz. Mrs. Gallipot). — Ib., (II, 517): Hush, sirrah! Goshawk flutters (addressed to Mrs. Openwork). — The Honest Whore, Part I, II, 1 (Middleton, ed. Dyce, III, 44): He's so malcontent, sirrah Bellafront. — Ib., Part II, III, 3 (Middleton, ed. Dyce, III, 186): Sirrah grannam. — Ram-Alley (Dodsley, ed. Hazlitt, X, 367 seqq.): —

> I hope thou knowest
> All wenches do the contrary: but, sirrah,
> How does thy uncle, the old doctor?

These lines are addressed to The First Woman by the chambermaid Adriana. — It remains to be added that Dyce in his Glossary, s. Sirrah, refers to Swift as having been fond of applying that humorous pet-name to Stella.

CCCII.

> Sirrah Biondello, go and entreat my wife
> To come to me forthwith; &c.

Ib., V, 2, 86 seqq.

This passage seems to have been imitated in Dekker's Honest Whore, Part II, II, 2 (Middleton, ed. Dyce, III, 164), although Dr. Ingleby in his 'Centurie of Prayse' and Dr. Furnivall in his 'Fresh Allusions' are silent about it: —

> *Can* [*dido*]. Luke, I pray, bid your mistress to come hither.
> *Lo* [*dovico*]. Luke, I pray, bid your mistress to come hither.
> *Can.* Sirrah, bid my wife come to me: why, when?
> *First Prentice* [*within*]. Presently, sir, she comes.
> *Lod.* La, you, there's the echo! she comes.

The second part of Dekker's Honest Whore was licensed in 1608, but published only in 1630.

CCCIII.

I have those hopes of her good that her education promises; her dispositions she inherits, which makes fair gifts fairer.

All's Well that Ends Well, I, 1, 45.

I suspect: I have those hopes of her that her education promises; her *good* dispositions she inherits, which makes fair gifts fairer. Compare Twelfth Night, III, 1, 146: —

> *Vio*[*la*]. Then westward-ho! Grace and good disposition
> Attend your ladyship.

See Al. Schmidt, Shakespeare-Lexicon, s. Disposition.

CCCIV.

Par[*olles*]. Save you, fair queen! &c.

Ib., I, 1, 100 seqq.

This well-known passage is another specimen, and none of the grossest, of what the conversation between ladies and gentlemen was in the days of the Virgin Queen, for there can be no reasonable doubt, that in this respect as well as in others our poet was the true interpreter and mouth-piece of his time; see my edition of The Tragedy of Hamlet, p. 192 seqq. The charge of indecency, therefore, ought not to be laid at his own door, but at that of the age in which he lived. Bad as the want of decency in conversation on the part of the women was in England, yet they are said to have been surpassed by the women in Holland. John Ray, F.R.S., in his Observations Topographical, Moral, and Physiological; made in a Journey through Part of the Low-Countries, Germany, Italy, and France (London, 1673), p. 55, reports the following remark made by his 'much-honoured friend Francis Barnham, Esq., deceased, at his being there [viz. in the Netherlands] in the Retinue of my Lord Ambassador Holles', (ib., p. 52). 'The common sort of Women', says Barnham *apud* Ray, 'seem more fond and delighted with lascivious and obscene Talk than either the English or the French.' That the 'ladies' were scarcely more decent than the 'common women' (at least in England) is sufficiently proved by the passages quoted in my second edition of 'Hamlet', l. c., and in my 'Abhandlungen zu Shakespeare', 405. Let us hope in charity that *(mutatis mutandis)* the saying *Pagina lasciva, vita proba,* may have held good with respect to the women of that age, in Holland as well as in France and England.

CCCV.

> My heart is heavy, and mine age is weak;
> Grief would have tears, and sorrow bids me speak.

Ib., III, 4, 41 seq.

Mr. P. A. Daniel in his Notes and Conjectural Emendations, p. 40 seq., has ingeniously pointed out, how odd it seems, that, 'her sorrow bidding the Countess to speak, she should thereupon leave the stage.' He, therefore, proposes to read *forbids* instead of *bids*, which is undoubtedly right, and to omit *and* before *sorrow*, which, although seemingly required by the metre, may yet be considered doubtful. *Sorrow*, M. E. *sorwe*, occurs in Chaucer as a monosyllable, *sorowful* or *sorwful* as a dissyllable; see Troylus and Cryseide, I, 1: —

> The dou|ble sorowe | of Tro|ylus | to tel|len;

ib., I, 2: —

> Help me; | that am | the sorow|ful in|strument, —
> And to | a sorw|ful tale | a sor|ry chere.

See also The Boke of the Duchesse, ll. 10, 213, and 462. Compare ten Brink, Studien, p. 13, and the Glossary in Dr. Morris' edition of Chaucer, Vol. I, s. Morwe. Perhaps also *arwe* = arrow (Canterbury Tales, 9079), *shadwe,* and similar words were pronounced as monosyllables. Moreover it is an undeniable fact that not only during the Elizabethan era but even as late as the middle of the last century the ending -*ow* was frequently slurred before a vowel, and if I am not much mistaken, sometimes even before a consonant. Compare, e. g., the following passages: —

Troilus and Cressida, I, 3, 80: —

> Hollow upon | this plain, | so man|y hol|low fact|ions.

Antony and Cleopatra, I, 3, 64: —

> With sorr'w|ful wa|ter? Now | I see, | I see.

Marlowe, Edward II., III, 2, 180 (ed. Tancock): —

> Edward | with fire | and sword | follows at | thy heels.

Fair Em (ed. Warnke and Prœscholdt), III, 6, 9: —

> My sor|rows afflicts | my soul | with e|qual pass|ion.

Mucedorus (ed. Warnke and Prœscholdt), II, 2, 122: —

> To-mor|row I die, | my foe | reveng'd | on me.

Ib., II, 4, 39: —

> As if | he meant | to swal|low us both | at once.

The Rambler, No CX, Apr. 6, 1751: —

> Or sor|row unfeign'd | and hu|milia|tion meek.

Paradise Lost, I, 558: —

> Anguish | and doubt | and fear | and sor|row and pain.

Compare Abbott and Seeley, English Lessons for English People (London, 1880), p. 203.

Ib., II, 518:

> By har|ald's voice | explain'd: | the hol|low Abyss.

Ib., V, 575: —

 Be but | the shad|ow of Heaven, | and things | therein.

Samson Agonistes, 958: —

 Cherish | thy has|ten'd widow|hood with | the gold.

Professor Masson (The Poetical Works of J. Milton, I, CXXI and CXXIII) quotes two more Miltonic lines in point, which he, however, scans very differently, viz.: —

 Of rain|bows and star|ry eyes. | The wa|ters thus,

and: —

 Wallowing, | unwield|y, enorm|ous in | their gait.

The Tempest, II, 1, 251: —

 We all were sea-swallow'd, though some cast again.

In this line Pope omits *all,* Spedding *we*; most editors, however, leave it unaltered. There seem to be two ways of scanning it, viz.: —

 We all | were sea-|swallow'd, | though some | cast 'gain,

or: —

 We all | were sea-|swallow'd, though | some cast | again.

Now, if this latter scansion be right, as I presume it to be, it will certainly reflect on the line in All's Well that Ends Well and justify us in reading and scanning it thus: —

 Grief would | have tears, | and sor|row forbids | me speak.

No doubt, some wiseacre of a copyist or compositor who felt called upon to improve the metre, altered *forbids* to *bids.* (Notes, privately printed, 1882, p. 15 seq.)

CCCVI.

 If there be here German, or Dane, low Dutch,
 Italian, or French, let him speak to me; I'll
 Discover that which shall undo the Florentine.

Ib., IV, 1, 78 seqq.

This is Capell's arrangement, adopted by the Cambridge Edd.; in the Ff *I'll* is wrongly joined to the following line. Malone divides the lines after *to me* and *undo.* According to Capell's division which, no doubt, has the greatest claim to be considered the poet's own, we have in l. 79 an extrasyllable before the pause after the first foot and the line is thus to be scanned: —

 Ital|ian, or French, | let him | speak to | me; I'll

It seems, however, well worthy of consideration, if preference should not be given to a different scansion, viz.: —

 Ital|ian, or French, | let'm speak | to me; | I will, &c.

Compare note XL. *Florentine* is, of course, a triple ending.

CCCVII.

Cap. It is perchance that you yourself were saved.

Twelfth Night, I, 2, 6.

This line should be spoken by one of the Sailors, to whom Viola
has expressly addressed herself; *what think you, sailors?*, she asks.
I have no doubt that the speech was transferred to the Captain by
the actors merely for want of a player capable of impersonating a
'*First Sailor*', the representatives of the Sailors being what were
called hired men and unfit to take part in the dialogue, such as
now-a-days are termed walking gentlemen. Similar combinations of
different characters for want of a sufficient number of actors are by
no means of rare occurrence; two very striking instances occur, the
one in A. II, sc. 4 of the present play (see *infra* note CCCXXI),
the other in K. Lear, IV, 7, where the Doctor and the Gentleman
'are distinct characters, and have separate prefixes' in the Quartos,
whilst 'according to the folio, the two parts were combined, and
played by the same actor' (see Collier's note *ad loc.*). — That *perchance* in this passage does not mean *perhaps,* but *by chance,* has
justly been remarked by Delius *ad loc.* and by Al. Schmidt, s. v.
Perchance.

CCCVIII.

After our ship did split,
When you and those poor number saved with you
Hung on our driving boat, I saw your brother.

Ib., I, 2, 9 seqq.

Instead of *those* Rowe (2nd ed.) reads *that*; Capell *this*; *the* Anon.
conj. Qy. read: —

After our ship did split,
When you and those — poor number! — saved with you
Hung on our driving boat, &c.?

CCCIX.

The like of him. Know'st thou this country?

Ib., I, 2, 21.

A catalectic verse; see note II. Dr. Abbott and his followers will no
doubt prefer to pronounce *country* as a trisyllable. With the help of
a slight alteration the verse might even be scanned as a syllable
pause line: —

The like | of him. | ᴗ Know|est thou | this coun|try?

I take the opportunity of adding that Twelfth Night is almost
entirely free from syllable pause lines, whereas they abound, e. g.,

in Antony and Cleopatra, in Cymbeline, Pericles, &c. To me this
seems to be a notable fact, apt to be made a starting-point for further
metrical disquisitions and to be admitted among what are called
metrical tests.

CCCX.

Sir And. What is 'pourquoi'? do or not do? I would I had
bestowed that time in the tongues that I have in fencing, dancing
and bear-baiting: O, had I but followed the arts!
Sir To. Then hadst thou had an excellent head of hair.
Sir And. Why, would that have mended my hair?
Sir To. Past question; for thou seest it will not curl by nature.
Sir And. But it becomes me well enough, does't not?
Sir To. Excellent; it hangs like flax on a distaff; &c.

Ib., I, 3, 96 seqq.

'The point of Sir Toby's jest', remarks Dr. Aldis Wright *ad loc.*,
'will be lost unless we remember that "tongues" and "tongs" were
pronounced alike, as was pointed out by Mr. Crosby of Zainsville
[Zanesville] in the American Bibliopolist, June, 1875 [p. 143].' —
This ingenious explanation, though it can hardly be disputed, does
not preclude the existence of a second quibble between *arts* and *hards*,
i. e. tow.

CCCXI.

Sir To. Wherefore are these things hid? wherefore have these
gifts a curtain before 'em? are they like to take dust, like Mistress
Mall's picture? *Ib., I, 3, 133 seqq.*

It seems chronologically impossible to me that this passage should
refer to Moll Cutpurse (Mary Frith). Moll Cutpurse is generally
said to have been born in 1584 (or even so late as 1589); consequently she was between 17. and 18. years old when Twelfth
Night was performed at the Middle Temple on Feb. 2, 1601—2.
At that time she did not yet enjoy the notoriety which made her
the heroine of John Day's 'Madde pranckes of mery Mall of the
Banckside' in 1610, and of Middleton and Dekker's 'Roaring Girl'
in 1611. These were no doubt the years when she had reached the
height of her disreputable career and become of sufficient interest to
have her portrait prefixed as a frontispiece to Middleton and Dekker's
play. I cannot think that she should ever have been thought a
worthy subject for the painter's brush; nor can I subscribe to the
explanations given by Dyce, but fully agree with Mr. John Fitchett
Marsh who shows that 'Mistress Mall' is Maria, Olivia's gentlewoman
(N. and Q., July 6, and Nov. 30, 1878). Maria is certainly not a
common servant, but in part at least the confidante of her mistress,

and her picture, executed not in oil, but in water-colours and done perhaps when she was in her teens, may well be imagined hanging in the room where Sir Toby and his weak-brained friend sit carousing, a room which does by no means belong to Olivia's drawing-rooms, but is something between a parlour and a buttery; perhaps it is even Maria's own parlour. Maria does not seem to care much for her picture; it is neglected and covered with dust. For be it remarked, Sir Toby does not at all say that Mistress Mall's picture is curtained, but that it has taken dust, a circumstance which, for all I know, has been overlooked or misinterpreted by all editors.

CCCXII.

Vio. On your attendance, my lord; here.

، *Ib., I, 4, 11.*

A slight transposition would certainly improve the line: —
On your attendance; *here, my lord.*

CCCXIII.

Oli. Cousin, cousin, how have you come so early by this lethargy? *Ib., I, 5, 131 seq.*

Either intentionally or unintentionally Olivia mistakes Sir Toby's belching for yawning.

CCCXIV.

I pray you, tell me if this be the lady of the house, for I never saw her. *Ib., I, 5, 182 seq.*

Before the words, *I pray you, &c.* a stage-direction, be it either, *To Maria,* or, *To the Attendants* should be added.

CCCXV.

Oli. Have you any commission from your lord to negotiate with my face? You are now out of your text: but we will draw the curtain and show you the picture. Look you, sir, such a one I was this present: is 't not well done? [*Unveiling.*

Ib., I, 5, 249 seqq.

Of all attempts at healing the corruption of the last sentence, the one made by Mr. P. A. Daniel comes nearest the mark. He proposes to read: *such a one, I, as this presents.* He should have added one more letter, viz.: I'*m* as, than which correction nothing can follow more closely the original *ductus literarum* (I'm as — I was). Read, therefore: 'such a one I'm, as this presents.' For the rest compare Westward Ho!, II, 3, init.: *Sir Gos[ling]*. So, draw those curtains, and let's see the pictures under them. [*The ladies unmask.*

CCCXVI.

Thy tongue, thy face, thy limbs, actions and spirit,
Do give thee five-fold blazon: not too fast: soft, soft!
Unless the master were the man. How now!
Even so quickly may one catch the plague?

Ib., I, 5, 311 seqq.

The twofold exclamation, *Soft, soft!* has been placed in an interjectional line by Dyce and regular metre has thus been restored. In my opinion, however, the chief break in Olivia's speech occurs in the next line and I should, therefore, prefer the following arrangement: —

Thy tongue, thy face, thy limbs, actions and spirit,
Do give thee five-fold blazon: not too fast!
Soft, soft! — unless the master were the man!
How now!
Even so quickly may one catch the plague?

Either of these two arrangements, Dyce's and mine, removes the Alexandrine and consequently one of them should be installed in the text.

CCCXVII.

Mal. She returns this ring to you, sir: you might have saved me my pains, to have taken it away yourself. She adds, moreover, that you should put your lord into a desperate. assurance she will none of him. *Ib., II, 2, 5 seqq.*

After *sir* Hanmer inserted the following clause: *for being your Lord's she'll none of it,* and some such insertion seems indeed to be required, as in I, 5, 321 Olivia charges Malvolio to tell Cesario, that she will none of it, viz. the ring, and in II, 2, 25 Cesario, in his soliloquy, repeats the words, *None of my lord's ring,* as having come from Olivia through her 'churlish messenger'. I, therefore, think it most likely that the missing words were, *she will none of your lord's ring.* This insertion, however, does not suffice to restore the passage, but at the same time renders a correction of the words, *she will none of him,* unavoidable, especially as they do not come from Olivia. Olivia says (I, 5, 323): *I am not for him,* and we expect to hear Malvolio repeat these very words. The passage as I imagine it to have been written by the poet, will then read thus: 'She returns this ring to you, sir; *she will none of your lord's ring.* You might have saved me my pains, to have taken it away yourself. She adds, moreover, that you should put your lord into a desperate assurance *she is not for him.'*

CCCXVIII.

Sir To. We did keep time, sir, in our catches. Sneck up!

Ib., II, 2, 101.

Theobald is quite right in adding the stage-direction: *Hiccoughs.* In order to produce the greatest possible similarity of sound we should write: *Snick up (Snick up — hiccup).*

CCCXIX.

Sir To. Out o' tune sir, ye lye:

Ib., II, 3, 122.

This reading of the Ff should never have been disturbed, except with respect to the pointing, in so far as an interrogation should be substituted for the comma after *sir,* and an exclamation for the colon after *lye*; moreover a comma is to be added after *tune.* The words are addressed to the clown who has roused Sir Toby's bile by telling him that he dares not 'bid him [Malvolio] go.' This impertinent remark, Sir Toby says, is 'out of tune' and a lie, and to prove it so he forthwith falls outh with Malvolio exhorting him not to overstep the bounds of his office as steward; after which he roundly bids him go: 'Go, sir, rub your chain with crums.' In order to exclude every doubt, two stage-directions might be added, viz.: *To the Clown* (before, *Out o' tune*) and *To Malvolio* (before, *Art any more &c.*).

CCCXX.

Sir To. She's a beagle, true-bred, and one that adores me: what o' that?
Ib., II, 3, 195 seq.

Dr. Aldis Wright has ingeniously pointed out that Maria is of diminutive stature and is chaffed on that account first by Viola (I, 5, 218: *Some mitigation for your giant, sweet lady*) and afterwards by Sir Toby (II, 3, 193: *Good night, Penthesilea*). He might have added the present line, for according to all old and modern authorities a beagle was — or is — a small dog. See Skeat, Etym. Dict., s. Beagle. It was used as a term of endearment and applied to persons of either sex; compare Dekker and Webster's Westward Ho, III, 4, init., where Mrs. Tenterhook says to Mr. Monopoly: *You are a sweet beagle.* The brevity of Maria's person is also alluded to in A. II, sc. 5, l. 16: *Here comes the little villain,* and in A. III, sc. 1, l. 70 seq.: *Look, where the youngest wren of nine comes.*

CCCXXI.

Now, good Cesario, but that piece of song,
That old and antique song we heard last night: &c.

Ib., II, 4, 2 seq.

This request of the Duke is replied to, not by Cesario, but by Curio,
a subordinate character, who informs his master that he who should
sing it, viz. Olivia's fool, is not here. But the Duke did not want
to hear the Clown sing, but Cesario, who in A. I, sc. 2, l. 67 seq.
has assured the Captain that he

'can sing
And speak to him [the Duke] in many sorts of music.'

And what business and right has Lady Olivia's fool to sing before
the Duke? After being introduced by Curio (l. 41) he is desired by
Orsino almost in the same words as Cesario was some minutes ago,
to sing 'the song we had last night.' Now, who was last night's
singer? Cesario or the Clown? And why does not Cesario sing
when desired by his master to do so? — It seems evident that
according to the poet's intention two singers were required for the
performance of our play: the one to sing in Orsino's palace (the
performer of Viola) and the other to do the same office in Lady
Olivia's house (the Clown). As, however, at some time or other,
the Lord Chamberlain's men could only boast of a single singer and
that one the Clown, they gave him access to the Duke's palace and
made him do the singing of both parts. Compare *supra* note CCCVII.

CCCXXII.

Sir To. Come thy ways, Signior Fabian.

Ib., II, 5, 1.

In A. II, sc. 3, l. 188 Maria proposes to plant the two knights, 'and
let the fool make a third', where Malvolio shall find the letter. In
the present scene they are being planted in Olivia's garden, but it
is not the fool who makes the third, but Fabian who is only now
introduced to the reader. As Fabian has been brought out of favour
with my lady by Malvolio, he is indeed a more legitimate partner
in the conspiracy, or, to say the least, a more deeply interested witness than the Clown of the severe joke practised on the puritanical
and malevolent steward whose name is by no means meaningless.
But if this was the poet's design from the beginning, why did he
make Maria mention the Clown as a third partaker? She might just
as well have hit on Fabian as companion of the two knights, so
much the more as she must have been aware how eager a spectator
he would be and that he would consider her joke a fit retribution.
I confess myself unable to clear away this difficulty.

12*

CCCXXIII.

Sir To. Here comes the little villain. [*Enter Maria.*] How
now, my metal of India?   *Ib., II, 5, 16 seq.*

'Metal' (*mettle*, in FA) cannot possibly be the true reading, for the
following reasons. 1. It cannot be shown that 'metal', without some
epithet intimating such a meaning, was ever used in the sense of
'gold'. Such a meaning, in my humble opinion, is a purely gratuitous assumption for the nonce. 2. India is not, and never was, rich
in gold, as California and Australia are now-a-days. It abounds,
however, in precious stones of the greatest beauty and value, and
Shakespeare, had he wished to compare Maria to some Indian treasure,
would certainly have bethought himself of those renowned Indian
jewels and diamonds instead of an Indian metal. 3. The metaphor
does not apply to Maria in a higher degree than to almost all persons of the female sex. 4. It is not at all in Sir Toby's vein to
compliment Maria in good earnest; on the contrary he keeps con-
tinually teasing her and has just now styled her 'a little villain'.
Under the circumstances I am fully persuaded that the later Ff exhibit the correct reading, viz. 'my *nettle* of India', and completely
agree with what has been advanced on this head by Singer in his
note *ad loc.* The nettle of India may possibly be the *Urtica crenu-
lata* which is a native of Bengal; see Heinr. Gräfe, *Handbuch der
Naturgeschichte der drei Reiche &c.* (Eisleben und Leipzig, 1838),
Vol. IIa, p. 630. However that may be, at all events Maria may well
be termed a little 'stinging nettle' (K. Richard II., III, 2, 18); by her
plot she stings Malvolio to the quick and she proves not much less
prickly to the Clown, to Sir Andrew and to Cesario whom in A. I,
sc. 5, l. 215 she desires to 'hoist sail'. Who knows but even Sir
Toby, with whom she is in love, may have experienced not only
her quick wit, but also her sharp tongue; that she is sharp-tongued
is admitted by Dr. Aldis Wright in his note on A. II, sc. 5, l. 139.
The Rev. Henry N. Ellacombe (The Plant-Lore and Garden-Craft of
Shakespeare, Exeter, 1878, p. 137) seems not to have been acquainted
with Singer's note.

CCCXXIV.

Mal. There is example for 't; the lady of the Strachy married
the yeoman of the wardrobe.   *Ib., II, 5, 44 seq.*

'The incident of a lady of high rank', Dr. Aldis Wright says in his
note *ad loc.,* 'marrying a servant is the subject of Webster's Duchess
of Malfi, who married the steward of her household, and would thus
have supplied Malvolio with the exact parallel to his own case of
which he was in search.' It seems most strange to me that Dr. Aldis

Wright should not have concluded this remark with substituting the *'lady of Malfy'* in the room of the 'lady of the Strachy' who owes her existence no doubt to a mistake of one of those privileged blunderers, viz. the transcribers and compositors. Why may not Shakespeare have read the story of the Duchess of Malfi in Paynter's Palace of Pleasure just as well as Webster? Certainly nothing could fall in more naturally with the context than the lady of *Malfi*, whereas the conjectural emendations on this passage chronicled in the Cambridge and Clarendon editions are singularly far-fetched and almost all of them worse than the lection of the Ff itself.

CCCXXV.

Fab. Now is the woodcock near the gin.
Sir To. O, peace! and the spirit of humours intimate reading aloud to him! *Ib., II, 5, 92 seqq.*

A nice discrimination between the characters of Fabian and Sir Toby leads to the suspicion that the prefixes of these two speeches have most likely been transposed and should be altered. Just as, according to the Cambridge Editors, ll. 39 and 43, in which peace is enjoined on Sir Andrew, belong to Fabian, so l. 92, which urges silence on Sir Toby, should be assigned to the same character, whose eagerness to hear the contents of the letter is naturally greater than Sir Toby's, this latter being in the secret. Read therefore: —

Sir To. Now is the woodcock near the gin.
Fab. O, peace! and the spirit of humours intimate reading aloud to him!

CCCXXVI.

Vio. Save thee, friend, and thy music: dost thou live by thy tabor? *Ib., III, 1, 1 seq.*

Thus FA; the true reading, however, is that of the later Ff: *dost thou live by* THE *tabor*, as there is certainly a play upon *tabor* which besides signifying a drum, was also used as the sign or name of an inn. According to Collier *ad loc.* 'the Clown's reply, "No, sir; I live by the Church", is not intelligible, if we do not suppose him to have wilfully misunderstood Viola to ask whether he lived near the sign of the tabor.' Very true, but if so, Collier should not have retained the reading of the first Folio, by which such a quibble is precluded.

CCCXXVII.

Grace and good disposition attend your ladyship.

Ib., III, 1, 146.

Hanmer most boldly reads *you* instead of *your ladyship* and the editors of the Globe Edition have adopted a different division of the lines, proposed by S. Walker, Crit. Exam., III, 87. However this deviation from the old copies seems to be unwarranted, as *ladyship* may well be taken to be a triple ending; scan: —

> Grace and | good dis|posi|tion attend | your la|dyship.

Compare A. III, sc. 3, l. 24 *(pardon me)*; A. III, sc. 3, l. 35 *(city did)*; A. III, sc. 4, l. 383 *(misery)*; A. IV, sc. 3, l. 17 *(followers)*; A. IV, sc. 3, l. 21 *(deceivable)*; A. V, sc. 1, l. 75 *(enemies)*; and A. V, sc. 1, l. 79 *(enemy)*. — It need hardly be added that the line has an extra syllable before the pause. Some editors print *'tend* or *tend,* which, after all, may be right.

CCCXXVIII.

Oli. O, what a deal of scorn looks beautiful &c.

Ib., III, 1, 157.

Staunton and the Rev. H. Hudson justly add the stage-direction: *Aside,* which cannot be missed.

CCCXXIX.

Oli. Yet come again; for thou perhaps mayst move
That heart, which now abhors, to like his love.

Ib., III, 1, 175 seq.

The editors, as far as I know them, keep *altum silentium* about this passage, which to them seems to offer no difficulty whatever. Schlegel and Gildemeister, both of them classical translators, refer 'that heart' to Olivia's heart, which perhaps may be moved to like his love, i. e. Orsino. But may not Olivia be presumed with far greater probability to express a hope that Cesario, if coming back, may move his own heart to like his love, i. e. Olivia, whom it now abhors? Schlegel renders the lines as follows: —

> "O komm zurück! Du magst dies Herz bethören,
> Ihn, dessen Lieb' es hasst, noch zu erhören.

In my judgment it should be: —

> O komm zurück! Du magst *dein* Herz bethören,
> *Sie, deren* Lieb' es hasst, noch zu erhören.

Gildemeister's version might no less easily be altered. According to him Olivia says: —

> Komm wieder nur, du rührst mein Herz vielleicht,
> Dass es für den Verhassten sich erweicht.

Should it not rather be: —

> Komm wieder nur, du rührst *dein* Herz vielleicht,
> Dass es für *die Verhasste* sich erweicht?

CCCXXX.

> *Oli.* I have sent after him: he says he'll come;
> How shall I feast him? what bestow of him?
> For youth is bought more oft than begg'd or borrow'd.
> I speak too loud.   *Ib., III, 4, 1 seqq.*

The words: *he says he'll come* are 'explained by Warburton to mean "I suppose now, or admit now, he says he'll come, &c."' Dyce, *ad loc.* According to Mr. Rolfe, *ad loc.*, they are 'apparently = Suppose he says he'll come.' In my opinion this is too strained an explanation as to be acceptable or even grammatically admissible. 'Theobald', Mr. Rolfe continues, 'made it read "*Say, he* will come."' The Rev. H. Hudson grants that 'the concessive sense is evidently required, not the affirmative' and 'that the simple transposition [*says he* instead of *he says*] gets the same sense [as Theobald's alteration] naturally enough; the subjunctive being often formed in that way.' I think differently. The first four lines are evidently spoken aside by Olivia, as confirmed by her own words, *I speak too loud*; only in the fifth line she addresses Maria. It is, however, in the natural course of things that she should have conversed with Maria on the subject before and that the latter should have tried to raise the drooping spirit of her enamoured mistress by consolatory words. I should accordingly feel no hesitation in reading: —

> *Oli.* [*Aside*]. I have sent after him: *she* says he'll come;
> How shall I feast him? what bestow of him?
> For youth is bought more oft than begg'd or borrow'd.
> I speak too loud.
> [*To Maria*] Where is Malvolio? &c.

Olivia may easily be imagined to accompany the words, *she says he'll come* with a slight motion of either hand or head towards Maria.

CCCXXXI.

> *Sec. Off.* Come, sir, I pray you, go.
> *Ant.* Let me speak a little. This youth that you see here
> I snatch'd one half out of the jaws of death &c.
>   *.Ib., III, 4, 392 seqq.*

All critical efforts notwithstanding l. 393 has remained a metrical
stumbling block. The words *a little,* besides spoiling the metre, im-
press the reader as ridiculously superfluous and have probably slipped
from their original place which was in the second half of the preceding line, for I have little doubt that in the poet's manuscript this
line was complete, exactly as it is the case with lines 381, 386,
and 391 of this very scene. In a word, I suspect the original
wording of the passage to have been somewhat to the following
effect: —

> *Sec. Off.* Come, sir, I pray you, go.
> *Ant.*   *Tarry a little*
> *And* let me speak. This youth that you see here &c.

Stay but a little would, of course, do equally well as *Tarry a little.*

CCCXXXII.

> *Sir To.* Hold, sir, or I'll throw your dagger o'er the house.
>
> *Ib., IV, 1, 30 seq.*

From these words it appears that Sebastian is belabouring Sir Andrew with his dagger; daggers, in the time of Elizabeth, were long
enough to be used for such a purpose.

CCCXXXIII.

> *Oli.* If it be aught to the old tune, my lord,
> It is as fat and fulsome to mine ear
> As howling after music.
> *Duke.*   Still so cruel? '
> *Oli.* Still so constant, lord?
> *Duke.* What, to perverseness? &c.
>
> *Ib., V, 1, 111 seqq.*

Mr. P. A. Daniel (Notes and Conjectural Emendations of Certain
Doubtful Passages in Shakespeare's Plays, 1870, p. 43) ingeniously
proposes to add '*lady*' to the Duke's question: *Still so cruel?*
Mr. Daniel is right in so far as he has felt the want of an even
balance in the two short speeches of the Duke and Lady Olivia, but
his addition is an incumbrance on the metre and the equipoise of the
two speeches may be attained just as well by the omission of '*lord*'
(after *constant*) as by the addition of '*lady*'. One of these two conjectural emendations, either Mr. Daniel's or mine, should be adopted;
if Mr. Daniel's, the Duke's speech should not be joined to the preceding verse, but form a short line by itself.

CCCXXXIV.

Vio. If nothing lets to make us happy both
But this my masculine usurp'd attire,
Do not embrace me till each circumstance
Of place, time, fortune, do cohere and jump
That I am Viola: which to confirm,
I'll bring you to a captain in this town,
Where lie my maiden weeds; by whose gentle help
I was preserved to serve this noble count.

Ib., V, 1, 256 seqq.

Viola is here made to speak nonsense. 'If nothing lets to make us happy', she says to Sebastian who, being now convinced of his sister's identity, is eager to embrace her as such, 'but my masculine attire, then do *not* embrace me' &c., instead of saying the very contrary, viz. then you may safely embrace me, for I have only usurped this boys' dress and my maiden weeds are lying at a captain's house in this town. Arrange, therefore: —

Vio. Do not embrace me till each circumstance
Of place, time, fortune, do cohere and jump
That I am Viola: which to confirm, —
If nothing lets to make us happy both
But this my masculine usurp'd attire, —
I'll bring you to a captain in this town,
Where lie my maiden weeds; by whose gentle help
I was preserved to serve this noble count.

I should add by the way, that the two conjectural emendations *maid's* and *preferr'd* instead of *maiden* and *preserved* seem to admit of little doubt.

CCCXXXV.

And leave you to your graver steps. Hermione.

The Winter's Tale, I, 2, 173.

Mr. Fleay, in his paper entitled 'Metrical Tests applied to Shakespeare' and incorporated in Dr. Ingleby's Occasional Papers on Shakespeare (London, 1881), gives a survey of all those lines in the poet's plays which he takes to be Alexandrines and therefore holds to constitute an important element in those Metrical Tests from which he proceeds to conclusions and inferences respecting the chronology and authorship of the plays. Now it was to be expected that all these lines should have been carefully examined and incontrovertibly scanned before being set down as Alexandrines; but, on the contrary, it can easily be shown that many of them have been misunderstood with respect to their metre and that, far from being Alexandrines, they are merely mistaken blank verse. At p. 90 seq. Mr. Fleay gives a list of all the apparent Alexandrines in The Winter's Tale. 'I have thought it desirable', he says, 'to print the Alexandrines [in The Winter's Tale] *in extenso* with the cesuras marked. I have, in this instance, included all possibly doubtful cases in which the endings are probably trisyllabic, that the reader may have all the evidence before him. The preponderance (next to the regular lines) of lines with pause after the fifth foot is very striking. Where no cesura is marked, I believe the line to be one of trisyllabic feminine ending.'

Although I have not taken the trouble of checking Mr. Fleay's list to satisfy myself of its completeness, yet I have lighted on the following three pseudo-Alexandrines which are not included in it, viz.: —

I, 2, 173: And leave you to your graver steps. Hermione

II, 2, 43: Your honour and your goodness is so evident

II, 3, 23: Take it on her; Camillo and Polixenes.

Pronounce, of course, *Hermi'ne, ev'dent,* and *Polix'nes.*

Mr. Fleay's list will be considerably reduced in number, if all lines with what he calls trisyllabic feminine endings are cut out, which lines, however, he takes to be Alexandrines, since be has marked their cesuras. They are the following: —

I, 2 [not 1], 33: He's beat from his best ward. Well said, Hermi'ne

I, 2, 55: My pris'ner? or my guest? by your dread 'Ver'ly'

I, 2, 263: Are such allowed infirmities that hon'sty.
Compare S. Walker, Versification, p. 206.

I, 2, 287 [not 286]: Of laughing with a sigh; a note infall'ble

I, 2, 344: As friendship wears at feasts, keep with Bohemia

II, 1, 20: Into a goodly bulk: good time encount'r her.
Compare S. Walker, Versification, p. 67.

II, 1, 53: So eas'ly open? By his great author'ty.
Compare S. Walker, Versification, p. 205.

II, 1, 163 [not 164]: Our forceful instigation! Our prerog'tive

II, 1, 185: Of stuff'd sufficiency: now from the or'cle

II, 2, 46: So meet for this great errand. Please your lad'ship

II, 3, 42: Away with that audacious lady! Antig'nus.
Besides a triple ending this line has an extra syllable before the pause.

II, 3, 189: Like offices of pity. Sir, be prosp'rous

III, 2, 209: Do not repent these things, for they are heavier

IV, 4, 476: More straining on for plucking back; not foll'wing

IV, 4, 518: I'll hear you by and by. He's irremov'ble.

> The anonymous conjecture *immovable* (recorded in the Cambridge Edition) would not influence the scansion, but requires the reading *He is*.

IV, 4, 576: There is some sap in this. A course more prom'sing.

 V, 1, 95: That e'er the sun shone bright on. O Hermi'ne

 V, 1, 112 [not 111]: The rarest of all women. Go, Cleom'nes

 V, 3, 3:   I did not well, I meant well. All my serv'ces

 V, 3, 144: And take her by the hand whose worth and hon'sty.

A second class of pseudo-Alexandrines consists of those lines that have a triple ending, or an extra syllable, before the pause. To this class belong the following instances in Mr. Fleay's list, viz.: —

I, 2, 19 [not I, 1, 68]: I'll no gainsaying. Press me not, b'seech
you, so.

> Hanmer's and Capell's conjectures are needless.

I, 2, 22 [not I, 1, 21]: Were there necess'ty in your request,
although.

> Should the pause after *necessity* be deemed too slight to admit of an extra syllable before it, the last syllable of *necessity* might, perhaps, be lost in the pronunciation of the following *in*.

I, 2, 161: Will you take eggs for money? No, m'lord, I'll fight.

> For the contraction *m'lord* Mr. Fleay may be referred to his own edition of Marlowe's Edward II., p. 122. Possibly, however, the arrangement of the Cambridge Edition (two short lines) is right.

I, 2, 391: As you are certainly a gentl'man; thereto.

> See S. Walker, Versification, p. 116 and 189. Capell's conjecture *are, certain, a* is needless.

I, 2, 410: I mean to utter 't, or both yourself and me.

> See S. Walker, Versification, p. 102.

I, 2, 454: Must it be vi'lent? and as he does conceive

II, 2, 11: Th' access of gentle vis'tors. Is't lawful, pray you

II, 3, 167: To save | the inn|'cent; an|y thing pos|sible.

> *Any thing* is to be pronounced as a dissyllable; compare Fair Em, ed. Delius, p. 48 (To any such as she is underneath the sun); ib., p. 50 (Nor heard any ways to rid my hands of them; see note LXXXII); Mucedorus, ed. Delius, p. 26 (If any body ask for me, make some excuse; see note CXLV); Hamlet, II, 1, 107 (What, have you given him any hard words of late?);
> . B. Jonson, Catiline, II, 1, 24 (Any way, so thou wilt do it, good impert'nence); Field, A Woman is a Weathercock, in Dodsley, ed. Hazlitt, XI, 15 (Whiter than any thing but her

neck and hands). Hanmer's conjecture *what's* for *any thing* is therefore needless.

III, 2, 5:   Of being tyr'nous, since we so openly

or: Of being tyrannous, since we so op'nly

III, 2, 241 [not 249]: Shall be my recreation: so long as nature

III, 3, 2:   The deserts of Bohemia? Ay, m'lord; and fear

V, 3, 25 [not 24]: Thou art Hermi'ne; or rather, thou art she.

See Abbott, s. 469.

A third class of lines will be reduced to regular blank verse by means of simple contractions; such are: —

I, 2, 108: Th' oth'r for some while a friend. Too hot, too hot!

For the monosyllabic pronunciation of *other* compare S. Walker, Versification, p. 108 (where this very line is quoted) and Abbott, s. 466.

I, 2, 227: Of head-piece extraord'n'ry? lower messes.

Compare As You Like It, III, 5, 42: I see no more in you than in the ord'n'ry.

I, 2, 408: That I think hon'rable: therefore mark my counsel

II, 1, 107: With an aspect more fav'rable. Good my lords.

See S. Walker, Versification, p. 274. There is no need of Hanmer's conjecture *aspect of more favour.*

IV, 4, 401: Contract us 'fore these witnesses. Come, your hand.

Pronounce *witness.* See S. Walker, Versification, p. 244, and Abbott, s. 471.

IV, 4, 504: As you've e'er been my father's honour'd friend.

See S. Walker, Crit. Exam., I, 81 *(As y' have e'er, &c.).*

IV, 4, 531: To have them recompensed as thought on. Well, m'lord.

Thus S. Walker, according to the Cambridge Edition.

The remaining number of Mr. Fleay's list is still farther lessened by the correction of those lines that are either wrongly arranged or manifestly corrupted. Thus, e. g., I, 2, 375 seq. (not I, 1, 371) should probably be printed as two short lines, as it has been done in the folio and in a number of modern editions, although *knów, m'lord* might be taken for a double ending: —

That changeth thus his manners. I dare not know, m'lord.

In II, 1, 182 seq. the words *in post* do not belong to the first, but to the second line and the preposition *to,* in the latter, is to be contracted with *Apollo's:* —

Most piteous to be wild, I have dispatched
In post to sacred Delphos, t' Apollo's temple.

In the line II, 3, 21 the connective *And* seems to be an interpolation and was therefore rightly omitted by Capell: —

in himself too mighty,
In's parties, his alliance; let him be, &c.

From line II, 3, 149 the words *we beg* have been justly transferred to the following line by Hanmer: —

So to esteem of us, and on our knees
We beg as recompense of our dear serv'ces.

Hanmer's correction *service* instead of *services* is needless. The lines IV, 4, 375 seq. should be arranged thus: —

Or Ethiopian's tooth, or the fanned snow
That's bolted by the northern blasts twice o'er.
    Pol. What follows this?
How prettily &c.

There is no need of Dyce's conjecture *Ethiop's*.

Thus almost all of Mr. Fleay's list of Alexandrines in The Winter's Tale has vanished like the banquet in The Tempest, and without any 'quaint device' having been resorted to. The remainder is, indeed, incomparably small; and possibly even these few exceptional lines may not have been originally Alexandrines. (Alexandrines in The Winter's Tale and K. Richard II. Privately printed, 1881.)

CCCXXXVI.

Here's a stay
That shakes the rotten carcass of old Death
Out of his rags.

King John, II, 1, 455 seqq.

This is the reading of the folio, of which W. N. Lettsom has justly remarked, that '*stay* is perhaps the last word that could have come from Shakespeare.' Johnson has conjectured *flaw* which S. Walker (Crit. Exam., II, 294) thinks 'is indisputably right'; it bears, however, too little resemblance to the old reading, and, besides, the idea of a gust of wind seems to be foreign to the context. The same objections lie against Mr. Spedding's conjectures of *storm* and *story*. Beckett and Singer propose *say* which is far too weak in the mouth of the Bastard. I think we should read, Here's a *bray*. The Heralds both of the besiegers and the besieged play a conspicuous part in this scene and have just opened the parley with the blowing of their trumpets; King Philip says (II, 1, 204 seq.): —

You loving men of Angiers, Arthur's subjects,
Our trumpet call'd you to this gentle parle.

Under such circumstances the citizen of Angiers may be said not inappropriately to 'bray out' his defiance to the kings like a 'harsh-resounding' trumpet (see K. Richard II., I, 3, 135: With harsh-resounding trumpets' dreadful bray) and, in the Bastard's language, by such a clang to shake 'the rotten carcass of old Death out of his rags.' Compare Hamlet, I, 4, 11 seq.: —

> The kettledrum and trumpet thus bray out
> The triumph of his pledge —

and Edward III., I, 2 (ed. Delius, 9): —

> How much they will deride us in the North;
> And in their vile, uncivil, skipping jigs,
> Bray forth their conquest and our overthrow,
> Even in the barren, bleak, and fruitless air.

See also Faerie Queene, I, 3, 23: —

> Whom overtaking, they gan loudly bray.

Greene, Dorastus and Fawnia (Shakespeare's Library, ed. Hazlitt, I, IV, 43): who as in a fury brayed out these bitter speaches. Milton's English Poems, ed. R. C. Browne (London, 1873) I, 228 and 367. Speeches of Lord Macaulay (London, 1875, p. 180 b): The Orangeman raises his war-whoop: Exeter Hall sets up its bray. (The Athenæum, June 22, 1867, 821. — Shakespeare's dramatische Werke nach der Uebersetzung von Schlegel und Tieck, herausgegeben von der Deutschen Shakespeare-Gesellschaft, I, 235. — Transactions of the New Shakspere Society, 1880—2, Part I, p. 107.)

CCCXXXVII.

> The grappling vigour and rough frown of war
> Is cold in amity and painted peace.

Ib., III, 1, 104 seq.

Hanmer reads *cool'd*; Capell, *clad*; Staunton proposes *coil'd*, and Mr. Collier's corrected folio has *faint in peace*. Mr. Collier's manuscript corrector, whoever he may have been, has rightly felt the want of symmetrical agreement between the two clauses of the second line, but the remedy by which he has meant to restore it, seems to be wrong. I rather incline to the belief that Shakespeare wrote: —

> Is *scolding* amity and painted peace.

Constance reproaches King Philip with perjury and denounces his warlike preparations as a sham; they are, she says, not more dreadful than amity that scolds a friend, or peace which is painted to look like war. The required harmony of the sentence is thus very naturally recovered; and I need not dwell on the easy misapprehension by which the words *Is scolding,* particularly when spoken, could be transmuted into *Is cold in.* (The Athenæum, June 22, 1867, 821. — Shakespeare's dramatische Werke nach der Uebersetzung von Schlegel und Tieck, herausgeg. von der Deutschen Shakesp.-Gesellsch., I, 238.)

CCCXXXVIII.

For I do see the cruel pangs of death
Right in thine eye.

Ib., V, 4, 59 seq.

Right in thine eye certainly gives a sense, but so weak and poor a sense that it is beneath Shakespeare. It can neither be supported by Coriolanus, III, 3, 70: —

Within thine eyes sat twenty thousand deaths,

nor by Byron, The Island, I, 4: —

Full in thine eyes is waved the glittering blade.

Right, in our passage, is merely an expletive. Hanmer and Warburton therefore conjectured *Pight in thine eye (eyes)*; Capell, *Fight in thine eye*; Collier's so-called manuscript corrector, *Bright in thine eye*; Brae, *Riot in thine eye.* This last suggestion has been cited by Dr. Ingleby (Shakespeare Hermeneutics, or The Still Lion, London, 1875) 116 with 'unqualified satisfaction'. Collier's conjecture, although approved by Singer and Knight, has been incontrovertibly refuted by Dyce *ad loc.* I think the compositor anticipated *right* from the following line ('that intends old right') and am convinced that the true reading is: —

For I do see the cruel pangs of death
Writhing thine eye.

(The Athenæum, June 22, 1867, 821. — Shakespeare's dramatische Werke nach der Uebersetzung von Schlegel und Tieck, herausgegeben von der Deutschen Shakespeare-Gesellschaft, 2. Aufl., I, 247. The first edition, I, 247, has the misprint *Whithin* for *Writhing.*)

CCCXXXIX.

Enter BASTARD *and* HUBERT, *seuerally.*

Hub. Whose there? Speake hoa, speake quickely, or I shoote.
Bast. A Friend. What art thou?
Hub. Of the part of England.
Bast. Whether doest thou go?
Hub. What's that to thee?
Why may not I demand of thine affaires,
As well as thou of mine?
Bast. Hubert, I thinke.
Hub. Thou hast a perfect thought.

Ib., V, 6, 1 seqq.

This is the reading of the folio and it need not be pointed out that, as far as the distribution of the speeches is concerned, it is a perfect tangle. Attempts at emendation have been made by W. W. Lloyd,

Dyce (3d Ed., V, 98), and Mr. H. H. Vaughan (New Readings and New Renderings of Shakespeare's Tragedies, London, 1878, I, 84 seq.). Dyce differs from the folio only in the following lines: —

> *Hub.* What's that to thee?
> *Bast.*   Why may not I demand
> Of thine affairs, as well as thou of mine?
> Hubert, I think.

He adopts, he says, as absolutely necessary, this portion of the new distribution of the speeches at the commencement of this scene which was recommended to him by W. W. Lloyd. Mr. Vaughan proposes the following arrangement: —

> *Hub.* Who's there? Speak ho! speak quickly, or I shoot.
> *Bast.* A friend: what art thou?
> *Hub.*   Of the part of England.
> Whither dost thou go?
> *Bast.*   What is that to thee?
> *Hub.* 'What's that to thee?' — Why may not I demand
> Of thine affairs — as well as thou of mine?
> *Bast.* Hubert, I think.
> *Hub.*   Thou hast a perfect thought.

Thus, Mr. Vaughan says, the metre becomes perfect, whereas, according to him, the metrical defect is not remedied by Dyce's arrangement. In my opinion both Dyce's and Mr. Vaughan's alterations are insufficient and do not improve the text; of Mr. Lloyd's arrangement, as it is not contained in his Critical Essays on the Plays of Shakespeare (London, 1875), I know nothing except what has been imparted by Dyce. If we bear in mind that throughout the play the Bastard is hot-headed, aggressive and over-bearing, whereas Hubert is of a sedate temperament and generally stands on his defence, it will seem quite natural that it is not the latter, but the former, who opens the dialogue with the impetuous question: 'Who's there? Speak, ho!', to which he immediately adds a threat. It speaks greatly in favour of this supposition that in the stage-direction the name of the Bastard is placed first. I feel therefore convinced that the verses should be distributed as follows: —

> *Bast.* Who's there? Speak, ho! speak quickly, or I shoot.
> *Hub.* A friend.
> *Bast.*   What art thou?
> *Hub.*   Of the part of England.
> Whither dost thou go?
> *Bast.* What's that to thee?
> *Hub.*   Why may not I demand
> Of thine affairs as well as thou of mine?
> *Bast.* Hubert, I think.
> *Hub.*   Thou hast a perfect thought.

(Shakespeare's dramatische Werke nach der Uebersetzung von Schlegel und Tieck, herausgegeben durch die Deutsche Shakespeare-Gesellschaft, I, 247. — The Athenæum, June 22, 1867, 821.)

CCCXL.

Let it be so: and you, my noble prince,
With other princes that may best be spared,
Shall wait upon your father's funeral.

Ib., V, 7, 96 seqq.

S. Walker (Crit. Exam., I, 293) believes the word *princes* to be a corruption, the transcriber's or compositor's eye having been caught by the word *prince* in the preceding line. Dyce and the Cambridge Editors concur in this opinion, without, however, making an attempt at restoring the passage. The compositor, in my opinion, by mistake repeated a wrong word from the preceding verse; instead of *princes* he ought to have repeated *nobles,* for Shakespeare in all probability wrote: —

With other *nobles* that may best be spared.

(The Athenæum, June 22, 1867, 821. — Shakespeare's dramatische Werke nach der Uebersetzung von Schlegel und Tieck, herausgegeben von der Deutschen Shakespeare-Gesellschaft, I, 248.) .

CCCXLI.

Gaunt. As near as I could sift him on that argument.

*Richard II., I, 1, 12.**

It gives me great pleasure to subscribe to Mr. Fleay's remark (*apud* Ingleby, p. 75) that this is not an Alexandrine, but a regular blank verse with a triple ending.

CCCXLII.

K. Richard.　　　　　　Rage must be withstood:
Give me his gage: lions make leopards tame.
Mow. Yea, but not change his spots.

Ib., I, 1, 173 seqq.

The Clarendon Press Editors remark on these lines: 'Pope altered this to "*their* spots"; but Mowbray is quoting the text, Jeremiah XIII, 23.' Besides this text the poet at the same time may have had in his mind Lyly's Epistle Dedicatorie (before his 'Euphues') to

---

* With a few exceptions the above notes on K. Richard II. were first published in Prof. Kölbing's Englische Studien, XII, 186—197.

Sir William West, Knight, Lord Delaware, where we meet with the following passage (according to the edition of 1579, in the British Museum): 'The fairest Leopard is sette downe with his spots, the sweetest Rose with his prickles, the finest Veluet with his bracke.' In the quarto 1581 (the Grenville copy) the wording is somewhat different, viz.: 'The fairest Leopard is made with his spots, the finest cloth with his list, the smoothest shooe hath his laste.' Compare Lyly's Euphues, ed. by Arber, p. 202, and Lyly's Euphues, &c. Ed. by Dr. Friedrich Landmann (Heilbronn, 1887), Preface, p. 3. 'The Leopard with his spots' would seem to have been a proverbial phrase.

CCCXLIII.

Lord marshal, command our officers at arms.

Ib., I, 1, 204.

In addition to his list of Alexandrines in The Winter's Tale Mr. Fleay (1. c., p. 72 seq.) prints a complete list of all the Alexandrines in K. Richard II. (54 in all) and is much surprised at their unusual number, which, he assures his readers, is twice as large as that in any unadulterated play anterior to Measure for Measure. He, moreover, declares many of the lines in this list to bc most unsatisfactory to the ear and would therefore 'rather see in this peculiarity a proof of incorrect printing or carelessness in revising the original 1593 copy for the press in 1597, than a sudden alteration of style hastily adopted and as hastily abandoned.' At p. 80 he declares these same Alexandrines to be 'printers' or editors' verse, not Shakespeare's'. Be it so; but what value can then be ascribed to them as metrical tests in the investigation of the chronology and authorship of the plays? 'A large number of these Alexandrines', he goes on to say, 'demand pitiless correction', and such correction he then applies to some of them, although on p. 76 he wishes it to be clearly understood, that he 'would not (except in re-arranging some few divisions of lines) on any account interfere with the received text editorially by inserting emendations on these hypothetical grounds.' In my opinion such emendations are much less needed than Mr. Fleay seems to think, and those that are needed should, of course, be inserted in the text. Let us take, for instance, the very first line adduced by Mr. Fleay (I, 1, 204): —

Lord mareshal, command | our officers at arms,

for thus Mr. Fleay prints it, whereas the folio reads *Marshall*. For my part, I have not the least doubt that this is no Alexandrine at all, but a regular blank verse with the familiar extra syllable before the pause; that the pause falls after the first foot can hardly be a matter of surprise. The line II, 1, 141 (No. 3): —

(I do) beseech your majesty | impute his words,

is to be corrected in Mr. Fleay's opinion by the omission of *I do*;
it requires, however, no change at all, *majesty* being a triple ending
before the pause. The same scansion occurs again in III, 3, 70
(No. 31): —

Controlling majesty: alack, alack for woe,

as also in V, 3, 25 (No. 47), where Mr. Fleay has found it out: —

God save your grace. I do beseech your majesty.

With respect to No. 6 (II, 1, 254) Mr. Fleay might likewise have
abstained from a change, although he shields himself by the reading
of the folio which omits the adjective *noble*: —

That which his (noble) ancestors achieved with blows.

May not the original scansion have been *anc'stors* or rather *ance'tors*
and *'chieved*? That the rapid dissyllabic pronunciation of *ancestors*
and *ancestry* was by no means owing to the straits of the versifiers
is proved by the notable fact that *ance'trie* occurs in a prose passage
in B. Jonson's Every Man in his Humour, I, 3 (Fol., Vol. I, p. 13):
'Mine ance'trie came from a kings belly, no worse man.' In the line
II, 2, 29 (No. 8): —

Persuades me it is otherwise: howe'er it be,

Mr. Fleay thinks it necessary to expunge *it is*. There can be no
doubt, however, that *otherwise* is to be pronounced as a dissyllable
just as in Beaumont and Fletcher's King and no King, III, 3 (quoted
by S. Walker, Versification, p. 108): —

Otherwise, I think, I shall not love you more.

Compare what has been remarked in the foregoing note on The Winter's Tale, I, 2, 108. Scan therefore: —

Persuades | me it | is oth'r|wise: howe'er | it be.

Nos. 10 (II, 2, 53) and 18 (II, 3, 55): —

The Lord Northumberland, his son young Henry Percy
And in it are the Lords of York, Berkley, and Seymour

may also be considered as blank verse, provided that in the former
Northumberland be pronounced as a trisyllable (compare Abbott, s. 469),
and that in the latter *in it* and *the Lords* be contracted: *in 't* and
th' Lords. How the next line (II, 3, 120; No. 19): —

A wandering vagabond; my rights and royalties

could have been mistaken for an Alexandrine by a critic who has
been taught by S. Walker and Dr. Abbott, it is difficult to understand; *royalties* is, of course, to be pronounced as a dissyllable.
Compare III, 3, 113: —

Than for his lineal royalties and to beg.

The same remedy provides for Nos. 24 and 35 (III, 1, 9 and IV, 1, 89): —

> A happy gentleman in blood and lineaments
> To all his lands and signories: when he's return'd.

In other words, *lineaments* and *signories* are to be pronounced as triple endings.

From the line III, 3, 30 (No. 28): —

> O belike it is the bishop of Carlisle

Mr. Fleay disjoins the interjection *O* (omitted altogether by Pope) and places it in a separate line; why not rather pronounce *belike* as a monosyllable *(b'like)*? See Note CCLV. An interjectional line is also resorted to by Mr. Fleay with respect to No. 30 (III, 3, 45): —

> The which | how far off from the mind of Bolingbroke.

In my opinion, the words *The which* are ill qualified for a separate line; pronounce *Bolingbroke* as a triple ending and the metre is unobjectionable.

In the line V, 2, 70 (No. 42): —

> I do beseech you, pardon me; I may not show it,

Mr. Fleay again omits *I do,* just as in No. 3; I think *pardon me,* both here and in A. II, sc. 2, l. 105, should be pronounced as a triple ending; *pardon'd thee* (V, 2, 117) is likewise used as a triple ending before the pause. Compare notes CLXXVII and CCCLXXIV.

By the arrangement proposed with respect to No. 46 (V, 3, 24): —

> What means our cousin, that he stares and looks so wildly?

the lines would be unwarrantably torn; the division of the lines as given in the Globe Edition seems far preferable. Perhaps, however, the words *and looks* should be omitted as an interpolation. A similar surplusage seems to be discernible in the adverb *freely* in No. 38 (IV, 1, 326: My lord, before I freely speak my mind herein) although no objection can be raised to either placing (with the Cambridge Editors) the vocative *My lord* in a separate line, or to omitting it, as it has been done in the later quartos and the folios.

I subjoin two more pseudo-Alexandrines taken at random from other plays which, in my opinion, Mr. Fleay has not succeeded in either scanning or correcting rightly.

The Merchant of Venice, II, 9, 28: —

> Which pries not to th' interior, but like the martlet.

Which pries, according to Mr. Fleay (p. 81), may stand in a separate line, or the cesura may be after the eighth syllable. Neither the one, nor the other. Scan: —

> Which pries | not to | th' inte|rior, but like | the mart|let.

The line has an extra syllable before the pause.

Antony and Cleopatra, II, 1, 38: —

The ne'er lust-wearied Antony. I cannot hope.

'Possibly', says Mr. Fleay (p. 87), 'pronounce *can't*, but I prefer making the line an Alexandrine.' The line will then be an Alexandrine of Mr. Fleay's making, but it is certainly none of Shakespeare's. *Antony* is a triple ending before the pause; see Abbott, s. 469. Compare l. 20 of the very same scene: —

Looking for Antony. But all the charms of love,

and Robert Garnier's Cornelia translated by Thomas Kyd (Dodsley, ed. Hazlitt, V, 232): —

Whom fear'st thou then, Mark Antony. — The hateful crew.

(Alexandrines in the Winter's Tale and K. Richard II. Privately printed, 1881.)

CCCXLIV.

Who, when they see the hours ripe on earth,
Will rain hot vengeance on offenders' heads.

Ib., I, 2, 7 seq.

All editors, as far as they are known to me, agree in declaring *hours,* which is the uniform reading of all old and modern editions, to be a dissyllable. I do not think so, but am convinced that Shakespeare wrote: —

Who, when they see the *hour is* ripe on earth, &c.

The singular *hour* is certainly required; compare 2 Henry IV., IV, 5, 97: 'Before thy hour be ripe', and 1 Henry IV., I, 3, 294: 'When time is ripe.' (The Athenæum, Sept. 3, 1887, p. 320.)

CCCXLV.

Of thy adverse pernicious enemy:
Rouse up thy youthful blood, be valiant and live.

Ib., I, 3, 82 seq.

S. Walker, Crit. Exam., I, 281, omits *adverse* and transfers *Rouse up* to the preceding line; Mr. Fleay declares the second line to be an Alexandrine. In my opinion, *Rouse up* belongs indeed to l. 82, there is, however, no occasion of expunging *adverse, enemy* being a triple ending before the pause. Arrange, therefore: —

Of thy adverse pernicious enemy: rouse up
Thy youthful blood, be valiant and live.

(Kölb., Engl. Stud., XI, 363.)

CCCXLVI.

K. Richard.   What says. he?
North.   Nay, nothing; all is said.
Ib., II, 1, 148.

Capell (followed by Steevens) inserted *now* after *he*, and S. Walker (Crit. Exam., III, 126) agrees with him, whilst Mr. Lettsom in a footnote offers a conjecture of his own. Abbott, s. 482, dissyllabizes *Nay.* In my conviction the verse either belongs to the category of syllable pause lines: ——

What says | he? *_* | Nay, no|thing; all | is said,

or *What* is a monosyllabic foot and the verse to be scanned thus: ——

What | says he? | Nay, no|thing; all | is said.

CCCXLVII.

Then thrice-gracious queen,
More than your lord's departure weep not: more's not seen;
Or if it be, 'tis with false sorrow's eye,
Which for things true weeps things imaginary.
Ib., II, 2, 24 seqq.

Qq: *more is,* instead of *more's.* Abbott, p. 402, takes l. 25 to be an Alexandrine. Arrange: ——

Then thrice-gracious queen,
More than your lord's departure weep not: more is
Not seen; or if't be, 'tis with false sorrow's eye,
Which for things true weeps things imaginary.

Not, in l. 25, and *be,* in l. 26, are extra syllables before the pause.

CCCXLVIII.

Queen.   Now God in heaven forbid!
Ib., II, 2, 51.

The tame and poor expletive *Now* does ill suit the agitated and disturbed state of mind of the Queen. May not the poet have written: *No!* God in heaven forbid!? The import of these two readings can best be shown on the stage by an intelligent actress.

CCCXLIX.

Sirrah, get thee to Plashy, to my sister Gloucester.
Ib., II, 2, 90.

Hazlitt justly places *Sirrah* in a line by itself. The same arrangement is advocated by Mr. Fleay, l. c., p. 74.

CCCL.

What, are there no posts dispatched for Ireland?

Ib., II, 2, 103.

'To make the metre smooth', say the Clarendon Press Editors, 'we might either omit "There", or place "What" as an exclamation in a line by itself, as "Well" and "No" in lines 135 and 141, reading "Ireland" as a trisyllable.' To me it seems to admit of no doubt that 'Ireland' is to be read as a dissyllable and 'What' as a monosyllabic foot. 'No' in l. 141 is another monosyllabic foot, whereas 'Well' in l. 135 forms indeed a separate line, unless the reading 'Well, I'll' &c., adopted by Singer, Hazlitt, R. Gr. White and other editors should be preferred. The two lines are to be scanned thus: —

No; | I will | to Ire|land to | his maj|'sty,

or: —

No; I'll | to Ire|land to | his maj|esty.
Well, I'll | for ref|uge straight | to Bris|tol cas|tle,

or: —

Well,
I will for refuge straight to Bristol castle.
Compare also Mr. Fleay, l. c.

CCCLI.

Gentlemen, will you go muster men?
If I know how or which way to order these affairs &c.

Ib., II, 2, 108 seq.

Several editors expatiate on the supposed irregularity of these lines, which, Collier asserts, 'is meant to accord with York's perturbed state of mind', whilst, according to R. Gr. White, it 'is doubtless due to accident or carelessness.' Mr. Rolfe compares Abbott, s. 507, whose scansion of l. 108 is not very satisfactory. For my part, I fail to see any metrical irregularity, except in the division of the lines, in so far as 'the old text ends the first of these lines with *men*, and puts *If — affairs* all into the next line.' All difficulty would seem to be removed by arranging either (with Mr. Hudson): —

Gentlemen, will you go muster men? If I
Know how or which way t'order these affairs, &c.

or (which I take to be the true arrangement): —

Gentlemen,
Will you | go mus|ter men? | ◡ If | I know
How or which way to order these affairs, &c.

Mr. Fleay proposes: —

Gent'men, | will you | go mus|ter men? | If *I* | know
How or which way to order these affairs, &c.

'*I*' should not stand in the accented part of the foot; but let the reader take his choice.

CCCLII.

Well, somewhat we must do. Come Cozen,
Ile dispose of you. Gentlemen, go muster vp your men,
And meet me presently at Barkley Castle:
I should to Plashy too: but time will not permit,
All is vneuen, and euery thing is left at six and seuen.

Ib., II, 2, 116 seqq.

This is the lection and arrangement of FA, in the faultiness of which
all editors are agreed, without, however, having been able to restore
the true reading. In my opinion, the words *Gentlemen, go* should
be transposed and the lines should be divided as follows: —

Well, somewhat we must do.
Come, cousin, I'll dispose of you. Go, gentlemen,
Muster up your men, and meet me presently
At Berkley Castle. I should to Plashy too;
But time will not permit: all is uneven,
And every thing is left at six and seven.

Gentlemen is, of course, to be pronounced as a triple ending. The
monosyllabic pronunciation of *Muster* needs neither explanation, nor
justification; compare Chaucer, ed. by Morris, I, 177 seq. Instead of
Barkley Castle the Qq read *Barkly* or *Barckly,* which suits the metre
just as well, only it makes the verse a syllable pause line; or it
must be read as a trisyllable *(Berkeley).*

CCCLIII.

I do remaiu as neuter. So, fare you well.

Ib., II, 3, 159.

In order to regulate the metre S. Walker (Crit. Exam., III, 127)
proposes to read *So farewell.* 'The extra syllable in the body of the
line', he says, 'would be in place in Macbeth or King Henry VIII.,
but is strange here.' — S. Walker is mistaken, for there is an
abundance of extra syllables before the pause in our play and the
line is perfectly right. By the way it may be added that it escaped
S. Walker that Pope made the same correction before him.

CCCLIV.

York. It may be I will go with you: but yet I'll pause.

Ib., II, 3, 168.

Pope omitted *with you.* Read, of course, with Mr. Fleay: —
May be | I'll go | with you: | but yet | I'll pause.

CCCLV.

Nor friends, nor foes, to me welcome you are.

Ib., II, 3, 170.

In accordance with Dr. Abbott, s. 490, some editors print *welcóme*.
Dr. Abbott adds the following remark: 'This particular passage may
be explained by a pause, but *"welcóme"* is common in other authors.'
Compare note CCXXIV and S. Walker, Crit. Exam., III, 127. In a
case like this we should look above all for the use of Shakespeare
himself before turning to other authors, and it remains to be seen,
whether or not a line is to be found in his plays by which the
accentuation of *welcome* on the last syllable can be established beyond
a doubt. In the present case there is certainly a pause after *me*
and *welcome* may be read as a trochee. Should this pause be thought
too slight by some one or other of my readers, he may perhaps be
better satisfied by a transposition which would remove all difficulty,
viz.: —

Nor friends, nor foes, wélcome to me you are.

The conjectural emendation proposed by Mr. Daniel in his Notes and
Conjectural Emendations, p. 49, (*or* friends *or* foes) has nothing to
do with the metre of the line and may be left to the reader's own
judgment.

CCCLVI.

The king reposeth all his confidence in thee.

Ib., II, 4, 6.

Pope changes *confidence* to *trust*; Capell reads *in thee all his confid-*
ence; Seymour omits *all his*; Singer, Hazlitt, and others end the line
at *confidence* and place *in thee* in a separate line; Mr. Fleay, l. c.,
suspects 'that *"reposeth"* should be *"rests"* or *"puts".*' This is
quite a chemist's shop full of remedies for the poor line that needs
no doctoring at all, provided *confidence* be pronounced as a dissyllable; scan: —

The king | repos|eth all | his con|f'dence ín | thee.

Compare note CXXXIII *(comb'tants).*

CCCLVII.

Boling. Thanks, gentle uncle. Come, lords, away,
To fight with Glendower and his complices:
Awhile to work, and after holiday.

Ib., III, 1, 42 seqq.

Pope inserted *my* before *lords*, an entirely gratuitous insertion, the
verse being obviously a syllable pause line. 'Theobald', remarks
Dr. Prœscholdt *ad. loc.,* 'ejected l. 43 as an interpolation; S. Walker

(Crit. Exam., III, 128), on the contrary, to avoid „the awkward vicinity of the final words *away* and *holiday* to each other", proposed to supply after l. 42 a verse to the following effect: —

And lead we forth our well-appointed powers.'

I cannot help thinking differently. I feel no doubt that in the poet's Ms. the scene concluded with a couplet and that we ought to read and arrange: —

Boling. Thanks, gentle uncle. To fight with Glendower
And his *accomplices*, come, lords, away:
Awhile to work and after holiday.

For the inverted position of the infinitive compare Dr. Abbott, s. 357. Dr. Abbott restricts this inversion to the infinitive in its 'indefinite signification', which restriction does not seem to be borne out by the facts. Mätzner (Engl. Gr., 2ᵈ Ed., IIb, 49 and 577 seq.) quotes amongst other instances the following sentence from Douglas Jerrold, Bubbles, 1: 'To obtain a certain good you would sell anything', where *to obtain* is certainly not equivalent to 'as regards obtaining', but to 'in order to obtain.' The same explanation may possibly hold good with respect to the line in Macbeth (II, 2, 73) quoted by Dr. Abbott: 'To know my deed, 'twere best not know myself.' — Line 42 is a syllable pause line both in the *textus receptus* and in my arrangement. — It should be added that two more couplets in our play have been spoiled by the ignorance and negligence of either transcribers or printers, viz. A. IV, sc. 1, l. 333 — 334 and A. V, sc. 3, l. 135 — 136; both were corrected by Pope — the task was indeed easy enough.

CCCLVIII.

High be our thoughts: I know my uncle York
Hath power enough to serve our turn. But who comes here?

Ib., III, 2, 89 seq.

The true arrangement of these lines has been given by Dr. Abbott, s. 506, p. 414; it is as follows: —

High be our thoughts:
I know my uncle York hath power enough
To serve our turn. But who comes here?

CCCLIX.

Boling. I know it, uncle, and oppose not myself
Against their will. But who comes here?
Enter Percy.
Welcome, Harry: what, will not this castle yield?

Percy. The castle royally is mann'd, my lord,
Against thy entrance.
   Boling. Royally!
Why, it contains no king?
   Percy.   Yes, my good lord,
It doth contain a king; &c.

Ib., III, 3, 18 seqq.

This is the reading and arrangement of the Cambridge Edition. It is of no use to repeat the various conjectures and arrangements to which the passage has given rise; suffice it to submit to the reader's judgment the following new division of the lines: —

   Boling. I know it, uncle, and not oppose myself
Against their will. But who comes here?
                Enter Percy.
Welcome Harry!
What, will not this castle yield?
   Percy.   The castle
Is royally mann'd, my lord, against thy entrance.
   Boling. Royally?
Why, it contains no king?
   Percy.   Yes, my good lord,
I doth contain a king; &c.

Line 18 has an extra syllable before the pause. As to the position of the negative before the verb compare The Tempest II, 1, 121; V, 38 and 303; Much Ado, IV, 1, 175; &c. See also Mätzner, Engl. Gr., 2^d Ed., IIb, 585. *What,* in l. 21, is a monosyllabic foot. *Is royally* is the lection of QBCD, whilst the rest of the old copies read *royally is.*

CCCLX.

To his most royal person, hither come.

Ib., III, 3, 38.

Pope omits *hither come*; Mr. Rolfe explains the words by 'having come hither.' Qy. read and scan: —

To his | most roy|al per|son; hither | come *I*?

CCCLXI.

Be rush'd upon! Thy thrice noble cousin.

Ib., III, 3, 103.

Pope inserted *No,* S. Walker (Crit. Exam., II, 260) *this,* before *thy*; no such insertion, however, is wanted. Scan: —

Be rush'd | upon! | ⏑ Thy | thrice no|ble cous|in.

CCCLXII.

And, as I am a gentleman, I credit him.

Ib., III, 3, 120.

Collier's Ms. corrector cut out *I am*; Mr. Fleay takes *credit him* to be
a triple ending. In my opinion the line has a triple ending before
the pause, or, in other words, *gentleman* is to be read as a dissyllable; see S. Walker, Versification, 189. Scan, therefore: —

And, as | I am | a gent|leman, I cred|it him.

CCCLXIII.

Thou, old Adam's likeness, set to dress this garden
How dares thy harsh rude tongue sound this unpleasing news?

Ib., III, 4, 73 seq.

Two lines of six feet which have been reduced to regular blank verse
in different ways. Pope struck out *old* and *harsh rude*; Hudson
omitted *Thou*; 'the Poet', he says, 'probably first wrote *Thou*, and
then substituted *Old*, and both words got printed together.' Mr. Rolfe
compares Abbott, s. 498, Steevens inserted *here* after *set*, and Malone
conjectured *dress out this garden. Say.* There can be no harm
done in adding another arrangement to this profusion of conjectural
emendations. Qy. read and arrange: —

Thou, old Adam's likeness,
Thou, set to dress this garden, how dares
Thy harsh-rude tongue sound this unpleasing news?

Apart from the division of the lines this arrangement contains only
one slight deviation from the *textus receptus*, viz. the repetition of
Thou, which can easily be shown to be in the poet's manner; compare, e. g., A. V, sc. 1, l. 11. The first *Thou* is, of course, a monosyllabic foot and the second verse a syllable pause line which is
thus to be scanned: —

Thou, set | to dress | this gar|den, ⏑ | how dares.

CCCLXIV.

Of good old Abraham! Lords appellants.

Ib., IV, 1, 104.

Pope altered the division of the lines and omitted *old*; Capell inserted
My before *lords*, and Keightley *father* before *Abraham*. S. Walker
(Crit. Exam., III, 130) has nothing better to offer than the following
makeshift: 'If all is right, we must pronounce *áppellants*. Are there
any traces of such a pronunciation'? Abbott, s. 485, justly describing
such a pronunciation as not Shakespearian, *more suo* dissyllabizes
Lords. In my conviction all these critical endeavours are mistaken,

as the verse shows not the slightest trace of corruption, but is either a regular syllable pause line: —

Of good | old A|braham! | ⌣ Lords | appel|lants,

or a catalectic verse (see note II): —

Of good | old A|br'am! Lords | appel|lants.

Abraham is used as a dissyllable not only by Shylock in The Merchant of Venice, but also by King Richard III. (IV, 3, 38): —

The sons | of Ed|ward sleep | in A᾿braham's bo|som.

For my own part I prefer this latter scansion.

CCCLXV.

And long live Henry, fourth of that name.

Ib., IV, 1, 112.

This is the lection of QABCD and has been adopted amongst others by the Clarendon Press Editors on the assumption that *fourth* is to be pronounced as a dissyllable. The Ff and QE read *of that name the fourth,* a palpable correction of which there is no need whatever, the verse, as printed in the Qq, being a regular syllable pause line; scan: —

And long | live Hen|ry, ⸜ | fourth of | that name.

CCCLXVI.

And he himself not present? O, forfend it, God.

Ib., IV, 1, 129.

Pope omitted *God*; Mr. Fleay strikes out *And he.* Dele, with Seymour, *O.*

CCCLXVII.

To Henry Bolingbroke.
K. Richard. Give me the crown. Seize the crown;
Here, cousin, on this side my hand, and on that side yours.

Ib., IV, 1, 180 seqq.

This is the reading and arrangement of QCD; it is evidently corrupt and that of the Ff (including QE) which has been adopted in the Cambridge, Globe, and Clarendon Press Editions is even more so. It was reserved for Singer to discover that *Seize the crown* is a stage direction that has crept into the text. I feel certain that we should arrange: —

To Henry Bolingbroke.
K. Richard. Give me the crown. [*Seizes the crown.*]
Here, cousin!
On this side my hand, and on that side yours.

CCCLXVIII.

With mine own breath release all duty's rites.

Ib., IV, 1, 210.

Among the various readings and conjectural emendations to which this line has given rise there is only one that deserves to be admitted into the text, namely that proposed by Collier: *duteous rites.*

CCCLXIX.

Transform'd and weaken'd? hath Bolingbroke
Deposed thine intellect? hath he been in thy heart?

Ib., V, 1, 27 seq.

This is the division of all Qq and Ff, whilst several modern editors, following the example set by Pope, end the first line at *depos'd.* Instead of *weaken'd* Pope reads *weak*; S. Walker (Crit. Exam., III, 113) proposes *weak'd*; Capell and Collier, ending the line as Qq Ff, inserted the former *proud,* the latter *this,* before *Bolingbroke.* As far as the metre is concerned, it may safely be asserted that l. 27 is a syllable pause line: —

Transform'd | and wea|ken'd? ⏑ | hath Bol|ingbroke,

and that *intellect* in l. 28 is a triple ending before the pause. A different question, however, has been started by the Clarendon Press Editors, who by the feebleness of l. 28 are led 'to suspect that it is corrupt, and that something of this sort occupied its place, dividing as in the early editions: —

Deposed thine intellect, benumb'd thy heart'.

There is, however, no occasion to omit *hath he,* and *benumb'd* seems too remote from the lection of the old copies both in spelling and sound; should we not make a somewhat nearer approach to it by reading: —

Deposed | thine in|t'llect? hath he | *bereaved* | thy heart?

CCCLXX.

And in compassion weep the fire out.

Ib., V, 1, 48.

A catalectic verse. According to the Clarendon Press Editors, *fire* is to be pronounced as a dissyllable. The metre would certainly be improed by a transposition: —

And weep | the fire | out in | compas|sión.

CCCLXXI.

Yea, look'st thou pale? let me see the writing.

Ib., V, 2, 57.

In order to regulate the metre Hanmer read *come, let,* Malone *boy, let.* Capell inserted *sir* after *pale,* and Abbott, s. 484, dissyllabizes this latter word. I take the verse to be a syllable pause line: —

Yea, look'st | thou pale? | ⏑ let | me see | the writ|ing.

Two lines *infra, satisfied* is to be pronounced as a dissyllable. The same pronunciation occurs again in l. 71 of the present scene: —

I will | be sat|'sfied; let | me see't, | I say.

CCCLXXII.

A dozen of them here have ta'en the sacrament.

Ib., V, 2, 97.

Sacrament is clearly a triple ending; cf. note CCXLVII.

CCCLXXIII.

Away, fond woman; were he twenty times my son,
I would appeach him.
    Duch.   Hadst thou groan'd for him
As I have done, thou wouldst be more pitiful.

Ib., V, 2, 101 seqq.

Arrange, with Mr. Fleay: —

Away, fond woman; were he twenty times
My son, I would appeach him.
    Duch.   Hadst thou groan'd
For him, as I have done, thou'ldst be more pitiful.

Pitiful is, of course, to be pronounced, as a triple ending.

CCCLXXIV.

Till Bolingbroke have pardon'd thee. Away, be gone;

Ib., V, 2, 117.

Pope struck out *be gone*; Mr. Fleay, l. c., wants either *Away!* or *be gone!* to be omitted; Singer, Hazlitt, and others end the line at *Away!* placing *Be gone!* in a separate line. In my opinion *pardon'd thee* is a triple ending, and no alteration whatever is requisite. Compare note CCCXLIII.

CCCLXXV.

Show minutes, times, and hours: but my time.

Ib., V, 5, 58.

Hours is not to be read *dissolutè*, the verse being a syllable pause line: —

Show min | utes, times, | and hours: | ⏑ but | my time.

The reading of the Ff and of QE: *O, but my time,* is an obvious correction, which, however, should be noticed as showing that the dissolution of *hour* was not in use at that time; it militates against Dr. Abbott and Mr. Fleay.

CCCLXXVI.

That staggers thus my person. Exton, thy fièrce hand.

Ib., V, 5, 110.

Pope omitted *Exton*, and Mr. Fleay, apparently without a knowledge of Pope's correction, proposes the same remedy in order to restore the metre. The line, however, has an extra syllable before the pause, and *Exton* is to be pronounced as a monosyllable, just like *pardon, reason, iron, &c.* Scan: —

That stag | gers thus | my per | son. Ext'n, thy | fierce hand.

CCCLXXVII.

North. First, to thy sacred state wish I all happiness.

Ib., V, 6, 6.

Happiness is, of course, a triple ending.

CCCLXXVIII.

Of Prisoners, Hotspurre tooke
Mordake Earle of Fife, and eldest sonne
To beaten Dowglas, and the Earle of Atholl,
Of Murry, Angus, and Menteith.

1 K. Henry IV., I, 1, 70 seqq.

This is the reading and arrangement of the first Folio. 'Some slight mutilation here', remarks Dyce *ad loc.* rather mildly. This mutilation or confusion, however, has nothing to do with the mistake into which the poet has been led concerning the Earl of Fife, who was son to the Duke of Albany, and not to Earl Douglas; which mistake, if need were, might easily be corrected by the substitution of *the* for *and*, before *eldest*. Without reviewing the different conjectures that have been proposed by Hanmer, Capell, Keightley, and Collier in

order to restore the original text, I content myself with increasing
the list by a conjectural emendation of my own. May not Shakespeare have written: —

Of prisoners, Hotspur took
The Earls of Murray, Angus, and Menteith,
Mordake the Earl of Fife, and eldest son
To beaten Douglas; and the Earl of Athol?

CCCLXXIX.

I tell you what
He held me last Night, at least, nine howres,
In reckning vp the seuerall Deuils Names
That were his Lacqueyes:
I cry'd hum, and well, goe too,
But mark'd him not a word.

Ib., III, 1, 158 seqq.

Thus FA. The second line is no doubt corrupt and has given rise
to a number of conjectures. Pope wrote *the last night*; Steevens,
but last night; an anonymous critic (according to the Cambridge
Edition) proposed *yesternight*; Capell *at the least*. In my opinion *fast*
dropped out before *last,* from its very similarity. The fourth and
fifth lines have been joined by the editors, so as to form an Alexandrine, which Pope attempted to reduce to five feet by the omission
of *go to*, whilst all modern editors have refrained from so unwarranted
an alteration and have preferred to preserve the Alexandrine. Ritson
(apud Dyce) even went so far as to declare that 'these two foolish [!]
monosyllables [*go to*] seem to have been added by some foolish player,
purposely [!!] to destroy the measure.' No such thing! Omit *and,*
and Shakespeare's authentic blank verse (with an extra syllable before
the pause) will at once present itself. The passage, therefore, should
be printed thus: —

I tell you what,
He held me fast last night at least nine hours
In reckoning up the several devils' names
That were his lacqueys; I cried 'hum', 'well', 'go to',
But marked him not a word.

As to the insertion of *fast* before *last* the reader is referred to note
CCXCVIII *(Her sister — tut!)*. Besides I have discovered in two
well-known German books two instances in point which go far to
establish almost beyond the reach of doubt the truth of this suggestion.
The first instance occurs in Eichendorff's celebrated novel 'Aus dem
Leben eines Taugenichts', Chap. IV, at the beginning of the last
paragraph but one. Of the five different editions which I have been
able to compare, the *Editio princeps* (Berlin, 1826, Vereinsbuch-

Elze, Notes.

14

handlung, p. 58), the illustrated edition published by M. Simion
(Berlin, 1842, p. 59), and the second edition of the 'Sämmtliche
Werke' (1864, Vol. III, p. 44) correctly read: 'Was war mir aber das
alles (Alles) nütze, wenn ich meine lieben lustigen Herrn (Herren)
nicht wieder fand?' In the more recent editions, however, which
were published by Ernst Julius Günther (Leipzig, 1872, p. 61) and
by C. F. Amelang (Leipzig, 1882, p. 61) we read: 'Was mir aber das
Alles nütze, wenn ich meine lieben lustigen Herren nicht wiederfand?'
In these editions *war* has dropped out, no doubt from its similarity
with the preceding *Was,* from which it differs only by a single
letter. Still more striking is the second instance, which is taken
from the 'Jugenderinnerungen eines alten Mannes (Wilh. v. Kügelgen)'
(Berlin, Hertz) of which I have looked up the second, fifth, and
ninth editions. In the second edition (Berlin, 1870) we read at p. 31:
'Nicht weniger befremdlich war es der Mutter, dafs Wetzel seine
würdige Frau nie anders nannte als "Henne" und sein niedliches
Töchterchen "Forelle". Er dagegen behauptete, unsere gewöhnlichen
Taufnamen seien gar zu albern und hätten nicht die geringste Be-
deutung. Unter Amalie, Charlotte, Louise, Franz und Balthasar, und
wie die Leute alle hiessen, könne sich kein Mensch was denken.
Namen müssten das Ding bezeichnen, gewissermassen abmalen, und
wenn er seine Frau "Henne" nenne, so hätte Jedermann damit ein
treues Bild ihres Wesens und ihrer Beschäftigungen, wie denn auch
seine Tochter eine veritable Forelle sei.' In the fifth and ninth
editions, however, (p. 31 in either edition), the word *Henne* before
nenne has been omitted, evidently from no other cause than from the
similarity between the two words, which differ merely in their initial
letters (*H* and *n*). In so far these two cases are completely analogous to: 'He held me fast last night' &c. (Kölb., Engl. Stud., VIII, 495.
Notes and Queries, June 18, 1881, p. 485. Reply by Dr. Brinsley
Nicholson, ib., Sept. 24, 1881, p. 245. Dr. Nicholson has misunderstood my scansion of the last line but one, and blames the conjecture
fast, before *last,* as 'a cacophony and jingle, unpleasant and therefore [!] un-Shakespearian.' As if Shakespeare were pleasantness
itself! Dr. Nicholson might have recollected not a few lines in Shakespeare that are by no means paragons of euphony and pleasantness;
and no wonder, that there are some black sheep among so many
thousand lines! Even jingles are not altogether foreign to Shakespeare's verses. Here is an instance, taken from Coriolanus, II, 1,
180 seq.: —

<blockquote>
Where he hath won
With *fame,* a *name* to Caius Marcius.
</blockquote>

The same 'unpleasant and therefore un-Shakespearian cacophony and
jingle', to borrow Dr. Nicholson's words, occurs also in Cymbeline,
III, 3, 51 (I' th' *name* of *fame*). Two more cases in point are met

with in K. Henry V., II, 3, 54 (And hold-fast is the only *dog,* my *duck*) and in Othello, IV, 3, 69 (it is a great *price* For a small *vice*). The list might easily be increased.)

CCCLXXX.

Swear me, Kate, like a lady as thou art,
A good mouth-filling oath.

Ib., III, 1, 258 seq.

In Marston's comedy What you will, III, 1 (Works, ed. Halliwell, I, 255) we meet with the following lines: —

What I know a number,
By the sole warrant of a lapy-beard,
A raine beate plume, and a good chop-filling oth,
With an odde French shrugge, and by the Lord, or so,
Ha leapt into sweete captaine with such ease
As you would feart not.

Are we to consider *a good chop-filling oath* as a customary expression, or is it a recollection taken from Shakespeare's line? In the latter case the passage should find admittance in a future edition of Dr. Ingleby's Centurie of Prayse. The first part of K. Henry IV. was first printed in 1598, Marston's What you will in 1607.

CCCLXXXI.

That English may as French, French Englishmen,
Receive each other. God speak this Amen!
All. Amen!

K. Henry V., V, 2, 395 seqq.

The meaning of this passage can be no other than this: That English may receive each other as French, French as Englishmen. This, however, is not what the poet intended to say; it is no meaning at all. The thought the poet wishes to express is no doubt the following: That the English may receive the French, the French the English each other as brethren. I cannot, therefore, help suspecting some corruption in l. 395; possibly *brethren* dropped out after *as,* and *Englishmen* is, in consequence, to be considered as a triple ending. In l. 396 we meet with another corruption, for there can be little doubt that the poet wrote *his* [not *this*] Amen; compare Henry VIII., III, 2, 45: *My amen to 't. All men's* [viz. *amen to it*]. The second *Amen* is not an interjectional line, but forms part of l. 396. It is a curious fact, that, so far as I am aware, as yet no editor has seen in these lines a difficulty that requires explanation, or rather, correction.

14*

CCCLXXXII.

Enter Will Kemp.

Romeo and Juliet, IV, 5 (QB).

The account of Will Kemp's life and doings as given by Dyce in
the Introduction to 'Kemp's Nine Daies Wonder' (printed for the
Camden Society, 1840), singular though it be, has yet been far surpassed by the wild hypotheses concerning it advanced by the late
R. Simpson (The School of Shakspere, II, 373 seq.). Simpson is the
only critic, as far as I am aware, who pretends to a knowledge of
Kemp's whereabouts before 1587. This knowledge he derives from
the pseudo-Shakespearean comedy of 'Fair Em' to which he imparts
a symbolical meaning and which he imagines to refer to events in
the history of the stage. William the Conqueror, the hero of that
comedy, according to Simpson, is no other than William Kemp, who,
he fancies, went to Denmark in 1586, at the head of a company of
actors, in order to marry the princess Blanch, that is, in order 'to
make himself the master of the Danish stage.' 'But on his arrival
there', continues Simpson, 'he was more struck with the chances of
another career, and very soon eloped to Saxony, to turn his histrionic
talents to more account there.' This fact, Simpson fancies, is
shadowed forth by the change that takes place in the sentiments of
William the Conqueror. 'Mounteney and Valingford', our critic goes
on to say, 'are two of his company whom he would have taken with
him, but who preferred to stay behind, and contend for the prize
of the Manchester stage, which Lord Strange's players were then
bringing into repute.' The second part of the plot carries on the
history of this Manchester contention. 'The windmill, with its clapper
and its grist, is the type of the theatre; the wind is either the
encouraging breath of the audience, or the voice of the actors, the
clapper the applause, and the grist the gains. The miller's daughter
is the prize; he who wins her bears the bell as play-wright.' — As
this second part of Simpson's explanation has nothing to do with
Will Kemp, I dismiss it with the question, what the verdict of
English critics might have been, had a German scholar started such
a theory.

There is not a single argument to support Kemp's supposed
journey to Denmark and Saxony; nay such a journey is utterly
improbable. Putting aside for the moment Kemp's 'Dutiful Inuective'
(1587) of which I shall speak more at large hereafter, we find Kemp
first mentioned in 1589, if we take it for granted that Nash's undated
tract 'An Almond for a Parrot' which is inscribed to William Kemp,
was published in this year. In the dedication Kemp is complimented
as the 'vice-gerent generall to the Ghost of Dicke Tarlton'; and in
Heywood's 'Apologie for Actors' (43) we are likewise told that Kemp
succeeded Tarlton, who died in September, 1588, 'as wel in the

favour of her majesty, as in the opinion and good thoughts of the
generall audience.' The question, therefore, arises whether it is likely
that Kemp, if he had really proceeded in 1586 to Denmark and
thence to Saxony, could have been back again in England as early
as the end of 1588 or the beginning of 1589; nay, if he really were
the author of the 'Dutiful Innective' which appeared in 1587, his
stay in foreign parts must dwindle down to less than a twelvémonth.
But travelling in those days was no such easy pastime as it is now-
a-days, and certainly we must allow Kemp some time both in Denmark and Germany for the exercise of his profession. Besides, Kemp
in 1588, in all probability, was a very young man, for he himself
tells us that in 1599 when performing his famous morris-dance from
London to Norwich, he 'judged his heart cork and his heels feathers,
so that he thought he could fly to Rome or at least hop to Rome,
as the old proverb is, with a mortar on his head.' We cannot possibly believe him to have been a man advanced in years in 1599,
else he would certainly not have been able to undergo the fatigues
of a feat so unheard of and never surpassed. Supposing then that
he was about thirty-five years old when dancing to Norwich, he
would in 1586 have numbered little more than twenty years, an age
at which we can hardly believe him to have gone abroad at the
head of a company of players. Moreover it is highly probable that
from 1589 to 1593 Kemp belonged to Edward Alleyn's company,
for his 'Applauded Merrimentes of the Men of Goteham' are contained
in the most pleasant and merry Comedy 'A Knacke to knowe a
Knaue', which was published in 1594 and acted in 1592 by Alleyn's
company; this, as Dyce justly remarks, would scarcely have been
the case, had not Kemp been a member of the company and himself
performed a part in his Applauded Merrimentes. Thus far every one
will be glad to side with so distinguished a critic as Dyce; but
when directly afterwards he ridicules Ritson for having inserted in
the catalogue of Kemp's 'Works', the 'Applauded Merrimentes',
nobody, it is true, will be ready to raise that fragment of buffoonery,
— even supposing it to have been amplified by improvisation, — to
the dignity of a 'Work', but nobody, on the other hand, I think,
will be justified in denying, with Dyce, that Kemp was its author.
On the contrary, this fact is supported by a testimony quoted by Dyce
himself (p. XXV), viz. a passage in Nash's 'Strange Newes, Of the
intercepting certaine Letters' (1592) where Nash advises Gabriel
Harvey to be on his guard lest Will Kemp should choose him one
of these days for the subject of one of his 'Merrimentes'.*

Beside the 'Applauded Merrimentes' three jigs are entered in
the Stationers' Registers (1591 and 1595) as 'Kemp's jig' or 'Kemp's

* Collier, H. E. Dr. P. (1st Ed.), III, 33, erroneously cites the passage in
question as taken from Nash's Apologie for Pierce Pennilesse (1593).

New Jig'. According to Dyce these jigs were ascribed to Kemp on
no other ground than because, by his consummate skill, he had succeeded in rendering them popular. His reasons for this assertion are
twofold. First, he alleges that Kemp himself speaks of his Nine
Daies Wonder (1600) as the first pamphlet published by him, which,
according to Dyce, would be an untruth if he had published not
only the 'Applauded Merrimentes' but also three jigs before that time;
for it would be a poor argument, Dyce adds, to distinguish between
the jigs and the Nine Daies Wonder, on the ground that the former
were not pamphlets. I do not see why this argument is to be rejected as a poor one; jigs were a species of plays, and written in
verse, as Dyce himself admits, whereas the Nine Daies Wonder is
written in prose as pamphlets generally are. Besides, are we quite
sure that Kemp's jigs were given to the world by the author himself, as we know his Nine Daies Wonder was? May not their publication have been effected in the same manner in which so many
Elizabethan plays were published, without the consent, nay, even
without the knowledge of the author? Granting this, it certainly
would have been an unimpeachable statement for Kemp to style the
Nine Daies Wonder 'the first pamphlet that ever Will Kemp offred
to the Presse.'

The second argument adduced by Dyce in support of his opinion
cannot lay claim to any greater cogency. Although Kemp, he says,
was not 'grossly illiterate', as is proved by his Nine Daies Wonder,
yet he could not boast of a faculty for poetry; for, 'if he had been
a practised jig-maker', he would not have needed the assistance of
a friend for the few verses inserted in the Nine Daies Wonder. If,
however, we peruse this pamphlet without prejudice we cannot doubt
but that Kemp himself, and no other, was the author of the two
little pieces in rhyme on p. 10 and p. 13 seq.; the good fellow, his
friend, to whom he ascribes them is nothing but a poetical fiction,
a mask or screen, common enough, the predecessor of the 'judicious
friend' in Lord Macaulay's Life and Letters. Both in matter and
style these verses entirely agree with Kemp's prose; in both we meet
with the same kind of wit and buffoonery, both are clearly from the
same pen.

But Dyce goes still farther. Not only the Merrimentes and the
Jigs, but everything else that bears Kemp's name, with the sole exception of the Nine Daies Wonder, he declares to be spurious. This
leads us back to the above-mentioned little volume 'A Dutiful Inuective &c.' which was published in 1587 with William Kemp's name on
the title-page. This poem, written in iambic lines of seven feet, is
termed 'the first fruites of his labour' by the author and inscribed
to the Lord Mayor of London. It is directed against the traitors
Ballard and Babington, and expresses an ardent enthusiasm for the
Queen. In this latter respect it is quite of a piece with the Nine

Daies Wonder, towards the end of which the author assures us that
'al his mirths (meane though they be) haue bin and euer shal be
imploi'd to the delight of my royal Mistris; whose sacred name ought
not to be remembred among such ribald rimes as these late thin-
breecht lying Ballet-singers haue proclaimed it.' This is the well-
known language of all players and play-wrights of the time, who
were abundantly thankful for the favour and patronage which the
Queen extended to the stage. Although in 1587 Kemp had not yet
succeeded to Tarlton, he may even at that time have attracted the
notice of the Queen and received marks of her favour. In spite of
all this Dyce does not hesitate to attribute the 'Dutiful Inuective' to
another William Kemp, who, as Dyce informs us, was a schoolmaster
at Plymouth, and who in the following year published a treatise
under the title 'The Education of Children in Learning'. As, however, on the title-page of this latter tract we read only the initials
W. K., there is nothing to assure us that they are meant for William
Kemp. May they not stand just as well for Walter King, or Knight,
or Kelly? But taking it for proven that there was a schoolmaster
of the name of William Kemp living at Plymouth and that he was
the author of the treatise in question, all. that we may infer from
this proposition is, that we have to deal with two William Kemps,
the one living at London, the other at Plymouth; the one an actor,
the other a schoolmaster; the one the author of the Nine Daies
Wonder, the other the author of the Education of Children in Learning, and one of them the author of the Dutiful Inuective. Now
what reason have we to ascribe this latter production to the schoolmaster rather than to the actor? Is he to be thought endowed with
a larger measure of the 'faculty divine' than his namesake the actor?
And living at Plymouth, as he did, what reason had he to inscribe
his treatise to the Lord Mayor of London? A London actor might
well be induced to flatter His Lordship by the dedication of some
document of dutiful loyalty and well-spent literary labour, as the
grim City-potentate did not usually look with a benign eye on theatres
and theatrical amusements, least of all jigs and clowns. Besides it
should be remembered that when several years after Kemp danced
his morris to Norwich, he began it before the Lord Mayor's house.
And for what reason should the heart of the Plymouth schoolmaster
have dilated with the same enthusiastic loyalty for the Queen, as
did that of the London actor? That William Kemp, the actor, came
before the public more than once in print is fairly to be inferred
from the wellknown words which the student Philomusus addresses
to him in The Return from Parnassus (1606): 'Indeed M. Kempe',
he says, 'you are very famous, but that is as well for workes in
print as your part in kue.' As we have seen, Dyce not only ridicules the expression 'workes' which may indeed be comically exaggerated, but he declares the whole statement to be incorrect and not

deserving of belief; 'I understand', he says, 'the ironical compliment as an allusion to his (viz. Kemp's) Nine Daies Wonder only; for I feel assured that all the other pieces have been erroneously attributed to his pen.' This assertion, in my opinion, is by no means borne out by the facts and is wholly gratuitous.

In the same spirit of overstrained criticism Dyce discusses the journeys, which on the testimony of several contemporaries were undertaken by Kemp; if we are to believe him, all of them, with the single exception of the morris to Norwich, are entirely fictitious. Now Kemp himself towards the end of the Nine Daies Wonder declares his intention of setting out on some journey; being not yet certain as to its aim, he mentions Rome, Jerusalem, and Venice as places where he should be most inclined to go. No account of such a journey is extant, and this fact is thought by Dyce a sufficient argument to deny its having been made at all. In the passage just quoted from The Return from Parnassus, however, Kemp is welcomed as having just come back from abroad and Philomusus and Studioso, the two Cambridge students, address him in the following words: '*Phil.* What, M. Kempe, how doth the Emperour of Germany? *Stud.* God save you, M. Kempe; welcome, M. Kempe, from dancing the morrice ouer the Alpes.' Kemp's reply is this: 'Well, you merry knaues, you may come to the honour of it one day: is it not better to make a foole of the world as I have done, then to be fooled of the world as you schollers are?' All this Dyce declares to be nothing but 'sportive allusions to Kemp's journey to Norwich', an assertion which hardly needs refutation. In what connection do the Emperor of Germany and the Alps stand to Norwich, and how can a mention of the former be taken for an allusion to the latter? According to the simplest rules of interpretation the question 'How doth the Emperour of Germany?' suggests the fact that Kemp saw the Emperor, or at least heard of him from persons attached to his court or train, as well he might if he had been in Germany. But if Kemp travelled at all he certainly did so in his capacity as a clown and dancer, and it was no doubt the aim of his journey to turn his histrionic talents to the best possible account. Why then may he not have acted before his Imperial Majesty? We know that John Spencer, who was at the head of a company of English actors in the service of the Elector of Brandenburg, travelled with his company in the South of Germany and performed several times before the Emperor and the Diet at Ratisbon in 1613.* If Kemp really should have done so before his countryman, he may very likely on his return have boasted of the honour and this boasting may have occasioned the comic exaggerations and railleries with which his friends and contemporaries bantered him, — a supposition which *mutatis mutandis* may likewise hold in regard to Kemp's so-called 'Works'.

* A. Cohn, Shakespeare in Germany, p. LXXXIV seq.

Our belief in Kemp's journey to Italy is greatly strengthened by several additional testimonies. In the above-mentioned dedication of the pamphlet 'An Almond for a Parrot' Nash tells us that about the year 1588 he was in Italy and that at Bergamo the Italian 'arlechini' inquired about the celebrated M. Kemp of whom they spoke in terms of highest eulogy. This, I think, could not but prove an inducement to Kemp to go to Italy himself and there to make the acquaintance of his Italian fellow-clowns and admirers. The international intercourse between England and Italy, especially Northern Italy, was highly flourishing and a journey to Italy was easily and cheaply to be accomplished, — according to the notions and customs of the time. Nevertheless, it must be owned that Nash's dedication is written in that style of buffoonery which seems to be inseparable from the dedicator and still more so from the dedicatee, and as we are not sure to what extent similar jokes may have been thought allowable in those merry days it may be as well not to lay too great a stress on this dedication. It is different, however, with a second testimony, also quoted by Dyce himself, viz. a passage in John Day's 'Travailes of the Three English Brothers' &c., an historical (!) play which was published in 1607, but, according to Dyce, written before that time, as it is not yet divided into acts and scenes. Here Will Kemp is introduced, *in propria persona,* in a scene laid at Venice. In this scene an Englishman desires to be presented to Sir Anthony Shirley who is staying at Venice as ambassador from the Sophy. 'An Englishman?' Sir Anthony asks his servant, 'what's his name? *Serv.* He calls himselfe Kempe. *Sir Ant.* Kemp! bid him come in [*Exit Seruant. Enter Kempe.*] Welcome, ·honest Will; and how doth all thy fellowes in England?' Then an Italian clown and his wife make their appearance and ask permission to perform before Sir Anthony, who prevails upon Kemp to join in this performance of the two Italians. Kemp, however, takes great offence at a woman exhibiting before spectators, and therefore makes her and her husband the butt of his jokes and satirical remarks. Now this scene in my opinion would have been meaningless, and insipid, and hardly tolerable on a London stage, if Kemp had not been really at Venice and had not been a partaker there in some such exhibition. For this same reason we must conclude that 'The Travailes of the Three English Brothers' was acted during Kemp's lifetime.

The fact of Kemp's journey into Italy and of his interview there with Sir Anthony Shirley is distinctly stated in a passage in Sloane Mss. 392, fol. 401, quoted by Mr. Halliwell-Phillipps in his edition of the Conventry Plays, and thence transferred to Mr. A. H. Bullen's edition of the Works of John Day (1881, privately printed), Vol. I, p. 100. This is the passage: '1601. September 2. Kemp, mimus quidam, qui peragrationem quandam in Germaniam et Italiam instituerat, per multos errores et infortunia sua reversus: multa refert de

Anthonio Sherley, equite aurato, quem Romae [!] (legatum Persicum
agentem) convenerat.' Another distinct statement that Kemp travelled
on the continent in his capacity as a dancer, is contained in Weelkes'
Madrigals (1608) No. XX, quoted by Sam. Neil, Shakespeare's Hamlet,
with Introduction and Notes (London and Glasgow, 1877), p. 174.
It is to the following effect: —

Since Robin Hood, Maid Marian, and Little John are gone-a
home-a,
The hobby-horse was quite forgot when Kempe did dance-a,
He did labour, after the tabor, for to dance them into France.
For he took pains
To skip it, to skip it;
In hope of gains, of gains,
He will trip it, trip it, trip it on the toe.
Diddle, diddle, diddle, do.

The date of Kemp's death is quite uncertain, the respective
conjectures of Malone and Chalmers not being supported by positive
evidence; according to Malone he died before 1609, according to
Chalmers as early as 1603. That he was dead in 1612, is generally inferred from the passage in Heywood's Apologie quoted above,
although Heywood's words are by no means explicit enough to remove
all doubts. If we follow Malone, who is generally a safe guide,
Kemp may very well have witnessed the performance of the 'Travailes' and it is evident, provided he did not perform the part himself, that the zest of the joke for the audience must have been in
seeing the real Kemp sitting amongst them opposite his counterfeit
on the boards.

CCCLXXXIII.

Tim. Thy backe I prythee.
Ape. Liue, and loue thy misery.
Tim. Long liue so, and so dye. I am quit.
Ape. Mo things like men,
Eate *Timon*, and abhorre then.   [*Exit Apemantus.*

Timon of Athens, IV, 3, 396 seqq.

This is the reading and arrangement of the folio. The last two lines
have rightly been given to Timon by the editors and in order to
complete the metre Hanmer and Capell have needlessly added *so*
before the words *I am quit.* In my opinion this is not sufficient to
restore the passage; the words *Long live so, and so die* do not belong
to Timon, but to Apemantus and the true arrangement, therefore,
seems to be the following: —

Tim. Thy back, I prythee.
Ape.   Live and love thy misery;

Long live so, and so die.   [*Exit Apemantus.*
   Tim.   I am quit.
Moe things like men?   Eat, Timon, and abhor them.

The last verse but one is a syllable pause line; scan: —

Long live | so, and | so die. | ⌣ I | am quit.

(Shakespeare's dramatische Werke nach der Uebersetzung von Schlegel und Tieck, herausgegeben durch die Deutsche Shakespeare-Gesellschaft, X, 439. — Notes and Queries, June 25, 1870, p. 594.)

———

CCCLXXXIV.

Your greatest want is, you want much of meat.

Ib., IV, 3, 419.

Various conjectures have been proposed to cure this corrupted verse, none of which, however, proves satisfactory. Dyce and the Cambridge Editors, therefore, have left the reading of the folio untouched as above. The word *much* is evidently owing to a dittography, the Banditti having just complained that they *much do want.* Steevens conjectures *much of me,* which would be most bald and trivial prose; he should have altered one more letter, for there seems to be little doubt that Shakespeare wrote *you want muck of me,* viz. gold, in which sense this word is frequently used. Compare the Ballad of Gernutus, the Jew of Venice (Percy's Reliques), st. 6: —

His heart doth thinke on many a wile,
  How to deceive the poore;
His mouth is almost ful of mucke,
  Yet still he gapes for more.

Coriolanus II, 2, 128 seqq.: —

       Our spoils he kick'd at,
And look'd upon things precious as they were
The common muck of the world.

Cymbeline, III, 6, 54 seqq.: —

All gold and silver rather turn to dirt!
As 'tis no better reckon'd, but of those
Who worship dirty gods.

Thomas Heywood, If you know not me, you know nobody, Pt. II (ed. Collier for the Shakespeare-Society, 149): 'But, madam, you are rich, and by my troth, I am very poor, and I have been, as a man should say, stark naught; — — and, though I have not the muck of the world, I have a great deal of good love, and I prithee accept of it.' — Nash, Summer's Last Will and Testament (Dodsley, 1825, IX, 23): 'If then the best husband has been so liberal of his best handy-work, to what end should we make much of a glittering excrement, or doubt to spend at a banquet as many pounds, as he spends men at a battle?' — Ib., IX, 25: '*Omnia mea mecum porto*, quoth Bias, when he had nothing but bread and cheese in a leathern bag, and two or three books in his bosom. Saint Francis, a holy saint, and never had any money. It is madness to doat upon mucke.' — Tell-Trothes New-yeares Gift (ed. Furnivall for the New Shakspere Society), 69: 'Many looke so long for aboundance of mucke, as they fall into a quagmire of miseries, hauing siluer to looke on, though wanting mony to supply many wants.' — Ib., 75: 'Indeede, what cannot money doo, that will buye any thing? and yet honestie will purchase that which all the muck in the world cannot compasse, namely, a good report for euer.' — Faerie Queene, III, 9, 4: —

But all his minde is set on mucky pelfe.

Pope, Essay on Man, IV, 279: —

Is yellow dirt the passion of thy life?

Compare Forby, Vocabulary of East-Anglia, s. v. Muckgrubber, 'a hunks; a sordid saver of money, who delves for it, as it were, in the mire.' 'Muckgrubbing, adj. sordidly avaricious.'

To revert to the passage in Timon. To the pretence of the bandits that they are no thieves, 'but men that much do want', Timon replies they could not possibly be in want, since nature, the bounteous housewife, on each bush laid her full mess before them; their only want was for muck, i. e. gold, and that was no real want. The same reproach is addressed to the painter and the poet afterwards (V, 1, 115): —

Hence, pack! Here's gold; you came for gold, ye slaves.

(Shakespeare's dramatische Werke nach der Uebersetzung von Schlegel und Tieck, herausgegeben durch die Deutsche Shakespeare-Gesellschaft, X, 439. — Notes and Queries, June 25, 1870, 594. Compare the ever-memorable reply by A. H[all], Notes and Queries, July, 16, 1870, 43.)

CCCLXXXV.

Cæs. Ha! who calls?
Casca. Bid every noise be still: peace yet again!
Cæs. Who is it in the press that calls on me?

Julius Cæsar, I, 2, 13 seqq.

According to the Cambridge Edition *ad loc.* Staunton seems to be the only editor that takes exception to these lines as transmitted by the folio. In his opinion either the whole of the second line ought to be added to Caesar's previous question *Who calls?* or the last

word of it should be connected with the following speech of Cæsar,
thus: —

> *Cæs.* Ha! who calls?
> *Casca.* Bid every noise be still: — peace yet!
> *Cæs.*   Again!
> Who is it in the press that calls on me?

This is even worse than the arrangement of the folio, and yet the
true reading lies so near at hand that it will seem almost miracu-
lous, if I have not been forestalled in finding it out. Read, of
course: —

> *Cæs.* Ha! who calls? [*To Casca*] Bid every noise be still!
> *Casca.* Peace yet again!
> *Cæs.* Who is it in the press that calls on me?

Once before, at the beginning of the scene, where Cæsar addresses
Calpurnia, Casca with marked officiousness silenced the crowd: —

> *Cæs.* Calpurnia!
> *Casca.*   Peace ho! Cæsar speaks.

Nothing, therefore, can be more simple and natural than that Cæsar
once more summons the assistance of Casca and that Casca again
proclaims silence. Compare 2 Henry VI., IV, 2, 39 seq.: *Cade.* — —
Command silence. *Dick.* Silence! (Anglia, herausgegeben von Wülcker
und Trautmann, I, 341.)

CCCLXXXVI.

For now this fearefull Night,
There is no stirre, or walking in the streetes;
And the Complexion of the Element
Is Fauors, like the Worke we haue in hand,
Most bloodie, fierie, and most terrible.

Ib., I, 3, 126 seqq.

This is the uniform reading of the folios, with the only exception
of 'Fauours' in the third and fourth. Mr. J. G. Herr, in his 'Scat-
tered Notes on the Text of Shakespeare', published at Philadelphia
(1879), proposes 'Is haviours', a conjecture which I think will hardly
anywhere be welcomed as a suitable substitute for Dr. Johnson's generally received correction, 'In favour's.' On the contrary, I feel convinced that not even those critics will accept Mr. Herr's new reading
that take exception to Dr. Johnson's emendation. Among the latter
Prof. Craik, in his edition of Julius Cæsar (5th Ed., p. 133 seq.), takes
a prominent place. After mentioning another emendation, proposed
either by Steevens (according to Prof. Craik) or by Capell (according
to the Cambridge Edition), viz., 'Is favoured', Prof. Craik continues:
'To say that the complexion of a thing is either featured like or

in feature like to something else is very like a tautology.' He is, therefore, strongly inclined to adopt Reed's (or, according to the Cambridge Edition, Rowe's) ingenious conjecture, 'Is feverous', to which, on the other hand, Dr. Aldis Wright, in his annotated edition, very properly objects, inasmuch as 'the word "complexion" in the previous line suits better with "favour's" than with "feverous".' In my humble opinion neither the one nor the other of these conjectures is what the poet wrote. Prof. Craik is quite right in remarking that "it may, perhaps, count for something, though not very much, against both "favour's like" and "favoured like" that a very decided comma separates the two words in the original edition.' If, as I imagine, the original reading was *Ill-favoured,* even the most decided comma may keep its place after it with propriety. As to the semicolon after 'streets' in the second line, it does not seem to be of any great moment whether it be retained or replaced by a comma, as has been done in the Cambridge Edition. There may perhaps be some one or other among my readers that will like to hear that *ill-favoured* is used with especial reference to the complexion in Fair Em, I, 3, 28 (ed. Warnke and Prœscholdt): —

Swart and ill-favoured, a collier's sanguine skin.

Compare also Titus Andronicus, III, 2, 66: it was a black ill-favoured fly. — Spenser, The Faerie Queene, I, 1, 15. (The Athenæum, Dec. 13, 1879, p. 762.)

CCCLXXXVII.

Cassi. Am I not stay'd for? tell me:
Cinna. Yes, you are. O Cassius,
If you could but winne the Noble Brutus
To our party —

Ib., I, 3, 139 seqq.

The arrangement of these lines as given in the folio cannot possibly have proceeded from the poet's pen, and the editors, therefore, have made various attempts to heal the evident corruption. Capell, e. g., reads: —

Yes,
You are. O Cassius, if you could but win
The noble Brutus to our party.

The words *Yes, you are,* however, should not be severed, and must no doubt be connected with the preceding speech of Cassius in one and the same line. S. Walker (Versification, 290), Craik (The English of Shakespeare, 5th Ed., 120), and Staunton arrange as follows: —

> *Cassi.* Am I not staid for? Tell me!
> *Cinna.* * Yes, you are.
> O Cassius, if you could
> But win the noble Brutus to our party.

But the incomplete line *O Cassius, if you could* does not harmonize with the metrical character of this play, which, it is well known, is of great regularity. Knight and Collier introduce an alexandrine: —

> Yes, you are.
> O Cassius, if you could but win the noble Brutus
> To our party.

In my opinion the difficulty might easily be removed by the addition of *Caius* before *Cassius,* — he is elsewhere addressed by both his names, just as we find Caius Ligarius (in Julius Cæsar), Caius Marcius (in Coriolanus) and Caius Lucius (in Cymbeline). The lines then might be regulated thus: —

> *Cas.* Am I not staid for? Tell me!
> *Cin.* Yes, you are.
> O Caius Cassius, if you could but win
> The noble Brutus to our party.

The last line is a catalectic verse (see note II). (Anglia, herausgegeben von Wülcker und Trautmann, I, 341 folg.)

CCCLXXXVIII.

Let us be sacrificers, but not butchers, Caius.

Ib., II, 1, 116.

In my remarks on this most perplexing line in Prof. Wülcker's Anglia, I, 343 seq., I intimated two emendations which, in my opinion, promise fair to remove the difficulties detailed both by former editors and myself l. c. The one is to omit *Caius,* as there can be little doubt that the names of the persons addressed were no less frequently added as left out by mistake at the end of the line. The other way of healing the corruption of this line is to discard the conjunction *but.* To all appearance this *but* is merely a faulty repetition from the preceding line: —

For Antony is *but* a limb of Cæsar.

At the same time the first syllable of *butchers,* following hard upon, may have contributed to mislead the copyist or compositor. At all events the omission of *but* would help us to a regular scansion of the line just as well as the omission of *Caius:* —

Let us | be sa | crifi | cers, not but | chers, Ca | ius.

* Instead of *Cinna* S. Walker, by an evident mistake, printed *Casca.*

The expedients proposed by S. Walker, Versification, p. 274, and by Craik *ad loc.* are of no avail and may be consigned to oblivion.

CCCLXXXIX.

And then, they say, no spirit dare stir abroad;
The nights are wholesome; then no planets strike,
No fairy takes, nor witch hath power to charm,
So hallow'd and so gracious is the time.

Hamlet, I, 1, 161 seqq.

I hope I may be allowed to repeat a conjectural emendation which, although inserted in the text of both my editions of Hamlet, has been left unnoticed by all subsequent editors — even by Dr Furness. The plural 'planets', which is the uniform reading of QB seqq. and all the Folios, does not harmonize well with the singulars 'fairy' and 'witch'. Moreover, in all parallel passages we meet with the singular, thus, e. g., in The Winter's Tale, I, 2, 201: —

It is a bawdy planet, that will strike
Where 't is predominant.

Ib., II, 1, 105: —

There's some ill planet reigns.

Titus Andronicus, II, 4, 14: —

If I do wake, some planet strike me down;

Othello, II, 3, 182: —

As if some planet had unwitted men.

Westward Ho!, V, 1 (Webster, ed. Dyce, 1857, in 1 vol., p. 238b): Sure, sure, I'm struck with some wicked planet, for it hit my very heart. — Ben Jonson, Every Man in his Humour, IV, 5: Sure I was struck with a planet thence, for I had no power to touch my weapon.

Under these circumstances I have no doubt that the text of QA 'no planet frikes' shows us the right way and that we should read, *no planet strikes.*

CCCXC.

Hor. Indeed? I heard it not; it then draws near the
season
Wherein the spirit held his wont to walk.

Ib., I, 4, 5 seq.

Seymour (*apud* Furness) remarks on this verse: 'This line is overloaded. "I heard it not" is implied in "indeed". Read: Indeed? why then it does draw near the hour!' It need hardly be added that a conjecture of such unwarranted boldness is not in accordance

with the rules of modern criticism and cannot but be rejected.
Nevertheless Seymour seems to have been on the right scent, for a
verse of six feet looks suspicious and out of place here. This was
evidently felt also by Rowe, who (according to the Cambridge Edition) expunged *Indeed*. In my opinion, the word *Indeed* does not
belong to Horatio, but should be given to Hamlet, so that the passage would run thus: —

> *Ham.* The air bites shrewdly; it is very cold.
> *Hor.* It is a nipping and an eager air.
> *Ham.* What hour now?
> *Hor.*   I think it lacks of twelve.
> *Mar.* No, it is struck.
> *Ham.* Indeed?
> *Hor.* I heard it not; it then draws near the season
> Wherein the spirit held his wont to walk.

Only on the stage the import of this arrangement can be fully shown.
Hamlet has evidently followed Horatio and Marcellus to the platform
in a state of dreaminess; his question *What hour now?* is uttered
rather listlessly and with no deeper motive than to break the silence.
On hearing, however, from Marcellus that it has just struck midnight, he is at once roused to the most anxious expectation as now
or never the appearance of the Ghost must be at hand. To this
expectation he gives expression by the exclamation *Indeed?* — By
the way, it may be added that the Editors of the Globe Edition,
and Mr. Moberly in their wake, give the words *No, it is struck*, in
opposition to the Quartos as well as Folios, to Hamlet; on what
grounds, it does not appear — at all events they ought to have been
'more relative'. Most likely it is only a mistake, the Cambridge
Edition being in accordance with the old copies. (The Athenæum,
Jan. 11, 1879, 40 seq. — Robinson's Epitome of Literature, Mar. 15,
1879, Vol. III, p. 48.)

CCCXCI.

> The dram of eale
> Doth all the noble substance of a doubt
> To his owne scandle.

Ib., I, 4, 36 seqq.

None of the numerous conjectural emendations to which this passage
has given rise, is a real improvement on the notoriously corrupt
text. I think we might obtain a very near approach to the reading
of the old copies, together with an unexceptionable sense, by printing: —

> The dram of evil
> Doth all the noble substance *often daub*
> To his own scandal.

Compare B. Jonsou, Every Man out of his Humour (Induction): —
My soul
      Was never ground into such oily colours
      To flatter vice, and daub iniquity.

Beaumont and Fletcher, The Knight of the Burning Pestle, V, 3: —
I shall never more
      Hold open, whilst another pumps both legs,
      Nor daub a sattin gown with rotten eggs.

A Warning for Fair Women, A. II, ll. 1448 seqq. (Simpson, The School
of Shakspere, II, 325): —

      Vile world, how like a monster come I soyld from thee!
      How have I wallowed in thy lothsome filth,
      Drunke and besmear'd with al thy bestial sinne.   ·

In regard to the sentiment expressed in Hamlet's words compare
Nash, Pierce Pennilesse (ed. Collier for the Shakespeare Society, 53),
a passage, which, as far as I know, has never yet been brought
into comparison with the lines in Hamlet: 'Let him bee indued with
neuer so manie vertues, and haue as much goodly proportion and
favour, as Nature can bestow vpon a man, yet if hee be thirstie
after his owne destruction, and hath no ioy nor comfort, but when
he is drowning his soule in a gallon pot, that one beastly imper-
fection wil vtterly obscure all that is commendable in him, and all
his goode qualities sinke like lead downe to the bottome of his car-
rowsing cups, where they will lye, like lees and dregges, dead and
vnregarded of any man.' — Pierce Pennilesse, to add this as a matter worthy of further consideration, was published in 1592, whilst
the above Shakespearean passage does not appear in the quarto of
1603, but is only found in that of 1604. —

   Eleven years after the first publication of this conjectural emendation (The Athenæum, Aug. 11, 1866, 186) Mr. Samuel Neil, in
his edition of Hamlet, apparently without any knowledge of my suggestion, proposed the following: —

This dram of talc
      Doth all the noble substance overdaube [sic!],
      To its own scandal.

Talc, which, Mr. Neil says, 'was a wonderful cosmetic and preser-
vative of the complexion, much in use in Shakespeare's time', would
be just the reverse of what is required by the context. Some Elizabethan authority for the verb overdaub would have been welcome.

   Notwithstanding these defects Mr. Neil's conjecture has led me
to re-consider the passage and I now imagine that my conjectural emendation might be improved by a slight alteration: instead of often daub,
we should write oft bedaub. The meaning of the passage is: 'A
single dram of evil is sufficient to bedaub (besmirch, besmear, or

soil) the whole of a noble substance and render it as scandalous
as it is itself.' The verb *to bedaub* occurs in Romeo and Juliet,
III, 2, 54 seqq.: —

> A piteous corse, a bloody piteous corse;
> Pale, pale as ashes, all bedaub'd in blood,
> All in gore-blood, &c.;

in Marlowe's Edward II, II, 2, 181 (ed. Tancock): —

> and thyself,
> Bedaub'd with gold, rode laughing at the rest;

and in Bishop Hall's Satires (Chiswick, 1824), Bk. IV, Sat. I, p. 78: —

> The close adultress, where her name is red,
> Comes crawling from her husband's lukewarm bed,
> Her carrion skin bedaub'd with odours sweet
> Groping the postern with her bared feet. — —
> She seeks her third roost on her silent toes,
> Besmeared all with loathsome smoke of lust,
> Like Acheron's steams, or smouldering sulphur dust.

Shakespeare frequently indulges in the metaphorical use of similar
verbs, such as *smirch, stain, smear, besmear,* and *bestain*; see Much
Ado about Nothing, IV, 1, 135; Love's Labour's Lost, II, 1, 47 seqq.;
The Merchant of Venice, V, 218 seq.; King John, IV, 3, 24; 1 K.
Henry IV., I, 1, 85 seq.; 1 K. Henry VI., IV, 7, 3; K. Henry VIII.,
I, 2, 121 seqq.; Timon of Athens, I, 1, 15 seqq.; The Rape of Lucrece,
55 seq.; ib., 195 seq.

CCCXCII.

> You know, sometimes he walks four hours together,
> Here in the lobby.　　　　　　　　　　*Ib., II, 2, 160 seq.*

Dr. Jacob Heussi in his edition of this tragedy (Parchim, 1868) has
inserted Hanmer's conjecture 'for' into the text and justifies this
reading by the following note: 'Alle alten Drucke lesen freilich *four*
st. *for,* und die Erklärer behaupten, *four* werde häufig als unbe-
stimmte Zahl gebraucht, wie *forty*; nirgends findet sich aber diese
Behauptung durch ein wirkliches Beispiel constatirt; dass *four* heut
zu Tage nicht in dieser Weise gebraucht wird, ist bekannt, ob es
früher der Fall war, ist noch abzuwarten. Ich setze hier die Präposition *for* statt des *four* der Ausgaben, da diese Präposition die
Zeitdauer bezeichnet.'* Benno Tschischwitz (Shakspere's Hamlet &c.
Halle, 1869) reads *four,* but seems to take this number in its literal
meaning. *'Four hours',* he says, 'wäre eine auffallend lange Zeit,

---

* The latest American editor of Shakespeare's Tragedy of Hamlet, the
Rev. Henry N. Hudson, also reads 'for', and does not even think it necessary
to justify it.

um sich zu ergehn, wenn sie nicht der Prinz, der gänzlich ohne die
noblen Passionen eines Laertes ist, mit Lectüre und Meditationen aus-
füllte.   Auch Ophelia wird später aufgefordert 'to walk' und dabei
in einem Buche zu lesen, es mag dies also wohl einer Zeitsitte ent-
sprechen.'   Mr. Collier's corrected Folio exhibits the correction *for*
and even Malone preferred this oft-repeated conjectural emendation
to the reading of the old editions, although he adduces the following
passage from Webster's Duchess of Malfi (IV, 1, 10 seq.), which is so
much to the point that it ought to have removed every doubt: —

> She will muse four hours together; and her silence,
> Methinks, expresseth more than if she spake.

Malone (Supplement, I, 352) goes so far as to suppose the same
mistake to have taken place here as well as in Hamlet and Mr. Collier
in his Supplemental Notes, I, 276 expresses the same conviction; 'the
same probable misprint', he says, 'of *four* for *for* is contained in
Webster's Duchess of Malfi, A. IV (ed. Dyce, I, 260), where Bosola is
giving to Ferdinand a description of the demeanour of the heroine' &c.

The fact is that *four,* as well as *forty* and *forty thousand,* is
used to denote an indefinite number and this use, dating from a very
remote period, is by no means confined to the English language, but
is also to be found in other languages.   As an indefinite number
generally supposes a large quantity it will not appear strange that
four occurs much less frequently in this sense than *forty*; the instances, however, are numerous enough to convince even Dr. Heussi.

After the remarks made by J. Grimm (Deutsche Rechtsalter-
thümer, 211 seqq.) on the number 'four' there can be little doubt as
to its early connection with the four cardinal points and their influence
on the construction of roads, the distribution of land and other matters
of custom.*   But in German, as well as in English, all local and
legal associations connected with this number have long ago vanished,
and when in the Lay of the Nibelungen (Lachmann, 2014; Zarncke,
4th Ed., p. 318) we read: —

> tûsent unde viere, die kômen dar in,

'tûsent' merely means an indefinite quantity and 'viere' a surplus
likewise indefinite.   In Ayrer's plays (ed. A. v. Keller, IV, 2796 and
2801) occur the following passages: —

> Er würd wol vier mahl vmb gebracht,
> Eh er ein mal drob thet erwachen,

and: —

> Ach Ancilla, ich bitt durch Gott
> Verlass mich nicht in dieser Noth!
> Vier Cronen geb' ich dir zu Lohn.

---

* According to Pott (Die quinare und vigesimale Zählmethode, Halle,
1847, S. 74 seq.) four is the primary number with the Hawaians, perhaps in
accordance with the four extremities of the human body.

The earliest instance in English I have met with, is in Robert
Mannyng's translation of Peter Langtoft's Chronicle (*apud* Wülcker,
Altenglisches Lesebuch, I, 64 and 153): —

    Sone in for yers perchance a werre shall rise.

Very near to the passage in Hamlet comes the following from Puttenham's Arte of English Poesie (ed. Arber, 307): 'laughing and
gibing with their familiars foure houres by the clocke.'   Other instances, no less striking, are supplied by the Elizabethan dramatists,
Shakespeare amongst the number.   In the Old Play of Timon (ed.
Dyce, p. 7) we read: —

    Timon, lend me a little goulden dust,
    To ffree me from this ffeind; some fower talents
    Will doe it.

S. Rowley, When you see me, you know me (ed. Elze, 22): 'The
lords has attended here this four days.' — Lilly's Endimion, IV, 2
(Dramatic Works, ed. F. W. Fairholt, I, 53): '*Sam.*   But how wilt
thou live? *Epi.* By angling; O 'tis a stately occupation to stand
foure houres in a colde morning, and to have his nose bitten with
frost before his baite be mumbled with a fish.' — Lord Cromwell, II, 2
(Malone's Supplement, II, 391): 'We were scarce four miles in the
green water, but I, thinking to go to my afternoon's nuncheon, felt
a kind of rising in my guts.' — Webster, The White Devil, or
Vittoria Corombona (The Works of John Webster, ed. Dyce, 1857,
47a): —

    I made a vow to my deceasèd lord,
    Neither yourself nor I should outlive him
    The numbering of four hours.

Ib., (ed. Dyce, 49b): —

    O could I kill you forty times a day,
    And use 't four years together, 'twere too little.

Fair Em (ed. Del., 17. — W. and Pr., 20): —

    I have not seen him this four days at the least.

The Winter's Tale, V, 2, 146 seqq.: '*Autolycus.*   I know you are
now, sir, a gentleman born. *Clown.* Ay, and have been so any
time these four hours.' — K. Henry V., V, 1, 42 seq.: 'I say, I will
make him eat some part of my leek, or I will peat his pate four
days.' — William Rowley, A Match at Midnight (Hazlitt's Dodsley,
XIII, 25): 'That, by four days' stay, a man should lose his blood!'
In Ellis' Specimens, II, 301, the giant Ferragus is thus described: —

    He had twenty men's strength;
    And forty feet of length
      Thilke paynim had;
    And four feet in the face
    Y-meten on the place,
      And fifteen in brede.

'Fifteen', in the last line, has evidently been introduced for want of another indefinite numeral.

These passages, I think, are amply sufficient for the vindication of the reading *four hours,* but in order fully to illustrate the subject the numbers *forty* and *forty thousand* must also be taken into consideration. As early as in the Old Testament 'forty' is used in an indefinite sense; the Deluge lasts forty days and forty nights; Moses with the Jews lives forty years in the wilderness (Acts, XIII, 18) and stays forty days and forty nights on Mount Sinai (Exodus, XXIV, 18). According to the Book of Judges (III, 11; V, 31; VIII, 28) the land had repeatedly rest for forty years and the children of Israel were delivered into the hands of the Philistines for forty years (Judges, XIII, 1).* Jesus fasted forty days and forty nights in the wilderness (Matth., IV, 2). The same use prevails in the popular poetry both of Germany and England. Thus in the ballad Das Schloss in Oesterreich (*apud* Scherer, Jungbrunnen, 3ᵈ Ed., 67) we read: —

> Darinnen liegt ein junger Knab
> Auf seinen Hals gefangen,
> Wol vierzig Klafter tief unter der Erd'
> Bei Ottern und bei Schlangen.

Jacob Ayrer (Dramatische Werke, herausgeg. von A. v. Keller, V, 3213) says: —

> Starb doch der gross Riess Goliat,
> Der deiner sterckh wol firtzigk hat.

In the English romance of Richard Cœur-de-Lion the hero winds forty yards of silk cloth round his arm before putting it into the lion's mouth and tearing out his heart; compare Percy's Reliques, Essay on the Ancient Metrical Romances.

Instances of the use of 'forty' in Elizabethan dramatists are exceedingly frequent. Webster, The White Devil, or Vittoria Corombona (Works, ed. Dyce, 26b): —

> Wilt sell me forty ounces of her blood
> To water a mandrake?

Heywood, If you know not me, you know nobody (ed. Collier, 71; cf. ib., 125): —

> Bid him by that token
> Sort thee out forty pounds' worth of such wares
> As thou shalt think most beneficial.

---

* Also the numbers *four, twenty* (the half of forty), *twenty two thousand, forty thousand,* and *four hundred thousand* seem to have been used in an indefinite sense in the Old Testament no less than in the Elizabethan dramatists; cf. Judges XI, 40. XIX, 2. IV, 3. XX, 21. XV, 20. XVI, 31. V, 8. XX, 2. XX, 17.

Ben Jonson, The Devil is an Ass, II, 3: —

> O, sir! and dresses himself the best, beyond
> Forty of your very ladies; did you never see him?

B. Jonson, Epicœne, IV, 1: I have not kissed my Fury these forty weeks. — Ib.: A most vile face! And yet she spends me forty pound a year in mercury and hogsbones. — Bartholomew Fair, II, 1: Like enough, sir; she'll do forty such things in an hour (an you listen to her) for her recreation. — Ib., III, 1: Put him a-top o' the table, where his place is, and he'll do you forty fine things. — Marlowe, The Jew of Malta, IV, 4 (ed. Dyce, 168b): Within forty foot of the gallows, conning his neckverse. — Beaumont and Fletcher, The Knight of Malta, III, 4: —

> Oh, 't was royal music!
> And to procure a sound sleep for a soldier,
> Worth forty of your fiddles.

The Merry Wives of Windsor, I, 1, 205: I had rather than forty shillings, I had my book of songs and sonnets here. — The Comedy of Errors, IV, 3, 84 and 97: —

> A ring he hath of mine worth forty ducats —
> For forty ducats is too much to lose.

A Midsummer-Night's Dream, II, 1, 175 seq.: —

> I'll put a girdle round about the earth
> In forty minutes.

Twelfth Night, V, 1, 180 seq.: I had rather than forty pound I were at home. — Henry VIII., V, 4, 53 seq.: When I might see from far some forty truncheoners draw to her succour.

Even now-a-days this use of 'forty' is by no means extinct. In Wordsworth's little poem 'Written in March' (Poetical Works, Moxon, 1850, 6 vols, II, 110) we read: —

> The cattle are grazing,
> Their heads never raising;
> There are forty feeding like one.

The well-known ballad 'Barbara Frietchie' by Mr. J. G. Whittier (Complete Poetical Works, Boston, 1879, 270) contains the following lines: —

> Forty flags with their silver stars,
> Forty flags with their crimson bars,
>
> Flapped in the morning wind: the sun
> Of noon looked down, and saw not one.

'Forty thousand' occurs in 1 Tamburlaine, II, 1 (ed. Dyce, 13b. — A. Wag., 508): —

> Our army will be forty thousand strong.

Edward III., IV, 6 (ed. Del., 78. — W. and Pr., 73): —

> No less than forty thousand wicked elders
> Have forty lean slaves this day ston'd to death.

Webster, The White Devil, or Vittoria Corombona (Works, ed. Dyce, 25a): I'd — — be entered into the list of the forty thousand pedlers in Poland. — The Winter's Tale, IV, 4, 279 seqq.: Here's another ballad of a fish, that appeared upon the coast on Wednesday the fourscore of April, forty thousand fathom above water and sung this ballad against the hard hearts of maids.

In Laȝamon, 25, 395 we have 'feouwer hundred thusende.'

It is a noteworthy fact that the halves of these numbers, from 'two' upwards, are likewise used in the same indefinite sense. K. Lear, I, 2, 169 seq.: *Edm.* Spake you with him? *Edg.* Ay, two hours together. — Greene's Tu Quoque (Hazlitt's Dodsley, XI, 207): I could have maintained this theme this two hours. — Heywood, The Four Ps (Hazlitt's Dodsley, I, 363): —

> Doubtless this kiss shall do you great pleasure;
> For all these two days it shall so ease you,
> That none other savours shall displease you.
>   *'Pothecary.* All these two days! nay, all these two years;*
> For all the savours that may come here
> Can be no worse.

The Old Play of Timon (ed. Dyce, 73): —

>   *Gelas.* Pseudocheus,
> How many miles think you that wee must goe?
>   *Pseud.* Two thousande, forty four.

Hamlet, IV, 4, 25: —

> Two thousand souls, and twenty thousand ducats.**

Nobody and Somebody, l. 1276 seqq. (Simpson, The School of Shakspere, I, 327): —

> Two thousand Souldiors have I brought from Wales,
> To wait upon the princely Peridure.
>   *Malg.* As many of my bold confederates
> Have I drawn from the South, to sweare allegiance
> To young Vigenius.

The use of 'twenty', as is to be expected, far exceeds that of 'two' in frequency. The Tempest, II, 1, 278 seqq.: —

>   twenty consciences
> That stand 'twixt me and Milan, candied be they
> And melt ere they molest.

---

* The rhyme clearly shows that we should write: *this two year.*

** S. Walker (Crit. Exam., III, 268) feels convinced, that an indefinite number is required here, but, not being aware of the true nature of 'two thousand', needlessly conjectures 'Ten thousand'.

The Merchant of Venice, II, 6, 66: —

    I have sent twenty out to seek for you.

Ib., III, 4, 74: —

    And twenty of these puny lies I'll tell.

Ib., III, 4, 84: —

    For we must measure twenty miles to-day,

where, however, 'twenty' may possibly have been used in its literal sense; see my Abhandlungen zu Shakespeare, 304. — The Taming of the Shrew, Induction, II, 37 seq.: —

             Apollo plays
    And twenty caged nightingales do sing.

Richard II., II, 2, 14: —

    Each substance of a grief hath twenty shadows.

Heywood, If you know not me, you know nobody (ed. Collier, 125): —

        Thou owest me but twenty pound
    I'll venture forty more.

Ib., (ed. Collier, 150): —

    Now, for your pains, there is twenty pound in gold.

The Return from Parnassus, III, 2 (Hawkins, Origin of the English Drama, III, 242): When he returns, I'll tell twenty admirable lies of his hawk. — Ib., (Hawkins, III, 249): —

    His hungry sire will scrape you twenty legs
    From one good Christmas meal on Christmas-day, &c.

S. Rowley, When you see me, you know me (ed. Elze, 36): King Harry loves a man and I perceive there's some mettle in thee, there's twenty angels for thee.* — In Chapman's Alphonsus (ed. Elze, 49) a poison is extolled because: —

    it is twenty hours before it works,

whilst in Marlowe's Jew of Malta, III (ed. Dyce, 163 b) it is said of another poison that no less than forty hours must elapse before its effect be perceived: —

    It is a precious powder that I bought
    Of an Italian, in Ancona, once,
    Whose operation is to bind, infect,
    And poison deeply, yet not appear
    In forty hours after it is ta'en.

A Warning for Fair Women, A. II, 1. 820 seq. (Simpson, The School of Shakspere, II, 300): —

    Roger, canst thou get but twenty pound,
    Of all the plate that thou hadst. from us both.

---

* A few lines before the King gives one of the prisoners 'forty angels', to 'drink to king Harry's health'.

Ib., A. II, 1. 1062 seqq. (Simpson, II, 310): —

> I have heard it told, that digging up a grave
> Wherein a man had twenty years been buried, &c.

A very curious instance occurs in Hamlet, V, 1, 257, where 'twenty' in the first Quarto (1603): —

> I lou'de Ofelia as deere as twenty brothers could,

has been increased in the later Qq and the Ff to the far larger number of 'forty thousand': —

> I lov'd Ophelia; forty thousand brothers
> Could not, with all their quantity of love,
> Make up my sum.

'Twenty-thousand' occurs hardly less frequently than 'twenty'. The Two Gentlemen of Verona, II, 6, 16: —

> With twenty thousand soul-confirming oaths.

The Merry Wives of Windsor, IV, 4, 90: —

> Though twenty thousand worthier come to crave her.

Love's Labour's Lost, V, 2, 37: —

> I am compared to twenty thousand fairs.

The Taming of the Shrew, II, 1, 123 and V, 2, 113: twenty thousand crowns. K. Richard II., IV, 1, 59: —

> To answer twenty thousand such as you.

2 K. Henry VI., III, 2, 141 seq.: —

> Fain would I go to chafe his paly lips
> With twenty thousand kisses.

Ib., III, 2, 206: —

> Though Suffolk dare him twenty thousand times.

Coriolanus, III, 3, 70: —

> Within thine eyes sat twenty thousand deaths.

Hamlet, IV, 4, 60: —

> The imminent death of twenty thousand men.

In Dryden's alteration of the Tempest, IV, 1, we meet with 'twenty hundred': —

> You cannot tell me, sir,
> I know I'm made for twenty hundred women
> (I mean if there so many be i' th' world), &c.

The very acme of indefinite numbers is reached, curiously enough, by a rather sedate and cool-headed character, viz. Friar Laurence in Romeo and Juliet, III, 3, 153: —

> and call thee back
> With twenty hundred thousand times more joy
> Then thou went'st forth in lamentation.

Also 'four and twenty' and 'two and twenty' may be mentioned as indefinite numbers; the former occurs in The Winter's Tale, IV, 3, 43: She hath made me four and twenty nosegays for the shearers; and in 1 K. Henry IV., III, 3, 85: and money lent you, four and twenty pound. 'Two and twenty' is found in 1 K. Henry IV., I, 1, 68 seqq.: —

> Ten thousand bold Scots, two and twenty knights,
> Balk'd in their own blood did Sir Walter see
> On Holmedon's plain.

Ib., II, 2, 16 seq.: I have forsworn his company hourly any time this two and twenty years, and yet I am bewitched with the rogue's company. — Ib., III, 3, 211: O for a fine thief, of the age of two and twenty or thereabouts.

Even 'eighty' ($=$ twice forty) occurs in an indefinite sense; see Hawkins, The Origin of the English Drama (Oxford, 1773), III, 233: Hark thou, sir; you shall have eighty thanks.

I am of course far from asserting that no other numbers but those here discussed are used to denote an indefinite quantity; on the contrary several others, such as 'three', 'seven', 'three and twenty' (Troilus and Cressida, I, 2, 255), 'three and twenty thousand' (1 K. Henry VI., I, 1, 113), 'five and twenty', 'five and twenty thousand' (3 K. Henry VI., II, 1, 181), are used more or less frequently in the same manner. (Jahrb. d. D. Sh.-G., XI, 288 seqq.)

CCCXCIII.

On Fortune's cap we are not the very button.

Ib., II, 2, 233.

In addition to what I have remarked on this line in my second edition of Hamlet (p. 156 seq.) I am now able to state that the Scotch cap was indeed worn in Shakespeare's time. This fact is proved by the following stage-direction in Locrine, A. IV, sc. 2: *Enter Strumbo, wearing a Scotch cap, with a Pitch-fork in his hand.* Whether or not it was decorated with a flowing ribbon, may still be doubted, although it would seem highly probable.

CCCXCIV.

When we have shuffled off this mortal coil.

Ib., III, 1, 67.

A non-English critic may well pause before questioning an expression which for a couple of centuries has been, as it were, a household word with all English-speaking people. I am, however, unable to silence the critical doubts to which the expression 'mortal coil' has given rise in me and which are greatly increased by the disagreement that prevails even among English commentators about it. Warburton takes 'coil' in the sense of 'turmoil, bustle', and Al. Schmidt (Shakespeare-Lexicon, s. v.) likewise defines it by 'this turmoil of mortality, of life'; Heath thinks 'mortal coil' means the 'incumbrance of this mortal body'; and Caldecott does not hesitate to claim two (or three) meanings at one and the same time for the' word, viz. that of 'turmoil' and that of 'ringlet' or 'slough'. 'It is here used', he says, 'in each of its senses: turmoil, or bustle, and that which entwines or wraps round. Snakes generally lie like the coils of ropes; and it is conceived that an allusion is here had to the struggle which that animal is obliged to make in casting his slough.' This explanation, though backed by no less an authority than Dr. Furness, in my opinion can hardly be maintained, since the meaning of the word 'coil' with Elizabethan writers can be shown to have been quite definite and unequivocal. Other critics think 'coil' in our passage to be equivalent to what Fletcher (Bonduca, IV, 1) calls the 'case of flesh'. 'It has been contended', says the late Dr. Ingleby (Shakespeare Hermeneutics, 88) 'that in Hamlet's speech, the "mortal coil" is the coil, i. e. the trouble or turmoil, incident to man's mortal state: but the analogies are too strong in favour of the "mortal coil" being what Fletcher calls the "case of flesh".' It is greatly to be regretted that Dr. Ingleby has not favoured his readers with some one or other of these strong analogies. In the same, or at least in a similar, sense the word seems to have been taken by R. Chambers in his Traditions of Edinburgh, 198 seq.: 'Or does the "mortal coil" in which the light of mind is enveloped, become thinner or more transparent by the wearing of deadly sickness?' The explanation of the passage given by James Henry Hackett (Notes and Comments upon Certain Plays and Actors of Shakespeare, New York, 1864, 21 and 25) comes nearly to the same. This supposed signification of the word, however, is not supported by testimony; it is rather a signification 'for the nonce', a *petitio principii*. Still less acceptable is that which a late English friend of mine imagined to be the meaning of 'coil' in the present passage; he understood it to denote a slough. But 'coil' nowhere occurs in this sense, and if it did, this sense would not fit the present passage, inasmuch as the poet does by no means speak of our mortal coil as of something which like a slough has already been cast off, but as of something which we are still wearing.

Apart from the line under discussion, the word 'coil' occurs eleven times in Shakespeare and in all these passages has the signification of 'turmoil, bustle, noise, disturbance'. To examine these instances which are enumerated both in Mrs. Cowden Clarke's Concordance and in Al. Schmidt's Shakespeare-Lexicon would be labour thrown away, especially since all editors agree with respect to their interpretation. As may be expected, the word is no less frequent with other dramatists and writers of the Elizabethan era, and in order to get firm ground· for our further inquiry it may, perhaps, be as well first to give a list of all those various passages which in the course of many years' reading I have been able to collect.

1. Marlowe, 2 Tamburlaine, IV, 1 (ed. Dyce, 61b. — Ed. A. Wagner, 3744, seqq.): *Caly.* I would my father would let me be put in the front of such a battle once, to try my valour! [*Alarms within.*] What a coil they keep! I believe there will be some hurt done anon amongst them.

2. Marlowe, Faustus, V, 1 (ed. Dyce, 129a. — Ed. W. Wagner, 94): —

> *Duke.* What rude disturbers have we at the gate?
> Go, pacify their fury, set it ope,
> And then demand of them what they would have.
>   [*They knock again, and call out to talk with Faustus.*
> *Serv.* Why, how now, masters! what a coil is there!
> What is the reason you disturb the Duke?

3. Marlowe, The Tragedy of Dido, A. IV init. (ed. Dyce, 265a): —

> I think it was the devil's revelling night,
> There was such hurly-burly in the heavens:
> Doubtless Apollo's axle-tree is crack'd,
> Or agèd Atlas' shoulder out of joint,
> The motion was so over-violent.
> *Iar.* In all this coil, where have ye left the queen?

4. Marlowe, Hero and Leander, Sixth Sestiad (ed. Dyce, 307a): —

> As when you descry
> A ship, with all her sail contends to fly
> Out of the narrow Thames with winds unapt,
> Now crosseth here, then there, then this way rapt,
> And then hath one point reach'd, then alters all,
> And to another crookèd reach doth fall
> Of half a bird-bolt's shoot, keeping more coil
> Than if she danc'd upon the ocean's toil.

5. Ben Jonson, Cynthia's Revels, IV, 1: Heart of my body, here's a coil, indeed, with your jealous humours.

6. Ben Jonson, Bartholomew Fair, I, 1: Do you hear! Jack Littlewit, what business does thy pretty head think this fellow may have, that he keeps such a coil with?

7. Ib., I, 1: And then he is such a ravener after fruit! — you will not believe what a coil I had t' other day to compound a business between Cather'ne pear woman and him, about snatching: 't is intolerable, gentlemen!

8. Ben Jonson, Volpone, II, 1 (Nano sings): —
You that would last long, list to my song,
Make no more coil, but buy of this' oil.

9. Edward III., IV, 6 (ed. Del., 76. — W. and Pr., 72): —
What need we fight, and sweat, and keep a coil,
When railing crows outscold our adversaries.

10. The Spanish Tragedy, A. III (Qu. 1618, 32a): —
How now, what noise?   What coyle is that you keepe?
                                        [*A noyse within.*

11. Lord Cromwell, I, 1 (Malone's Supplement, II, 374): He keeps such a coil in his study, with the sun, and the moon, and the seven stars, that I do verily think he'll read out his wits.

12. Middleton, The Mayor of Quinborough, III, 3 (Dodsley, 1780, XI, 127): Here's no sweet coil, I am glad they are so reasonable. (Some lines *antè* we have the stage-direction: *A noise without.*)

13. S. Rowley, When you see me, you know me (ed. Elze, 11): Dost thou hear, Harry, what a coil they keep?

14. Eastward Ho! IV, 1 (The Works of George Chapman: Plays. Ed. R. H. Shepherd, 470a): 'S light! I think the devil be abroad, in likeness of a storm, to rob me of my horns! Hark, how he roars! Lord! what a coil the Thames keeps!

15. Arden of Feversham, III, 6 (ed. Del., 49. — W. and Pr., 46): —
'Zounds! here's a coil;
You were best swear me on the interrogatories,
How many pistols you have took in hand,
Or whether I love the smell of gunpowder,
Or dare abide the noise the dag will make,
Or will not wink at flashing of the fire?

16. Rob. Chester's Loves Martyr, ed. Grosart (for the New Shakspere Society), 94: —
Then Rage and Danger doth their senses haunt,
And like mad Aiax they a coile do keepe,
Till leane-fac'd Death into their heart doth creepe.

17. Histrio-Mastix, A. III, 1. 92 (Simpson, The School of Shakspere, II, 47): What a coyle keepes those fellows there?

18. Jack Drum's Entertainment, A. II (Simpson, The School of Shakspere, II, 162): —
What harsh, vnciuill tongue keeps such a coyle?

19. Marston, Antonio and Mellida, A. II init. (Works, ed. Halliwell, I, 20): Slud (cri'd Signior Balurdo) O for Don Bessiclers armour, in the mirror of knighthood: what coil's here? O for an armour, canon proofe: O, more cable, more fetherbeds, more fether-

beds, more cable, till hee had as much as my cable hatband, to fence him.

20. Hugh Holland, quoted in Malone's Shakespeare by Boswell (1821), II, 221 (according to S. Walker, Crit. Exam., II, 116): —

Here no need is of my sorry charmes
To boast it, though my braines Apollo warmes;
Where, like in Jove's, Minerva keeps a coile.

21. Nash, Summer's Last Will and Testament (Hazlitt's Dodsley, VIII, 30): Heigh ho. Here is a coil indeed to bring beggars to stocks.

22. Ib., (Hazlitt's Dodsley, VIII, 47): Here is a coil about dogs without wit.

23. Nash, Pierce Pennilesse, ed. Collier (for the Shakespeare Society), 48: Lord! what a coyle have we, this course and that course, removing this dish higher, setting another lower, and taking away the third. A generall might in lesse space remove his camp, than they stand disposing of their gluttony.

24. Nash, A Private Epistle of the Author to the Printer &c. before the second edition of Pierce Pennilesse (ed. Collier, XIV): And, lastly, to the ghost of Robert Greene, telling him what a coyle there is with pampheting [*sic, read pamphleting*] on him after his death.

25. Gascoigne's Princely Pleasures with the Masque intended to have been presented before Qu. Elizabeth at Kenilworth Castle, 1575. With an Introductory Memoir and Notes (London, 1821), p. 6: —

What stir, what coil is here? come back, hold, whither now?
Not one so stout to stir, what harrying have we here?

26. Beaumont and Fletcher, The Humorous Lieutenant, V, 4: —

And such a coil there is
Such fending and such proving.

To these instances of the substantive 'coil' I join three passages in which the verb 'to coil' occurs, once in the signification 'to wind, to form ringlets', twice in the signification 'to beat, to drub'. They are: —

27. Beaumont and Fletcher, The Knight of Malta, II, 1: —

Third Sol. We have seen the fight, sir.
Nor. Yes; coil'd up in a cable, like salt eels,
Or buried low i' th' ballast: do you call that fighting?

28. A Comedy of K. Cambises (Hawkins, Origin of the English Drama, I, 266): Here draw and fight. Here she must lay on and coyle them both, the Vice must run his way for feare &c.

29. The Wife Lapped in Morel's Skin (The Old Taming of a Shrew, ed. Th. Amyot for the Shakespeare Society, 79): —

Except she turne and change her minde,
And eake her conditions euerichone,

> She shall fynde me to her so vnkinde,
> That I shall her coyle both backe and bone,
> And make her blew and also blacke,
> That she shall grone agayne for woe.

This is the whole number of instances of 'coil' which I have come across in Elizabethan literature; there may, no doubt, be many more, but I have no knowledge of them. I hardly need assure the reader that I do not withhold a single instance, least of all one where 'coil' might be taken in a different sense. As to the modern use of the word the influence of the Hamlet-passage, in many cases, is distinctly discernible, even where we have not to deal with a mere quotation of, or an intentional allusion to, it. I continue my list, beginning this, its second series with the era of the Restoration.

30. Davenant, The Playhouse to be Let, A. V (Works, 1673, II, 118): —

> Widow, be friends, make no more such a hot coyle;
> We'll find out rich Husband to make the pot boyl.

31. Butler, Hudibras, Part I, Canto 3, l. 183 seqq.: —

> He rag'd, and kept as heavy a Coil as
> Stout Hercules for Loss of Hylas;
> Forcing the Vallies to repeat
> The Accents of his sad Regret.

32. Scott, The Lady of the Lake, Canto III, 24: —

> The signal roused to martial coil
> The sullen margin of Loch Voil.

33. Ib., Canto V, 16: —

> Like adder darting from his coil,
> Like wolf that dashes through the toil,
> Like mountain-cat who guards her young,
> Full at Fitz-James's throat he sprung.

34. Scott, Rokeby, Canto III, 6: —

> Thus circled in his coil, the snake
> When roving hunters beat the brake,
> Watches with red and glistening eye,
> Prepared, if heedless step draw nigh,
> With forked tongue and venom'd fang
> Instant to dart the deadly pang;
> But if the intruders turn aside,
> Away his coils unfolded glide
> And through the deep Savannah wind,
> Some undisturb'd retreat to find.

35. Scott, The Lord of the Isles, Canto I, Introd.: —

> Where rest from mortal coil the mighty of the Isles.

36. Leigh Hunt, The Story of Rimini, init.: —

> And when you listen you may hear a coil
> Of bubbling springs about the grassier soil.

37. R. Chambers, Traditions of Edinburgh (New Edition) p. 111: She now became alarmed, screamed for help, and waved her arms distractedly; all of which signs brought a crowd to the shore she had just left, who were unable, however, to render her any assistance, before she had landed on the other side — fairly cured, it appeared, of all desire of quitting the uneasy coil of mortal life.

Another passage in the same book has already been mentioned on p. 236.

38. Carlyle, History of Friedrich II. of Prussia (Tauchn. Ed.) I, 192: The marriage was done in the Church of Innspruck, 10. Feb. 1342 (for we love to be particular), Kaiser Ludwig, happy man, and many Princes of the Empire, looking on; little thinking what a coil it would prove.

The verb 'to coil' has only thrice occurred to me in modern writers, viz.:

39. Southey, The Life of Nelson, Chap. I (London, Bell, 1876), p. 21: He started up, and found one of the deadliest serpents of the country coiled up at his feet.

40. Galt, The Life of Lord Byron (Paris, Baudry, 1835) p. 232: —

> I felt the many-foot and beetle creep,
> And on my breast the cold worm coil and crawl.

41. J. G. Whittier, Complete Poetical Works (Boston, 1879) p. 1: —

> The moonlight through the open bough
> > Of the gnarl'd beech, whose naked root
> > Coils like a serpent at his foot,
> Falls, checkered on the Indian's brow.

After all these instances there can hardly remain a doubt as to the signification of the substantive 'coil' and it is evident that during the Elizabethan period it occurs exclusively in the meaning of 'turmoil, bustle, tumult, noise'; its second meaning (= ringlet, winding) being only to be met with in modern authors. The fact is, that we have to distinguish between two different words of entirely different origin. Messrs. Wedgwood and Skeat are agreed in deriving 'coil' No. 1 from the Celtic; 'Gael. *goil*, boiling, fume, battle, rage, fury; O. Gael. *goill*, war, fight; Irish *goill*, war, fight; Irish and Gael. *goileam*, prattle, vain tattle; Gael. *coileid*, a stir, movement, noise. — Gael. and Ir. *goil*, to boil, rage.' As to 'coil' No. 2 there is as yet no proof that during the Elizabethan era it was used as a substantive; with the writers of this period it only occurs as a verb (see No. 27) which according to Dr. Skeat originally means 'to gather together'; Dr. Skeat and Mr. Stratmann (Old English Dictionary,

3ᵈ Ed., 128a) rightly derive it from O. F. *coillir, cuillir, cueillir,* Lat. *colligere.* Thus it appears that the substantive 'coil' in the sense of 'ringlet, winding' is a recent formation, derived from the verb. Even 'coil' No. 1 does by no means seem to be an old English word; it is not contained in either Stratmann's Dictionary or in Mætzner's Sprachproben (Glossary). Now, if critics are justly required to be conservative, commentators, in my opinion, ought to be possessed of the same quality, and ought by no means to ascribe any other signification to a word than that in which it is used, without exception, by the writers of the period. In the above line of Hamlet, therefore, a methodical critic has no choice left but to take 'mortal coil' simply, and unequivocally, in the sense of 'mortal turmoil, bustle, noise', which we are required or expected some day to shuffle off.

Under these circumstances I cannot refrain from thinking our passage corrupt. M. Mason, who was of the same opinion, proposed to read *this mortal spoil*; but neither Shakespeare, nor any other Elizabethan dramatist, seems to have used 'spoil' in the sense of 'slough', in which sense Mason wishes it to be understood. An anonymous critic in the Appendix to Shakespeare's Dramatic Works (Leipsic, 1826) p. 106 conjectures *foil* or *clay*, whilst I myself, in my first edition of Hamlet (Leipzig, 1857), have been led to·suggest 'vail' instead of 'coil'. I have, however, withdrawn this suggestion since I am convinced that the passage may be corrected in a much easier, and, at the same time, more satisfactory manner. Steevens, *ad loc.*, quotes a similar passage from 'A dolfull discours of two Straungers, a Lady and a Knight' (in The firste Parte of Church-yardes Chippes, London, 1575, fol. 32 v.), without, however, profiting of the opportunity for correcting the Hamlet-passage, which to him seems to have presented no difficulty whatever. Churchyard's verses are these: —

> Yea, shaking of this sinfull soyle
> Me thincke in cloudes I see
> Amonge the perfite chosen lambs,
> A place preparde for mee.

It is certainly not assuming too much that Shakespeare had read Churchyard's Chippes, which were published when he was eleven years of age, and that the lines may have flashed through his memory when he was writing his most celebrated soliloquy. At all events our passage does not offer the least difficulty if we substitute 'soil' for 'coil'. The expression 'mortal soil' would on the contrary perfectly agree not only with the poet's own sentiments, but also with those of his contemporaries who love to represent the human body as a piece of earth or a heap of dirt or loam. Who does not remember Hamlet's words in the churchyard-scene (V, 1, 231):

'Alexander died, Alexander was buried, Alexander returneth to dust; the dust is earth; of earth we make loam, and why of that loam, whereto he was converted, might they not stop a beer-barrel?' — Similar passages occur in The Tempest, I, 2, 313: —

> Caliban,
>
> Thou earth, thou! speak —

and ib., I, 2, 345: —

> I have used thee
> Filth as thou art with human care.

Still more to the point is the well-known line in Sonnet CXLVI, which forms, as it were, a transition from the Dolefull Discourse to our passage in Hamlet: —

> Poor soul, the centre of my sinful earth.

Compare also Much Ado about Nothing, II, 1, 63 seqq.: Would it not grieve a woman to be overmastered with a piece of valiant dust? to make an account of her life to a clod of wayward marl?

The Merchant of Venice, V, 1, 63 seqq.: —

> Such harmony is in immortal souls;
> But whilst this muddy vesture of decay
> Doth grossly close it in, we cannot hear it.

Compare also K. John, V, 7, 57 seq.: —

> And then, all this thou seest is but a clod
> And module of confounded royalty.

K. Richard II., I, 1, 177 seqq.: —

> The purest treasure mortal times afford
> Is spotless reputation: that away,
> Men are but gilded loam or painted clay.

2 K. Henry IV., I, 2, 8 seqq.: The brain of this foolish-compounded clay, man, is not able to invent any thing that tends to laughter, more than I invent or is invented on me.

Julius Cæsar, III, 1, 254: —

> O pardon me, thou bleeding piece of earth.

Among Shakespeare's contemporaries only the following may be quoted: Dekker, Old Fortunatus (Dekker's Dramatic Works, London, 1873, I, 91): —

> I set an Ideots cap on vertues head,
> Turne learning out of doores, clothe wit in ragges,
> And paint ten thousand Images of Loame,
> In gawdie silken colours.

Th. Heywood's Love's Mistress I, 5 (Dramatic Works, London, 1874, V, 106): —

> A piece of mooving earth —

16*

S. Rowley, When you see me, you know me, ed. Elze, 13: —

> The child is fair, the mother earth and clay.

Appius and Virginia (Hazlitt's Dodsley, IV, 142 seq.) where Virginius exclaims: —

> O man, O mould, O muck, O clay!
> O hell, O hellish hound,
> O false judge Appius, &c.

Whetstone's Remembraunce of the wel imployed Life, and godly End, of George Gascoigne, Esquire (G. Gascoigne, ed. Arber, 24): —

> And what is man? Dust, slime, a puf of winde,
> Conceiued in sin, &c.

Glapthorne, Albertus Wallenstein, III, 3 (Plays and Poems, II, 49): —

> They'r (viz. these desires) all fleshly
> Sordid, as. is the clay this frame's compos'd of.

Sir Philip Sidney, An Apologie for Poetrie, ed. Arber, 29: The final end is, to lead and draw vs to as high a perfection, as our degenerate soules, made worse by theyr clayey lodgings, can be capable of.

To these English writers a German contemporary of Shakespeare may be joined, who passed a great part of his life in London, viz. the poet Rudolf Weckherlin. His poem 'Elend des menschlichen Lebens' (W. Müller's Bibliothek deutscher Dichter des siebzehnten Jahrhunderts, IV, 81) begins with the following lines: —

> Du wenig Koth, du wenig Staub,
> Hochmüthig durch ein wenig Leben,
> Durch welches Leben, wie ein Laub,
> Du kannst ein' Weil' allhie umschweben.

All these instances are of too striking a character not to lend the strongest support to the emendation 'mortal soil'. But also in respect to the *ductus literarum* the alteration is most easy, for Quartos as well as Folios write both 'foyle' and 'foile', 'coyle' and 'coile' indifferently, and an *ſ*, negligently written, or damaged in printing, could be easily taken for a *c.'* At all events, thus much seems certain that if the old editions had read 'mortal soil', nobody would have taken the least exception to this reading, and the most presumptuous of emendators would never have so much as dreamt of proposing 'mortal coil' for 'mortal soil'. (Jahrb. d. D. Sh.-G., II, 362.)

CCCXCV.

> *Ham.* So long? Nay then, let the devil wear black, for I'll have a suit of sables.   *Ib., III, 2, 136 seq.*

In the Jahrb. d. D. Sh.-G., XI, 294 seq., I have tried to show that the contrast between a suit of sables and a mourning garment does not so much lie in the color as in the costliness and splendor of the material. In accordance with the immemorial Biblical usage of mourning in sackcloth and ashes, mourning garments to this day are made of coarse and dull-coloured material, whereas for a suit of sables the most sumptuous stuff was selected. Since I wrote that note I have, however, come across some passages in our Middle High-German poets, from which it would appear, that usually garments of brightest colour especially scarlet and green were trimmed with sable, so that the contrast between a suit of sables and a black mourning garment would be complete even as to colour. I subjoin these passages in their original wording.

1. Seyfried Helbling, XIII, 179 (Haupt, Zeitschrift für deutsches Alterthum, Leipzig, 1844, Vol. IV, p. 214): —

> Wirt mir niht *scharlach* unde *zobel*
> ez wirt mir eins gebûren hobel
> von eim guoten Pöltingære.

2. Maier Helmbrecht 1343 — 1352 (Haupt, Zeitschrift für deutsches Alterthum, Vol. IV, p. 366): —

> Der dritte sac der ist vol,
> ûf und ûf geschoppet wol,
> fritschâl brûnât, vêhe veder
> dar under zwô, der ietweder
> mit *scharlât* ist bedecket,
> und dâ für gestrecket
> einez, heizet *swarzer zobel:*
> die hân ich in einem tobel
> hie nâhen bî verborgen;
> die gibe ich ir morgen.

3. Parzival, herausgegeben von Lachmann, 63, 24: —

> *Grüene samît* was der mandel sîn:
> ein *zobel* dâ vor gap *swarzen* schîn.

It seems that our ancestors — as far as they belonged to the Upper Ten Thousand — delighted in these brilliant garments, particularly in the contrast between bright-coloured materials and dark sable-trimmings. — Compare Westward Ho!, I, 1 and V, 3 (Webster, ed. Dyce, 1857, in 1 vol., p. 210a and 240b).

CCCXCVI.

Look here upon this picture and on this.

Ib., III, 4, 53.

Some light is thrown on this passage by an incident in Marlowe's Edward II., A. I, sc. 4, 1. 127, where the king and his minion Gaveston exchange pictures; the king says: —

> Here, take my picture, and let me wear thine.

It would, therefore, seem most conformable to the usage of Shakespeare's time and stage that the Queen should wear the portrait of her second husband, with whom she may justly be supposed to have exchanged pictures, whereas Hamlet wears a miniature of his father. According to our modern notions, however, it seems far more impressive on the audience to have two half length pictures hung on the wall of the Queen's closet.

CCCXCVII.

For use almost can change the stamp of nature,
And either the devil, or throw him out
With wondrous potency.

Ib., III, 4, 168 seqq.

This is the reading of the quarto of 1604. The later quartos read: —

And master the devil, or throw him out,

whilst in the first quarto, as well as in the folios, the passage is wanting. Whether we follow QB, or its successors, the second line is incomplete and the editors therefore have very properly endeavoured to fill it up. Believing the copyist or compositor of the second quarto to have been deceived by the similarity of the sound of two successive words I formerly suggested: —

And either *usher* the devil, or throw him out.

Although Messrs. Clark and Wright, in their annotated edition of the play, are likewise of opinion 'that something is omitted which is contrasted with *throw out*', yet I have now come to the conviction that most likely such an antithesis was not in the poet's mind, but that his thoughts turned exclusively on the fact that by constant habit the vicious stamp of nature may be reformed. The reading most likely to have come from the poet's pen seems therefore to be: —

And *either master* the devil or throw him out.

This reading is erroneously attributed to the quarto 1604 by S. Walker (Versification, 75). It is true, there is some slight tautology in it, but a tautology which is by no means foreign to Shakespeare. The compositor of the second quarto, I imagine, overlooked the second, those of the later quartos overlooked the first word of the two. As to the metre, I cannot agree with those critics who think it necessary that a monosyllable should be added after *either*, e. g. *curb* or *wean*. S. Walker is quite right in scanning: —

And either master th' devil [pronounce de'il], &c.

(The Athenæum, Aug. 11, 1866, p. 186.)

CCCXCVIII.

The rabble call him lord;
And, as the world were now but to begin,
Antiquity forgot, custom not known,
The ratifiers and props of every word,
They cry, 'Choose we: Laertes shall be king!'

Ib., IV, 5, 102 seqq.

Though this is the uniform reading of the old editions, yet the last
line but one has given rise to a number of conjectural emendations;
Warburton proposed *of every ward*, Johnson, *of every weal*, and
Tyrwhitt, *of every work*. Caldecott (*apud* Furness) and Al. Schmidt,
on the other hand, declare against all alteration of the passage.
Caldecott takes 'word' to mean 'term, appellation or title; as "lord"
and "king";' 'in its more extended sense,' he continues, 'it must
import "every human establishment".' In Al. Schmidt's opinion
(Shakespeare-Lexicon, s. v.) 'every word' signifies 'every thing that
is to serve for a watchword and shibboleth to the multitude.' This
is certainly wrong, whereas the explanation given by Caldecott would
in part be acceptable, if it could be shielded by some authority; in
extending, however, the meaning of 'every word' to 'every human
establishment' he overshoots the mark. Perhaps we should read *of
every worth*, which would at once remove all difficulty. As far as
worth is concerned, Laertes would be a proper person indeed to be
elected king. But the king is not to be chosen, as in primeval
times, for his worthiness alone; antiquity and custom come in for
their share also; they are 'the ratifiers and props of every worth'.
Compare Pericles, II, 3, 6: —

Since every worth in show commends itself.

Thomson's Seasons, III, 943 seq.: —

At home the friend
Of every worth and every splendid art,

and IV, 468: —

Thee, Forbes, too, whom every worth attends.

(Shakespeare's Hamlet, herausgegeben von Elze, Leipzig, 1857, 230. —
The Athenæum, Aug. 11, 1866, 186. — Shakespeare's dramatische
Werke nach der Uebersetzung von Schlegel und Tieck, herausgegeben
durch die Deutsche Shakespeare-Gesellschaft, VI, 177.)

CCCXCIX.

Who, dipping all his faults in their affection,
Would, like the spring that turneth wood to stone,
Convert his gyves to graces.

Ib., IV, 7, 19 seqq.

The corruption of this passage does not lie in *gyves*, as Theobald and others have imagined, but in *graces*. How can *gyves*, a very material object, be converted into abstract *graces*? Not even the Knaresborough spring can effect such an illogical conversion. The context, in a word, will not bear an abstract noun in this place, which would entirely spoil the metaphor. Logical symmetry indeed might be restored, if *gyves* were replaced by an abstract noun, but the comparison then would be deprived of all force, of all sensible, not to say palpable, distinctness and Shakespeare would certainly never have introduced the Knaresborough spring in order to compare two abstract qualities. *Gibes* which has been proposed instead of *gyves* is fairly insufferable. I feel convinced that we ought to correct *graces* to *graves* (according to modern orthography *greaves*), which, at the same time, would give the verse a regular flow. According to the Folio, *graves* occurs in another passage of the poet, which, in some respect, bears a surprising similarity to ours, viz. 2 Henry IV., IV, 1, 50: —

> Turning your books to graves, your ink to blood.*

In both passages something feeble or despicable is to be turned into *graves*, which not only form part of chivalric armour, but, at the some time, are emblems of knighthood. Who does not recollect Homer's ἐϋκνήμιδες Ἀχαιοί and Chapman's *fair greaves* (Iliad XVIII, 415)? *Gyves*, in our passage, stands of course metonymically for those crimes and misdemeanours which ought to be punished by them, *graves* metonymically for those merits and signal deeds, which ought to be rewarded and distinguished by them, or, in a word, which ought to be knighted. The simile of the spring becomes most appropriate if we remember that gyves were originally made of wood. It is true, that in order to render it perfect, graves should have been made of stone instead of steel; but so far it may be conceded that *omne simile claudicat*. *Graces* is, to all appearance, a sophistication of the compositor who hesitated at the unusual word *graves*, provided it be not a simple mistake, which is still likelier. As to the orthography, *graves* instead of *greaves* is quite analogous to *thraves* (for *threaves*) and *stale* (for *steale* or *stele*); compare Mr. Hooper's note on Chapman's Iliad, XI, 477; Chapman's Iliad, IV, 173 and Nares s. *Stele*. On the other hand, *hames* in South Warwickshire becomes *eames* according to Mr. Halliwell - Phillipps, Dict. Arch. and Prov. Words, and Mrs. Francis, South Warwickshire Provincialisms (in Original Glossaries &c. ed. by Walter W. Skeat for

---

* In this line *graves* has an obelus in the Globe Edition. Warburton conjectured *glaives* which has been highly commended by Dr. Ingleby in the Jahrb. d. D. Sh.-G., II, 220, whereas in his Shakespeare Hermeneutics, 61, he feels much less certain. *Glaives* is not a Shakespearean word and *graves*, in my opinion, is the true reading.

the English Dialect Society).   (The Athenæum, Feb. 20, 1869, 284. Jahrb. d. D. Sh.-G., XI, 295 seq.)

Since writing the above I have come across two passages that bid fair to confirm my conjecture *graves*.   In The Merry Wives of Windsor, I, 1, 294 seq. Slender says: 'I bruised my shin th' other day with playing at sword and dagger with a master of fence.'   In Mr. Saintsbury's Life of Dryden in Mr. John Morley's well-known collection of English Men of Letters, at p. 119 seq., we read the following: 'He has exposed. his legs to the arrows of any criticaster who chooses to aim at him.'   Do not these two passages imply that the legs were frequently chosen as an aim by fencers and archers and therefore had to be protected from the enemy's sword and arrows? And by what other means could they be protected than by greaves? At all events this seems to be a track which should be pursued, if we wish to arrive at a thorough understanding and consequent emendation of the king's speech in Hamlet.   Compare my second edition of Hamlet (1882), p. 221 seq. — At the same time I embrace the opportunity of adding *wale* to the list of those words that are spelt with either *a* or *ea*; in Chapman's Iliads, ed. Hooper, Bk. II, 1. 232, it is written *wale,* whereas nowadays it is pretty frequently spelt *weal.*   Compare also S. Walker, Crit. Exam., II, 118 (*wave* and *weave*).

CD.

Where be his quiddities now, his quillets, his cases, his tenures, and his tricks.   *Ib., V, 1, 107 seqq.*

Tenures undoubtedly stands in the wrong place; it is by no means synonymous with quiddities, cases and tricks, but belongs to the law-terms relative to the acquisition and transfer of property, and should accordingly be inserted four lines *infra,* between *recognisances* and *fines.*   This suspicion is strongly confirmed by the Quarto of 1603, in however crude a state the passage may be given there. That this edition reads *tenements* instead of *tenures* is of no importance, inasmuch as our concern lies only with the position of the word, and in this respect the first Quarto exhibits the right text. The passage there runs thus: 'Where is your quirks and quillets now, your vouchers and double vouchers, your leases and freehold, and tenements?'   (The Athenæum, Feb. 20, 1869, 284.)

CDI.

Now pile your dust upon the quick and dead,
Till of this flat a mountain you have made,
To o'ertop old Pelion, or the skyish head
Of blue Olympus.   *Ib., V, 1, 274 seqq.*

> And, if thou prate of mountains, let them throw
> Millions of acres on us, till our ground,
> Singeing his pate against the burning zone,
> Make Ossa like a wart! *Ib., V, 1, 303 seqq.*

Compare Richard Brome, The Court Begger, IV, 3, init. (The Dramatic Works of Rich. Brome &c., London, 1873, Vol. I, p. 245): —

> *Fer[dinand].* Heape yet more Mountaines, Mountaines upon
> Mountaines, Pindus on Ossa, Atlas on Olympus,
> I'le carry that which carries Heaven, do you
> But lay't upon me!

This passage is not contained in either the late Dr. Ingleby's Centurie of Prayse (second edition, by Miss Lucy Toulmin Smith), or in Dr. Furnivall's Fresh Allusions. By the way it may be remarked, that the first two lines are wrongly divided; arrange, of course: —

> Heape yet more Mountaines, Mountaines upon Mountaines,
> Pindus on Ossa, Atlas on Olympus, &c.

CDII.

Woul't drink up esile? eat a crocodile?

Ib., V, 1, 299.

It is a matter of surprise to me that after all that has been written on this line there should still be found so many defenders of the old reading (QB *Esill,* FA *Esile,* not to speak of vessels in QA). Several critics have justly observed that it would not only be 'tame and spiritless', but 'inconsistent and even ridiculous' (Nares s. v.) to make Hamlet dare Laertes to drink 'large draughts of vinegar' in a scene whose every line is teeming with emphasis and hyperbole — nay, even bombast; and it was reserved to Al. Schmidt (Shakespeare-Lexicon s. *Eysell*) to think there was no hyperbole in the case and Hamlet's questions were meant to be ludicrous. 'Hamlet's questions', he says, 'are apparently ludicrous, and drinking vinegar, in order to exhibit deep grief by a wry face, seems much more to the purpose than drinking up rivers.' This is even less acceptable than the explanation given by Theobald, that Hamlet means to say, 'Wilt thou resolve to do things the most shocking and distasteful? and behold, I am resolute.' The other passages in which 'eysell' is mentioned do not bear in the least on the line under discussion; 'eysell' being there only spoken of as a medicine (thus, e. g., in Sonnet CXI) or as 'an ingredient of the bitter potion given to our Saviour on the Cross' (Hunter, Illustrations, II, 263); nowhere is drinking eysell mentioned as a feat of courage and strength, as it would seem to be in the present passage. Mr. Moberly in his edition of 'Hamlet' (Rugby Edition, Lon., Oxf., and Cambr., 1873) *ad loc.*

assures his readers that 'a large draught of vinegar would be very dangerous to life'; he might have added that roast crocodile would not be a very wholesome dish either. This is certainly so far-fetched and tame a thought, that Shakespeare cannot have been guilty of it; it reminds the reader involuntarily of Capell's humorous remark that 'if Eisel be the right reading, it must be because 't is wanted for sauce to the crocodile.'

There are critics who would willingly give up the vinegar and side with those who are convinced that 'esile' is meant for a river, if it were not that in their opinion a Danish river must be referred to, or at least one that is not too far removed from Denmark; in default of a Danish river they are ready to put up with the Polish Weisel* or the Dutch Yssel, but they strongly object to the Nile as being at variance with the scenery of the play. This ill-founded objection has been refuted by Dr. Furness who justly observes that Shakespeare 'who did not hesitate to make Hamlet swear by St. Patrick, would have been just as likely to mention a river in farthest Ind as in Denmark, if the name flashed into his mind, and would have been intelligible to his audience.' It may be added that the Nile is' (and was) no less known in Denmark than in any other European country; I cannot conceive why the mention of so world-renowned a river should be inappropriate in the mouth of a Danish prince: but if so, the dramatic unity is just as much violated by the crocodile; in order to be consistent these critics should substitute some Danish — or at least some Baltic — beast for the crocodile. It may be safely asserted that Shakespeare never cared for Danish, Polish, or Dutch rivers, and that the name of a Danish river in this passage would indeed be the last that could have come from his pen.

It was certainly not only allowable to Shakespeare to introduce the Nile without violating the locality of his play, but it can be easily shown that he had the strongest motives for so doing. The grief of Laertes at the untimely and tragical death of his sister is uttered with such an emphasis that Hamlet cannot refrain from objecting to such clamorous woe and from overawing him who utters it; he entirely gives the rein to hyperbole and bombast; he challenges Laertes to do whatever feat he may to express his sorrow and to be assured that he, Hamlet, will do the same, nay, more. Nothing can be more intelligible, more explicit: —

> And, if thou prate of mountains, let them throw
> Millions of acres on us; till our ground,
> Singeing his pate against the burning zone,
> Make Ossa like a wart! Nay, an thou'lt mouth,
> I'll rant as well as thou.

* Does this form of the name occur elsewhere or has it been coined for the nonce? I greatly suspect the latter.

One of the feats thus enumerated is drinking up the Nile, a feat
than which nothing can better befit the occasion, as the Nile was
considered in the days of Elizabeth not only as the home of wonders
and monsters, but also as the mightiest, nay, even as a measureless
stream; our poet himself in Titus Andronicus, III, 1, 71, says: —

>   And now, like Nilus, it disdaineth bounds.

Besides, drinking up a river, or even the ocean, is an hyperbole
very familiar to Elizabethan poets. Various passages have been quoted
in support of these facts, both by English editors, and myself in my
editions of 'Hamlet'; and I am now able to increase their number.
The vast extension of the Nile is extolled by Marlowe in the first
Part of Tamburlaine, V, 2 (ed. Dyce, 36b. — Ed. A. Wagner, 2221
seq.): —

>   Which had ere this been bath'd in streams of blood,
>   As vast and deep as Euphrates or Nile.

In the same play, Part 1, II, 3 (ed. Dyce, 15a. — A. Wag., 606 seqq.)
the poet makes Tamburlaine say: —

>   The host of Xerxes, which by fame is said
>   T' have drunk the mighty Parthian Araris,
>   Was but a handful to that we will have.

In the second part of Tamburlaine, III, 1 (ed. Dyce, 54a. — A. Wag.,
3141 seqq.) Orcanes even mentions Nilus itself: —

>   I have a hundred thousand men in arms:
>   Some, that in conquest of the perjur'd Christian,
>   Being a handful to a mighty host,
>   Think them in number yet sufficient
>   To drink the river Nile or Euphrates,
>   And for their power enow to win the world.

Can it be doubted that Shakespeare was acquainted with these passages? He who is known to have inserted in the second part of his
K. Henry IV. (II, 4) the famous lines from the second part of Tamburlaine (IV, 3): —

>   Holla, you pampered jades of Asia,
>   What, can you draw but twenty miles a-day?

In Dawbridgecourt Belchier's Invisible Comedy of Hans Beer Pot
(London, 1618, E, 3c) we meet with these lines: —

>   Enough my ladde, wilt drink an Ocean?
>   Methinks a whirlpool cannot ore drinke me.

Edward III., III, 1 (ed. Delius, 39. — W. and Pr., 37): —

>   By land, with Xerxes we compare of strength,
>   Whose soldiers drank up rivers in their thirst.

Richard II., II, 2, 145 seq.: —

>   The task he undertakes
>   Is numbering sands and drinking oceans dry.

The Dramatic Works of Rob. Greene, ed. Dyce (London, 1831), Vol. I, p. 43: —

 And drink up overflowing Euphrates.

Westward Ho!, II, 3 (Webster, ed. Dyce, 1857, in 1 vol., p. 222b): Come, drink up Rhine, Thames, and Meander dry! [An exhortation to drink Rhenish wine at the Steelyard.])

Chaucer, The Romaunt of the Rose, l. 5712 seq.: —

 He undirfongith a gret peyne,
 That undirtakith, to drynke up Seyne.

Locrine, IV, 4 (Malone's Supplement, II, 246; Hazlitt, Supplementary Works, 93; Doubtful Plays, Tauchn. Ed., 179): —

 O what Danubius now may quench my thirst?
 What Euphrates, what light-foot Euripus
 May now allay the fury of that heat,
 Which raging in my entrails eats me up?

Chapman's Revenge for Honour, III, 2 (The Works of George Chapman: Plays, edited, with Notes, by Richard Herne Shepherd, London, 1874, 433b): —

 Sol. Let go round:
 I'd drink 't, were it an ocean of warm blood
 Flowing from th' enemy.

 Delius, *ad loc.,* gives it as his opinion that all difficulties would be removed, if the reading of the old editions was: —

 Woo't drink up Nilus? eat a crocodile?

but he finds it difficult to believe that so familiar a word as *Nilus* could have been sophisticated into *vessels, Esill,* and *Esile.* To me this seems to be a *cura posterior*; provided we have got the right word, the word which is imperatively required by the context, we need not trouble ourselves with the inquiry as to how the corruption may have crept into the text. It is certainly very gratifying and adds to the force of an emendation if we are able to show the origin of the corrupted reading, but there are many passages in Shakespeare and his contemporaries where such an endeavour is, and ever will be, vain, whereas the emendation itself cannot be doubted. Let any one try to explain the printers' mistakes that are committed even at this day! Many of them may certainly be accounted for by a foul case and in other ways, but no less a number will still baffle all explanation. Or has a critic ever yet been able to explain how the famous *Vllorxa* found its way into the text? Yet who will defend it? The Cambridge Editors, in their Preface, p. XII, justly insist on the frequent 'causelessness of the blunders', which they illustrate by the following instance taken from A Midsummer Night's Dream, I, 1, 139: —

 Or else it stood upon the choice of merit.

This reading of the Folios is certainly wrong. 'But if we compare', the Cambridge Editors go on to say, 'the true reading preserved in the Quartos, "the choice of friends", we can perceive no way to account for the change of "friends" to "merit", by which we might have retraced the error from "merit" to "friends". Nothing like the "ductus literarum", or attraction of the eye to a neighbouring word, can be alleged here.' This case is even more glaring than the corruption of *Nilus* to *Esile*, where we may fancy without great difficulty that *Es* originated in an indistinctly written *N*, and that *Esile*, therefore, is merely a misread *Nile*.

There remain two points still to be mentioned. First the words *drink up*. Notwithstanding what has been said to the contrary by Dr. Furness and others, I still believe that this phrase means something more than simply 'to drink'; the preposition *up* 'conveys the sense of totality or completeness' to use Mr. Richard Grant White's words; *up*, says Al. Schmidt, s. v., 'imparts to verbs the sense of completion, by indicating that the action expressed by them is fully accomplished.' I feel convinced that 'to drink up', to say the very least of it, is applied much more fitly to a river than to vinegar. The parallel passages cited above are eloquent on this head too; nevertheless I hope I may be allowed to add two more instances. Dekker, The Honest Whore, Part II, 1 (Middleton, ed. Dyce, III, 137): —

Drink up this gold, good wits should love good wine.

[*Gives money*.

Puttenham, The Arte of English Poesie, ed. Arber, p. 88: 'one a horsebacke calling perchance for a cup of beere or wine, and hauing dronken it vp rides away and never lights.' 'To drink up Nilus' is, in my opinion, equivalent to 'to drink Nilus dry.'

My second, — and last, — remark is on the crocodile. If drinking up Nilus (that 'disdaineth bounds') be conceded to be an hyperbole of the first water as it expresses a pure impossibility, it may be objected, that eating a crocodile would be a rather weak anti-climax and could not be placed on a level with the first-named feat of strength. I cannot admit such an objection to be just, as eating a crocodile, on account of its impenetrable scales which our poet's contemporaries imagined to be not only spear-proof, but even cannon-proof, is no less an impossibility than drinking up the river in which it lives.* In Locrine, A. III, init. Ate says: —

* The source of these hyperbolical descriptions may be found in the forty first chapter of Job, where we read: 'The sword of him that layeth at him [viz. leviathan] cannot hold: the spear, the dart, nor the habergeon. He esteemeth iron as straw, and brass as rotten wood. The arrow cannot make him flee: slingstones are turned with him into stubble. Darts are counted as stubble: he laugheth at the shaking of a spear.' — Compare also Job XL, 23: 'Behold, he [viz. behemoth] drinketh up a river, and hasteth not: he trusteth that he can draw up Jordan into his mouth.'

> High on a bank, by Nilus' boisterous streams,
> Fearfully sat the Egyptian crocodile,
> Dreadfully grinding in her sharp long teeth
> The broken bowels of a silly fish:
> His back was arm'd against the dint of spear,
> With shields of brass that shone like burnish'd gold.

Another passage brings us still nearer to Shakespeare, viz. 1 Tamburlaine, IV, 1 (ed. Dyce, 25a. — A. Wag., 1374 scqq.): —

> While you, faint-hearted, base Egyptians,
> Lie slumb'ring on the flow'ry banks of Nile,
> As crocodiles that unaffrighted rest,
> While thund'ring cannons rattle on their skins.

Now let Laertes try his teeth on such a skin! In short, my conviction, that Shakespeare wrote: —

> Woul't drink up *Nilus*? eat a crocodile?

is more confirmed than ever it was before. (Compare Jahrb. d. D. Sh.-G., XV, 437 seq. and XVI, 250.)

CDIII.

> May be prevented now. The princes, France and Burgundy.
>
> *K. Lear, I, 1, 46.*

There are few instances in Mr. Fleay's list of Alexandrines in King Lear that cannot be shown without difficulty to be either regular blank verse or what Dr. Abbott terms trimeter couplets. The safest and most correct way will be to follow Mr. Fleay step by step (with some few omissions), in order to enable the reader to judge for himself. As to the line quoted above, it contains two triple endings, the one at the end of the first hemistich (*prevented now*; see Abbott, s. 472), the other at the end of the line (*Burgundy*; see S. Walker, Versification, 240 seqq.). Hanmer needlessly suggested to omit *now*.

I, 1, 94: My heart | into | my mouth: | I love | your maj | 'sty.

See S. Walker, Versification, 174 seq.

I, 1, 109: So young, and so untender? So young, my lord, and true.

These are two short lines that should not be joined into one; the arrangement of the Cambridge and Globe Editions is right.

I, 1, 134: That troop | with maj | 'sty. Ourself, | by month | ly course.

I, 1, 139: The swáy, | revén | ue, ex'cú | tion óf | the rést.

Compare my edition of Shakespeare's Tragedy of Hamlet (1882), p. 182, where a different, but less correct, scansion of this line has been given.

I, 1, 156 (not 155): Reverbs | no hol|l'wness. Kent́, on | thy life, |
                                                           no more.

> See *supra* note CCCV.

I, 1, 158: To wage | against | thy en|'mies; nor fear | to lose | it..
I, 1, 196: Or cease | your quest | of love? | Most roy|al maj|'sty.
I, 1, 198: Nor will | you ten|der less. | Right no|ble Bur|g'ndy.
I, 1, 226: Could nev|er plant | in me.   I yet ·| beseech | your
                                             maj|'sty.

Triple endings both before the pause *(plant in me)* and at the
end of the line *(majesty)*. Possibly, however, another scansion
might be set up against the triple ending of the first hemistich,
viz.: —

Could ne'er | plant in | me.   I yet | beseech | your maj|'sty.

I, 1, 228: To speak | and pur|pose not; since what | I well | intend.
Triple ending before the pause; compare Abbott, s. 471.

I, 1, 247 (not 248): Duchess of Burgundy. — Nothing: I have
                                     sworn; I am firm.
Either two short lines, as printed in the Cambridge and Globe
Editions, or *Burgundy* to be read as a triple ending before the
pause and *I have* and *I am* to be contracted: —

Duchess | of Bur|g'ndy. Nothing: | I've sworn; | I'm firm.

I, 1, 250: That you | must lose | a hus|band. Peace be | with
                                             Bur |g'ndy.

I, 1, 270: Come, no|ble Bur|g'ndy. — Bid fare|well to | your
                                             sis|ters.

I, 2, 4: The cu|rios'ty | of na|tions to | deprive | me.
Pope reads *nicely*; Thirlby suggested *curtesie,* which was adopted
by Theobald. Mr. Fleay's scansion is right; compare S. Walker,
Versification, 201, and *supra* note XXIII.

I, 3, 23: What grows | o't, no mat|ter; advise | your fel|lows so.
Grows of it is a triple ending before the pause. The line
admits, however, of another scansion, viz.: —

What grows | of it, | no mat|ter; advise | your fel|lows so.
Fellows so to be read as a triple ending.

I, 4, 223: In rank and not-to-be endurèd riots. Sir.
Sir was rightly thrown out by Theobald. S. Walker, Versification, 270, would place it in an interjectional lino.

I, 4, 265: Shows like | a ri't|'s inn: epi|curism | and lust.
Steevens omitted *riotous*. *Riotous inn* is a triple ending before
the pause.

I, 4, 347: At point | a hund|red knights: yes, that, | on ev|'ry dream.
At point, omitted by Pope. *Hundred knights* seems to be a triple ending.

II, 1, 118 seq. Rightly arranged by Jennens: —

> You we first seize on. I shall serve you truly,
> However else. — For him I thank your grace.

II, 2, 79: Who wears | no hon|'sty. Such smi|ling rogues | as these.
Pope transferred *as these* to the beginning of the following line, whilst Hanmer omitted these words.

II, 2, 91: Two short lines, as printed in the Globe Edition.

II, 2, 121: The same.

II, 2, 144: You should | not use | me so. Sir, being | his knave,|
I will.

Use me so is a triple ending before the pause.

II, 2, 177: Losses | their rem|'dies. All wea|ry and | o'erwatch'd.

II, 4, 157: Age is | unne'|ss'ry: on | my knees | I beg.
This is S. Walker's scansion (Versification, 275), rightly adopted by Mr. Fleay.

II, 4, 234: I and | my hund|red knights. | Not al|toge'er | so.
See S. Walker, Versif., 103 seq. and note on IV, 7, 54.

III, 2, 67: Their scant|ed court|'sy. My wits | begin | to turn.

III, 4, 176: I do beseech your grace. — O, cry you mercy, sir.
The Qq rightly omit *sir*.

III, 4, 179: In, fellow, there, into the hovel: keep thee warm.
QA and Ff: *there, into th'*; QB: *there in't*; Capell: *there, to the*. — Read, point, and scan: —

In, fel|low: there | i' th' ho|vel keep | thee warm.

IV, 6, 145: And my | heart breaks | at it. Read. What, | wi' th'
case | of eyes?

Breaks at it is a triple ending before the pause.

IV, 6, 198: Scan either: —

I'm cut | to th' brains. | You shall | have an|ything.
or: —
I am | cut to | the brains. | You shall | have an|'thing.
See note on The Winter's Tale, I, 2, 173.

IV, 6, 256: Upon | the Brit|ish par|ty. O, untime|ly death.
Hanmer: *On th' English, English* being the reading of the Ff. The first two syllables of *O, untimely* 'coalesce or are rapidly pronounced together.' Abbott, s. 462.

IV, 7, 54: To see | ano'cr | thus. I know | not what | to say.
> *To say,* omitted by Hanmer. See Abbott, s. 466 and *supra* note on II, 4, 234.

V, 3, 45: May equally determine. Sir, I thought it fit.
> Read, with Pope, *thought fit.*

V, 3, 178: Did hate thee or thy father! Worthy prince, I know 't.
> *I know 't* is to be transferred to the beginning of the following line, as printed by Hanmer, who moreover completes l. 179 by reading, *I know it well.*

V, 3, 271: Corde|lia! Corde|lia, stay | a lit|tle. Ha!
> The line has an extra syllable before the first pause. ·

V, 3, 295: Edmund | is dead, | m'lord. That's but | a tri|fle here.
> Pope, Theobald, Hanmer, and Warburton omit *here.* Compare Pericles, I, 2, 101: —
>
> Well m' lord, | since you | have given | me leave | to speak.

V, 3, 313: Vex not his ghost. Oh, let him pass! he hates him much.
> *Much,* which is only contained in QB, has been justly omitted by almost all editors and should not have been conjured up again by Mr. Fleay.

CDIV.

Iago. 'S blood, but you will not hear me.

Othello, I, 1, 4.

Complete the line by adding *Roderigo.* Iago and Roderigo address each other by their names in order thus to introduce themselves to the spectators who were not provided, as now-a-days, with printed play-bills from which they could learn the names of the *Dramatis Personæ.* Of course it is chiefly in the introductory scenes that the Elizabethan dramatists had to resort to this mode of acquainting their audiences with the characters of the play. Print therefore: —

Iago. 'S blood, but you will not hear me, *Roderigo.*

CDV.

And, in conclusion,
Nonsuits my mediators; for, 'Certes', says he,
'I have already· chose my officer.'
And what was he?
Forsooth, a great arithmetician, &c.

Ib., I, 1, 15 seqq.

The words *And, in conclusion,* are wanting in the Ff. Arrange, with the late Mr. Hudson: —

> And, in conclusion, nonsuits my mediators;
> For, 'Certes', says he, 'I have already chose
> My officer.' And what was he, *Roderigo?*
> Forsooth, a great arithmetician, &c.

For the addition of *Roderigo* I must answer myself.

CDVI.

A fellow almost damn'd in a fair wife.

Ib., I, 1, 21.

I am convinced that for this once there is no woman in the case; Cassio has no wife, and no critic, I think, will agree with Theobald in assigning the 'fair wife' to Iago. Cassio is sneered at by Iago as an arithmetician, a counter-caster, an expert in bookish theory, whose soldiership is 'mere prattle, without practice.' Thus the context distinctly shows, that the word which originally stood in the place of *a fair wife* like the rest had reference in some way or other to Cassio's commercial calling and unsoldierlike life and behaviour. Perhaps some commentator that possesses a more intimate knowledge of commerce and business life than I can boast of, may be fortunate enough to hit on the true word. The conjectural emendations of *life, wise, face,* and *phyx* are hardly worth mentioning.

CDVII.

Is all his soldiership. But he, sir, had the election.

Ib., I, 1, 27.

Soldiership is a triple ending before the pause. Such triple endings before the pause occur also in the following lines of our play, viz.: —

By debitor and *creditor:* this counter-caster.   *(I, 1, 31.)*

For nought but *provender,* and when he's old, cashier'd.
   (I, 1, 48.)

Sir, I will answer *anything.* But, I beseech you.   *(I, 1, 121.)*

Compare note on The Winter's Tale, I, 2, 173.

Of here and *every where.* Straight satisfy yourself.   *(I, 1, 138.)*

For thus *deluding you.* Strike on the tinder, ho!   *(I, 1, 141.)*

'Tis oft with *difference* — yet do they all confirm.   *(I, 3, 7.)*

And sold to *slavery,* of my redemption thence.   *(I, 3, 138.)*

To assist my *simpleness.* What would you, Desdemona.
   (I, 3, 248.)

Does tire the *ingener.* How now! who has put in? *(II, 1, 65.)*

Players in your *housewifery,* and housewives in your beds.
(II, 1, 113.)

Hold! the general *speaks to you;* hold, hold, for shame!
(II, 3, 168.)

This is the reading of the Qq. The first *Hold!* is a monosyllabic foot. As to *speaks to you* compare note on Antony and Cleopatra, I, 4, 7. Those editors that adopt the lection of the Ff must scan: —

Hold! | the gen|'ral speaks | t' you; hold, | for shame!

From her *propriety,* What is the matter, masters? *(II, 3, 176.)*

And great *affinity,* and that in wholesome wisdom. *(III, 1, 49.)*

Farewell, my *Desdemon:* I will come to thee straight.
(III, 3, 87.)

The uniform reading of the old copies is: —

Farewell, my Desdemona: I'll come to thee straight.

Desdemon was diffidently suggested by S. Walker, Crit. Exam., I, 231, and inserted in the text by Dyce (2ᵈ Ed.); *I will* is Capell's correction. It must be admitted, however, that the line allows of a correct scansion without this latter alteration, viz.: —

Farewell, | my Des|d'mon: I'll | come to | thee straight.

Mr. Fleay (*apud* Ingleby, l. c.) proposes either to transfer *Farewell* to l. 86 (which would make that line an Alexandrine), or to read *Desdemon.*

Matching thy *inference.* 'Tis not to make me jealous.
(III, 3, 183.)

For too much *loving you.* I 'm bound to thee for ever.
(III, 3, 213.)

And, lo, the *happiness!* go and importune her. *(III, 4, 108.)*

Save you, worthy *general!* With all my heart, sir. *(IV, 1, 229.)*

Save is a monosyllabic foot.

Lay on my bed my *wedding sheets:* remember; and call.
(IV, 2, 105.)

Remember has an extra syllable before the pause. — In all copies and editions, from the first quarto down to Dr. Furness's Variorum Edition, this line ends at *remember.* Six feet are thus allotted to the following line, whereas two regular lines are obtained by transferring *and call* to l. 105. Some editors print l. 106 as two incomplete lines.

And sing it like poor *Barbara.* Prithee, dispatch. *(IV, 3, 33.)*

Do you see, *gentlemen?* nay, guiltiness will speak. *(V, 1, 109.)*

The line begins with a trochee.

Kind *gentlemen*, let us go see poor Cassio dress'd.　　*(V, 1, 124.)*
　　Old copies (and modern editions) *let's;* Pope omitted *go.*
To this *extremity.* Thy husband knew it all.　　　　*(V, 2, 139.)*
　　Steevens, *extreme.*

I do not vouch for the completeness of this list and merely add that part of the lines quoted are declared to be Alexandrines by Mr. Fleay (e. g. I, 1, 27; I, 1, 48; I, 1, 138; I, 1, 141; I, 3, 248; II, 1, 65; II, 1, 113; III, 1, 49; III, 3, 183; III, 4, 108), whilst others have been left unnoticed.

CDVIII.

And such a one do I profess myself.　For, sir,
It is as sure as you are Roderigo, &c.

Ib., I, 1, 55 seq.

Pope omitted *For, sir*; Capell, followed by subsequent editors, placed it in a separate line. I imagine *sir* to be an actors' addition, so much the more so, as it stands at the end of the line. *'Sir'*, says S. Walker, Versification, p. 177, 'I have reason to suspect, is frequently interpolated.' Another case in point occurs in A. I, sc. 2, l. 10: —

I did full hard forbear him.　But, I pray you, sir,

where the metre clearly requires the omission of *sir.* Compare also A. IV, sc. 2, l. 114 *(lady)*; A. V, sc. 1, l. 105 *(mistress)*; and *infra* note DLXXXII. May not Shakespeare have written: —

And such a one do I profess myself.
For it 's [or, *'t is*] as sure as you are Roderigo, &c.?

This alteration certainly helps us to two regular lines of blank verse.

CDIX.

To start my quiet.
　Rod.　Sir, sir, sir, —
　Bra.　　　　　　　　But thou must needs be sure.

Ib., I, 1, 101.

Hazlitt combines the second and third line, and by repeating *sir* four times produces a regular blank verse. In my humble opinion the third line is to be joined to the first; they form one of those verses that are continued in spite of interruptions, a metrical peculiarity with which Hazlitt seems not to have been acquainted. Compare note CDXXII and Abbott, s. 514.

CDX.

Bra.   Thou art a villain.
Iago.   You are — a senator.

Ib., I, 1, 119.

Scan either: —

    Thou árt | a víl|lain.   You áre | a sén|atór,

or (as a syllable pause line with a triple ending): —

    Thou art | a vil|lain.   ◡ | You are | a sen|ator.

Compare, amongst other instances, Coriolanus, III, 1, 92 and IV, 5, 138: —

    You grave | but reck|less sen|ators, have | you thus.

    And take | our friend|ly sen|ators by | the hand.

Triple endings occur also in the following lines of our play: —

But with a knave of common hire, a *gondolier.*   (I, 1, 126.)

> Qy. *gondoler*? just like *pioner*, *muleter* &c.   See my second
> edition of Hamlet (1882) p. 114 and note on Cymbeline, IV, 2,
> 100 seq.   Compare Dr. Furness, *ad loc.*; S. Walker, Versification,
> 218; and Abbott, s. 497.

I thus would play and trifle with your *reverence.*   (I, 1, 133.)

To do no contrived murder: I lack *iniquity.*   (I, 2, 3.)

> Besides a triple ending this line has an extra syllable before
> the pause.

My services which I have done the *signiory.*   (I, 2, 18.)

> Compare S. Walker, Versification, 243; Abbott, s. 471.

What is the news?   The duke does greet you, *general.*

(I, 2, 36.)

Abased her delicate youth with drugs and *minerals.*   (I, 2, 74.)

For an abuser of the world, a *practiser.*   (I, 2, 78.)

A messenger from the galleys.   Now, what 's the *business.*

(I, 3, 13.)

> This line has at the same time an extra syllable before the
> pause.

Of Venice hath seen a grievous wreck and *sufferance.* (II, 1, 23.)

> See *infra* note CDXVIII.

'Tis one Iago, ancient to the *general.*   (II, 1, 66.)

Away, I say; go out and cry a *mutiny.*   (II, 3, 157.)

Hold, ho! Lieutenant, — sir, — Montano, — *gentlemen.*

(II, 3, 166.)

> Differently arranged by Mr. Fleay.

Shall nothing wrong him.   Thus it is, *general.*   (II, 3, 224.)

> Scan: —

    Shall noth|ing wrong | him.   ◡ | Thus it | is, gen|eral.

However, *general* may be pronounced as a trisyllable and *him* may be considered as an extra syllable before the pause: —

Shall noth|ing wrong | him.   Thus it | is gen|eral.

To execute upon him.   Sir, this *gentleman.*   *(II, 3, 228.)*

Something that 's brief; and bid 'Good morrow', *general.*
          (III, 1, 2.)

And for I know thou'rt full of love and *honesty.*   *(III, 3, 118.)*

In order to regulate the metre Hanmer omitted *love and.*

To spy into abuses, and oft my *jealousy.*   *(III, 3, 147.)*

This line has also an extra syllable before the pause.

For, sure, he fills it up with great *ability.*   *(III, 3, 247.)*

With any strong or vehement *importunity.*   *(III, 3, 251.)*

Compare S. Walker, Versification, 201.

Look, where he comes.   Not poppy, nor *mandragora.*
          (III, 3, 330.)

Fie, there is no such man; it is *impossible.*   *(IV, 2, 134.)*

Compare S. Walker, Versification, 272.

Why should he call her whore? who keeps her *company?*
          (IV, 2, 137.)

Speak of me as I am; nothing *extenuate.*   *(V, 2, 342.)*

For they succeed on you.   To you, lord *governor.*   *(V, 2, 367.)*

I do not claim the praise of completeness for this list, although it comprises a greater number of lines than that compiled by Mr. Fleay.

As has been remarked, the line at the head of this note comes under our notice not only on account of its triple ending, but also as a syllable pause line and as such offers a welcome opportunity of subjoining a list (whether complete or not) of syllable pause lines in 'Othello', viz.: —

Marry, | to ⏑ | Come, cap|tain, will | you go?   *(I, 2, 53.)*

I would | keep from | thee.   ⏑ | For your | sake, jew|el.
          (I, 3, 195.)

O my | fair war|rior?   ⏑ | My dear | Othel|lo.   *(II, 1, 184.)*

According to S. Walker, Versification, 175, *warrior* should be pronounced *dissolutè.*

Shall lose | me.   ⏑ | What! in | a town | of war.   *(II, 3, 213.)*

'Tis mon|strous.   ⏑ | Ia|go, who | began 't?   *(II, 3, 217.)*

Shall noth|ing wrong | him.   ⏑ | Thus it | is gen|eral.
          (II, 3, 224.)

See *supra.*

I will | not.   ⏑ | Should you | do so, | my lord.   *(III, 3, 221.)*

Must be | to loathe | her.   ⏑ | O curse | of mar|riage.
          (III, 3, 268.)

S. Walker, Versification, 176, is of opinion that *marriage* should be pronounced *dissolutè*.

A frank | one. ∠ | You may, | indeed, | say so.   *(III, 4, 44.)*

I thank | you. ∠ | How does | Lieuten|ant Cas|sio? *(IV, 1, 235.)*

And will | not have | it. ∠ | What sin | commit|ted. *(IV, 2, 80.)*

Here as well as in ll. 72 and 76 I think the insertion of *sin* proposed by Keightley indispensable.

That mar|ried with | Othel|lo. ∠ | You, mis|tress. *(IV, 2, 90.)*

S. Walker, Versification, 48, pronounces *mist(e)ress*.

Nay, that 's | not next. | Hark! ∠ | Who is 't | that knocks?

(IV, 3, 53.)

O vil|lain! ∠ | Most heath|enish and | most gross. *(V, 2, 313.)*

Ritson says, that 'for the sake of both sense and metre' we ought to read *villainy*, and S. Walker, Crit. Exam., II, 45, agrees with him. Certainly not for the sake of metre.

To these lines a passage (IV, 1, 270 seqq.) must be added which evidently requires a different arrangement than that given in all old and modern editions, an arrangement which introduces one more syllable pause line into the text. The uniform division of the lines in question is: —

I'll send for you anon. Sir, I obey the mandate,
And will return to Venice. Hence, avaunt!
Cassio shall have my place &c.

The first line is an Alexandrine. Arrange: —

I'll send for you anon. Sir, I obey
The man|date, ∠ | and will | return | to Ven|ice.
Hence, avaunt!   [*Exit Desdemona.*
Cassio shall have my place &c.

The reader will have observed that in all these cases it is the accented syllable for which the pause serves as a substitute, whereas those instances where the pause takes the place of an unaccented syllable are comparatively rare, and not exempt from doubt. The first occurs in A. II, sc. 1, l. 40: —

An in|distinct | regard. | ◡ Come, | let 's do | so.

Who knows but the poet wrote: —

An in|distinct | regard. | Come *let* | *us* do | so?

The second instance is A. III, sc. 4, l. 183: —

Is 't cóme | to thís? | Well, wéll! | ◡ Gó | to, wóm|an.

The rather unusual accentuation *Gó to* occurs also in A. III, sc. 3, l. 208, in K. John IV, 1, 97 and in K. Henry VIII., IV, 2, 103. In the first named line Pope, by the omission of *why*, not only restored the common accentuation *(Go tó)*, but at the same time reduced the Alexandrine to a blank verse: —

She loved | them most. | And so | she died. | Go to, | then.

The same effect, as far as the accentuation is concerned, might be produced in the line under discussion by a slight transposition: —

Is 't come | to this? | Well, well! | Woman, | go to!

The third case in point (IV, 1, 90) admits of no other scansion than this: —

And noth|ing of | a man. | ⌣ Dost | thou hear, | Ia|go?

An Alexandrine with a double ending and therefore not to be taken upon trust. Capell omitted *thou*; perhaps rightly, if it should not be thought preferable to omit *Iago*. Or we may have to deal with two incomplete lines. After all it would appear that no incontrovertible instance can be found in our play where the pause takes the place of an unaccented syllable, whereas in the number of cases where an accented syllable has been left out, our play excels many others. This seems a noteworthy fact and should be looked into more closely.

CDXI.

Bra. O heaven! How got she out? O treason of the blood!

Ib., I, 1, 170.

O heaven! should form a separate line.

CDXII.

I had thought to have yerk'd him here under the ribs.

Ib., I, 2, 5.

FA *t' have.* *Under the ribs* is placed in a separate line in the Qq. Pope, followed by subsequent editors, omitted *had*. Read *I'd* and either *t'have* or *to've*, as printed by Pope and others. The pause is after *here*, and a trochee *(under)* follows it.

CDXIII.

The senate hath sent about three several quests.

Ib., I, 2, 46.

Hath is only in the Ff. I have little doubt that Shakespeare wrote: —

The *senate 's* sent about three several quests.

The *'s* was lost by way of absorption (compare notes CCLVIII and CCLXIII) and *hath* was added by either the editors or printers of FA.

CDXIV.

The Ottomites, reverend and gracious, &c.

Ib., I, 3, 33.

A catalectic verse (see note II). *Reverend and gracious,* without a noun, seems, however, too familiar an address in the mouth of a messenger. Is it likely, that so mean a person should address the highest tribunal of the republic less formally than their renowned general, who some thirty lines lower down begins his speech most respectfully: —

Most potent, grave, and reverend signiors.

The two well-known passages in Hamlet (III, 1, 43: *Gracious, so please you,* and IV, 7, 42: *High and mighty*) do not come from subordinate characters, but from the Lord Chamberlain Polonius and Prince Hamlet. Under the circumstances I cannot but think that *signiors* was lost at the end of the line, so much the more so as by this addition the verse is completed.

CDXV.

After your own sense, yea, though our proper son.

Ib., I, 3, 69.

Which is the true scansion of this line? Is it: —

Aft'r yoúr | own sénse | yea, thoúgh | our próp|er són?

For the monosyllabic pronunciation of *after* compare S. Walker, Versification, 64 seqq.; Abbott, s. 465; Mr. Fleay, l. c., p. 75 (who is wrong in saying that 'this is unusual'); note CCLV; and K. Richard II., III, 2, 3. Or should we scan: —

Áfter | your ówn | sense, yea, thóugh | our próp|er són?

Sense to be read as an extra syllable before the pause. Or are we to retain the reading of the first quarto which omits *yea*? I take the opportunity to remark that the text not only of the first quarto, but of the quartos in general, in not a few cases is preferable to that of the folios, although it has mostly been displaced by the latter.

CDXVI.

Even fall upon my life.
    Duke.   Fetch Desdemona hither.

Ib., I, 3, 120.

Printed as two incomplete lines by Rowe, Theobald, Hanmer, Capell, and Hazlitt. Mr. Fleay enlists the line among his Alexandrines. Read *Desdemon* and scan: —

E'en fall | upon | my life. | Fetch *Des*|*d'mon* hith|er.

CDXVII.

       I therefore beg it not,
To please the pallate of my Appetite:
Nor to comply with heat the yong affects
In my defunct, and proper satisfaction.
But to be free, and bounteous to her minde: &c.

            Ib., I, 3, 262 seqq.

This is the reading of the first folio, and there cannot be the least
doubt about the fact that it is corrupt. As Dr. Furness has chronicled most fully and most judiciously the different opinions and inter-
pretations of critics and commentators, it would be tedious to repeat
them. To come to the point at once, I am firmly convinced that
Bailey's conjecture *th' heat of young affects* is right, and that instead
of *defunct* we ought to read *discreet*. The meaning is: 'I beg it not
in order to please my own appetite, nor to comply with the heat of
my wife's young affects, as, in accordance with my age, my satisfaction is discreet and proper, "but [I beg it] to be free, and bounteous to her mind".' It will not escape the reader's notice, that
contrary to the discretion which the Moor here claims for himself,
Iago gives him a very different and no doubt slanderous character;
he calls him the 'lusty Moor', the 'lascivious Moor', and suspects
him of having 'done his office 'twixt his sheets'. The passage should
no doubt be printed: —

       I therefore beg it not
To please the palate of my appetite;
Nor to comply with th' heat of young affects
In my *discreet* and proper satisfaction;
But to be free and bounteous to her mind: &c.

CDXVIII.

That their designment halts: a noble ship of Venice
Hath seen a grievous wreck of sufferance.

            Ib., II, 1, 22 seq.

Hanmer omitted *noble* in order to regulate the metre. Arrange: —

That their designment halts: a noble ship
Of Venice hath seen a grievous wreck of sufferance.

Venice is to be pronounced as a monosyllable (see S. Walker, Versification, 64 seqq.) and *sufferance* as a triple ending (see *supra* CDX.)
Compare *Lewis* which is frequently, if not generally, a monosyllable
with Shakespeare. S. Walker, Versification, 4 seqq.

CDXIX.

The Moor himself at sea
And is in full commission here for Cyprus.

Ib., II, 1, 27 seq.

Himself has rightly been altered to *himself's* by Rowe. Instead of
here Mr. P. A. Daniel (Notes and Conjectural Emendations, 78) proposes *bound,* to which conjectural emendation Dr. Furness justly
objects, that 'the *ductus literarum* is against it.' Read: —

The Moor himself 's at sea
And *in his* full commission *steers* for Cyprus.

This, I think, comes as near the *ductus literarum* (Qq as well as Ff
read *heere*) as can be wished. Compare I, 3, 34: —

Steering with due course towards the isle of Rhodes,

and Cymbeline III, 7, 9 seq.: 'he commends His absolute commission.'

CDXX.

Even till we make the main and the aerial blue.

Ib., II, 1, 39.

A regular blank verse; *the aerial* is to be pronounced as two syllables. Compare Richard II., III, 1, 9 (*lineaments* as a dissyllable).

CDXXI.

And chides with thinking.
Emil. You have little cause to say so.

Ib., II, 1, 108 seq.

Printed as two incomplete lines not only in the old copies, but also
in almost all modern editions (except those by Singer and Staunton).
They form, however, a regular blank verse with an extra syllable
before the pause; read and scan: —

And chides | with think|ing. You 've lit|tle cause | to say | so.

CDXXII.

And this and this, the greatest discords be
That e'er our hearts shall make.
Iago.   [*Aside*] O, you are well tuned now!
But I'll set down the pegs that make this music,
As honest as I am.
Oth.   Come, let us to the castle.

Ib., II, 1, 200 seqq.

Mr. Fleay reads lines 201 and 202 as one line and thus obtains a
welcome item in his list of Alexandrines. The Ff, followed by Rowe

and other editors, print Iago's speech as prose and Othello's words
Come, let us to the castle as a short line. As it appears to me,
these words (rightly printed *Come, let's to the castle* in Rowe's
second edition) complete the last line of Othello's antecedent speech,
which seems so much the likelier as Iago's speech is spoken aside
and, apart from the interjectional *Oh!*, consists of two regular lines
of blank verse. See Abbott, s. 514, and note CDIX. Compare also
The Dramatic Works of Massinger and Ford, with an Introduction
by Hartley Coleridge (London, 1839, in 1 vol.) p. 161 b and Ed. Hanne-
mann, Metrische Untersuchungen zu John Ford (Halle, 1888), p. 51.
The passage should therefore be printed: —

> And this and this the greatest discords be
> That e'er our hearts shall make. [*Kissing her.*]
>   *Iago.* [*Aside*] Oh!
> You 're well tuned now! But I'll set down the pegs
> That make this music, as honest as I am.
>   *Oth.*   Come, let 's to the castle.

CDXXIII.

Nay, good lieutenant, — alas, gentlemen.

Ib., II, 3, 158.

This line shows most strikingly the deterioration which the text has
only too frequently undergone in the folios. The first quarto reads
godswill, the second and third *Gods-will.* No doubt in pursuance
of the well-known act of King James this invocation of God had to
make room in the Ff to the tame interjection *alas,* an alteration
which is so much the worse as it spoils the metre. The corrector
who was no doubt more conspicuous for his piety than for his pro-
ficiency in the doctrine of metre, ought to have placed the interjection
at the end of the line, if he wanted to produce a regular blank
verse: —

Nay, good | lieuten|ant -- gent|lemen, | alas.

Of course, we must abide by the reading of the quartos.

CDXXIV.

When you yourself did part them.

Ib., II, 3, 239.

This line should be completed by the addition of *general.* Compare
l. 224 of this very scene.

CDXXV.

Iago.   You have not been a-bed, then?

Ib., III, 1, 33.

Another of those lines at the end of which the name of the person addressed has been dropped.   Read: —

Iago.   You have not been a-bed then, *Cassio?*

CDXXVI.

With Desdemona alone.

Pray you, come in.

Ib., III, 1, 56.

This reading of the Qq has been retained by the Cambridge and Globe Editors, by Hudson, Rolfe, &c.   Of course, this can only be done on the condition that the last syllable of *Desdemona* and the first syllable of *alone* 'coalesce or are rapidly pronounced together' (Abbott, s. 462).   Critics that do not approve of thus running two syllables into one another, must decide in favour of the lection of the Ff, *Desdemon.*   Compare Furness, *ad loc.*

CDXXVII.

Certain, men should be what. they seem.

Ib., III, 3, 128.

As in A. III, sc. 1, l. 33 and elsewhere, here too the name of the person addressed *(Iago)* has been lost at the end of the line.

CDXXVIII.

Emil.   I am glad I have found this napkin.

Ib., III, 3, 290.

A catalectic verse (see note II).   *Am* is to be emphasized.   Hanmer completed the line by adding *here.*   Or should we write: —

Emil.   I'm glad I've found this napkin?

CDXXIX.

To kiss and talk to. I'll have the work ta'en out,
And give't Iago: what he will do with it
Heaven knows, not I;
I nothing, but to please his fantasy.

Ib., III, 3, 296 seqq.

This division of the lines in FA was altered by Dr. Johnson to: —

> To kiss and talk to. I'll have the work ta'en out,
> And give't Iago:
> What he will do with it heaven knows, not I;
> I nothing, but to please his fantasy.

Hanmer arranged: —

> To kiss and talk to. *I will* have the work
> Ta'en out, and *give it* to Iago; *but*
> What *he'll* do with it, heaven knows, not I:
> I nothing, but to please his fantasy.

This is taking unwarrantable liberties with the text. In my opinion the break is after *talk to,* and we ought to divide: —

> To kiss and talk to.
> I'll have the work ta'en out, and give't Iago:
> What he will do with it heaven knows, not I;
> I nothing, but to please his fantasy.

CDXXX.

> That handkerchief
> Did an Egyptian to my mother give;
> She was a charmer, and could almost read
> The thoughts of people: — —
> 'T is true: there's magic in the web of it:
> A sibyl, that had number'd in the world
> The sun to course two hundred compasses,
> In her prophetic fury sew'd the work;
> The worms were hallow'd that did breed the silk;
> And it was dyed in mummy which the skilful
> Conserved of maidens' hearts.

> *Ib., III, 4, 55 seqq.*

A parallel passage which as far as I know has never been referred to occurs in Ben Jonson's Sad Shepherd, II, 1: —

> But, hear ye, Douce, because ye may meet me
> In mony shapes to-day, where'er you spy
> This browder'd belt with characters, 't is I.
> A Gypsan lady, and a right beldame,
> Wrought it by moonshine for me, and star-light,
> Upon your grannam's grave, that very night
> We earth'd her in the shades; when our dame Hecate
> Made it her gaing night over the kirk-yard,
> With all the barkand parish-tikes set at her,
> While I sat whyrland of my brazen spindle:
> At every twisted thrid my rock let fly

Unto the sewster, who did sit me nigh,
Under the town turnpike; which ran each spell
She stitched in the work, and knit it well.
See ye take tent to this, and ken your mother.

Can it be doubted that this is an imitation, by which Jonson intended, more or less, to ridicule Shakespeare? Gifford, of course, would never have allowed the truth of such a remark. (Jahrb. d. D. Sh.-G., XI, 299 seq.)

CDXXXI.

I' faith, sweet love, I was coming to your house.

Ib., III, 4, 171.

No reader, however little versed in Shakespearian criticism, will be surprised to learn that instead of *I' faith,* which is only in the Qq, the Ff read *Indeed.* — S. Walker, Crit. Exam., II, 203, thinks that '*I was* must have been pronounced as one syllable, in whatever manner the contraction was effected.' I cannot but think differently; in my conviction either *sweet,* or *love* ought to be omitted.

CDXXXII.

She is protectress of her honour too.

Ib., IV, 1, 14.

The context proves Capell's ingenious emendation *proprietress* to be indubitably right.

CDXXXIII.

O, 'tis the spite of hell, the fiend's arch-mock.

Ib., IV, 1, 71.

Arch-mock? No! I do not entertain the least doubt that Shakespeare wrote: —

O, 'tis the spite of hell, the *arch-fiend's* mock.

Arch-enemy occurs in 3 Henry VI., II, 2, 2 though not in its usual meaning of *satan.* Milton uses *arch-enemy* in Paradise Lost, I, 81; *Arch-Fiend,* ib., I, 156 and 209 (*arch-fiénd* and *árch-fiend*). *Arch* was evidently omitted by an oversight of the transcriber, was then added in the margin and thence transferred to a wrong place by the compositor.

CDXXXIV.

And knowing what I am, I know what she shall be.

Ib., IV, 1, 74.

Differently, but wrongly, arranged by S. Walker, Crit. Exam., III, 289; left unnoticed by Mr. Fleay. *Knowing* is to be pronounced as a monosyllable (see Abbott, s. 470) and there is an extra syllable before the pause *(am)*. Scan: —

And knowing | what I | am, I know | what she | shall be.

Compare A. I, sc. 1, l. 52, where *throwing* is used as a monosyllable.

CDXXXV.

Oth.   O, thou art wise; 'tis certain.
Iago.   Stand you awhile apart.

Ib., IV, 1, 75.

An Alexandrine according to Mr. Fleay. I rather incline to the belief that we have to deal with two short lines, unless the omission of the interjection *O!* should be preferred; or it might be placed in a separate line as in A. II, sc. 1, l. 203: —

Oth.   Oh!

Thou 'rt wise; 'tis certain.
Iago.   Stand you awhile apart.

The whole passage (down from l. 70) has been differently arranged by Hanmer and S. Walker.

CDXXXVI.

To fetch her fan, her gloves, her mask, nor nothing.

Ib., IV, 2, 9.

Although this line, so far as my knowledge goes, has never been queried, yet I cannot but think it faulty; I feel certain that Shakespeare wrote: —

To fetch her fan, her gloves, her mask, *her* nothing.

Compare Coriolanus, II, 2, 81: —

To hear my nothings monster'd,

although it seems doubtful whether *nothing* is to be understood in the same sense in these two passages. The Winter's Tale, I, 2, 295: —

— nor nothing have these nothings,

If this be nothing.

. (The Athenæum, June 11, 1881, p. 783.)

CDXXXVII.

Your mystery, your mystery; nay, dispatch.

Ib., IV, 2, 30.

Scan: —

Your myst|ery, | your myst|'ry; nay, | dispatch.

The following lines may be aptly compared, viz: —
Richard II., I, 2, 73: —

Desolate, desolate, will I hence and die.

Here is room for two scansions, either: —

Déso|late, dés|'late, will | I hénce | and díe.

or: —

Dés'late | déso|late will | I hénce | and díe.

Antony and Cleopatra, IV, 9, 23: —

O Án|toný! | O Án|t'ny! Let's speák | to hím.

Or, may be: —

O Án|t'ny! | O Án|toný! | Let's speák | to hím.

Compare note *ad loc.*

Cymbeline, IV, 2, 26: —

Cow'rds fa|ther cow|ards and | base things | sire base.

See note *ad loc.*

John Ford, ed. Hartley Coleridge (The Lover's Melancholy, I, 3,
p. 6 b): —

Di'monds cut diamonds; they who will prove.

Id., ('Tis Pity She's a Whore, IV, 1, p. 40 a): —

Yet, ere | I pass | away — | cru'l, cru|el flames.

Compare also Abbott, s. 475, and what has been said on The Tempest, I, 2, 53, by S. Walker, Versification, 138, and in note CCXXXIX.

CDXXXVIII.

That the sense aches at thee, would thou hadst ne'er been born!

Ib., IV, 2, 69.

Printed as two lines ending *thee ... born* in Qq and Ff. Mr. Fleay,
as usual, takes the line to be an Alexandrine, and S. Walker, Crit.
Exam., III, 289, says: 'Dele *that!*' The line, if scanned rightly, is
a regular blank verse with an extra syllable before the pause: —

That th' sense | aches at | thee, would thou | hadst ne'er |
been born!

CDXXXIX.

I am a child to chiding.
Iago.   What 's the matter, lady?

Ib., IV, 2, 114.

Omit *lady.* Iago's question is not addressed to Desdemona, but
to Emilia, and a stage-direction to that effect should be inserted.
Having received no satisfactory answer from Desdemona Iago very

naturally turns to his wife from whom he gets the information he requires. The omission of *lady* at the same time restores the metre; read, therefore: —

> I am a child to chiding.
> *Iago* [*to Emilia*].   What 's the matter?

CDXL.

> *Iago.* Here, stand behind this bulk; straight will he come.
> *Ib., V, 1, 1.*

Bulk (bulke) is the reading of the quartos; FAB *barke,* FCD *bark.* Collier's manuscript-corrector gives *balk* and an anonymous critic (the Cambridge Editors?) proposes *bulwark.* *Bulk* is right; compare Coriolanus, II, 1, 226, and Gay's Trivia, Bk. II, l. 140 (Poems, London, 1762, I, 154): —

> Alone, beneath a bulk she dropt the boy.

This latter quotation is not contained in Dr. Murray's Dictionary.

CDXLI.

> Here, at thy hand: be bold and take thy stand.
> *Ib., V, 1, 7.*

Hand has clearly intruded from the preceding line *(Be near at hand)* and cannot be right. According to the Cambridge Edition an anonymous critic (perhaps the Cambridge Editors themselves) suggests *at thy side* or *at thy left.* I imagine the original reading to have been *at thy heel,* which would certainly come nearer to the *ductus literarum* than either *side* or *left.*

CDXLII.

> *Iago.* Who is 't that cried?
> *Bian.* O, my dear Cassio.
> My sweet Cassio: O Cassio, Cassio, Cassio.
> *Ib., V, 1, 75 seqq.*

This is the arrangement of FA, whereas in the Qq the passage is printed as prose. Lines 75 and 76 are to be joined into one and *My* in l. 77 is a monosyllabic foot. *Cassio* at the end of l. 75 is to be pronounced as a trisyllable, at the end of l. 76 as a dissyllable, an incongruity which, if need be, may be backed by Richard II., II, 1, 22; 2 Henry VI., I, 2, 80 — 82; Henry VIII., IV, 2, 70; Romeo and Juliet, III, 2, 41; and IV, 3, 26 and 30.

CDXLIII.

Some good man bear him carefully from hence.

Ib., V, 1, 99.

Read *men,* as one man would hardly be able to bear Cassio 'carefully from hence' in a chair.

CDXLIV.

Stay you, good gentlemen. Look you pale, mistress?

Ib., V, 1, 105.

Qq *gentlewoman* instead of *gentlemen*; justly. The words are addressed to Bianca who offers to follow her wounded lover, and on whom Iago endeavours to lay all guilt. The lection of the Qq, however, is not sufficient to restore regular metre, if we do not at the same time omit *mistress,* which is an evident interpolation, just like *sir* (A. I, sc. 1, l. 55 and A. I, sc. 2, l. 10) and *lady* (A. IV, sc. 2, l. 114). It crept in, when *gentlewoman* was wrongly altered to *gentlemen* and another word of address to Bianca was wanted in its stead. Read: —

Stay you, good gentlewoman. Look you pale?

CDXLV.

It strikes, where it does loue. She wakes.
Des.   Who's there?   *Othello?*
Oth.   I *Desdemona.*
Des.   Will you come to bed, my Lord?
Oth.   Haue you pray'd to night, *Desdemon?*
Des.   `I my Lord.

Ib., V, 2, 22 seqq.

From this reading and arrangement of FAB the two later folios and the quartos only differ in reading *Desdemona* instead of *Desdemon.* The words '*She wakes*' have justly been declared by the Cambridge Editors, or whoever else the anonymous critic may have been, to be a stage-direction that has crept into the text. Similar instances of such an intrusion occur in As You Like It, IV, 2, 13 and K. Richard II., IV, 1, 181. The Cambridge Editors accordingly print *It ... Othello?* as one line, but are silent about the next, which should be corrected thus: —

Oth.   Ay, *Desdemon.*
Des.   Will you come to bed, my lord?

The rest of the passage is anything but metrically correct, and I see but one way to make it so, viz. by transferring *Desdemon* to the beginning of the line. The passage will then read thus: —

It strikes where it does love.
    Des.   Who 's there? Othello?
    Oth.   Ay, Desdemon.
    Des.   Will you come to bed, my lord?
    Oth.   Desdemon, have you pray'd to-night?
    Des.   Ay, m' lord.

Should this arrangement find no acceptance, the last resort will be
to print the passage exactly as it stands in the first folio, that is to
say as short lines.

CDXLVI.

Since guiltiness I know not; but yet I feel I fear.
    Oth.   Think on thy sins.
    Des.   They are loves I bear to you.
                          Ib., V, 2, 39 seq.

In the first line Pope, followed by subsequent editors, wrote *guilt*
instead of *guiltiness* and omitted *but*. I should prefer to strike out
I feel. In the second line Pope, Dyce (3ᵈ Ed.), and Hudson read
They're. Qy.: *They are the loves I bear you?*

CDXLVII.

That sticks on filthy deeds.
    Emil.   My husband!
    Oth.   What needs this iteration, woman? I say, thy husband.
                          Ib., V, 2, 149 seq.

Iteration is the reading of the Qq; Ff *itterance.* Compare S. Walker,
Crit. Exam., II, 241, where Mr. Lettsom, in a foot-note, declares
iterance 'necessary for the metre.' This lection certainly sets the
last line right, but leaves the preceding verse incomplete. The correct arrangement seems to be: —

    That sticks on filthy deeds.
    Emil.   My husband!
    Oth.   What needs
    This iteration, woman? I say, thy husband.

CDXLVIII.

Though I lost twenty lives. Help! help, ho! help!
                          Ib., V, 2, 166.

The punctuation of the Qq cannot be fully gathered from either the
Cambridge Edition or Dr. Furness's Variorum Edition. FA: *helpe,*
helpe, hoa, helpe. Rowe, followed by later editors: *Help! help! hoa!*

help! The great majority of modern editions point (as above): *Help!
help, ho! help!* This is contrary to the rhythm, which requires the
pointing: *help! help! ho, help!*

CDXLIX.

To the Venetian state. Come, bring him away.

Ib., V, 2, 337.

This is the reading of the Qq; the Ff omit *him.* The text of the
Qq is right; *him* should be pronounced as an enclitic; compare
note XL.*

CDL.

Call in the messengers. As I am Egypt's queen.

Antony and Cleopatra, I, 1, 29.

Messengers, in this line, and *homager,* in the next but one, are
triple endings before the pause; compare note CCLXXVII (p. 154).
Mr. Fleay has added l. 31 to his list of Alexandrines in Shakespeare,
but makes no mention of l. 29.

CDLI.

We stand up peerless. Excellent falsehood.

Ib., I, 1, 40.

A syllable pause line with a trochee after the pause; scan: —
 We stand | up peer|less. ⏑ | Excel|lent false|hood.
Seymour needlessly proposed to read, *O excelling falsehood.*

CDLII.

Char. Lord Alexas, sweet Alexas, most any thing Alexas,
almost most absolute Alexas, where's the soothsayer that you praised
so to the queen?   *Ib., I, 2, 1 seqq.*

Any thing, like *every thing,* frequently serves as conclusion to a succession of synonym or other nouns, enumerated without connectives
and frequently assuming the character of a climax; it is, if I am
allowed to borrow a simile from card-playing, the last trump, after

---

* With a few exceptions these notes on Othello (CDIV—CDXLIX) were
first published in Professor Kölbing's Englische Studien, XI, 217—235.

all the rest have been played. Some examples will distinctly show what is meant. In As You Like It, II, 7, 166, we read: —

> Sans teeth, sans eyes, sans taste, sans' every thing.

The Taming of the Shrew, III, 2, 234 seqq.: —

> She is my house,
> My household stuff, my field, my barn,
> My horse, my ox, my ass, my any thing.

Twelfth Night, III, 1, 161 seq.: —

> Cesario, by the roses of the spring,
> By maidhood, honour, truth, and every thing.

Twelfth Night, III. 4, 389, where Steevens has restored the true pointing: —

> Than lying, vainness, babbling, drunkenness,
> Or any taint of vice whose strong corruption
> Inhabits our frail blood.

Macbeth, III, 5, 18 seq. (no asyndeton): —

> Your vessels and your spells provide,
> Your charms and every thing beside.

Hamlet, IV, 7, 8 (compare my note on this line in my second (English) edition of 'Hamlet', p. 221): —

> As by your safety, greatness, wisdom, all things else,
> You mainly were stirr'd up.

Othello, I, 3, 96 seqq.: —

> and she, in spite of nature,
> Of years, of country, credit, every thing,
> To fall in love with what she fear'd to look on!

Dekker and Middleton, The Honest Whore, III, 1 (The Works of Thomas Middleton, ed. Dyce, III, 65): —

> Put on thy master's best apparel, gown,
> Chain, cap, ruff, every thing.

Mucedorus, III, 3, 44 seq. (ed. W. and Pr.): Here's a stir indeed, here's message, errand, banishment, and I cannot tell what.

These instances throw a vivid light not only on the passage under discussion, but also on that well-known speech of Gonzalo in The Tempest, I, 1, 69 seq., where the concluding *any thing* plainly requires the previous enumeration of several synonyms following each other without connectives, or, to say it in a word, a previous asyndetic series. This asyndetic series is supplied by Hanmer's ingenious conjecture than which nothing can be more convincing or possess a more valid claim to be admitted into the text: 'Now would I give a thousand furlongs of sea for an acre of barren ground, *ling,* heath, *broom,* furze, any thing.'

Missing Page

Missing Page

known to enjoy the freest possible rhythmical movement. 'Antony and Cleopatra' bears ample testimony to this fact, and it may be as well to gather from it a few more cases in point where trisyllabic words are used as dissyllables, be it either at the end of the line, before the pause, or anywhere else. I purposely select such lines as may be thought more or less harsh and may be construed into Alexandrines, omitting those that admit of no doubt. Compare, e. g., I, 3, 91 *(royalty)*; I, 4, 46 *(lackeying)*; I, 5, 46 *(opulent)*; II, 1, 10 *(auguring)*; II, 1, 33 (both *amorous* and *surfeiter)*; II, 1, 43 *(enmities)*; II, 2, 92 *(penitent* and *honesty)*; II, 2, 96 *(ignorant)*; II, 2, 122 *(widower)*; II, 2, 166 *(absolute)*; II, 2, 202 *(amorous)*; II, 3, 26 *(natural)*; III, 1, 7 *(fugitive)*; III, 10, 24 *(violate)*; III, 10, 29 *(there-abouts)*; III, 12, 19 *(hazarded)*; III, 12, 26 *(eloquence)*; III, 13, 23 *(ministers)*; III, 13, 30 *(happiness)*; III, 13, 36 *(emptiness)*; III, 13, 63 *(Antony)*; III, 13, 165 *(discandying* and *pelleted)*; IV, 1, 3 *(personal)*; IV, 4, 36 *(gallantly)*; IV, 8, 35 *(promises)*; IV, 12, 4 *(augurers)*; IV, 12, 23 *(blossoming)*; IV, 13, 10 *(monument)*; IV, 14, 76 *(for-tunate)*; IV, 14, 117 *(absolute)*; V, 1, 17 *(citizens* and *Antony)*; V, 1, 63 *(quality)*; V, 2, 23 *(reference)*; V, 2, 142 *(treasurer)*; V, 2, 237 *(liberty)*; V, 2, 239 *(purposes)*.

At a later date the works of Dryden and Pope, those great masters of versification, abound with similar contractions. The following are culled at random from Dryden: *fav'rites* (On Cromwell, st. 8); *emp'ric* (To Clarendon, 67); *spir'tual* (Absalom and Achitophel, I, 626); *med'cinally* (The Medal, 150); *rhet'ric* (Mac Flecknoe, 165); *orig'nal* (Religio Laici, 278); *Test'ments* (ib., 283)*; *diff'rence* (ib., 348); *med'c'nal* (Threnodia Augustalis, 111 and 170); *Presb'tery* (The Hind and the Panther, I, 233); *congl'bate* (Death of Lord Hastings, 35); *liqu'rish* (Wife of Bath, 319); *med'cinable* (Sigismonda and Guiscardo, 707).

With respect to Pope I cannot do better than by introducing a remark made by Dr. Edwin A. Abbott in his Introduction (p. V) to Edwin Abbott's Concordance to the Works of Alexander Pope (London, 1875). 'Words', he says, 'are often abbreviated by Pope to an extent not now customary. Thus *Penny-worth* is pronounced *penn'orth* [The Basset-Table, 30; the same abbreviation occurs in Dryden's Prologue to Oedipus, 33. Compare also *ha'porth* (Life and Letters of William Bewick, ed. by Thomas Landseer. London, 1871, II, 177)]; *casuistry* is pronounced as a trisyllable [Rape of the Lock, V, 121]

---

* It is a strange fact, that the editors of Dryden should have found a difficulty in scanning this line. Derrick and others omitted *and* before *cast*, and Mr. W. D. Christie (Dryden, &c., 2ᵈ Ed., Oxford, Clarendon Press, 1874, p. 273) attempts to make things square by accenting *Testaments* on the second syllable *(Testáments*, like *testátor)*. No such thing! Scan: —

'Twere worth | both Test | 'ments, and | cast in | the creed.

and *influence* as a dissyllable [Moral Essays, I, 142]. (*Stúrgeón* is an exception). This abbreviation is often expressed in the spelling. Hence *confus'dly* [Rape of the Lock, V, 41]; *cov'nant*; *dev'l* as well as *devil*; *clam'rous* [Windsor Forest, 132]; *di'mond* as well as *diamond* [the same in Dryden]; *flatt'rer* (except twice); *gall'ry* [Epistle to Arbuthnot, 87]; *gen'ral* seventeen times, *general* once; *ign'rance* [Essay on Criticism, 508]; *immac'late* [Donne Versified, IV, 253]; *intemp'rate*; *int'rest*; *Marybone*; *'Pothecaries. Though* is, I believe, almost always spelt *tho'*, and *through*, *thro'*. Many of these abbreviated pronunciations are common in the Elizabethan Poets [nay, many more than these; in fact, the abbreviations in the Elizabethan Poets are numberless].'

Bunyan (The Pilgrim's Progress, 1678, p. 155) uses *Vanity* as a monosyllable (!); *Bartholomew* and *Claverhouse* occur as dissyllables (*Bartlmew* and *Claver'se*) in Percy's Folio Manuscript, II, 186 and in Whitelaw's Book of Scottish Ballads, 543 a, respectively; *Bartlemy* in The Essays of Elia (1862, Moxon), p. 12; compare S. Walker, Versification, 186. The name of *Westmorcland* is generally spelt *Westmerland* in the old copies of Shakespeare, a spelling which is strikingly indicative of the abbreviated pronunciation of the word.

The triple endings employed by Shakespeare do not always consist of a single word, but frequently of two and three words. This can hardly be a matter of surprise as even at the present day a large number of such dactyls occur in dactylic verse. In Charles Wolfe's celebrated poem 'The Burial of Sir John Moore' the following dactyls are found: *corpse to the*; *sods with our*; *sheet or in*; *spoke not a*; *face that was*; *tread o'er his*; *Lightly they'll*; *o'er his cold*; *little he'll*; *reck if they*; *let him sleep*; *Briton has*; *half of our*; *clock struck the*; *fame fresh and.* These dactyls are certainly not a whit less harsh than the triple endings in Shakespeare which are objected to by English critics for their pretended harshness.

The reader may also be reminded of Lord Byron's triple rhymes in Don Juan, such as: *wishing all* (I, 31); *war again* (I, 38); *tombing all* (IV, 101); *tune it ye* (IX, 9); *gloom enough* (IX, 48); *accuse you all* (XII, 28); *talk'd about* (XII, 47); *term any* (XV, 36); and numerous others. However comically exaggerated these rhymes sometimes may be, yet they serve to show what the bent of English pronunciation is in this respect, and it cannot be doubted, that abbreviations and contractions, even such as are thought harsh now-a-days, are far less foreign to the genius of dramatic verse in Elizabeth's time than Alexandrines, which fell from Shakespeare's pen far more rarely, than English critics would make us believe.

In conclusion a few instances (out of many) of triple endings that consist of two or three words may be added. Compare, e. g., A. III, sc. 1, l. 15 (before the pause): —

Acquire | too *high* | a *fame,* when him | we serve 's | away.

A. IV, sc. 14, l. 80: —

> Most use│ful for │ thy coun│try. O, │ sir, *par*│*don me!*

It is well known, however, that *pardon* is frequently pronounced as a monosyllable; see *supra* note CLXXVII. Perhaps, therefore, it would be more correct to scan: —

> Most use│ful for │ thy coun│try. O, │ sir, *pard'n* │ *me!*

A Winter's Tale, I, 2, 117 (before the pause): —

> As in │ a *look*│*ing-glass,* and then │ to sigh, │ as 'twere.

S. Walker (Crit. Exam., III, 91) needlessly conjectured *glass* for *looking-glass*, although he thinks it 'dangerous to alter without stronger reason than there appears to be in the present case.'

Richard III., I, 2, 89 (before the pause): —

> Say that │ I *slew* │ *'em not.* Why, then │ they are │ not dead.

Perhaps, however, this line may be taken for a 'trimeter-couplet' as well; see Abbott, s. 500. The same may be said of Troilus and Cressida, III, 3, 127 (before the pause): —

> That has│ he *knows*│ *not what.* Nature,│ what things│ there are,

and of Coriolanus, IV, 1, 27 (before the pause): —

> As 'tis │ to *laugh* │ *at 'em.* My moth│er, you │ wot well.

Julius Cæsar, II, 1, 285. In all old and modern editions this line is uniformly printed: —

> And talk to you sometimes? Dwell I but in the suburbs.

Pope omitted *sometimes* and I once sided with him (Anglia, I, 347). 'The true prosodical view of this line', says Craik (The English of Shakespeare, &c. 5th Ed., London, 1875, p. 174) 'is to regard the two combinations "to you" and "in the" as counting each for a single syllable. It is no more an Alexandrine than it is an hexameter.' Although the same scansion is given by S. Walker (Crit. Exam., I, 221), yet I am unable to acquiesce in it. It now seems to me that *sometimes* has slipped out of its place and should be transposed, and that *talk to you* is a triple ending before the pause: —

> And some│times *talk* │ *t'you?* Dwell I │ but in │ the sub│urbs.

CDLIX.

> So much as lank'd not.
>   *Lep.*   'Tis pity of him.
>   *Cæs.* Let his shames quickly
> Drive him to Rome: 'tis time we twain
> Did show ourselves i' the field.

Ib., I, 4, 71 seqq.

Arrange (with Mr. Fleay) and scan: —

    So much | as lank'd | not. 'Tis pit|y of him. | Let's shames
    Quickly | drive him | to Rome. | 'Tis time | we twain
    Did show ourselves i' th' field.

Let's = let his; compare III, 7, 12: 'from's time'; Twelfth Night, III, 4, 326: 'for's oath sake.' Mr. Fleay, of course, declares l. 71 to be an Alexandrine with the cesura at the ninth syllable: —

    So much as lankt not. ‖ 'Tis pity of him. | Let his shames.

I wonder, how he scans this so-called Alexandrine.

CDLX.

    Eno. Go to, then; your considerate stone.

Ib., II, 2, 112.

Read either: —

    Go to, then, *you* considerate stone,

or, though I suggest it with hesitation: —

    Go to, then; *you're* considerate stone.

The meaning is: You are indeed considerate (= discreet, circumspect), but at the same time 'senseless as a stone', inaccessible to conciliatory and tender emotions.

CDLXI.

    Would then be nothing: truths would be tales.

Ib., II, 2, 137.

A syllable pause line; scan: —

    Would then | be noth|ing: ⏑ | truths would | be tales.

All conjectures are needless; the best of them is that by Staunton: *half tales.*

CDLXII.

    By duty ruminated.
       Ant.   Will Cæsar speak?
      Cæs. Not till he hears how Antony is touch'd
    With what is spoke already.
       Ant.   What power is in Agrippa.

Ib., II, 2, 141 seqq.

Already, in l. 143, is omitted by Hanmer. Arrange and scan: —

    By du|ty rum|'natèd. |
      Ant.   Will Cæ|sar speak?

> *Cæs.* Not till | he hears | how An | tony is touch'd | with what
> I spoke | alread | y.
>   *Ant.*   What power | is in | Agrip | pa.

Antony is is to be pronounced as a dissyllable (= *Ant'ny's*); compare III, 3, 44 (creature's); III, 7, 70 (leader's); &c. Thus the Alexandrine is got rid of.

CDLXIII.

> Her people out upon her; and Antony.   *Ib., II, 2, 219.*

Scan either: —

> Her peo | ple out | upon | her. And An | tony,

or (as a syllable pause line with a triple ending): —

> Her peo | ple out | upon | her; ∠ | and An | tony.

CDLXIV.

> Whom ne'er the word of 'No' woman heard speak.
>   *Ib., II, 2, 228.*

Capell's conjecture (*never the word — no*) does not improve the line; the only means to render it smoother would be by a transposition: —

> Whom *woman* ne'er the word of 'No' heard speak.

CDLXV.

> Her infinite variety: other women cloy
> The appetites they feed, but she makes hungry.
>   *Ib., II, 2, 241 seq.*

Arrange: —

> Her infinite variety: other women
> *Cloy* th' appetites they feed, but she makes hungry.

Variety is, of course, to be read as a trisyllable. Another Alexandrine is thus done away with.

CDLXVI.

> There saw you labouring for him. What was't.
>   *Ib., II, 6, 14.*

This line may be differently scanned; either: —

> There saw | you la | bouring | for him. | What was't.

or: —

> There saw | you la | b'ring for | him. ∠ | What was't.

To me this latter scansion seems preferable.

CDLXVII.

Then so much have I heard.

Ib., II, 6, 68.

A mutilated line; add: *Mark Antony:* —

Then so much have I heard, *Mark Antony.*

CDLXVIII.

It nothing ill becomes thee.

Ib., II, 6, 81.

Another defective line, to be completed by the addition of *Enobarbus:* —

It nothing ill becomes thee, *Enobarbus.*

CDLXIX.

And, as I said before, that which is the strength of their amity shall prove the immediate author of their variance.

Ib., II, 6, 136 seqq.

The context clearly shows that the poet did not write, 'the strength of their *amity*', but, 'the strength of their *unity*', referring the words not to l. 130: 'the very strangler of their amity', but to l. 122 seqq.: 'Then is Cæsar and he for ever knit together. *Eno.* If I were bound to divine of their unity, I would not prophesy so.' *Variance,* in l. 138, is not a suitable antithesis to *amity*, but it is to *unity.*

CDLXX.

These drums! these trumpets, flutes! what!

Ib., II, 7, 138.

A badly mutilated line which is far from being restored by Hanmer's omission of *flutes.*   Qy. read: —

These drums! | these trum|pets! ⸽ | *these* flutes! | what *ho!*?

That the exclamation *ho!* originally formed part of Menas's speech and most probably of this very line results from the words of Enobarbus: 'Ho! says a'. There's my cap!,' to which Menas replies: 'Ho! noble captain, come.'

CDLXXI.

And in his offence
Should my performance perish.
Sil.   Thou hast, Ventidius, that.

Ib., III, 1, 26 seq.

I feel no doubt that we should either read: *Thou'st that, Ventidius,*
or adopt the arrangement proposed by Steevens; in my eyes, the
former correction is preferable because it places *that* in the accented
part of the measure.　Steevens's arrangement is this: —

> Thou hast, Ventidius,
> That without which a soldier, and his sword, &c.

CDLXXII.

> This creature's no such thing.
> 　*Char.*　　　　　　　　　　　Nothing, madam.
> 　　　　　　　　　　　　　　　　　　　　　*Ib., III, 3, 44.*

A syllable pause line; scan: —

> This crea|ture's no | such thing. | ⌣ Noth|ing, mad|am.

Pope's and Keightley's conjectures are unnecessary.

CDLXXIII.

> *Cæs.*　Most certain.　Sister, welcome: pray you,
> Be ever known to patience: my dear'st sister!
> 　　　　　　　　　　　　　　　　　　　　*Ib., III, 6, 97 seq.*

Critics that will not allow the first line to pass for a catalectic verse
as defined in note II, may perhaps prefer the following arrangement: —

> *Cæs.*　Most certain.　Sister, welcome: pray you, *be*
> *E'er* known | to pa|tience: ⌣́ | my *dear*|*est* sis|ter;

or: —

> E'er known | to pa|ti-ence: | my dear|est sis|ter.

Compare Abbott, s. 510 (p. 419).

CDLXXIV.

> Hoists sails and flies.
> 　*Eno.*　That I beheld.　　　　　　*Ib., III, 10, 15 seq.*

A complete blank verse may be restored by the insertion of *Enobarbus*: —

> Hoists sails | and flies, | *En'bar*|*bus.*
> 　*Eno.*　　　　　　　　　　That I | beheld.

For the trisyllabic pronunciation of *Enobarbus* see note CDLV.
According to the Cambridge Edition Capell proposed *sail* for *sails;*
compare, however, the concluding song in Westward Ho! (Webster,
ed. Dyce, 1857, in 1 vol., p. 245 b): —

> Hoist up sails, and let's away.

·CDLXXV.

Why then good night indeed. *Ib., III, 10, 30.*

Another defective line; read: —

> Why then | good night | indeed, | *Canid* | *iús.*

CDLXXVI.

Which leaves itself: to the sea-side straightway.

Ib., III, 11, 20.

Either a catalectic verse (see note II), or a syllable pause line: —

> Which leaves | itself: | ⌣ to | the sea- | side straight | way.

CDLXXVII.

Frighted each other, why should he follow?

Ib., III, 13, 6.

The attempts made by Pope and an anonymous critic to correct this seemingly corrupt verse are needless; it is either a catalectic verse, or a syllable pause line and as such to be scanned: —

> Frighted | each oth | er, ∠ | why should | he fol | low?

CDLXXVIII.

Hear it apart.

   Cleo. None but friends: say boldly.

Ib., III, 13, 47.

A syllable pause line again; scan: —

> Hear it | apart. |
>   *Cleo.* ⌣ None | but friends: | say bold | ly.

All conjectures on this line recorded in the Cambridge Edition are needless.

CDLXXIX.

>   Your Cæsar's father oft
> When he hath mused of taking kingdoms in.

Ib., III, 13, 82 seq.

Arrange: —

>   Your Cæsar's father
> *Oft,* when he hath mused of taking kingdoms in.

He hath is to be contracted into one syllable; compare IV, 1, 3: 'He hath whipped'; IV, 15, 14: —

> Not Cæ | sar's val | our hath o'er | thrown An | tony,

(unless the pause after *valour* be deemed of sufficient strength to
admit of an extra syllable); Twelfth Night, V, 1, 372: 'he hath
married her'; Pericles, I, 1, 143: 'He hath found'; ib., II, 1, 132: 'it
hath been a shield.' — Another Alexandrine is thus eliminated.

CDLXXX.

Authority melts from me: of late, when I cried 'Ho!'
Like boys unto a muss, kings would start forth,
And cry 'Your will?' Have you no ears?
I am Antony yet. Take hence this Jack and whip him.

Ib., III, 13, 90 seqq.

With respect to the division of these lines I completely agree with
Hanmer, whose arrangement is as follows: —

Authority melts from me: of late, when I
Cried 'Ho!' like boys unto a muss, kings would
Start forth, and cry 'Your will?' Have you no ears?
I'm Antony yet. Take hence this Jack and whip him.

CDLXXXI.

Laugh at his challenge. Cæsar must think.   *Ib., IV, 1, 6.*
All attempts at completing this line recorded in the Cambridge
Edition are needless; scan: —

Laugh at | his chal|lenge. | Cæsar | must think.

CDLXXXII.

For I spake to you for your comfort; did desire you.

Ib., IV, 2, 40.

'In IV, 2, 40', says Mr. Fleay, who declares the line to be an
Alexandrine, 'cesura after ninth syllable.' In my opinion we have
to deal with a regular blank verse; scan: —

For I | spake to | you for | your com|fort; did d'sire | you.
The line has an extra syllable before the pause. For the monosyllabic pronunciation of *desire* see notes CCLV and CDLIV.

CDLXXXIII.

Eros.   Sir, his chests and treasure
He has not with him.
     Ant.   Is he gone?
     Sold.   Most certain.

Ib., IV, 5, 10 seq.

The words *Most certain* are erroneously ascribed to the Soldier; they belong to Eros. The Soldier has already informed Antony that Enobarbus *is with Cæsar*, but Antony, unwilling to believe him, appeals to the higher authority of Eros, asking him whether Enobarbus be really gone (*Is he gone?*) and is answered by Eros, *Most certain.*

CDLXXXIV.

Make it so known.
    Agr. Cæsar, I shall.   *Ib., IV, 6, 3.*

Not two short lines, as printed in the Cambridge and Globe Editions, by Dyce, Delius, &c., but a defective blank verse which is to be completed by the addition of *Agrippa*: —

    Make it | so known, | *Agrip*|*pa*. Cæsar, | I shall.

CDLXXXV.

I tell you true: best you safed the bringer.
        Ib., IV, 6, 26.

A syllable pause line; scan: —

    I tell | you true: | ⌣ best | you safed | the bring|er.

All conjectures (see Cambridge Edition) may be dispensed with.

CDLXXXVI.

Each man's like mine: you have shown all Hectors.
        Ib., IV, 8, 7.

Another syllable pause line; scan: —

    Each man's | like mine: | ⌣ you | have shown | all Hect|ors.

S. Walker's and the anonymous critic's conjectures recorded in the Cambridge Edition are needless.

CDLXXXVII.

He has deserved it, were it carbuncled.
        Ib., IV, 8, 28.

This line admits of no less than three different scansions. Firstly it may be considered as a catalectic verse (see note II) with an extra syllable before the pause. Secondly it may be taken to be a syllable pause line: —

    He has | deserv'd | it, ⟋ | were it | carbun|cled,

and thirdly it may be scanned: —

    He has | deser|vèd it, | were it | carbun|cled.

CDLXXXVIII.

Make mingle with our rattling tabourines.   *Ib., IV, 8, 37.*

After this verse a line has evidently been lost in which those sounds
were mentioned that heaven 'strikes together' with the sounds of the
earth, the trumpets and rattling tabourines.

CDLXXXIX.

O Antony! O Antony!
　　Sec. Sold.　　　　　　' Let's speak
To him.
　　First Sold. Let's hear him, for the things he speaks
May concern Cæsar.

Ib., IV, 9, 23 seqq.

Qy. read, arrange, and scan: —

　　O An|tony! | O An|t'ny!
　　Sec. Sold.　　　　　　Let's speak | to him.
　　First Sold. Nay, let | *us* hear | him, for | the things | he
　　　　　　　　　　　　　　　　speaks
May con|cern Cæ|sar?

Capell inserted *further* after *hear him.* Compare note on Cymbeline, V, 5, 238.

CDXC.

I learn'd of thee. How! not dead? not dead?

Ib., IV, 14, 103.

There is no need of Pope's conjecture, *not* YET *dead.* Scan: —

　　I learn'd | of thee. | ◡ How! | not dead? | not dead?

CDXCI.

His guard have brought him hither. O sun.

Ib., IV, 15, 9.

Here too there is no need of filling up the line as has been done
by Pope's and Capell's conjectures (*O* THOU *sun* and *O sun,* SUN).
Scan: —

　　His guard | have brought | him hith|er. ∠ | O sun!

CDXCII.

I lay upon thy lips.
　　Cleo.　　　　　　I dare not, dear, —
Dear my lord, pardon, — I dare not.   *Ib., IV, 15, 21 seq.*

Read and arrange: —

> I lay upon thy lips. *Come down.*
> *Cleo.*   I dare not,
> Dear, dear my lord, pardon, — I dare not *come.*

Come down, in l. 21, has been added most happily by Theobald; the context shows that it cannot be dispensed with. For *come,* in l. 22, I must answer myself; without this addition the line must either be considered to be a catalectic verse, or a line of four feet: —

> Dear, dear | my lord, | pard'n, I | dare not,

or a syllable pause line: —

> Dear, dear | my lord, | ◡ par|don, — I | dare nót.

The two latter scansions will hardly receive the approval of competent critics, as they place *not,* instead of *dare,* in the arsis.

CDXCIII.

Splitted the heart. This is his sword.

Ib., V, 1, 24.

According to the Cambridge Edition Hanmer added *itself* after *heart;* Collier's Ms. corrector: 'Split that self noble heart.' If the line is to be filled up, it would seem more probable that the name of the person addressed was lost and should be inserted: —

> Splitted the heart. *Cæsar,* this is his sword.

Or we might read: —

> Splitted *that very* heart. This is his sword.

After all, however, I think the line should be left as it stands, since verses of four feet are pretty frequent when there is a break in the line or a change of thought; see Abbott, s. 507.

CDXCIV.

The gods rebuke me, but it is tidings.

Ib., V, 1, 27.

Rowe, *a Tiding.* There is, however, no need of correction; it is either a catalectic verse (see note II), or a syllable pause line: —

> The gods | rebuke | me, ⌣ | but it | is ti|dings.

CDXCV.

> His voice was propertied
> As all the tuned spheres, and that to friends;
> But when he meant to quail and shake the orb,
> He was as rattling thunder.   *Ib., V, 2, 83 seqq.*

Instead of *and that to friends*, Theobald reads: WHEN *that to friends,*
and an anonymous critic (the Cambridge Editors?) proposes, *addrest
to friends.* I think we should read either, *and soft to friends* or,
and sweet to friends; *low* would not come near enough to the *ductus
literarum.* Antony's voice when speaking to friends is forcibly contrasted to the 'rattling thunder' to which it is likened when he is
speaking to enemies. Shakespeare repeatedly praises a low voice in
woman; of Cordelia her father says (V, 3, 272 seq.): —

> Her voice was ever soft,
> Gentle, and low, an excellent thing in woman.

May not what is an excellent thing in woman, be an excellent thing
in Antony too, when he is speaking to his friends?

CDXCVI.

> What should I stay —
>   *Char.* In this vile world? So, fare thee well.
>
> *Ib., V, 2, 316 seq.*

The words: *In this vile world* do not belong to Charmian, but to
Cleopatra who already before (IV, 15, 60 seq.) has complained of
'this dull world' which, she says, in Antony's absence is 'no better
than a sty.' Arrange, therefore: —

> What should I stay in this vile world —
>   *Char.*   So, fare thee well.

Shakespeare certainly wrote *vilde*, not *wilde*. *Fare thee well* would
appear to be a triple ending.*

CDXCVII.

> Unto a poor but worthy gentleman: she's wedded;
> Her husband banished; she imprison'd: all
> Is outward sorrow; though I think the king
> Be touch'd at very heart.
>   *Sec. Gent.*   None but the king?
>
> *Cymbeline, I, 1, 7 seqq.*

This is the arrangement of the Folios; it is quite correct and all
conjectures to which the passage has given rise are gratuitous; nor
is Mr. Fleay right in declaring l. 7 to be one of six feet. *Gentleman*
may be read either as a trisyllable, or as a dissyllable (see S. Walker,

----

* These notes on 'Antony and Cleopatra' (CDL — CDXCVI) were first
published in Prof. Kölbing's Englische Studien, IX, 267—278.

Versification, 189 scq.); in the former case we have a triple ending, in the latter an extra syllable, before the pause.*

CDXCVIII.

Of the king's looks, hath a heart that is not.

Ib., I, 1, 14.

S. Walker, according to the Cambridge Edition, suspects a corruption here. The line would indeed be intolerably harsh, if scanned: —

. Of the | king's looks, | hath a | heart that | is not.

In my opinion, however, there is no need of correction, the verse being either a syllable pause line: —

Of the | king's looks, | ◡ hath | a heart | that is | not,

or *Of* taking the place of a monosyllabic foot: —

Of | the king's | looks, hath | a heart | that is | not.

CDXCIX.

To his protection, calls him Posthumus Leonatus.

Ib., I, 1, 41.

Neither of the two names can be dispensed with, both of them being required by the context. The correct explanation of the line has been given by Dyce and Staunton *ad loc.* 'Various passages in these plays', says Dyce, 'show that Shakespeare (like his contemporary

---

* With the exception of a few additions the above notes on Cymbeline (CDXCVII—DCIV) were first printed in Professor Wülker's Anglia, Vol. VIII, p. 263—297, and were embodied in a Letter to C. M. Ingleby, Esq., M. A., LL. D., V. P. R. S. L. The introductory words of this Letter which I hope I shall be allowed to reproduce, were to the following effect: 'Dear Ingleby! When, in October last, at the beginning of our winter-term, I entered upon a course of lectures on Shakespeare's 'Cymbeline', I was surprised by the unexpected news that you were engaged in preparing a new edition of this most attractive, though at the same time most thorny play. You will easily believe that under these circumstances my thoughts turned to you whenever I was beset by one of those perplexing difficulties both critical and oxegetical with which this play abounds. It was natural that I should have wished to talk such passages over with you in your genial study at Valentines and thus to clear away *viribus unitis* some of those *cruces interpretum*. This privilege, however, was denied me, and a continued correspondence on the subject of our studies would have been too heavy a tax not only on your time, but also on mine. The next best thing, therefore, I can do, is to lay before you in print all those notes and conjectural emendations that have presented themselves to me in the course of my lectures. As your edition has been unavoidably postponed they may still prove serviceable to you in the revision and explanation of the badly corrupted text; your friendly disposition towards me will no doubt prompt you to gather from them all the critical honey they may contain and to favour me with your opinion of what you approve and of what you disapprove. Here, then, they are.'

dramatists) occasionally disregarded metre when proper names were to be introduced.' He then refers his readers to his note on 2 K. Henry VI., I, 1, 7: —

> The Dukes of Orleans, Calaber, Bretagne, and Alençon.

'I may observe', he says there, 'that Shakespeare has allowed this line to stand just as he found it in The First Part of the Contention, &c.; and, indeed, even in the plays which are wholly his own, he, like other early dramatists, considered himself at liberty occasionally to disregard the laws of metre in the case of proper names: e. g., a blank verse speech in Richard II., Act II, sc. 1, contains the following formidable line: —

> Sir John Norbery, Sir Robert Waterton, and Francis Quoint.'

To this instance Dyce, in his second edition, has added three similar lines, but has been singularly unfortunate in their choice, as they can be scanned without the least correction or difficulty. The first of them is taken from The Two Gentlemen of Verona, II, 4, 54, and is to be scanned in the following manner: —

> Know | ye Don | Anto|nio, your coun|tryman?

The line begins with a monosyllabic foot and has an extra syllable before the pause. The second line is from A. V, sc. 1 of the same play and its only irregularity is an extra syllable before the pause: —

> That Sil|via, at Fri|ar Pat|rick's cell, | should meet | me.

The third instance, also from the same comedy (V, 2, 34), may certainly be considered as one line, as printed by Dyce, in which case *Valentine* is to be read as a triple ending; there is, however, no occasion to depart from the arrangement of the first Folio, which, amongst others, has been adopted by the Cambridge and Globe Editors: —

> *Duke.* Why then,
> She's fled unto that peasant Valentine.

Even the 'formidable' and perhaps corrupt passage in Richard II., II, 1, 281 seqq. may be reduced to something like metre: —

> That late | broke from | the Duke | of Ex|eter,
> His broth|er, Archbish|op late | of Can|terbur|y,
> Sir Thom|as Er|pingham, | ◡ Sir | John Ram|ston,
> Sir | John Nor|bery,
> Sir Rob|ert Wa|terton | and Fran|cis Quoint.

Should S. Walker, Versification, 100, be right in maintaining that *Archbishop* is generally accented on the first syllable, a slight transposition of the word will meet the requirements of the case: —

> His broth|er, late Arch|bishop | of Can|terbur|y.

To revert to 'Cymbeline'. Staunton's note on the line in question is to the following effect: 'The old poets not unfrequently introduce proper names without regard to the measure.' To this he adds another remark of no little import: 'occasionally indeed', he says, 'as if at the discretion of the player, the name was to be spoken or not.' The truth, in my opinion, is, that the names of the interlocutors as well as titles and other words of address seem frequently either to have been wrongly left out or wrongly added by the carelessness of the players and copyists, especially at the end of the line. Indeed a great number of verses may be corrected either by the addition, or (though less frequently) by the omission of the name of the person addressed. See my note on Hamlet (second edition), s. 59 (Reynaldo); *supra* note CCXIII; &c.

D.

Could make him the receiver of; which he took.

Ib., I, 1, 44.

Scan: —

    Could make | him the | recei'er | of; which | he took.
See Abbott, s. 466. Compare also l. 72 of this very scene: —

    Evil [*E'il*]-eyed | unto | you: you're | my pris|'ner, but,
wrongly altered by Pope to *Ill-eyed* &c. See S. Walker, Crit. Exam., II, 196.

DI.

As we do air, fast as 'twas minister'd,
And in 's spring became a harvest, lived in court.

Ib., I, 1, 45 seq.

Both Mr. Fleay and Mr. Ellis (On Early English Pronunciation, III, 946) register l. 46 among what they are pleased to call Alexandrines. Hertzberg (Shakespeare's Dramatische Werke nach der Uebersetzung von Schlegel und Tieck, herausgegeben durch die Deutsche Shakespeare-Gesellschaft, XII, 453) likewise thinks that it would be the easiest expedient to read *And in his spring &c.* and thus to make the line one of those Alexandrines, of which, he says, there is no want in Cymbeline. In my conviction Capell has come nearest to the truth by adding *And* to the preceding line; only he should not have dissolved *in's*. Arrange and read accordingly: —

    As we do air, fast as 'twas minister'd, and
    In's spring became a harvest, lived in court, &c.

Minister'd is, of course, to be pronounced as a dissyllable (*min'ster'd*); see Abbott, s. 468.

DII.

A sample to the youngest, to the more mature.

Ib., I, 1, 48.

Mr. Fleay has no doubt that this is an Alexandrine, and I have no
doubt that it is not. *Youngest* is either to be pronounced as a
monosyllable, like *eldest* ten lines *infra*; or, if the dissyllabic pronunciation should be preferred, it contains an extra syllable before the
pause. The article before *more* is to be elided (or read as a pro-
clitic) just as it is the case eight lines lower down: *to th' king*, and
l. 59: *I' th' swathing-clothes*. Scan, therefore, either: —

A sam|ple to | the young'st, | to th' more | mature,

or: —

A sam|ple to | the young|est, to th' more | mature.

DIII.

I' th' swathing-clothes the other, from their nursery.

Ib., I, 1, 59.

No Alexandrine, *nursery* being a triple ending. Compare the scansion of *imagery* in Spenser's Faerie Queene, VII, 7, 10: —

That richer seem'd than any tapestry,
That Princes bowres adorne with painted imagery.

DIV.

That could not trace them!
 First Gent.   Howsoe'er 'tis strange.

Ib., I, 1, 65.

Qy. *that't* or *that' could not trace them?* Compare III, 4, 80: *That*
[qy. *that't?*] *cravens my weak hand.* See S. Walker, Versification,
77 seqq.

DV.

I will be known your advocate: marry, yet.

Ib., I, 1, 76.

S. Walker, Versification, 187, endeavours to show that *marry* 'is commonly a monosyllable' and that it 'would have been irregular' to
scan: —

I will | be known | your ad|v'cate: mar|ry, yet.

Nevertheless I own that I prefer this scansion, so much the more
as S. Walker has not succeeded in proving his case. Apart from a
line in Hudibras (III, 3, 644), in which the *y* of *Marry* is to be

contracted with the following *hang,* he only instances K. Richard III., III, 4, 58, where *marry* may just as well be read as a trochee and *he is* may be contracted: —

Marry, | that with | no man | here he's | offend|ed.

If some reader or other should object that by this scansion *no* is placed in the unaccented, instead of the accented part of the measure, he may be referred to note XV. In support of his theory S. Walker also adduces *sirrah,* which, he says, is 'frequently at least' pronounced as a monosyllable, e. g., 3 K. Henry VI., V, 6, 6. But may not this line be read and scanned: —

, Sirrah, | leave's to | ourselves: | we must | confer?

In conclusion the reader's attention may be called to the fact that in all the lines quoted, a pause follows after both *marry* and *sirrah* which would seem to speak in favour of my scansions. That in the line quoted from Hudibras the pause does not impede the contraction of the two vowels, cannot be a matter of surprise.

DVI.

Imo. O blest, that I might not! I chose an eagle,
And did avoid a puttock.

Ib., I, 1, 139 seq.

'A puttock', says Singer *ad loc.,* 'is a mean degenerate species of hawk, too worthless to deserve training.' This note re-appears in the Rev. H. Hudson's edition in a slightly altered shape: 'A puttock', he says, 'is a mean degenerate hawk, not worth training.' Delius has nothing better to say; his note is to the following effect: 'Puttock, ein Habicht schlechter Art.' What does a 'degenerate hawk' mean? I am unable to attach a meaning to this phrase. The fact is that the puttock does not belong to the *falcones nobiles,* as they are termed in natural history, but is a species of kite (*Milvus ictinus,* the glede). According to Naumann und Gräfe, Handbuch der Naturgeschichte der drei Reiche &c. (Eisleben und Leipzig, 1836), I, 362 the *Milvi* are 'von traurigem Ansehn, träge und feig, und können den Raub nicht fliegend ergreifen, sondern nur sitzende und kriechende Thiere fangen, und fressen auch Aas.' 'Der rothe Milan (Gabelweihe, Königsweihe, *Falco Milvus*)', the same authors continue, 'jagt junge Hühner, Enten, Gänse und andere. junge oder des Flugvermögens beraubte Vögel, Mäuse, Maulwürfe, Amphibien, indem er niedrig über den Boden wegstreicht, fällt gern auf Aas.' The chief point, as I take it, is that the *Milvi* cannot catch birds on the wing, but only when sitting or walking about. This is the reason why they were held in disregard by all lovers of hawking and why all attempts at training cannot but be lost on them, since training may improve, but cannot alter the natural gifts of bird or beast. Thus the name of 'puttock' passed into a by-word and an expression of contempt. The derivation of the word serves as an eloquent confirmation of this theory, *puttock* being by no means a diminutive, but a corruption of *poot-hawk,* i. e. a hawk that preys on poots or pouts; *pout,* as Prof. Skeat has shown, standing for *poult* = *pullet* (Fr. *poulet*) from Lat. *pullus.*

DVII.

Leave us to ourselves; and make yourself some comfort.

Ib., I, 1, 155.

Scan either: —

Leave us | t' ourselves; | and make | yourself | some com|fort,

or, which I think preferable: —

Leave's to | ourselves; | and make | yourself | some com|fort.

DVIII.

Queen.   Fie, you must give way.

Ib., I, 1, 158.

This is the punctuation of all the Ff. Modern editors punctuate either: Fie! you must &c., or: Fie! — you must &c., thus awakening the belief, as if in their opinion the words were addressed to two different persons. Not content with such an indirect hint, Delius explicitly refers the interjection *Fie!* to the preceding speech of Cymbeline, whereas he declares only the rest of the words to be addressed to Imogen. I cannot subscribe to such a division of the Queen's admonition. On hearing her father's terrible malediction Imogen very naturally gives expression to her wounded feelings by some gesture of impatience and horror and is reproved by her stepmother rather energetically, as only in l. 153 she has been desired to keep quiet ('Peace, Dear lady daughter, peace!'). She does not utter her grief and dismay in words, but her continued gesticulation shows that her mother's first injunction has been of little avail and requires repetition. The only words addressed to the King by the Queen are in l. 153: ,Beseech your patience.'

DIX.

Pray you speake with me;
You shall (at least) &c.   *Ib., I, 1, 177.*

This is the arrangement and reading of the Ff. Almost all editors since Capell have adopted his suggestion to add *I* before *pray,* which,

they say, has been lost. Nevertheless it may be submitted that the
line is quite correct, if scanned as a syllable pause line: —

> Pray you, | ◡ speak | with me: | you shall | at least.

I adopt, of course, the arrangement of the lines as proposed by Capell
and think the Ff as well as Rowe faulty in this respect.

DX.

Clo. You'll go with us?
First Lord. I'll attend your lordship.
Clo. Nay, come, let's go together.
Sec. Lord. Well, my lord.

Ib., I, 2, 40 seqq.

Capell, Dyce, and the Rev. H. Hudson have assigned the words:
'I'll attend your lordship' to the Second Lord. Delius, on the other
hand, suspects that the concluding speech: 'Well, my lord', should
be given to the First Lord. In my conviction both parties are wrong.
In reply to Cloten's invitation, addressed to the two lords conjointly,
to accompany him to his chamber, the First Lord who is a flatterer
and a flunkey, at once declares himself ready to attend his lordship;
the second, however, who knows and dislikes his master thoroughly,
either offers to stay behind, or to leave the stage by a different door,
but is prevented from doing so by Cloten's reiterated summons: 'Nay,
come, let's go together', to which he cannot but reply in the affirmative: 'Well, my lord.' Only on the stage the correctness of this
explanation can be made fully apparent. Compare note on II, 1, 48.

DXI.

Imo. Then waved his handkerchief?
Pis.   And kiss'd it, madam.
Imo. Senseless linen! happier therein than I!
And that was all?
Pis.   No, madam, for so long &c.

Ib., I, 3, 6 seqq.

This is the arrangement of the folios. Line 7 is thus to be scanned: —

> · Sense | less lin | en! Happier | therein | than I,

a scansion which exhibits indeed three deviations from the normal
type, viz. a monosyllabic foot, an extra syllable before the pause, and
a trochee after it. The scansion given by Dr. Abbott, s. 453: —

> Senseless | linen! | Happier | therein | than I

looks very plausible at first sight, but on second thoughts appears
too abnormal to find assent; it contains no less than three con-

secutive trochees!   S. Walker, Crit. Exam., III, 316, would arrange
as follows: —

    Imo.   Then waved his handkerchief?
    Pis.   And kiss'd it, madam.
    Imo.   Senseless linen, happier
Therein than I!
And that was all?
    Pis.   No, madam; for so long &c.

If, however, the division of the old copies is to be departed from,
the following arrangement seems preferable: —

    Imo.   Then waved his handkerchief?
    Pis.   And kiss'd it, madam.
    Imo.   Senseless linen!
Happier therein than I!   And that was all?
    Pis.   No, madam; for so long
As he could make &c.

DXII.

When shall we hear from him?   Be assured, madam.

Ib., I, 3, 23.

Scan: —

    When shall | we hear | from him? | Be assur|èd, mad|am.

I shall disbelieve the pretended accentuation *madám*, until convinced
by a case, where *mádam* is simply impossible.   The very next passage on which I shall comment is a case in point, in so far as here
the poet would seem to have accented the word on the last syllable,
but has not.   This passage is: —

DXIII.

Shakes all our buds from growing.
Enter a Lady.
    Lady.   The queen, madam.
Desires your highness' company.   *Ib., I, 3, 37 seq.*

The first line admits of a twofold scansion, either: —

    Shakes all | our buds | from grow|ing.   The queen, | madám,
or: —

    Shakes all | our buds | from grow|ing.   The | queen, mad|am.

But what, if neither of these two scansions should have been the
poet's own?   The above arrangement of the Ff has indeed been
retained by all editors, as far as I know; however, the words spoken

by the Lady form a complete blank verse by themselves and the lines should be divided accordingly: —

Shakes all our buds from growing.

Enter a Lady.

Lady.   The queen, | madam, | desires | your high|ness com|pany. Need I add, that *madam*, although in the second place, is a trochee (compare Abbott, s. 453 and my second edition of 'Hamlet', s. 118), and *company* a triple ending? By this division the incomplete line is shifted from the speech of the Lady which it does not fit at all, to that of Imogen where it finds a far more appropriate place. As to *madam*, Mr. Fleay, in his edition of Marlowe's 'Edward II.', p. 120, thinks it a strong argument in favour of the accentuation *madâm*, that the old texts write *Madame*, which spelling, in his opinion, is plainly indicative of the French accentuation of the word. In the present passage, however, as well as in I, 1, 23, the Ff uniformly write *Madam*, whilst in other passages (e. g. in Love's Labour's Lost, V, 2, 431) we read *Madame*, although the word be undoubtedly accented on the first syllable. Compare *supra* note CCXXIX. — In order to prevent a mistaken scansion one more line may be added, viz. A. I, sc. 5, l. 5: —

Pleaseth | your high|ness, ay: | here they | are, mad|am.

DXIV.

But, though slow, deadly.
  Queen.   I wonder, doctor.

Ib., I, 5, 10.

Theobald and, independently of him, S. Walker, Versification, 24: I *do* wonder. There is, however, no need of such an insertion, the verse being a syllable pause line; scan: —

But, though | slow, dead|ly. ⌣ | I won|der, doc|tor.

Or should we come still nearer to the poet's own scansion by reading *But* as a monosyllabic foot: —

But, | though slow, | deadly. | I won|der, doc|tor?

DXV.

Think on my words. [*Exeunt Queen and Ladies.*
  Pis.   And shall do.

Ib., I, 5, 85.

According to the Cambridge Edition Steevens suspects an omission here. Singer adds the following note: 'Some words, which rendered this sentence less abrupt, and perfected the metre, appear to have

been omitted in the old copies.' Add *gracious madam* after *shall do*,
and all will be right: —

> Think on | my words. |
>
> And shall | do, *gra*|*cious mad*|*am.*

Compare note on I, 1, 41.

. DXVI.

> What, are men mad? Hath nature given them eyes
> To see this vaulted arch, and the rich crop
> Of sea and land, which can distinguish 'twixt
> The fiery orbs above and the twinned stones
> Upon the number'd beach? and can we not
> Partition make with spectacles so precious
> 'Twixt fair and foul?   *Ib., I, 6, 32 seqq.*

Instead of *the number'd* Theobald reads rightly: *th' unnumber'd.*
Compare K. Lear, IV, 6, 20 seqq.:

> the murmuring surge
> That on the unnumbered idle pebbles chafes,
> Cannot be heard so high.

The 'crop of sea and land' means the crop of the sea on the land,
or the crop on the margin between the sea and land, i. e. that profusion of pebbles, shells, seaweeds, &c. that are. washed on shore by
the waves and constitute, so to say, the harvest which the land reaps
from the ocean. The poet places side by side those two natural
phenomena where an innumerable abundance of similar, nay almost
undistinguishable (I beg pardon for coining the word) objects are
gathered together: the firmament with its myriads of stars and the
unnumbered beach with its pebbles that are as like to each other as
twins. Now, he continues, if men's eyes are capable of distinguishing
some individual star or pebble from its twin, can they not, on
beholding the divine form of Imogen, make partition between fair
and foul, between an untainted virtuous lady and one of the common
sort, persons that even in their outward appearance are so wide apart?

DXVII.

> An eminent monsieur, that, it seems, much loves.
>
> *Ib., 1, 6, 65.*

Scan: —

> An em|'nent mon|sieur, that, | it seems, | much loves.

Compare Love's Labour's Lost, II, 1, 196: —

> A gal|lant la|dy. Mon|sieur, fare | you well;

K. Henry VIII., I, 3, 21: —

I'm glad | 'tis there: | now I | would pray | our mon|sieurs;

Ib., V, 2, 325: —

This is | the ape | of form, | mónsieur | the nice.

In this last line the word might indeed be read as an iambic, but it is a trochee after the pause. That *monsieur*, in Shakespeare's time, was generally accented on the first syllable, seems also to be confirmed by four of its six different spellings which occur in the first Folio, viz. *mounsieur, mounseur, mounsier,* and *monsier;* the fifth and sixth being *monsieur (passim)* and *monsieuer* (in As You Like It, I, 2, 173). The diphthong *ou* in the first syllable (which replaces the original *o*), recalls such words as *counsel (consilium), fountain (fontana), mountain (montana),* &c., and shows that the word was brought under the Teutonic accentuation. Also Dryden (Heroic Stanzas upon the Death of Oliver, &c. st. 23) accents it on the first syllable: —

Than the | light Món|sieur the | grave Don | outweighed,

and in 1663 we meet with the spelling *Mounser* which admits of no other accent but on the first syllable; see Rye, England as seen by Foreigners, p. 187. In more recent times, however, the French accentuation of the word has been re-instated and has kept its ground to the present day, just as it has been the case with the adjectives *divine, extreme, obscure,* &c. It should be added that all other passages in Shakespeare where *monsieur* occurs, are in prose.

<hr>

DXVIII.

Iach.   They are in a trunk,

Attended by my men.   *Ib., I, 6, 197.*

Qy. read: Attended by my *man?* Only in l. 53 of this very scene Iachimo has spoken of his man and informed us that he is strange and peevish.

<hr>

DXIX.

Sec. Lord. You cannot derogate, my lord.

Ib., II, 1, 48.

There can be little doubt that these words belong to the First and not to the Second Lord, and that Dr. Johnson's alteration of the prefix is right. Eight lines lower down the common text should be replaced by the following arrangement: —

First [instead of *Sec.*] *Lord.* I'll attend your lordship.

[*Exeunt Cloten and First Lord.*

Sec. Lord. That such a crafty devil &c.

Compare note on I, 2, 40 seqq.

<hr>

DXX.

Ah, but some natural notes about her body,
Above ten thousand meaner moveables
Would testify, to enrich mine inventory.

Ib., II, 2, 28 seqq.

Qy. read and point: —

Ah, but some natural notes about her body, —
Above ten thousand meaner moveables
They'ld testify, — t' enrich mine inventory?

DXXI.

The treasure of her honour. No more. To what end?

Ib., II, 2, 42.

No Alexandrine, but a blank verse with an extra syllable before the
pause; scan: —

The treas|ure of | her hon|our. No more. | T'what end?

Two lines *infra memory* is to be read as a dissyllable, which makes
the line a regular blank verse. Mr. Fleay declares l. 44 to be an
Alexandrine, but makes no mention of l. 42.

DXXII.

Swift, swift, you dragons of the night, that dawning
May bare the raven's eye!   *Ib., II, 2, 48 seq.*

In my conviction the last words should neither be understood literally,
nor can we suppose, as Dyce justly remarks, that Shakespeare would
turn night to a raven at the same moment when introducing her as
a goddess. Shakespeare, who was conversant with so many facts of
natural history, may possibly have been aware that the raven, to
introduce Mr. R. Gr. White's remark *ad loc.*, 'is the most matinal
[*sic,* read *matutinal*] bird, even more so than the lark.' But I greatly
doubt that his audience, unadulterated cockneys as they were, should
have been so intimately acquainted with the ways and habits of the
raven as to understand an allusion so far-fetched and altogether
foreign to the context. To me Sir Thomas Hanmer seems to have
hit the mark in attributing the raven's eye (or raven-eye) to dawning
itself; Iachimo expresses the wish that dawning might soon bare
or ope its eye which is as dark as the raven. Hanmer proposes to
read: *its* raven eye, but no alteration is needed; least of all Collier's
suggestion, *blear* the raven's eye, which has been energetically rejected
by Dyce as being 'most ridiculous.'

DXXIII.

> And winking Mary-buds begin
> To ope their golden eyes:
> With every thing that pretty is,
> My lady sweet, arise:
> Arise, arise.　　　　　　　*Ib., II, 3, 25 seqq.*

Read, of course, *that pretty bin,* as printed by Hanmer and Warburton; Hanmer's alteration of *every thing* to *all the things,* however, is not needed, although *bin* is the third person plural; see Morris, Outlines of English Accidence, s. 295, p. 182; Mätzner's Engl. Grammatik (2ᵈ Ed., I, 408); Al. Schmidt, Shakespeare-Lexicon, s. *Be. Every* and *each* are not unfrequently used as collectives, and as such govern the plural; compare, e. g., Much Ado about Nothing, III, 4, 60 seq.: Nothing I; but God send every one their heart's desire! Lucrece, 125: —

> And every one to rest themselves betake.

Thomas Heywood, The English Traveller (Dramatic Works, London, 1874, IV, 26): '*Wife.* But in all this, How did the Women scape? *Clo[wn].* They fared best, and did the least hurt that I saw; But for quietnesse sake, were forc'd to swallow what is not yet digested, yet euery one had their share, and shee that had least, I am sure by this time, hath her belly full.'

Dryden, Annus Mirabilis, st. 15: —

> It seems as every ship their sovereign knows.

Richard Bentley, A Dissertation upon the Epistles of Phalaris, &c. (London, 1699), Preface, p. LXXXV: 'The words in my Book, which he excepts against, are *Commentitious, Repudiate, Concede, Aliene, Vernacular, Timid, Negoce, Putid,* and *Idiom*: every one of which were in Print, before I us'd them; and most of them, before I was born.'

Lucrece, 404: —

> Each in her sleep themselves so beautify.

Pope, Imitations of Horace, The Second Satire of the Second Book, ll. 75 — 76: —

> How pale, each Worshipful and Rev'rend quest
> Rise from a Clergy, or a City feast!

Compare also the following passages in Childe Harold, viz. III, 62: —

> All that expands the spirit, yet appals,
> Gather around these summits,

and IV, 162: —

> 　　　　　　　Are exprest
> All that ideal beauty ever bless'd.

DXXIV.

The one is Caius Lucius.
Cym.   A worthy fellow.

Ib., II, 3, 60.

Mr. Fleay scans this line: —

Th' one's Ca|ius Lu|cius. | A wor|thy fel|low.

But the verse has evidently an extra syllable before the pause and is to be scanned: —

The one | is Ca|ius Lu|cius. A wor|thy fel|low.

DXXV.

Yet you are curb'd from that enlargement by
The consequence o' the crown, and must not soil
The precious note of it with a base slave,
A hilding for a livery, a squire's cloth,
A pantler, not so eminent.   *Ib., II, 3, 125 seqq.*

The only critic that has queried this passage, is Collier. 'We may', he says rather hesitatingly, 'also suspect a misprint in the word "note".' *Note* is surely a misprint; read *robe*. What the poet here calls the *'precious robe of the crown'* in K. Henry V., IV, 1, 279, is styled: —

The intertissued robe of gold and pearl,

and is there enumerated among the king's attributes. What reader of Shakespeare does not also recall Cleopatra's words: —

Give me my robe, put on my crown; I have
Immortal longings?

'You must not soil', says Cloten, 'the regal robe, with a base slave, a hilding born to wear a livery, or a squire's cloth at best.' The context sufficiently shows that this is what the poet had in his mind and wanted to express, and I need not dwell on the circumstance that, throughout our play, garments play a conspicuous part in Cloten's thoughts and even influence his actions. — The misprint *foyle* for *foyle* in the Ff would not be worth mentioning, but for the fact that Dr. Al. Schmidt, who in his Shakespeare-Lexicon has proved a stickler for the correctness of the first Folio, upholds the lection *foil*.

DXXVI.

I am sprited with a fool,
Frighted, and anger'd worse.   *Ib., II, 3, 144 seq.*

The meaning which has been missed in the late Professor Hertzberg's translation, is: I am not only sprited by a fool, but what is still

worse, frighted and angered by the loss of my bracelet; the anonymous conjecture on l. 141: —

How now! [*missing the bracelet*].   Pisanio!
having indeed hit the mark.

DXXVII.

But the worst of me.   So, I leave you, sir.

Ib., II, 3, 159.

A syllable pause line; scan: —

But th' worst | of me. | ⌣ So, | I leave | yòu, sir.

The same scansion occurs in the first hemistich of the next line *(To
th' worst | of dis|content)*.

DXXVIII.

In these fear'd hopes,

I barely gratify your love.   *Ib., II, 4, 6 seq.*

This is the reading of all the Ff; according to Collier (2nd Ed.) *ad
loc.* the words mean 'in these hopes which I fear may never be
realised' [!].   Dyce has adopted Tyrwhitt's conjecture *sear'd,* as he
(most justly) 'cannot think that the original reading here is to be
defended on the supposition that "fear'd hopes" may mean "fearing
hopes" or "hopes mingled with fears".'   The Rev. H. Hudson reads
'*sere hopes*'; '*sere hopes*', he explains, 'are withered hopes; as they
would naturally be in their Winter's state.'   The hopes of Posthumus,
however, are neither *feared* (by whom?), nor *seared* or *withered,* but
they are *dear hopes*, and this, in my humble opinion, is what the
poet wrote.

DXXIX.

Let it be granted you have seen all this, — and praise.

Ib., II, 4, 92.

Mr. Fleay wrongly reckons this line among the Alexandrines.   Read
and scan:—

Let it | be grant|ed you've seen | all this, | — and praise.

There is a pause after *granted* considerable enough to allow of an
extra syllable before it.

DXXX.

Iach.   Then, if you can,
[*Showing the bracelet.*

Be pale: I beg but leave to air this jewel; see!
And now 'tis up again.   *Ib., II, 4, 95 seqq.*

'In II, 4, 96', says Mr. Fleay, 'arrange "be pale" in l. 95.' — This, of course, would only be transferring the Alexandrine from l. 96 to l. 95. To me it seems to admit of no doubt, that *'See'* forms a most energetic interjectional line. Arrange: —

Then, if you can,

Be pale: I beg but leave to air this jewel;
See!   [*Showing the bracelet.*
And now 'tis up again.

DXXXI.

Must be half-workers? We are all bastards.

Ib., II, 5, 2.

The conjectures of Pope, Capell (S. Walker, Crit. Exam., III, 322), and Keightley are needless. The verse is a syllable pause line; scan: —

Must be | half-work|ers? ⌣ | We are | all bast|ards.

DXXXII.

For wearing our own noses. That opportunity.

Ib., III, 1, 14.

This line, left unnoticed by Mr. Fleay, has both an extra syllable before the pause and a triple ending.

DXXXIII.

Cym. You must know,
Till the injurious Romans did extort &c.

Ib., III, 1, 47 seqq.

I have no doubt that this speech does not belong to Cymbeline, but to the Queen who has been interrupted rather uncourteously by her son and whom the king expressly wishes to end, especially as by her action she undoubtedly indicates her desire of saying something more. My suspicion is confirmed by the following remarkable metrical fact. Dr. Abbott, s. 514, has ingeniously shown that 'interruptions are sometimes not allowed to interfere with the completeness of the speaker's verse.' Now the first line of the speech in question exactly completes the last line of the Queen's antecedent speech (l. 33), although an interruption by no less than three speeches, two from Cloten and one from the king, has taken place. This is the line: —

And Britons strut with courage. — You must know.

Compare *supra* notes III and CDXXII. — The words *We do* in l. 54 are assigned to *'Cloten'* by Collier and Dyce, to *'Cloten and Lords'* by

the Cambridge Editors. Either prefix may be right, yet I own that
this once I think it safer to side with Collier and Dyce than with
the Cambridge Editors; the Lords, in my opinion, expressing their
assent merely by gestures.

DXXXIV.

Though Rome be therefore angry: Mulmutius made our laws.

Ib., III, 1, 59.

One of Mr. Fleay's Alexandrines. I have no hesitation in accepting
Steevens's emendation, i. e., in discarding the words 'made our laws'
which are evidently either a marginal gloss intended to explain or
to replace 'Ordained our laws', or a dittography. The verse is a
syllable pause line: --

Though Rome | be there|fore an|gry: $\smile$ | Mulmu|tius.

DXXXV.

Thyself domestic officers — thine enemy.

Ib., III, 1, 65.

According to Mr. Fleay an Alexandrine with 'the cesura after the
eighth syllable.' I take it to be a blank verse with a triple ending
(enemy). Three lines farther on Mr. Fleay would make his readers
believe in another Alexandrine with the cesura after the ninth syllable (!). In my conviction it is a blank verse with an extra syllable
before the pause; *defied* is to be pronounced as a monosyllable; see
note CCLV. Scan: —

For fu|ry not | to be | resist|ed. Thus d'fied.

DXXXVI.

Pis. How! of adultery? Wherefore write you not
What monster's her accuser? Leonatus!

Ib., III, 2, 1 seq.

Adultery is to be pronounced as a trisyllable. The Ff have an interrogation after *accuse* (*accuser* in Capell's correction) and a colon after
Leonatus, which latter has been replaced by an exclamation in all,
or almost all, modern editions, a dash being moreover introduced
before *Leonatus.* Point: —

Wherefore write you not
What monster's her accuser, Leonatus?

DXXXVII.

O, not like me;
For mine's beyond beyond — say, and speak thick.

Ib., III, 2, 57 seq.

The meaning is, My longing is beyond being beyond yours. Compare Macbeth, I, 4, 21: —

More is thy due than more than all can pay.

DXXXVIII.

And our return, to excuse: but first, how get hence.

Ib., III, 2, 66.

The Rev. H. Hudson reads on his own responsibility: how *to* get hence. 'As *hence'*, he says in his Critical Note *ad loc.*, 'is emphatic here, *to* seems fairly required; and *get* is evidently in the same construction with *excuse*. To be sure, the insertion of *to* makes the verse an Alexandrine; but the omission does not make it a pentameter [Mr. Hudson clearly means to say a *blank verse*]. The omission was doubtless accidental.' — I do not see, why the line without Mr. Hudson's addition, should not be taken for a blank verse; scan: —

And our | return, | t'excuse: | but first, | how get | hence.

A closely analogous ending occurs in l. 17 of the following scene: —

But be|ing so | allow'd: | to ap|prehend thus.

DXXXIX.

Prithee, speak,
How many score of miles may we well ride
'Twixt hour and hour?   *Ib., III, 2, 70.*

''Twixt hour and hour', according to the Rev. H. Hudson, means: 'Between the same hour of morning and evening; or between six and six, as between sunrise and sunset, in the next speech.' — But Imogen's longing that is 'beyond beyond' and wishes for a horse with wings, would not have been satisfied with such a slow rate of travelling; what she wishes to know is, how many score of miles she may ride from the stroke of one hour to that of the next, and Pisanio makes the disheartening reply, only one score from one rising of the sun to the next. Compare III, 4, 44: 'To weep 'twixt clock and clock.'

DXL.

That run i' the clock's behalf. But this is foolery.

Ib., III, 2, 75.

Not an Alexandrine as Mr. Fleay would have it, but a blank verse
with a triple ending *(foolery)*. Line 77 which has not been noticed
by Mr. Fleay, has likewise a triple ending and the words *to her* are
to be run into one another: —

She'll home | t' her fa|ther: and | provide | me pres|ently.

Possibly, however, *She'll* had better be added to the preceding line: —

Go bid |.my wom|an feign | a sick|ness: say, | she'll
Home to | her fa|ther: and | provide | me pres|ently.

DXLI.

To see me first, as I have now. Pisanio! man!
Where is Posthumus?   *Ib., III, 4, 3 seq.*

Arrange with S. Walker, Crit. Exam., III, 323, and Mr. Fleay: —

To see me first, as I *crave* now. Pisanio!
Man! Where's Posthumus?

Crave, proposed by the Cambridge Editors (?), is no doubt the true
reading.

DXLII.

Some jay of Italy
Whose mother was her painting, hath betray'd him.

Ib., III, 4, 51 seq.

'The figure', says Mr. R. Grant White *ad loc.,* 'here approaches extra-
vagance', and in the Globe Edition the passage is marked with an
obelus. Nevertheless the true blue conservatives in Shakespearian
criticism uphold the old text against those wild conjecturing folks
that are not willing to kiss the first Folio; they even reckon such
strained figures among the beauties of the poet's diction. In support
of their interpretation they refer the reader to IV, 2, 81 seqq., where
Cloten's tailor is termed his 'grandfather': —

he made those clothes
Which, as it seems, make thee.

There is, however, this difference between the two passages that the
tailor, mentioned in the latter, is a real human being, whereas the
painting is not. It is true that, if the tailor is to be considered as
Cloten's grandfather, Cloten's dress must be taken to be his father;
but the poet does not startle us by such a grotesque figure — it is

merely implied. Besides it is a common proverbial saying that 'Fine feathers make fine birds', whilst nobody ever heard it said, that 'Fine painting makes a fine harlot.' Still less can the phrase be countenanced by the well-known passage in K. Lear, II, 2, 60: 'a tailor made thee.' A similar thought occurs strangely enough in A. V, sc. 4, l. 123 seq. of our play: —

> Sleep, thou hast been a grandsire, and begot
> A father to me;

but this is indeed the natural father of Posthumus. The Rev. R. Roberts (in Notes and Queries, Sept. 29, 1883, p. 241 seq.) has discovered two passages manifestly bearing upon the present line; the one occurs in Shelton's Translation of Don Quixote (2ᵈ Ed., 1652, lib. I, pt. 4, chap. 24, p. 133), the other in a pamphlet entitled: 'Newes from the New Exchange; or, The Commonwealth of Ladies. London, printed in the Yeere of Women without Grace, 1650.' From the former passage it would appear that somebody 'said that his arm was his father, his works his lineage'; nothing certain, however, can be said of it, since Mr. Roberts has not favoured his readers with the context. The second passage is to the following effect: 'If Madam Newport should be linkt with these Ladies, the chain would never hold; for she is sister to the famous Mistress Porter . . . . . and to the more famous Lady Marlborough (whose Paint is her Pander).' I am greatly surprised to find that neither Mr. Roberts, nor Dr. Brinsley Nicholson who has reproduced the above extracts in The New Shakspere Society's Transactions 1880 — 2, p. 202, should have thought of the possibility that here we may have got the clue to the line under discussion and that Shakespeare probably wrote: —

> Some jay of Italy
> Whose *pander* was her painting, hath betray'd him.

DXLIII.

And thou, Posthumus, that didst set up.

Ib., III, 4, 90.

In order to regulate the metre Capell has repeated *thou* after *Posthumus*, and all editors after him have followed in his wake. I have no doubt that Capell's division of the lines is right, but there is no need of an insertion, as the verse clearly belongs to the much-discussed class of syllable pause lines; scan: —

> And thou, | Posthu|mus, ◡ | that didst | set up.

DXLIV.

Pis. I'll wake mine eye-balls blind first.

Ib., III, 4, 104.

The lection of the Ff: 'I'll wake mine eye-balls first' cannot possibly be right, and most editors have therefore adopted Hanmer's addition *blind* after *eye-balls*. Staunton defends the old reading on the strength of a passage in Lust's Dominion (I, 2; Dodsley, ed. Hazlitt, XIV, 104): —

> I'll still wake,
> And waste these balls of sight by tossing them
> In busy observations upon thee.

Dyce, however, cannot think (and very properly too) that *wake,* in this passage, should govern *eye-balls*; he conceives the meaning to be, 'I'll still keep myself awake, and waste these balls', &c. He is, therefore, convinced that in the line under discussion some such word as *blind* seems to be required after *eye-balls* in order to complete both sense and metre. To me the very passage from Lust's Dominion seems to point in a very different direction, in as much as it suggests the conjectural emendation: —

> I'll *waste* mine eye-balls first.

Compared to this almost imperceptible alteration the insertion of *blind* is no doubt one of great boldness. As to the metre, the verse is to be numbered with the syllable pause lines; scan: —

> I'll *waste* | mine eye-|balls first. | ⌣ Where|fore then.

A confusion between *waste* and *wake* seems also to have taken place in Timon of Athens, II, 2, 171: 'I have retired me to a wasteful cock', instead of which unintelligible twaddle Mr. Swynfen Jervis has most ingeniously proposed to read: 'I have retired me to a *wakeful couch.*'

DXLV.

> Nor no more ado
> With that harsh, noble, simple nothing,
> That Cloten, whose love-suit hath been to me
> As fearful as a siege.   *Ib., III, 4, 134 seqq.*

Dr. Brinsley Nicholson proposes to read, *ignoble noble* (Notes and Queries, Sept. 29, 1883, p. 241). This conjecture spoils the metre, although *ignoble* seems to be the word wanted instead of *noble*, but not conjointly with it. Perhaps we should read: —

> With that | harsh, *that* | *igno*|*ble,* sim|ple noth|ing,
> That Cloten, &c,

All other conjectures to which this line has given rise, from Rowe
to Collier's so-called MS-Corrector downwards, may be passed over
with silence.   Compare S. Walker, Crit. Exam., I, 33. — Schipper,
Neuenglische Metrik, Erste Hälfte (Bonn, 1888), S. 313.

DXLVI.

Pis.   If not at court,
Then not in Britain must you bide.
  Imo.   Where then?
Hath Britain all the sun that shines? Day, night,
Are they not but in Britain? I'the world's volume
Our Britain seems as of it, but not in't;
In a great pool a swan's nest: prithee, think
There's livers out of Britain.
  Pis.   I am most glad
You think of other place.   *Ib., III, 4, 137 seqq.*

The words *Where then?* have been continued to Pisanio by Hanmer,
but Pisanio has 'consider'd of a course' and has made up his mind;
he has no occasion to ask *'Where then?'* Imogen, on the contrary,
has just put the question to Pisanio: —

What shall I do the while? where bide? how live?

She now asks again: *Where then?*, but she cannot possibly be the
speaker of the two following lines. The original distribution of the
lines, in my opinion, was this: —

Pis.   If not at court,
Then not in Britain must you bide.
  Imo.   Where then?
  Pis. Hath Britain all the sun that shines? Day, night,
Are they not but in Britain?
  Imo.   I'the world's volume
Our Britain seems as of it, but not in't;
In a great pool a swan's nest: prithee, think
There's livers out of Britain.
  Pis.   I am most glad
You think of other place.

It may be left to the reader to form his own opinion of Capell's
conjecture, *What then?* and of Mr. P. A. Daniel's transposition of *of
it* and *in it.*

DXLVII.

Now, if you could wear a mind
Dark as your fortune is, &c.
                                          Ib., III, 4, 146 seq.

In my opinion Warburton's conjecture *mien* for *mind* should be installed in the text without reserve, so much the more as it would appear that *mien* was frequently spelt and pronounced *mine* and could therefore easily be mistaken for *mind*; compare Dryden, ed. W. D. Christie (Clarendon Press, 1874), p. 228. — Al. Schmidt, Shakespeare-Lexicon, s. *Mien,* thinks differently.

DXLVIII.

Beginning nor supplyment.
    Imo.   Thou art all the comfort.
                                        Ib., III, 4, 182.

Mr. Fleay wrongly classes this line with the Alexandrines; scan: —
    Begin|ning nor | supply|ment. Thou'rt all | the com|fort.

DXLIX.

A prince's courage. Away, I prithee.
                                        Ib., III, 4, 187.

Either a catalectic verse with an extra syllable before the pause: —
    A prin|ce's cour|age. Away, | I pri|thee,
or a syllable pause line: —
    A prin|ce's cour|age. _ | Away, | I pri|thee.

DL.

Appear unkinglike.
    Luc.   So, sir: I desire of you.
                                        Ib., III, 5, 7.

Scan: —
        Appear | unking|like.
        Luc.   So, sir: | I d'sire | of you.

See note CCLV. I think it merely owing to an oversight that this line has not been brought forward as an Alexandrine by Mr. Fleay. Compare S. Walker, Crit. Exam., III, 325.

DLI.

Madam, all joy befall your grace.
    Queen.   .   And you!
                                        Ib., III, 5, 9.

The Ff continue the words *And you!* to Lucius. To me the conjectural emendation introduced into the text of the Globe Edition by the Cambridge Editors seems indeed palmarian. Lucius bids farewell to the King, the Queen, and Cloten successively and it seems obvious that all three should reply, especially the Queen who appears to be fond of speaking not only in her own name, but even in that of others. The words *And you* cannot, therefore, belong to any other character but to her.; least of all can they be addressed to Cloten by the Roman ambassador, as only in l. 12 the latter turns to Cloten and takes his leave from him by a cordial shaking of the hand.

DLII.

>She looks us like
>A thing more made of malice than of duty.
>
>*Ib., III, 5, 32 seq.*

Here too the Cambridge Editors (for I hope I shall not be wrong in fathering this anonymous emendation upon them) have hit the mark in suggesting *on's* for *as* in FA, or *us* in FBCD: —

>She looks *on's* like
>A thing more made of malice than of duty.

DLIII.

>That will be given to the loudest noise we make.
>
>*Ib., III, 5, 44.*

FA: *th' lowd of noise.* I think Rowe's conjecture *the loudest noise* preferable to that of Capell, *the loud'st of noise*, as, in accordance with Rowe and Singer, I feel convinced that *of* is a misprint for *'st* or *st*. Singer wrongly prints *th' loud'st noise,* instead of *th' loudest noise.*

DLIV.

>Prove false!
>   *Queen.*   Son, I say, follow the king.
>
>*Ib., III, 5, 53.*

Rowe's division of the lines is right, the conjectures suggested by Steevens, Jackson, S. Walker, &c., however, are needless. Scan: —

>Prove false! |
>   *Queen.*   ◡ Son, | I say, | fóllow | the king.

DLV.

>Pisanio, thou that standst so for Posthumus!
> He hath a drug of mine; &c.   *Ib., III, 5, 56 seq.*

The transition in these lines from the second to the third person,
abrupt and awkward though it be, yet seems to have proceeded from
the poet's own pen, especially as the same irregularity has already
occurred before (III, 3, 104): —

> they took thee for their mother,
> And every day do honour to her grave.

A third instance of a cognate kind (a transition from the third to
the second person) occurs in A. IV, sc. 2, l. 217 seq.: —

> With female fairies will his tomb be haunted,
> And worms will not come to thee.

'Alack, no remedy!' (III, 4, 163), is the only remark to be made on
these and similar deviations from correct and grammatical diction, by
which not only 'Cymbeline', but Shakespeare's latest plays in general,
are marked. See Dyce's note on I, 1, 118 (While sense ·can keep
it on).

DLVI.

> *Clo.* I love and hate her: for she's fair and royal,
> And that she has all courtly parts more exquisite
> Than lady, ladies, woman; from every one
> The best she hath, and she, of all compounded,
> Outsells them all.

Ib., III, 5, 70 seqq.

Line 71, left unnoticed by Mr. Fleay, has a triple ending (*exquisite*).
In the next line, this dreadful *crux,* I suspect, though not without
diffidence, that we should read: —

> Than lady, *lass, or* woman; &c.

except it should be deemed admissible to introduce into the text of
Shakespeare the diminutive *lassie,* in which case the reading. 'Than
lady, *lassie,* woman' would come nearest to the old text. I am well
aware that *lass* (or *lassie*) is chiefly a pastoral word, its use, however,
is not restricted exclusively to ·that homely kind of poetry, as it is
proved by a signal instance in Shakespeare. In Antony and Cleopatra, V, 2, 318 seq. Charmian, speaking of the dead Queen of
Egypt, says: —

> Now boast thee, death, in thy possession lies
> A lass unparallel'd.

Cleopatra is certainly anything but pastoral, and Imogen deserves the
praise of being 'a lass unparallel'd' in a far higher and nobler sense
than she. In our passage the poet evidently alludes to the different
classes of womankind, of every one of which Imogen has the best.
She possesses the nobleness and dignified manners of a lady, the
innocence and sprightliness of a young girl, and the true womanly

feeling of a matron, and thus, of all compounded, outsells them all. The strained explanation of the old text given by Singer cannot find favour in the eyes of scholars trained to the strict exegetical rules of classical philology. According to him Shakespeare means to say that Imogen has the courtly parts more exquisite 'than any lady, than all ladies, than all womankind.' The passage from All's Well that Ends Well (II, 3, 202: to any count; to all counts; to what is man) quoted by Singer, is not to the point, in so far as it is intelligible and correct, two distinguishing qualities of which the passage in Cymbeline cannot boast.

DLVII.

I will not ask again. Close villain,
I'll have this secret from thy heart, or rip
Thy heart to find it.   *Ib., III, 5, 85 seqq.*

L. 85 is a catalectic verse (see note II) and there is no need of adopting the division of Dyce's second edition, viz.: —

Close villain, I
Will have this secret &c.

DLVIII.

Pis. [*Aside*] I'll write to my lord she's dead. O Imogen.
                    Ib., III, 5, 104.

S. Walker, Crit. Exam., III, 326, needlessly proposes to omit *to*; scan: —

I'll write | to m'lord | she's dead. | O Im|ogen.
Compare note CCCXXXV.

DLIX.

Be but duteous, and true preferment shall tender itself to thee.
                    Ib., III, 5, 159 seq.

S. Walker, Crit. Exam., III, 326, very properly asks: 'What has "*true* preferment" to do here?' and proposes to point: 'be but duteous and true, preferment' &c. *True* certainly cannot be joined to *preferment*, but must necessarily refer to Pisanio, as Cloten in l. 110 has required *true service* from Pisanio and repeats his admonition immediately after (l. 162: Come, and be true) to which admonition Pisanio in his soliloquy replies: —

true to thee
Were to prove false, which I will never be,
To him that is most true.

On the other hand, the omission of *and* before *preferment* seems harsh; perhaps a slight transposition may help us to the true reading, viz.: *be but duteous-true, and preferment &c.* Compare S. Walker, Crit. Exam., I, 21 seqq. Merchant of Venice, III, 4, 46 *(honest-true)*; Cymbeline, V, 5, 86 *(duteous-diligent)*.

DLX.

> *Pis.* Thou bid'st me to my loss: for true to thee
> Were to prove false, which I will never be,
> To him that is most true.
>
> *Ib., III, 5, 163 seqq.*

Collier's MS-Corrector: 'to *thy* loss', which lection has been introduced into the text by the Rev. H. Hudson who thinks *my loss* 'little better than unmeaning here.' Quite the contrary. To Cloten's exhortation 'be but duteous-true, and preferment shall tender itself to thee', Pisanio replies: 'no, the way thou bidst me go, would not lead to my preferment, but to my loss, in so far as it would make me false to 'my master who is the truest of all.'

DLXI.

> *Imo.* To Milford - Haven.
> *Bel.* What's your name?   *Ib., III, 6, 59 seq.*

These two short lines should be joined into one, which is to be scanned and read: —

> *Imo.* To Mil|ford Ha|ven. ∠ |
> *Bel.*   What *is* | your name? ·

The reading *What is* was proposed by Capell. — Two lines further on we have no choice left but to adopt Hanmer's correction *embarks* instead of *embark'd*, so much the more as in A. IV, sc. 2, l. 291 seq. we learn from Imogen that she has by no means given up her journey to Milford-Haven and consequently is still in hopes of joining Lucius there. By the way it may be remarked, that Hanmer's edition (Oxford, 1770) does not read *embarques*, as reported in the Cambridge Edition, but *embarks*.

DLXII.

> I should woo hard but be your groom. In honesty.
>
> *Ib., III, 6, 70.*

This line, not noticed by Mr. Fleay, is not an Alexandrine, but has a triple ending *(honesty)*.

DLXIII.

Bel. He wrings at some distress.
Gui. Would I could free 't!
Arv. Or I, whate'er it be,
What pain it cost, what danger. Gods!
Bel. (whispering). Hark, boys.

Ib., III, 6, 79 seq.

The exclamation 'Gods!' is uncalled for and meaningless in the mouth of Arviragus, whereas it would be most appropriate and fraught with meaning when coming from Imogen, who cannot but be deeply moved by the noble ardour with which the two young men declare themselves ready to relieve her of her secret distress, whatever danger or pain it may cost; she calls the gods to witness of their touching and high-minded intents. A few lines lower down she is again prompted by her feelings to invoke the gods. 'Pardon me, gods!', she exclaims, 'but I would change my sex to be companion 'with these two young men.' Compare also her exclamation: 'O Gods and Goddesses' in IV, 2, 295. Arrange, therefore: —

Arv. Or I, whate'er it be,
What pain it cost, what danger.
Imo. (aside). Gods!
Bel. (whispering). Hark, boys.

(The Athenæum, Dec. 17, 1887, p. 836. Replies by A. Hall and Dr. Brinsley Nicholson, ib., Dec. 31, 1887, p. 904.)

DLXIV.

Cowards father cowards and base things sire base.

Ib., IV, 2, 26.

S. Walker, Versification, 145, and Crit. Exam., I, 153 dissyllabizes *sire.* There is, however, room for two other scansions, viz.: —

Cow'rds fa|ther cow|ards and | base things | sire base;
Cowards | fath'r cow|ards and | base things | sire base.

DLXV.

Know'st me not by my clothes?
Gui. No, nor thy tailor, rascal.

Ib., IV, 2, 81.

One of Mr. Fleay's Alexandrines. Pope omitted *rascal,* no doubt on purely metrical grounds. There is, however, another argument which speaks in favour of this omission, and this is the marked contrast between the two characters of Cloten and Guiderius. Cloten, from

the very moment of his entrance, heaps the most abusive language
on his adversary, whereas Guiderius studiously refrains from retaliating.
Guiderius says (l. 78 seq.): —

> Thy words, I grant, are. bigger, for I wear not
> My dagger in my mouth.

Only twice he retorts: in l. 72 seqq. (A thing more slavish &c., which
is moderate language enough) and in l. 89 (thou double villain).   I
am, therefore, inclined to agree with Pope, not only because *rascal*
spoils the metre, but at the same time because it contradicts the well-
defined character of Guiderius.   It is no doubt an actor's addition.

DLXVI.

> Yield, rustic mountaineer.   [*Exeunt fighting.*
>   *Re-enter* BELARIUS *and* ARVIRAGUS.
>   *Bel.*   No companies abroad?

Ib., IV, 2, 100 seq.

Metrically considered this is a very curious line, as it admits of no
less than three different scansions.   First the two hemistichs may be
considered as two short lines and as such they are printed by Dyce,
in the Cambridge and Globe Editions, &c.   Or they may be connected
so as to form an Alexandrine, which has been done by Mr. Fleay,
and here it must be owned that such Alexandrines (or trimeter
couplets) are by no means of rare occurrence.   The third way of
scanning the line is to read *mountainer* and pronounce the word
as a triple ending before the pause.   We shall then have to deal
with a regular blank verse, and I need scarcely add that in my conviction this is the true scansion.   The Ff certainly read *mountaineer*,
but in l. 71 of our scene they exhibit the spelling *mountainers* which
S. Walker, Versification, 224, is mistaken in declaring an erratum, as
according to his own showing it occurs also in Chapman's The
Widow's Tears, IV, 1.   Besides it corresponds exactly with the spellings *pioner* and *enginer* in Hamlet, I, 5, 163 and III, 4, 207; compare my second edition of Hamlet, p. 114 (note on *Climatures*) and
supra note CDX (Othello, I, 1, 126).

DLXVII.

> And burst of speaking, were as his: I am absolute.

Ib., IV, 2, 106.

A Spenserian Alexandrine according to Mr. Fleay; I think it a blank
verse with a triple ending *(absolute)*.

21*

DLXVIII.

Bel. Being scarce made up,
I mean, to man, he had not apprehension
Of roaring terrors; for defect of judgement
Is oft the cause of fear. But, see, thy brother.

Ib., IV, 2, 109 seqq.

Theobald's conjectural emendation *th' effect* instead of *defect* has been admitted into the text of the Globe Edition; the other attempts at correcting this evidently corrupted passage are hardly worth men-'
tioning. Perhaps we should read and arrange: —

for defect of judgment
Is oft the cause of *fearlessness.* But see!
Thy brother!

I cannot attach any great weight to the objection which will probably be raised against this conjectural emendation, that *fearlessness* does not belong to Shakespeare's vocabulary, since *fearless, fearful,* and *fearfulness* do; besides the word comes nearer to the *ductus literarum* of the old copies than if *courage* or *valour* should be suggested instead. At all events I feel sure that this is the thought that was in the poet's mind.

DLXIX.

So the revenge alone pursued me! Polydore.

Ib., IV, 2, 157.

No Alexandrine, but a blank verse with a triple ending *(Polydore).*
Mr. Fleay does not mention this line.

DLXX.

Is Cadwal mad?
Bel. Look, here he comes.

Ib., IV, 2, 195.

A defective line thus completed by S. Walker, Crit. Exam., II, 145: —
Is Cadwal mad?
Bel. Cadwal! — Look, here he comes!

However ingenious this conjecture may be, yet I cannot refrain from giving it a somewhat different turn by assigning the exclamation *Cadwal!* to Guiderius: —
Is Cadwal mad? Cadwal!
Bel. Look, here he comes.

DLXXI.

Yea, and furr'd moss besides, when flowers are none,
To winter-ground thy corse.

Ib., IV, 2, 228 seq.

The late Dr. C. M. Ingleby and myself have independently conjectured *wind around* for *winter-ground*. See Shakespeare's Cymbeline: The Text Revised and Annotated by C. M. Ingleby, LL. D. (London, 1886), p. 143 and 212.

DLXXII.

Gui. Cadwal, I cannot sing: I'll weep and word it with thee.

Ib., IV, 2, 240.

An Alexandrine, if we are to believe Mr. Fleay; but *Cadwal* palpably forms an interjectional line and is printed as such by Dyce, in the Cambridge and Globe Editions, &c.

DLXXIII.

Gui. Nay, Cadwal, we must lay his head to the east;
My father has a reason for it.

Ib., IV, 2, 255 seq.

'What was Belarius' "reason"', says Mr. R. Gr. White *ad loc.*, 'for this disposition of the body in the ground I have been unable to discover.' — Belarius' reason is no doubt to be found in the custom which prevailed in the Christian church to bury the dead with their heads looking to the East, where the Saviour had lived and from whence he is believed to re-appear on the day of the last judgment. This custom has even continued as late as the present century, as will be seen from the following passage in Thomas Carlyle's 'Reminiscences' (ed. by J. A. Froude, London, 1881, Vol. I, p. 39). 'My father', he writes, 'is now in his grave, sleeping by the side of his loved ones, his face to the east, under the hope of meeting the Lord when He shall come to judgment, when the times shall be fulfilled.' From the same motive the early Christians turned their face to the East when praying and the churches face the same part of the horizon, in so far as the chancel which contains the altar, the consecrated wafers, the crucifix, &c. generally occupies the eastern end of the building. See J. Kreuser, *Der christliche Kirchenbau* (Bonn, 1851), I, 42 seqq. Id., *Wiederum christlicher Kirchenbau* (Brixen, 1868), I, 338 seqq. and II, 416 seqq. Even the temples of classical antiquity are shown to have been constructed according to the same plan by Heinrich Nissen (*Das Templum.* Berlin, 1869). Our passage proves that Shakespeare was conversant with some one or other of these facts, though nobody can tell exactly with which; most probably

with the mode of making the dead in their graves look to the East.
Compare also Dr. Johnson's note on Hamlet, V, 1, 4: make her grave
straight; Dr. Johnson, however, is wrong in so far as *straight* in this
passage means *immediately*.

DLXXIV.

But, soft! no bedfellow! — O gods and goddesses.

Ib., IV, 2, 295.

Not noticed by Mr. Fleay, although this verse might be pronounced
to be an Alexandrine just as well as the rest. I need scarcely say
that I declare in favour of a blank verse *versus* Alexandrine. Two
different scansions would seem to be admissible, viz.: —

But, soft! | no bed|fellow! O gods | and god|dessés,

or: —

But, soft! | no bed|fellow! | O gods | and god|desses.

In the former case *bedfellow,* in the latter (which I cannot but think
preferable) *goddesses* is to be read as a triple ending.

DLXXV.

For so I thought I was a cave-keeper.

Ib., IV, 2, 298.

Rightly corrected by Collier's so called MS-Corrector: —

For *lo!* I thought I was a cave-keeper.

DLXXVI.

Struck the main-top! O Posthumus! alas.

Ib., IV, 2, 320.

The transposition proposed by Capell (according to the Cambridge
Edition): *Posthumus, O! alas* seems needless. Scan either: —

Struck the | maintop! | ◡ O, | Posthum's! | alas,

or: —

Struck | the main|top! O, | Posthum's! | alas.

DLXXVII.

Which he said was precious
And cordial to me, have I not found it
Murderous to the senses? That confirms it home.

Ib., IV, 2, 326 seqq.

Scan: —

> Which he said was precious
> And cor|dial to | me, ⸚ | have I | not found | it
> Murd'rous | to th' sen|ses?   That | confirms | it home.

It seems surprising that the last line has not been mentioned by Mr. Fleay in his list of Alexandrines.

DLXXVIII.

Cap. To them the legions garrison'd in Gallia
After your will, have cross'd the sea.

Ib., IV, 2, 333 seq.

In my eyes the anonymous conjecture (by the Cambridge Editors?), according to which *To them* does not form part of the text, but of the stage-direction (*and a sooth-sayer to them*) is both above doubt and above praise. Compare amongst other passages the stage-direction in Coriolanus I, 4: *To them a Messenger*.

DLXXIX.

Attending
You here at Milford-Haven with your ships.

Ib., IV, 2, 334 seq.

FACD: *with your ships*; FB: *with you ships* (not *your*, as Dyce erroneously says). Neither of these two lections can be right. Qy. *with yon ships?* It may safely be assumed that Milford-Haven with its ships is to be seen from the spot where Lucius is conversing with the officers, as we have heard from Imogen (III, 6, 5) that Pisanio showed it to her before parting with her. Or is recourse to be had to the correction *with their ships?*

DLXXX.

And gentlemen of Italy, most willing spirits.

Ib., IV, 2, 338.

This line which Mr. Fleay takes to be an Alexandrine, in my opinion has a triple ending before the pause; scan: —

> And gen|tlemen | of It|aly, most wil|ling spir|its.

DLXXXI.

Cap. With the next benefit o' the wind.
Luc.   This forwardness.

Ib., IV, 2, 342.

Scan: —

     Cap. With the | next ben | 'fit of | the wind. |
     Luc.   This for | wardness.

Forwardness is to be read as a triple ending. The line might have figured among Mr. Fleay's Alexandrines.

DLXXXII.

They 'll pardon it. — Say you, sir?
     Luc.   Thy name?
     Imo.   Fidele, sir.
                                Ib., IV, 2, 379.

I subscribe unhesitatingly to Hanmer's omission of the second *sir*; as to his contraction of *pardon it (pardon 't),* however, I think it more correct to scan: *pard'n it*: —

     They 'll pard'n | it. Say | you, sir?]
     Luc.   Thy name? |
     Imo.   Fide | le.

Compare notes CLXXVII and CDVIII.

DLXXXIII.

My friends,
The boy hath taught us manly duties: let us
Find out the prettiest daisied plot we can,
And make him with our pikes and partisans
A grave.
                                Ib., IV, 2, 396 seqq.

S. Walker, Crit. Exam., III, 327, proposes to omit *thee* after *father* in the preceding line (l. 395) and to arrange the passage as in the Ff. I should prefer to join *My friends* with l. 397; to contract *let us* and transfer it to the following line; and to omit *out* in l. 398: —

     My friends, the boy hath taught us manly duties:
     Let's find the prettiest daisied plot we can,
     And make him with our pikes and partisans
     A grave.

DLXXXIV.

The hope of comfort. But for thee, fellow.
                                Ib., IV, 3, 9.

Capell: *But for thee, thee, fellow*; compare S. Walker, Crit. Exam., II, 146. Dr. Abbott, s. 453, scans: —

     The hope | of com | fort. But | for thee, | fellow.

Thus the line is made to end in a trochee, since, according to
Dr. Abbott, 'the old pronunciation "fellów" is probably not Shakespearian.' The verse is undoubtedly a syllable pause line: —

    The hope | of com|fort. ⸗ | But for | thee, fel|low.

DLXXXV.

    Pis.   Sir, my life is yours;
I humbly set it at your will; but, for my mistress,
I nothing know where she remains, why gone,
Nor when she purposes return. Beseech your highness,
Hold me your loyal servant.
    First Lord.   Good my liege,
The day that she was missing &c.

                             Ib., IV, 3, 12 seqq.

Arrange: —

    Pis.   Sir, my life is yours;
I humbly set it at your will; but for
My mistress, I nothing know where she remains,
Why gone, nor when she purposes return.
Beseech your highness, hold me your loyal servant.
    First Lord. Good my liege,
The day that she was missing &c.

Thus we get rid of the two apparent Alexandrines in lines 13 and 15.
Lines 14 and 16 have extra syllables before the pause *(mistress*
and *highness)*.

DLXXXVI.

    All parts of his subjection loyally. For Cloten.

                             Ib., IV, 3, 19.

The words *For Cloten* have been placed in a separate line by Capell.
According to Mr. Fleay the line is an Alexandrine with the cesura
after the tenth (!) syllable. I have no doubt that *loyally* is to be
read as a triple ending before the pause: —

    All parts | of his | subject|ion loy|ally. For Clo|ten.
Troublesome in line 21, and *jealousy* in l. 22 are triple endings too.

DLXXXVII.

    We grieve at chances here. Away!

                             Ib., IV, 3, 35.

Hanmer completes this line by adding: *Come let's* before *Away!*,

which involves an unpleasant repetition of *Let's withdraw* in l. 32.
S. Walker, Versification, 273, would arrange: —

> We grieve at chances here.
> Away.

This seems even more unlikely than Hanmer's addition. I do not
see the necessity of filling up the line; if, however, such a completion should be deemed indispensable, I should suggest to read: —

> We grieve at chances here. Away, *my lords.*

DLXXXVIII.

> Wherein I am false I am honest; not true, to be true.
>
> *Ib., IV, 3, 42.*

A Spenserian Alexandrine, if we are to believe Mr. Fleay. I suspect
that we ought to scan: —

> Wherein | I'm false | I'm hon|est; not true | to be | true.

DLXXXIX.

> Revengingly enfeebles me; or could this carl.
>
> *Ib., V, 2, 4.*

An Alexandrine according to Mr. Fleay. The line, I think, has a
triple ending before the pause; scan: —

> Reveng|ingly | enfee|bles me; or could | this carl.

DXC.

> *Post.* Still going? [*Exit Lord.*] This is a lord! O noble misery.
>
> *Ib., V, 3, 64.*

Not noticed by Mr. Fleay. Pope, Theobald, and Hanmer omit *Still
going?,* whilst S. Walker (Crit. Exam., III, 327), Dyce, and the Rev.
H. Hudson place these words in a separate line. In my humble
opinion both parties are wrong. Instead of *this is* read *this'* (see
Abbott, p. 343) and pronounce *misery* as a triple ending: —

> Still go|ing? This' | a lord! | O no|ble mis|ery.

DXCI.

> And so I am awake. Poor wretches that depend.
>
> *Ib., V, 4, 127.*

One of Mr. Fleay's Alexandrines. I strongly suspect: —

> And so | I'm 'wake. | Poor wretch|es that | depend.

Compare Abbott, s. 460.

DXCII.

Tongue and brain not; either both or nothing.

Ib., V, 4, 147.

Tongue is to be read as a monosyllabic foot; the conjectures proposed by Rowe, Pope, Johnson, Steevens, and others may be stowed away in the critical lumber-room. Scan: —

Tongue | and brain | not; eith|er both | or noth|ing.

DXCIII.

O'ercome you with her show, and in time.

Ib., V, 5, 54.

Here too all conjectures are needless; scan: —

O'ercome | you with | her show, | ◡ and | in time.

A similar scansion holds good with respect to 1. 62, where Hanmer inserted *Yet* before *Mine eyes*; scan: —

We did, | so please | your high|ness. ⊥ | Mine eyes.

Both verses are syllable pause lines.

DXCIV.

Cym. All that belongs to this.
Iach.   That paragon, thy daughter.

Ib., V, 5, 147.

Another of Mr. Fleay's Alexandrines. The line has a triple ending before the second pause. Scan: —

Cym. All that | belongs | to this. |
Iach.   That par|agon, thy daugh|ter.

DXCV.

For feature, laming
The shrine of Venus, or straight-pight Minerva,
Postures beyond brief nature.

Ib., V, 5, 163 seqq.

'By a sharp torture' something like a meaning may be 'enforced' from these lines, *shrine,* in the opinion of the editors, being used here · and elsewhere in the sense of *statue.* The only critics, as far as I know, that take exception against this awkward metonymy in the present passage and declare the line to be corrupt, are Bailey (who absurdly suggests *shrinking Venus*) and the late Prof. Hertzberg in the notes on his translation of our play; but his attempts at healing the corruption are inferior to his arguments and unsatisfactory

even in his own eyes. I imagine that Shakespeare wrote *swim*
instead of *shrine,* thus contrasting the swimming gait of Venus with
the stiff and strait-built stature of Minerva, a contrast well known
to every student of ancient art. It must be admitted that the substantive *swim* does not belong to Shakespeare's vocabulary; it is used,
however, by B. Jonson, Cynthia's Revels, II, 1: Save only you
wanted the swim in the turn, and: Both the swim and the trip are
properly mine. Compare note CCLXXXVIII.

DXCVI.

O, get thee from my sight.

Ib., V, 5, 236.

A mutilated line to which the name of *Pisanio* should be added: —
    O, get | thee from | my sight, | *Pisa*|*nio.*
See note on I, 1, 41.

DXCVII.

Breathe not where princes are.
    Cym.   The tune of Imogen.

Ib., V, 5, 238.

Declared to be an Alexandrine by Mr. Fleay. *Imogen,* however, is
clearly a triple ending; compare *ante* l. 227, where the second *Imogen*
is to be pronounced as a dissyllable: —
    Imo|gen, Im||'gen! Peace, | my lord; | hear, hear.
Compare also note on Antony and Cleopatra, IV, 9, 23 seqq., where
the first *Antony* is likewise a trisyllable, the second a dissyllable.

DXCVIII.

Think that you are upon a rock; and now
Throw me again.

Ib., V, 5, 262 seq.

Mr. R. Grant White has hit the mark in suggesting the emendation,
Think she's upon your neck, only he should have conformed it to the
metre; read: —
    Think *that she is* upon your neck; and now
    Throw me again.

DXCIX.

With unchaste purpose and with oath to violate.

Ib., V, 5, 284.

Not mentioned by Mr. Fleay; *violate* is a triple ending. Compare
Childe Harold, IV, 8: —

The invi|'late is|land of | the sage | and free,

and Tennyson, Idylls of the King (London, 1859) p. 160: —

Not vi|'lating | the bond | of like | to like.

DC.

 Arv.   In that he spake too far.
 Cym. And thou shalt die for 't.
 Bel.   We will die all three:
But I will prove that two on's are as good
As I have given out him.

            Ib., V, 5, 309 seqq.

Arrange: —

 Arv.   In that he spake too far.
 Cym. [*To Bel.*] And thou shalt die for it.
 Arv.   We will die all three.
 Bel. But I will prove that two on's are as good
As I have given out him.

Cymbeline's speech *(And thou &c.)* is shown by the context to be
addressed to Belarius, and not to Arviragus, who has committed no
offence whatever. The two persons condemned to death by the King
are Guiderius and Belarius, whilst Arviragus is allowed to live; consequently he is the only person to whom the words, 'We will die
all three' can be assigned.

DCI.

 Gui. And our good his.
 Bel.   Have at it then, by leave.
Thou hadst, great king, a subject who
Was call'd Belarius.

            Ib., V, 5, 314 seqq.

All endeavours of healing this manifestly corrupt passage have proved
insufficient. I refrain, therefore, from reproducing them and merely
beg to offer a contribution of my own. I suspect that we should
read and arrange: —

 Gui. And our good *is your good.*
 Bel.   Have at it then.
By leave! Thou hadst, great king, a subject who
Was call'd Belarius.

Of this I feel certain that the words *By leave!* are not addressed to
Guiderius and Arviragus, but to the king, and so Capell and Dyce

seem to have understood the passage. For greater perspicuity's sake the stage-direction: [*To Cym.*] might be added at the beginning of l. 315.

DCII.

Your pleasure was my mere offence, my punishment.

Ib., V, 5, 334.

Not noticed by Mr. Fleay; *punishment* is a triple ending. — The same scansion occurs in l. 344 (also left unnoticed by Mr. Fleay) where *loyalty* is a triple ending.

DCIII.

Unto my end of stealing them. But, gracious sir.

Ib., V, 5, 347.

Pope omits *gracious* and Mr. Fleay takes the line to be an Alexandrine with the cesura after the eighth syllable. I have no doubt that the verse, like so many others, has a triple ending before the pause; scan: —

Unto | my end | of steal|ing 'em. But, gra|cious sir.

DCIV.

The thankings of a king.
    Post.   I am, sir.   *Ib., V, 5, 407.*

A syllable pause line; scan: —

The thank|ings of | a king. |
    Post.   ⌣ I | am, sir.

There is no need whatever of conjecturing or correcting.*

---

* As at p. 295 I have reproduced the introductory words of my Letter to C. M. Ingleby, Esq., I must here make room for the concluding words too. They were these: 'This, my dear Ingleby, is my critical mite on "Cymbeline". I am perfectly aware that the revision and explanation of this play will still be a match for ages to come and wish above all that the state of your health may shortly allow you to do your part and complete your edition. Not even the stanchest defender of the Folio can go so far as to deny that by the continued efforts of editors and critics the text of Shakespeare has been brought a great deal nearer to its original purity than when it was printed by Isaac Jaggard and Ed. Blount in 1623. Shakespeare's versification too is far better understood by the commentators of to-day than by Nicholas Rowe and the rest of the eighteenth-century-editors. "Step by step the ladder is ascended." These facts justify the hope that the twentieth century may enjoy a still more correct text of the immortal dramatist and possess a deeper insight into his language and metre than we can boast of. May we then be remembered as having assisted in handing down the torch from one generation to the other. *Vale faveque.* Always believe me, dear Ingleby, Yours very sincerely K. E. Halle, On the Ides of March, 1885.'

DCV.

Bring in our daughter, clothed like a bride,
For the embracements even of Jove himself.

Pericles, I, 1, 6 seq.

Line 6 admits of a twofold scansion: —

Bring in | our daugh|ter, cloth|èd like | a bride,

or, which I think preferable: —

Bring in | our daugh|ter, ⏑́ | clothed like | a bride.

In the following line the conjecture *Fit for* (by the Cambridge Editors?) should unhesitatingly be installed in the text and the article *the*, inserted by Malone, but omitted by the anonymous conjecturer, as unhesitatingly be retained: —

Fit for *the* embracements even of Jove himself.

DCVI.

Per. See where she comes, apparell'd like the spring,
Graces her subjects, and her thoughts the king
Of every virtue gives renown to men!

Ib., I, 1, 12 seqq.

Qy. read either: —

Graces her subjects, and her *thought* the king,

or: —

Grace is her *subject,* and her *thought's* the king?

Thought's is a conjecture by the Cambridge Editors (?). The *s* in *thoughts* may have intruded by way of a ὁμοιοτέλευτον (Graces, subjects, thoughts). See note CCLXIII.

DCVII.

Good sooth, I care not for you.   *Ib., I, 1, 86.*

Add the stage-direction: [*Pushes the Princess back*]. Compare A. V, sc. 1, l. 127: when I did push thee back. The stage-direction: *Takes hold of the hand of the Princess,* added by Malone after l. 76, in my opinion misses or rather contradicts the intention of the poet as expressed in the text.

DCVIII.

Ant. He hath found the meaning, for which we mean
To have his head.
He must not live to trumpet forth my infamy,
Nor tell the world Antiochus doth sin
In such a loathed manner.   *Ib., I, 1, 143 seqq.*

Arrange and read: —

> *Ant.* He hath found the meaning,
> For which we mean to have his head; he must
> Not live to trumpet forth my infamy,
> Nor tell the world Antiochus doth sin
> In such a loathed manner *with his daughter.*

He hath is to be contracted into a monosyllable; see note CDLXXIX. *For which* is the reading of all the old editions; Malone, in consequence of his wrong division of the lines, added the article before *which,* an addition which, although very well compatible with my arrangement, yet seems needless.

DCIX.

> Because we bid it. Say, is it done?
>   *Thal.*   My lord,
> 'Tis done.
>   *Ant.* — Enough.   *Ib., I, 1, 158 seqq.*

This division was introduced by Steevens and has even been adopted by the Cambridge (and Globe) Editors. The arrangement of the old copies, however, is quite correct and should not have been altered; it is this: —

> Because | we bid | it. ⌣ | Say, is | it done?
>   *Thal.* My lord, 'tis done.
>   *Ant.* Enough.

DCX.

> I'll make him sure enough: so farewell to your highness.
>   *Ib., I, 1, 169.*

Sure enough is a triple ending before the pause: —

> I'll make | him sure | enough; so fare | well to | your high | ness.

See notes CDVII and CDLVIII.

DCXI.

> And danger, which I fear'd, is at Antioch.   *Ib., I, 2, 7.*

S. Walker, Versification, 100, suggests, *fear'd, 's at Antioch,* which on account of the pause after *fear'd,* does not seem likely. I think we should omit *at* before *Antioch* and read: —

> *The* danger, which I fear'd, is Antioch.

The comma at the end of the preceding line should be altered to a colon, if not a full stop.

DCXII.

And then return to us. [*Exeunt Lords.*] Helicanus, thou
Hast moved us: what seest thou in our looks?

Ib., I, 2, 50 seq.

Helicanus is to be pronounced as a trisyllabic word (= *Hel'canus*);
compare *Pericles* which is several times used as a dissyllable (see
note DCXXII) and *Leonine* which in A. IV, sc. 1, l. 30 and A. IV,
sc. 3, l. 9 has likewise the quality of a dissyllable, whereas in A. IV,
sc. 3, l. 30 it is a trisyllable.   See note CDLV (*Enobarbus*). —
Line 51 is a syllable pause line; scan: —

Hast moved | us: ｰ | what seest | thou in | our looks?

DCXIII.

   Per.   Thou know'st I have power
To take thy life from thee.
   Hel. [*Kneeling*] I have ground the axe myself;
Do you but strike the blow.
   Per.   Rise, prithee, rise.
Sit down: thou art no flatterer:
I thank thee for it: and heaven forbid
That kings should let their ears hear their faults chid.

Ib., I, 2, 57 seqq.

Arrange, read, and scan: —

      Per.   Thou know'st *I've* power
To take thy life from thee.
      Hel. [*Kneeling*]   *I've* ground the axe
Myself; do you but strike the blow, *my lord*.
      Per. Rise, prithee, rise. Sit down: thou art no flatterer;
I thank | thee for | it; ｰ | and heaven | forbid
That kings should let their ears hear their faults chid.

In all old and modern editions, as far as I know, *myself* belongs to
l. 58; for the transfer of this word to the next line, I must answer
as well as for the addition of *my lord. Flatterer,* in l. 60, is a triple
ending.   L. 61 is a syllable pause line and does not stand in need
of Steevens's conjecture *high heaven*.   With respect to l. 62 I entirely
agree with Dyce.

DCXIV.

   Hel. Well, my lord, since you have given me leave to speak.

Ib., I, 2, 101.

Pronounce *m'lord*. Compare *supra* notes CCCXXXV (p. 187) and DLVIII.

DCXV.

Freely will I speak. Antiochus you fear,
And justly too, I think, you fear the tyrant,
Who either by public war or private treason
Will take away your life.   *Ib., I, 2, 102 seqq.*

A perfect muddle. Read and scan either: —

Freely | will I | speak. ⏑ | You fear | the ty|rant
Antiochus, and justly too, I think,
Who either by public war or private treason
Will take away your life,

or: —

I will speak freely. Antiochus you fear,
The ty|rant, ⏑ | and just|ly too, | I think,
Who either &c.

That *either* is frequently contracted into a monosyllable, need hardly be mentioned; compare S. Walker, Versification, 103.

DCXVI.

Or till the Destinies do cut his thread of life.
Ib., I, 2, 108.

This line is by no means an Alexandrine, but has a triple ending before the pause; scan: —

Or till | the Dest|'nies do cut | his thread | of life.

DCXVII.

But should he wrong my liberties in my absence.
Ib., I, 2, 112.

Can the meaning be: What, if he should encroach on my princely rights in my absence? Or is *my liberties* to be regarded as a corruption? Collier assures his readers that 'we may be reasonably sure that "my liberties" ought to be "*thy* liberties."' This, however, is anything but an improvement. By the context I am led to imagine that Shakespeare wrote *Tyre's liberties*; *liberties* to be pronounced as a dissyllable. In the reply which Helicanus makes to this speech, a line seems to have been lost, the purport of which apparently was: *In order to prevent such a misfortune* we shall mingle our bloods together &c.

DCXVIII.

And so in ours: some neighbouring nation.   *Ib., I, 4, 65.*
Qy.: *and so is ours?*

DCXIX.

Lord. That's the least fear; for, by the semblance.
Ib., I, 4, 71.

How are we to scan: —

    That's the | least fear; | for by | the semb|(e)lance,

or: —

    That *is* | the least | fear; ⌣ | for by | the semb|lance?

DCXX.

And to fulfil his prince' desire.
Ib., II, Gower, 21.

The majority of the old editions exhibit the reading *princes desire* which has been altered by Rowe to *prince's Desire.* Malone and all editors after him read *prince' desire.* To me Rowe's correction seems no less admissible than Malone's. For the monosyllabic pronunciation of *desire* compare notes CCLV, CDLIV, CDLXXXII and DCXXVII.

DCXXI.

    Thanks, fortune, yet, that, after all my crosses,
    Thou givest me somewhat to repair myself.
Ib., II, 1, 127 seq.

Should not Pericles have begun as well as ended his speech with a rhyming couplet? May not Shakespeare have written: —

    Thanks, fortune, yet, that after all *thy* [not *my*] crosses,
    Thou givest me somewhat to repair *my losses*?

Thy crosses is the reading of Delius, derived from Wilkins's novel; Malone, *my*; Qq and Ff, *all crosses. Heritage,* in the following line, is a triple ending.

DCXXII.

    Keep it, my Pericles; it hath been a shield.
Ib., II, 1, 132. ·

Scan either: —

    Keep it, | my Per|icles; | it hath been | a shield,

or: —

    Keep it, | my Per|'cles; it | hath been | a shield.

For the contraction of *it hath* compare note CDLXXIX. *Pericles,* as a dissyllable, occurs in A. II, sc. 3, l. 81: —

    A gent|leman | of Tyre; | ⌣ my | name, Per|'cles;

in A. II, sc. 3, l. 87 (according to my arrangement; see note *ad loc.*); A. III, Gower, l. 60 (a four-feet line with an extra syllable before

22*

the pause); A. IV, sc. 3, l. 13, a line which seems to admit of a
twofold scansion, viz.: —

    When no|ble Per|'cles shall | demand | his child,

or: —

    When no|ble Per|icles | shall d'mand | his child;

and A. IV, sc. 3, l. 23: —

    · And o|pen this | to Per|'cles. I | do shame.

Compare note DCXII.

DCXXIII.

Sim. Opinion's but a fool, that makes us scan
The outward habit by the inward man.

Ib., II, 2, 56 seq.

To the various conjectures proposed in order to heal l. 57 (which is
undoubtedly corrupt) the following transposition of the preposition *by*
may be added: —

    By th' out|ward hab|it ⏑ | the in|ward man.

DCXXIV.

Per. You are right courteous knights.
Sim.   · Sit, sir, sit.

Ib., II, 3, 27.

A syllable pause line; scan: —

    You are | right court|eous knights. | ⏑ Sit, | sir, sit.

Steevens's repetition of the first *Sit,* adopted by Singer, is unnecessary.

DCXXV.

All viands that I eat do seem unsavoury,
Wishing him my meat. Sure, he's a gallant gentleman.

Ib., II, 3, 31 seq.

Unsavoury and *gentleman* are triple endings.

DCXXVI.

Sim. He's but a ′country gentleman.

Ib., II, 3, 33.

The line may easily be completed by the addition of *daughter*: —
    Sim. Daughter, he's but a country gentleman.

DCXXVII.

Sim. And furthermore tell him, we desire to know of him.
Ib., II, 3, 73.

The metre of this line, if rightly understood, is completely right and no correction whatever is wanted. After the analogy of *father, mother, either, whether, &c., further* in *furthermore* is to be pronounced as one syllable; scan therefore: —

And furth'r|more tell | him, we d'sire | to know | of him.

As to *d'sire* see notes CDLIV and DCXX.

DCXXVIII.

Thai. He thanks your grace; names himself Pericles,
A gentleman of Tyre,
Who only by misfortune of the seas
Bereft of ships and men, cast on this shore.
Ib., II, 3, 86 seqq.

Read and arrange: —

Thai. He thanks your grace;
Names himself Pericles, a gentleman of Tyre,
Who *newly,* by misfortune of the seas
Bereft of ships and men, *was* cast on *th'* shore. ·

Only, the reading of all old and modern editions in l. 88, is decidedly wrong. *On this shore,* in l. 89, is the reading of the first Quarto and the Museum-copy of the second Quarto, whereas all the other old copies read *on the shore.* Perhaps we had better read *on shore* or *ashore* (see The Tempest, II, 2, 128 — not 129, 121 [as printed in the Globe Edition] being a misprint for 120).

DCXXIX.

Even in your armours, as you are address'd,
Will very well become a soldier's dance.
Ib., II, 3, 94 seq.

Qy. read *You'll* for *Will?*

DCXXX.

Come, sir;
Here is a lady that wants breathing too:
And I have heard, you knights of Tyre
Are excellent in making ladies trip.
Ib., II, 3, 100 seqq.

The words *Come, sir* have been placed in a separate line by Steevens and other editors, which to me seems to be an unnecessary deviation from the old copies. I rather think that *sir* is misplaced and belonged originally to l. 102 which is thus promoted to the rank of a legitimate syllable pause line: —

> Come, here's a lady that wants breathing too:
> And I | have heard, | *sir,* ⏑ | you knights | of Tyre
> Are excellent in making ladies trip.

All other conjectural emendations on this passage do not come half so near to the text of the old editions as this.

DCXXXI.

> *Hel.* No, Escanes, know this of me.   *Ib., II, 4, 1.*

This is the reading of the old copies. Malone: *know, Escanes*; Steevens: *No, no, my Escanes.* Read: —

> *Now,* Escanes, know this of me.

DCXXXII.

> Soon fall to ruin, — your noble self.   *Ib., II, 4, 37.*

A syllable pause line; scan: —

> Soon fall | to ru|in, ⏑ | your no|ble self.

Eight lines further on we meet with another syllable pause line of the same category: —

> A twelve|month long|er, ⏑ | let me | entreat | you.

DCXXXIII.

> Which yet from her by no means can I get.
>
>   *Ib., II, 5, 6.*

The first and second Folios read, *Which from her &c.*; the third and fourth, *Which yet from her &c.*, an unnecessary correction, which nevertheless has found admission into the text of the Globe Edition, whilst the Cambridge Edition follows the two earlier Folios. In my humble opinion we have to deal with a syllable pause line, however slight the pause may appear: —

> Which from | her ⏑ | by no | means can | I get.

Compare notes CLXXXVII, CCXI, &c.

DCXXXIV.

> One twelve moons more she'll wear Diana's livery.
>
>   *Ib., II, 5, 10.*

Livery is a triple ending.

DCXXXV.

Third Knight. Loath to bid farewell, we take our leaves.
Ib., II, 5, 13.

Steevens: *Though loath*; Anon.: *Right loath*; Anon.: *will we.* No expletive, however, is wanted, as the verse may safely be reckoned among the syllable pause lines; scan: —

    Loath to | bid fare|well, ⸜ | we take | our leaves.

In the same scene (1. 74) another syllable pause line occurs, the pause of which is still slighter than that of l. 13: —

    I am | glad on | it ⸜ | with all | my heart.

DCXXXVI.

    Will you, not having my consent.   *Ib., II, 5, 76.*

If a blank verse should be thought requisite, the line may easily be completed by the addition of *thereto*: —

    Will you, not having my consent *thereto*.

DCXXXVII.

    As great in blood as I myself. —
    Therefore hear you, mistress; either frame
    Your will to mine, — and you, sir, hear you,
    Either be ruled by me, or I will make you —
    Man and wife.
Ib., II, 5, 80 seqq.

No conjectural emendation of l. 81 is required. Arrange: —

    As great in blood as I myself. Therefore
    Hear you, mistress; either frame your will to mine, —
    And you, sir, hear you, either be ruled by me, —
    Or I will make you — man and wife.

DCXXXVIII.

    I nill relate, action may.   *Ib., III, Gower, 55.*

A syllable pause line; scan: —

    I nill | relate, | ⸣ act|ion may.

DCXXXIX.

    Thy nimble, sulphurous flashes! O, how, Lychorida,
    How does my queen? Thou stormest venomously.
Ib., III, 1, 6 seq.

Line 6 has an extra syllable before the pause and a triple ending. *Sulphurous* is to be pronounced as a dissyllable. The trisyllabic pronunciation of *Lychorida* occurs again in l. 65 of this very scene: —

    Lying | with sim|ple shells. | ⌣ O | Lychor|ida.

Venomously, in l. 7, is a triple ending.

DCXL.

    At careful nursing. Go thy ways, good mariner.

Ib., III, 1, 81.

Mariner is a triple ending.

DCXLI.

Death may usurp on nature many hours,
And yet the fire of life kindle again
The o'erpress'd spirits. I heard of an Egyptian
That had nine hours lien dead,
Who was by good appliance recovered.
    Re-enter a Servant, *with boxes, napkins, and fire.*
    Cer. Well said, well said; the fire and cloths.

Ib., III, 2, 82 seqq.

This passage which in the Globe Edition is marked with an obelus before the words: *I heard of an Egyptian,* seems to admit of a remedy as satisfactory as it is easy. It strikes me that the lines: *I heard of an Egyptian . . . . . recovered,* do not belong to Cerimon, but should be assigned to either the First or Second Gentleman. Cerimon's words, *Well said, well said,* are by no means addressed to the Servant and are not equivalent to *Well done,* as Collier, Delius, and the Rev. H. Hudson will have it, but form the reply to the Gentleman's appropriate and encouraging remark; their meaning is 'well or timely remarked.' That Shakespeare has given the thought a different turn from what it is in the novel can hardly be a matter of surprise or cause any difficulty to the critic. In order to restore the metre the words *Who was* should be transferred from the beginning of l. 86 to the end of l. 85, and in l. 86 Dyce's emendation *(appliances)* should be adopted: —

    That had | nine hou|(e)rs li|en dead, | who was
    By good appliances recover**è**d.

I admit that the blank verse (l. 85) thus recovered, though metrically correct, yet has little to recommend it, but is rather lame and heavy. Critics of less strict observance may, perhaps, be better pleased by the insertion of the words *like this,* taken (with a slight variation) from the respective passage in Wilkins's novel. For the scansion of l. 86 *(recovered)* compare Titus Andronicus, V, 3, 120 *(delivered)*. The passage, then, will read thus: —

>Death may usurp on nature many hours
>And yet the fire of life kindle again
>The o'erpress'd spirits.
>　　*First Gent.*　　　　I heard of an Egyptian
>That had nine hours lien dead *like this,* who was
>By good appliances recoverèd.
>　　*Re-enter a* Servant, *with boxes, napkins, and fire.*
>　　*Cer.* Well said, well said. [*To the Servant*] The fire aud
>　　　　　　　　　　　　　　　　cloths.

DCXLII.

The rough and woeful music that we have.

Ib., III, 2, 88.

Collier proposes *slow* for *rough*; most unlikely. Qy. either *soft, low,* or *sweet*? Add the stage-direction: *Music behind the scene.*

DCXLIII.

The viol once more: how thou stirr'st; thou block.

Ib., III, 2, 90.

Read *vial.* Dyce concludes from the context that Cerimon means the musical instrument, not a small bottle. The more I have been thinking of the passage, the more fully am I convinced that the very contrary is true and that we must side with R. Grant White against Dyce. Cerimon is in a flutter and speaks abruptly to the different bystanders; first he approves of the well-timed remark of the First Gentleman; then turns to the Servant; then orders the music to be sounded; then impatiently calls for the vial; then incites the music again. Let a trial be made on the stage, and I have no doubt that the decision of the audience will be in favour of *vial* against *viol,* although it may be admitted that the latter does not absolutely contradict the context. *Stirrest,* in the same line, is an evident corruption from *starest.* As Cerimon repeatedly exhorts the servant to bestir himself, it seems impossible that he should blame him for obeying his command. Besides, a block is not in the habit of stirring, but of staring. Mr. Fleay, in the Transactions of the New Shakspere Society, 1874, p. 217, reads and scans: —

>The vi|ol once | more; how | thou stirr'st, | thou block.

But had not the verse be better scanned as a syllable pause line: —

>The *vial* | once more; | ⌣ how | thou *starest,* | thou block?

DCXLIV.

Into life's flower again!
    First Gent.   The heavens.

Ib., III, 2, 96.

A catalectic line (see note II) to which Steevens proposed to add
sir. In my opinion the addition of *my lord* (instead of *sir*) would
bestow a more rhythmical movement on the line; there is, however,
no need of any correction whatever. Two more defective lines follow
at short intervals, viz. III, 2, 103 and III, 2, 110. In the former
verse, where the arrangement of the old editions seems preferable to
that of Malone, *again*, in the latter, *neighbours* would seem to have
been the word that has dropt out: —

> To make | the world | twice rich. | ◡ Live | *again*;
> For her relapse is mortal. Come, come, *neighbours*.

Dyce thinks it most probable that the last line should be completed
by a third repetition of *come*; perhaps it is a catalectic verse just
as well as l. 96.

DCXLV.

To have bless'd mine eyes with her!
    Per.   We cannot but obey.

Ib., III, 3, 9.

Mr. Fleay declares this line to be an Alexandrine. I rather think
that *eyes with her* is a triple ending before the pause; scan: —

> T' have blest | mine eyes | wi' her. We can|not but | obey.

Compare IV, 1, 50 and see note CDLVIII.

DCXLVI.

> *Cle.* We'll bring your grace e'en to the edge o' the shore,
> Then give you up to the mask'd Neptune and
> The gentlest winds of heaven.

Ib., III, 3, 35 seqq.

Instead of the nonsensical *mask'd Neptune* Dyce proposes *vast Neptune*; S. Walker, (Crit. Exam., III, 336) *moist Neptune*. The context,
I think, sufficiently shows that a wish for a happy voyage is
implied and that we should read *calm* or *calmest Neptune*: —

> *Cle.* We'll bring your grace e'en to the edge o' th' shore,
> Then give you up to the *calmest* Neptune and
> The gentlest winds of heaven.

The calmest Neptune would strictly correspond with *the gentlest winds*
which, if Cleon's prayer take effect, will this once waft the 'sea-tost'
Pericles safely and smoothly back to Tyre.

DCXLVII.

Deliver'd, by the holy gods.

Ib., III, 4, 7.

A mutilated line; add: *of a child*: —
Deliver'd *of a child,* by the holy gods.
Or should we be allowed to supply, *of child*: —
Deliver'd, by the holy gods, *of child?*

DCXLVIII.

Where you may abide till your date expire.

Ib., III, 4, 14.

A syllable pause line; scan: —
Where you | may 'bide | ⌣ till | your date | expire.
Malone's conjecture is unnecessary.

DCXLIX.

Might stand peerless by this slaughter.

Ib., IV, Gower, 40.

A catalectic line, in which *Might* stands for a monosyllabic foot. An acceptable improvement of the metre might be derived from a similar passage in Antony and Cleopatra, I, 1, 40 (We stand up peerless), viz.: —
Might stand *up* peerless by this slaughter.

DCL.

Leon. I will do't; but yet she is a goodly creature.
Dion. The fitter, then, the gods should have her. Here she comes weeping for her only mistress' death. Thou art resolved?
Leon. I am resolved.

Ib., IV, 1, 9 seqq.

Malone's conjectural emendation *I'll* for *I will,* in l. 9, admits of no doubt. He is also decidedly right in printing (1790) Dionyza's speech as verse and in ending the first line at *Here.* Add to these corrections Percy's ingenious emendation *old nurse's* instead of the nonsensical *only mistress'* and the original text will be restored: —
Leon. I'll do't; but yet she is a goodly creature.
Dion. The fitter, then, the gods should have her. Here She comes, weeping for her old nurse's death.
Thou art resolved.
Leon.				I am resolved.

DCLI.

Mar. No, I will rob Tellus of her weed. *Ib., IV, 1, 14.*

No is certainly wrong and both Steevens's and Malone's conjectures (*No, no* and *Now*) are anything but improvements. Qy. read and scan: —

> *So*; | I will | rob Tel|lus of | her weed?

So is a monosyllabic foot; compare The Works of John Marston, ed. J. O. Halliwell (Lon., 1856) Vol. III, p. 135: —

> *Tha*[*is*]. So, | there's one | fool shipt | away. | Are your Cross-points discovered? Get your breakfast ready.

Marina, in uttering this exclamation of 'acquiescence or approbation', as Al. Schmidt, s. v. *So,* defines it, casts a contented glance at the flowers in her basket. Compare note CXCVI.

DCLII.

> Lord, how your favour's changed
> With this unprofitable woe!
> Come, give me your flowers, ere the sea mar it.
> Walk with Leonine; the air is quick there,
> And it pierces and sharpens the stomach. Come,
> Leonine, take her by the arm, walk with her.
>   *Mar.* No, I pray you;
> I'll not bereave you of your servant.
>   *Dion.*   Come, come;
> I love the king your father, and yourself,
> With more than foreign heart.   *Ib., IV, 1, 25 seqq.*

Come, in l. 27, should be transferred to l. 26, which by this transposition becomes a regular blank verse: —

> With this | unprof|ita|ble woe. | ⏑ Come!

The way to the restoration of the rest of l. 27 has been shown by the Rev. H. Hudson who supplanted the stupid lection of the old copies, *ere the sea mar it,* by the most ingenious emendation: *on the sea-margent,* which may be brought still nearer to the original *ductus literarum* by being altered to, *there the sea-margent.* I am well aware that *on the sea-marge walk,* or *there the sea-marge walk,* would lend the line a smoother flow, but these readings would be two or three steps farther removed from the old text, so that no choice is left to a strict critic. Instead of *quick,* which is the uniform reading of all the old copies, the Cambridge Editors (?) have proposed to read *quicker.* *Pierces,* in l. 29, is to be pronounced as a monosyllable, like *belches* (III, 2, 55), *breathes* (III, 2, 94), and similar words; see Abbott, s. 471. In the same line *well* has been inserted by Steevens; I should willingly do without this expletive, if I felt sure that no objection would be raised to the completion of the line by the archaic form *sharpeneth.* Line 30 is a syllable pause line; scan: —

Leonine, | take her | by th' arm; | ◡ walk | with her.

The pronunciation of *Leonine* has been discussed *supra*, note on I, 1, 50. Marina's reply has hitherto been printed either as prose or in two lines, both of which arrangements are certainly wrong and may be avoided by the omission of *I* before *pray*; the blank verse thus restored admits of two different scansions, either with an extra syllable before the pause *(you)*, or *bereave* to be pronounced as a monosyllable.

Being thus corrected, the passage will stand as follows: —

Lord, how your favour's changed

Will this unprofitable woe. Come!
Give me your flowers; *there* the sea-margent walk
With Leonine; the air is quick there, and
It pierces and sharpens *well* the stomach. Come!
Leonine, take her by the arm; walk with her.
   Mar. No, pray you; I'll not bereave you of your servant.
   Dion. Come, come!
I love the king your father, &c.

DCLIII.

What! I must have a care of you.
   Mar.   My thanks, sweet madam.
Ib., IV, 1, 50.

Just like *eyes with her* in III, 3, 9 the words *care of you* are to be read as a triple ending before the pause; scan: —

   What! I | must have | a care | o' you.
   Mar.   My thanks, | sweet mad|am.

DCLIV.

That almost burst the deck.
   Leon. When was this?   *Ib., IV, 1, 58 seq.*

The words spoken by Leonine should be joined to the preceding line: —

   That al|most burst | the deck. |
   Leon.   ◡ When | was this?

DCLV.

And yet we mourn: her monument.   *Ib., IV, 3, 42.*

A defective line which should be completed by the insertion of *for her*: —

   And yet we mourn *for her*: her monument.

It is a well-known fact that words immediately repeated or doubled (*her* : *her*) frequently mislead the copyist or compositor and are written or set up only once instead of twice. See my 'Grundriss der englischen Philologie' (2ᵈ ed., Halle, 1889), S. 75.

DCLVI.

> *Cle.*   Thou art like the harpy,
> Which, to betray, dost, with· thine angel's face,
> Seize with thine eagle's talons.   *Ib., IV, 3, 46 seqq.*

An evidently mutilated passage on which although several conjectures have been wasted already, yet I cannot refrain from increasing their number. The sense undoubtedly requires the addition of *allure*; read therefore: —

>   Thou art like the harpy,
> Which, to betray, dost with thine angel's face
> *Allure, and then* seize with thine eagle's talons.

Thus both the sentence and metre are completed. Compare V, 1, 45 seq.: —

> She questionless with her sweet harmony
> And other chosen attractions, would allure, &c.

DCLVII.

> *Lys.* How's this? how's this? Some more; be sage.
>   *Ib., IV, 6, 102.*

Some more; be sage — Rowe conj.; *Some more, beseech.* Collier conj. Mr. P. A. Daniel proposes to read either *No more; be sage!* or, *Come now; be sage!* I strongly suspect: *Once more, be sage!*

DCLVIII.

> *Lys.*   I did not think
> Thou couldst have spoke so well; ne'er dream'd thou couldst.
>   *Ib., IV, 6, 109 seq.*

Qy. read: Thou *wouldst* have spoke so well; &c.?

DCLIX.

> Had I brought hither a corrupted mind,
> Thy speech had alter'd it. Hold, here's gold for thee:
> Persever in that clear way thou goest,
> And the gods strengthen thee!
> *Mar.*   The good gods preserve you!
>   *Ib., IV, 6, 111 seqq.*

Arrange, scan, and read: —

> Had I brought hither a corrupted mind,
> Thy speech | had al|ter'd it. | Hold, here's | gold for | thee:
> Persever in that clear way thou goest, and
> The good gods strengthen thee!
> *Mar.*   The gods preserve you.

Although l. 112 is metrically correct, yet I should prefer to read *alter'd it* as a triple ending before the pause and to scan: —

> Thy speech | had al|ter'd it. Hold, here | *is* gold | for thee.

The transposition of *and* from l. 114 to l. 113, and of *good* from Marina's speech to that of Lysimachus seems to be imperatively demanded by the metre.

DCLX.

Hear from me, it shall be for thy good.

Ib., IV, 6, 123.

Either a syllable pause line: —

> Hear from | me, ⏑ | it shall | be for | thy good,

or *Hear* to be considered as a monosyllabic foot: —

> Hear | from me, | it shall | be for | thy good.

DCLXI.

Empty
Old receptacles, or common shores, of filth.

Ib., IV, 6, 185 seq.

I cannot imagine on what ground Malone's ingenious emendation *sewers* for *shores* can be denied admission into the text.

DCLXII.

And in it is Lysimachus the governor.

Ib., V, 1, 4.

Governor is a triple ending.

DCLXIII.

> *Mar.* If I should tell my history, it would seem
> Like lies disdain'd in the reporting.
> *Per.*   Prithee, speak.

Ib., V, 1, 119 seq.

Two different arrangements may be offered, both of which will
remove the Alexandrine (l. 120). The first is to the following
effect: —

> If I | should tell | my hist|ory, 't would seem | like lies
> Disdain'd in the reporting.
> *Per.*   Prithee, speak.

History is to be read as a triple ending before the pause. The
second arrangement begins at l. 118: —

> You make more rich to owe?
> *Mar.*   If I should tell
> My history, it would seem like lies disdain'd
> In the reporting.
> *Per.*   Prithee, speak.

History to be read as a dissyllable. It seems hard to tell which of
these two arrangements possesses the better claim to be considered
the poet's own.

DCLXIV.

> *Mar.* My name's Marina.
> *Per.*   O, I am mock'd.
>> *Ib., V, 1, 143.*

Steevens needlessly inserted *sir*. It is a syllable pause line; scan: —

> My name's | Mari|na. ‿ | O, I | am mock'd.

Another syllable pause line of the same kind occurs five lines *infra*: —

> To call | thyself | Mari|na. ‿ | The name.

In the Globe Edition this latter passage (l. 148) is printed as two
short lines, whereas the two speeches at the head of this note are
printed as one line.

DCLXV.

> *Per.*   O, I am mock'd,
> And thou by some incensed god sent hither
> To make the world to laugh at me.
> *Mar.*   Patience, good sir,
> Or here I'll cease.
> *Per.*   Nay, I'll be patient.
>> *Ib., V, 1, 143 seqq.*

Scan: —

> To make | the world | to laugh | at me.
> *Mar.*   Patience, | good sir,
> Or here | I'll cease. |
> *Per.*   Nay, I'll | be pa|ti-ent.

Laugh at me is to be read as a triple ending. Critics who do not

think this scansion satisfactory, will be obliged to arrange differently
and to transpose in order to remove the Alexandrine: —

> To make the world to laugh at me.
>   *Mar.*   *Good sir,*
> *Patience,* or here I'll cease.
> *Per.*   Nay, I'll be patient.

DCLXVI.

> You have been noble towards her.
>   *Lys.*   Sir, lend me your arm.
>   *Per.*   Come, my Marina.

Ib., V, 1, 264 seq.

Line 264 is an apparent Alexandrine which may be reduced to
regular metre in a twofold manner. First by the omission of *Sir:* —

> You have | been no|ble tow|ards her. Lend me | your arm.

Towards her may either be read as a triple ending, or *her* be considered as an extra syllable before the pause, as *towards* is frequently
pronounced as a monosyllable; see S. Walker, Versification, 119 seqq.;
Al. Schmidt, Shakespeare-Lexicon, s. *Toward.* The second way of
restoring the passage lies in a different arrangement, viz.: —

> You have | been no|ble tow|ards her. |
>   *Lys.*   Sir, lend | me
> Your arm. |
>   *Per.*   Come, my | Mari|na.

Towards, in this case, to be pronounced as a dissyllable.

DCLXVII.

> Who, frighted from my country, did wed.   *Ib., V, 3, 3.*

The metrical difficulty of this line may be solved in a threefold way.
The first is to insert *once* before *did*; secondly, *country* may be pronounced 'as though an extra vowel were introduced between the *r*
and the preceding consonant' (Abbott, s. 477); and lastly, the verse
may be read as a syllable pause line: —

> Who, fright|ed from | my coun|try, ⏑ | did wed.

The reader may choose for himself.

DCLXVIII.

> She at Tarsus
> Was nursed with Cleon; who at fourteen years
> He sought to murder: but her better stars
> Brought her to Mytilene.   *Ib., V, 3, 7 seqq.*

For *who* in l. 8, which is the reading of all the old copies, Malone substituted *whom*. Qy. read: —

> who at fourteen years
> *Her* sought to murder: &c.?

DCLXIX.

> A birth, and death?
> *Per.*   The voice of dead Thaisa!
> *Thai.* That Thaisa am I, supposed dead
> And drown'd.
> *Per.* Immortal Dian!
> *Thai.*   Now I know you better.
>
> *Ib., V, 3, 34 seqq.*

Arrange: —

> A birth, and death?
> *Per.* The voice of dead Thaisa!
> *Thai.*   That Thaisa
> Am I, supposèd dead and drown'd.
> *Per.* Immortal Dian!
> *Thai.*   Now I know you better.

Thaisa is regularly used by the poet as a word of three syllables with the accent on the penult; compare II, 3, 57; V, 1, 213; V, 3, 27; V, 3, 34; V, 3, 46; V, 3, 55; and V, 3, 70. Apart from the line under discussion (according to the received text) two passages would seem to contradict this rule, viz. V, 1, 212: —

> To say my mother's name was Thaisa,

and V, 3, 4: —

> At Pentapolis the fair Thaisa.

Both passages, however, are manifestly corrupted. The former has been ingeniously restored by the Cambridge Editors (?): —

> To say my mother's name? *It* was Thaisa,

whilst the correction of the second is due to Malone: —

> The fair Thaisa at Pentapolis.

Thus all three seeming exceptions are cleared away.*

---

* These notes on 'Pericles', with the exception of notes DCLVII and DCLVIII, were first published in Prof. Kölbing's Englische Studien, IX, 278—290.

Index.

Abraham 364.

accent, rhythmical 15.

accentuation: aloug 221; appellants 364; curiosity 23; delectable 255; detestable 255; discoursing 255; familiarity 23; farewell 274; madam 2. 115. 186. 229. 512. 513; monsieur 517; proper names 215. 287; welcome 224. 355; without 4.

addresses, addition of —: 164. 186. 404. 405. 424. 425. 427. 467. 468. 474. 475. 484. 499; omission of —: 177. 186. 213. 408. 439. 444. 499. 582.

pseudo-Alexandrines (compare: triple endings): 23. 24. 29. 31. 51. 133. 198. 218. 270. *277. 316. *335. 341. *343. *403. 410. 416. *458. 534. 562.

ancestry, ancestors (dissyllables) 343.

antithesis 15. 41.

any thing, every thing as conclusion to a succession of synonym nouns 452.

appearance 81.

argument 13.

aromatic (gums) 197.

article, definite, omitted 6. 14. 17. 59. 166.

beagle 320.

beautiful (for bountiful) 24.

bedaub 391.

Belchier, Dawbridgecourt 402.

Bentley 523.

Bible 279. 283. 392. 402.

blear-eyed, blue-eyed 254.

Borde 81.

Brome 125. 401.

Bryant 288.

bulk 440.

bum (Dutch or Scotch?) 191.

Bunyan 458.

Butler 394. 505.

buzzard 125.

Byron 140. 211. 338. 458. 523.

Carlyle 394.

catalectic blank verse: *2. 71. 76. 81. 112. 128. 164. 206. 208. 215. 309. 387. 414. 428. 473. 476. 487. 494. 549. 557. 644.

Chambers 394.

Chaucer 4. 215. 305. 402.

Chester, Rob. 394.

coil 394.

compare (for comparison) 21.

couplets 97. 118. 144. 150. 182. 183. 294.

Cowper 263.

creature 40. 43.

Croydon 19.

dampish 103.

dankish 103.

daub 391.

Davenant 394.

dexteriously 81.

dittography 36. 50. 61. 96. 241. 292. 655.

drink up a river 402.

Drum, Jack 394.

Dryden 268. 458. 523. 547.

east: to bury the dead with their heads looking to the east 573.

Elliot 285.

enginer 566.

enjambement 34. 104.

errand (arrand) 162.

-es 89. 176.

esile 402.

excellence (for excellency) 59.

execution of pirates and robbers 251.

falls (Dutch or Scotch?) 191.

farewell (omitted) 233.

for to 168.

Galt 394.

Gascoigne 394.

Gay 440.

Getuly 193.

gondoler 410.

Gunpowder Plot 98.

him (enclitic) 35. 40. 449.

his = 's 459.

Holland 394.

Hunt, Leigh 394.

importuning (for importing) 74.

interjectional lines: 30. 32. 43. 51. 59. 66. 74. 115. 124. 132. 135. 138. 167. 178. 186. 316. 411. 435. 530.

Irving 66. 125.

ivory (= ivy) 162.

jealious 81.

jealousy 40.

lass 556.
letherne 8.
looby 129.
Lyly 342.

many a time and often 284.
measure (= dance) 107.
Merchant Royal 286.
metal 323.
metre (= verse) 107.
Milton 125. 208. 336; 81. 239. 240.
  305; 153. 177. 244. 263. 305. 433.
misprints: 50. 156. 189. 190. 193.
  241. 262. 263. 379. 394. 419. 525.
  655; n for m 10; s omitted 16.
  102. 153. 169. 241. 258. 413. 419;
  s added 52. 263. 606; s for l 154;
  r for t 194; s for n 196; t added
  241. 263; t omitted 160; s for f
  525; n for s 618.
Moll Cutpurse 311.
monosyllabic feet: 1. 5. 26. 55. 56.
  58. 70. 88. 89. 101. 108. 113. 116.
  117. 122. 127. 146. 150. 163. 165.
  166. 167. 170. 172. 174. 196. 211.
  214. 239. 259. 274. 299. 359. 514.
More, Thomas 183. 255.
mountainer 566.
muck 384.
muleter 410.
nettle 323.
numbers 282. 392.
oft 74. 140. 188.
orthography 8. 399.
- ow 305.

parle, parley 214. 336.
perchance 307.
perfume 240.
pioner 410. 566.
Pope 263. 384. 394. 458. 523.
prayers for the sovereign 183.
prefixes: 29. 45. 106. 127. 156. 177.
  183. 210. 255. 262. 305. 327. 343.
  454. 482. 535. 550. 620. 627. 648. 652.
puttock 506.

regardiant 81.
regorious 81.
rushes 160.
sable 395.
sanguine 19.
Scott 394.
shadow 268.
sheepbiter 136.
shoeptick (shintick) 162.
Sincklo 290.
sirrah 301.
Southey 394.

stage directions: 65. 71. 78. 171. 241.
  271. 314. 328. 367. 642.
state (for estate) 137.
Stirling, Earl of 266.
stoop 15.
studient 81.
stupendious 81.
substance 268.
syllable pause lines: unaccented syllable *4. 18. 45. 57. 60. 70. 75. 87.
  108. 128. 146. 173. 187. 200. 201.
  202. 203. 209. 211. 234. 236. 239.
  267. 300. 309. 361. 364. 371. 375.
  383. *410. 457. 472. 478. 485. 486.
  490. 492. 496. 498. 509. 527. 476.
  593. 604. 638. 639. 643. 644. 648.
  652. 654; accented syllable 2. *4.
  22. 64. 70. 101. 112. 115. 165.
  204. 205. 208. 230. 232. 236. 239.
  296. 346. 363. 365. 369. *410. 451.
  456. 461. 463. 470. 477. 481. 487.
  491. 494. 514. 531. 534. 543. 549.
  561. 577. 584. 593. 605. 609. 612.
  615. 623. 630. 632. 635. 660. 664. 667.
tabor 326.
Taylor, Thom. 258.
Thomson 398.
Thrasymene 211.
to, for too 15.
transition from the second to the third
  person 555.
treasure 40.
triple endings: 4. 33. 45. 49. 54. 56.
  113. 122. 212. 222. 223. 277. 327.
  343. 372. 373. 374. 377. 410. 418.
  453. 532. 535. 540. 562. 567. 569.
  574; before the pause: 48. 51. 110.
  247. 275. 277. 345. 363. 407. 450.
upsee Freese 250.
verses, printed as prose: 3. 31. 42.
  78. 96. 142; incomplete: 37. 99;
  wanting: 12. 20. 38. 39. 42. 86.
  143; interrupted: 3. 409. 422. 533.
very, added 121. 184. 296; omitted 121.
Whittier 394.
Will Kemp 382.
wis, woos, wusse 28.
with' (= with the) 6. 14. 17.
words, lengthening of —: 2. 4. 18.
  40. 43. 57. 75. 81. 187. 208. 211.
  230. 232. 233. 236. 274. 309. 364.
  375. 641; shortening of —: 133.
  177. 183. 187. 217. 255. 260. 305.
  343. 356. 415. 458; transposition
  of —: 62. 127. 208.

your (for you) 193.